THAT BABY

THAT BABY

JILLIAN DODD

Jillian Dodd Inc.
Madeira Beach, FL
Jillian Dodd is a registered trademark of Jillian Dodd, Inc.

ISBN: 978-1-946793-81-2

Books by Jillian Dodd

The Keatyn Chronicles®
USA TODAY bestselling young adult contemporary romance set in an East Coast boarding school.

Stalk Me
Kiss Me
Date Me
Love Me
Adore Me
Hate Me
Get Me
Fame
Power
Money
Sex
Love
Keatyn Unscripted
Aiden

That Boy Series
Small-town contemporary romance series about falling in love with the boy next door.

That Boy
That Wedding
That Baby
That Divorce
That Ring

The Love Series
Contemporary, standalone romances following the very sexy Crawford family.

Vegas Love
Broken Love

Spy Girl™ Series
Young adult romance series about a young spy who just might save the world.

The Prince
The Eagle
The Society
The Valiant
The Dauntless
The Phoenix
The Echelon

I know that the wait for this book has been long.

But when you write a book, you put pieces of yourself into it.

And, quite honestly, I wasn't ready for that.

Every time I sat down and tried to write it, I couldn't.

Because sometimes life doesn't go the way you planned.

And, as a warning, this book may not go the way you imagined it should.

But it's like life.

Tragedy can strike when you least expect it.

This book is dedicated to all the women who have lost a baby, suffered a miscarriage, or struggled with infertility—

and felt like they lost pieces of themselves in the process.

I know how you feel.

THE
FIRST
TRIMESTER

your MacDaddy

JANUARY 22ND

I AM MRS. Phillip Mackenzie.

Jadyn James Mackenzie.

Gosh, I love the way that sounds.

We came back from our amazing honeymoon, ready to move into our dream house.

Phillip unlocked the door and carried me over the threshold. Then, we started unpacking.

We've been unpacking all day, and we are tired, but I'm down in the basement, excitedly pulling the plastic off our gorgeous new sectional sofa. I'm practically in tears over how amazing it looks in the fabric I chose.

You know men.

They prefer function over form, and women typically will give up comfort for fashion. I mean, look at the way we contort our feet into fabulous shoes. Neither one of us had to compromise on this couch. It's the perfect combination of style and comfort. I ordered it in the softest ultra suede, and it's like lying on melted butter.

"I'm tired," Phillip says, sliding down onto the new couch. "Moving is a lot of work."

So, what is the very first thing Phillip decides to do on our couch?

Does he go over, lie down, look at me all sexy, and say, *Baby, come see your Mac Daddy, so we can properly break this in?*

No.

Does he run his hand across the gorgeous fabric and say, *Wow, this is amazing?*

No.

Does he comment on how cool it looks and what a statement it makes in the room?

No.

He flops on it with his shoes on, turns on the TV, and proceeds to fart on the new couch.

Yes, you heard me right.

He *farted* on my new suede sofa!

Seriously, who does that?

Who spends good money on something and then farts on it?

Who does that?

"PHILLIP! Why did you just do that?"

"It must have slipped out," he tells me with a little giggle.

"Phillip Mackenzie, that is our brand-new couch!"

He dismisses my horror. "Chill, it's not going to hurt it."

"It's a *brand-new* couch!" I say again.

"And it was one stupid fart."

"Well, it's the couch's first day here. If it has feelings, it must be terribly offended."

"You're being ridiculous."

I change course because I can see I need to speak in terms he can understand. "Phillip, are you telling me, if a skunk sprayed your car, it wouldn't hurt it?"

"Well, it wouldn't hurt it, no; it would just smell horrible."

"Exactly my point! The fabrics in your car are permeable. They hold in scents. Just like our new couch. One of the reasons you liked it is it reminded you of a sports car, remember?"

"Yeah."

"So, do you want people to come sit on our gorgeous, new couch in our brand-new house and have it smell like skunks live here?"

"Jadyn, it didn't even smell; it was just air."

"No farting on the furniture, Phillip."

He stares at me.

So, I say, "I'm serious. I'm adding it to our vows."

He rolls his eyes at me but says, "Fine. I won't fart on the couch."

"Good."

As I turn around to start putting wineglasses in the bar, I hear him mumble, "In front of you."

Okay, so I get farts.

I understand that our bodies were designed to do this as a way to let air escape when it needs to.

And I lived with two boys. I get that boys fart. I get that boys think farts are always hilariously funny.

But I thought maybe this was something they just did in a group. Like, when you fart alone, it's not as funny. I seriously cannot think of a time that Phillip has ever farted in front of me when we've been alone.

And he chooses this as the way to start off in our new home?

Is this what happens after you get married? The magic is gone?

It's stressful enough, trying to get everything unpacked.

And, to make matters worse, my pregnant best friend, Lori, decided—today of all days—that the baby in her belly can hear us, and she was encouraging—snarling/bitching at—us to watch our language all day.

I survived living with two boys without developing a farting habit, but when you hang out with people a lot, you tend to talk in a similar fashion. I think it's kind of like picking up an accent when you move down South.

You can't really help it.

So, I happen to have a pretty colorful repertoire of curse words in my vocabulary. The F-word being the tip of the iceberg really. I have to be very mindful of what I say at work, but around the boys, I let loose and talk like them. Lori has been my best friend since college. She knows that I cuss. And, even though she swears like a sailor, she's officially joined the F-Bomb Patrol.

She told me I couldn't say the F-word in front of the baby.

And I was about ready to buy her a fucking badge.

Oh shit. See? It just comes out.

And, to make it worse, I said *shit*.

Damn.

Oh my. See my point?

So, I realize that, if my swearing comes out naturally, maybe Phillip's fart did in fact accidentally slip out. But I can't let him get away with it.

I dive-bomb on top of him and say, "Mac Daddy is a bad boy."

He gets a grin on his face, that naughty gleam in his eye, and says, "But, Princess, on the brand-new couch?"

I reconsider that. "Uh, maybe not."

He rolls us off the couch, causing me to let out a scream and then laugh. Phillip smothers my laughter with his lips, and then, well, I let him be a little naughtier.

Thank goodness the F-Bomb Patrol is gone because I'm pretty sure we would have gotten arrested for this.

Tiny little F-bomb.

JANUARY 23RD

LORI AND DANNY, our best friends and neighbors, are over this morning to help us finish unpacking.

I'm pretty sure Lori must have completed some covert training last night because she seems to be off basic patrol and is now on the F-Bomb Special Forces.

I accidentally move the coffee table on my toe while trying to roll a rug out under it, and, well, it really hurts. So, maybe I let a tiny little F-bomb fly.

Quietly.

Lori glares at me. "Jade, really?"

"Fine. I hurt my *freaking* toe."

She smiles at me.

But, later, when I hammer my finger—rather than a nail—into the wall, I might say the F-word again.

Because, ouch, it hurts.

Apparently, I am not skilled at home improvement.

Lori scowls at me and covers her stomach with her hand. "Seriously? Did we not just talk about this?"

"Lori, I just hammered my, uh, *fricking* finger into the wall, and it *fricking* hurts. Shouldn't you be offering me some *fricking* sympathy?"

"Um," she says, "I really don't think *fricking* is appropriate either. Can you picture sending a child who says fricking to preschool?"

No, I can't really picture that, so I come up with a better idea. "Okay then, how about, I hammered my *effing* finger into the wall?"

She scowls at me. "Do you really think that's better? Effing? Are you kidding me? You can't say that either."

So, I do what any sane person with a hammered finger and a sore toe would do at this point. I become extremely frustrated and throw my hands in the air. "What the freak am I supposed to say then?"

She glares at me.

"What? I can't change the way I talk overnight. I also find it very hard to believe that you've stopped Danny from swearing. He's the freaking king of the F-bomb!"

"Well, I'm working on that," she says with a slightly maniacal grin. "See the rubber band?"

I glance over and notice a skinny blue rubber band around Danny's wrist. "Uh, yeah?"

"Every time he cusses, I snap him, and it hurts."

"Isn't that like husband abuse?"

She laughs at me.

"Where's your rubber band?"

"I don't need it. I can control myself." She digs a rubber band out of her pocket and dangles it in front of me.

And I'm like, "No."

And she's like, "Yes."

"This is bullshit, Lori. Sorry, but it is." I'm gearing up for a big fight, but Danny stands behind her, begging me with his eyes to let her put the rubber band on.

And I'll be damned, but I do it. I must be a really good friend.

LATER, HE'S LIKE, "Jay, come help me figure out where you want this ... blah, blah."

I don't even hear what he says.

He might have said *blah, blah*, but when we are both upstairs, he goes, "Thank you for not arguing with her. After the whole bleeding thing, seriously, Jay, no stress for her, okay? I think she gets some wicked little pleasure out of snapping me with the band. Like I'm in the pregnancy boat with her or something. She has had a time with it. Constantly sick and then the spotting that scared us to death. So, just try."

"Fine," I say, hanging my head in defeat.

He gets his Devil Danny grin. "Call her every dirty name in the book if you have to, just do it all in your head."

"Is that how you're surviving this?"

"Well, that, and I'm being trained."

"Danny, I'm sorry. I love her, but this is bullshit."

He leans over and snaps the rubber band on my wrist—hard.

"Oww! That hurts!"

He grins at me. "Yeah, I know."

"Then, why did you do it?"

"'Cause you said bullshit."

"Oh, really? So did you." I snap him back.

Pretty soon, Danny and I have our rubber bands off and are shooting them at each other, having a rubber-band war. I manage to nail his arm just as he's trying to duck behind the kitchen island.

But then the Fun Nazi comes upstairs. "What the hell are you two doing?"

Danny and I share a smirk.

"Um, Lori, do you need a rubber band, too?" I giggle.

"No," she says. "What I need is for you two to grow up."

Then, we all just laugh. This is sort of ridiculous.

After she goes back downstairs, Danny gets the sneaky look

again and pulls a little flask from his hoodie pocket.

"Oh, you're bad," I say.

"How do you think I'm surviving this?"

We do a shot together.

Lori is downstairs, fluffing—whatever that means—my bookshelves.

Phillip ran to get us some pizza since we have zero food in the house.

So, instead of Danny helping me maneuver the mattress pad and sheets onto our big, new bed, we are back to our rubber-band war.

Every time he hits me, he makes me do a shot. I've gotten hit a couple of times, but he's a good friend, and he has been drinking with me.

But no food and a few shots is not a good idea.

When Phillip gets home with the pizza, I quickly scarf some down.

It tasted great, but now, I'm feeling a bit nauseous.

Next thing I know, I'm throwing it all up, and I don't feel well.

At first, I thought it was from the alcohol, but I'm feeling achy and feverish. I must have the flu.

And you're puking?

JANUARY 24TH

NEXT MORNING, I eat some cereal and toast, and it's the same deal. I'm in the bathroom, throwing up. While I'm brushing my teeth, I see my birth control pills lying on the counter. I took one before breakfast.

Crap, I probably just threw it up.

Then, I look closer at the pills, and two things come to mind.

One, *I should have gotten my period a few days ago.*

And two, *WTF?*

Where the heck is my period?

But I try not to freak.

I know Lori would chew my ass if she heard me thinking this because, yes, I know there are a lot of people who want to get pregnant but can't. I know they try everything, and here I am, complaining *because* I am not thrilled with this combination of lateness and puking.

And, of course, this is the exact moment that Phillip chooses to walk into the bathroom to check on me.

"Are you okay? I thought I heard you throwing up again."

"Yeah, I'm not feeling so great."

He studies the pill package in my hand and stands frozen for a good thirty seconds.

I'm telling you, I can see the wheels turning in his brain.

And I don't think I will like the question that he's going to ask next.

"Oh my God, are you late? And you're puking?"

"Just a couple of days late, and that's not unusual."

Actually, it is unusual. But come on! I'm stressed. I've just gone through some major life changes. Planned a wedding. Designed a building. Packed. Got married. Traveled. It's happy stress, but it's still stress. So, it's natural that my body would freak out like my mind did. I mean, they do work in tandem most of the time.

Phillip gets a big grin on his face and pulls me into his arms. "It would be *so awesome* if you were pregnant. Do you think you could be?"

"Phillip, no! It would not be. We're not ready. We just got back from our honeymoon. What would your parents think?"

He laughs. "My parents got married in August, and Ashley was born in February. Do the math."

So, I do.

I count it out on my fingers. "September, October, November, December, January, February—Phillip, that's only six months!"

He laughs.

"Your mom was pregnant when they got married?"

"Ya think?"

"Did she trap your dad into marrying her?"

"I don't think so. They dated for over two years before they got married."

I get hit with another wave of nausea.

And I can't decide what's making me feel sicker—the thought of being pregnant, the flu, or an actual pregnancy.

It's got to be the flu.

Please, please, let it be the flu.

And, um, excuse me, while I go puke again.

Phillip is a sweetie, of course, and tells me I should lie back down and try to sleep.

But HA! You really think I'm going to be able to sleep? Now? At a time like this?

My body might be shaking and tired, but my mind is on freaking overdrive.

So, let's be rational and think this through.

I'm on the pill.

I take it every day.

I never miss a day.

I take it at the same exact time every single day just to be extra cautious.

But then I remember that I was on antibiotics for a sinus infection, and I very specifically told that boy we should use a condom.

What did he do?

He laughed at me and proceeded anyway.

And I stupidly didn't stop him.

I have that thing my parents used to say young people have. That stupid thing in the back of their mind that says, *It could never happen to me. It's just this one time.*

But, uh, well, it wasn't exactly just once, was it?

All month, we were not careful like we should've been.

Why did I listen to him?

Where was my willpower?

I'm really, really not ready for a baby.

Sure, I want to have kids.

I really do, but they are still a someday in my mind.

Not the far-off someday that they used to be, but in the foreseeable future someday.

I can't wait to have kids with Phillip, but I want it to be the right time. We need to be married for a little while. I have so much on my plate. Phillip's temporary office space is complete, but construction on the new building will start soon. And we need to get settled in our new house and our new city.

Truth be told, if I couldn't drink, I might not be able to get through it all.

And no.

No need to give me the whole alcoholic speech. It's not like that.

But I admit, there have been days recently where the only thing that has gotten me through is the thought of being able to come home and soak in a hot bubble bath with a glass of wine and some chocolate.

I seriously cannot be pregnant right now.

Please, God, please, don't let me be pregnant. And please don't hold it against me, like, in a few years from now when I want it to happen.

Apparently, I exhaust my brain with all this thinking, so it shuts up and goes to sleep.

I WAKE UP, feeling chilled and feverish.

Not good.

I shuffle into the kitchen and find Phillip unloading a grocery store's worth of bags. Lori is neatly organizing his purchases in my pantry. She waves at me over the bags piled on the island.

"Jade, how are you *feeling*?" she asks with a singsong, happy-bird-in-the-park quality to her voice as she scurries around, getting me crackers and 7Up and placing them in front of me with a flourish.

I sit at the bar with my blankie still wrapped around me and bite into a cracker. I'm delighted to discover that it tastes wonderfully salty and good.

"So, how is it?" she asks, pointing to my snack.

"It tastes good, thanks."

"Normal people don't really like saltines; only pregnant women do."

Oh, great. She now seems to think I just passed some litmus test for pregnant women.

"I lived on them during my first few months." Now, she's acting like we're in some secret saltines club together.

And it hits me. Her ultra-cheerful voice. Her being so nice.

"Phillip! You *told* her?"

He grins and holds up his hands. "I'm sorry. She wanted to know what was wrong with you, and I'm just so excited about what it could be that I let it slip that you're a few days late."

"I am *not pregnant!*"

And I am willing both them and the fertility gods to believe me.

Or, wait, would it be the non-fertility gods?

Is there such a thing?

"Please stop this ridiculousness. You're upsetting me."

"See, Phillip? I told you. *Mood swings,*" Lori says, acting like she is some kind of pregnancy expert.

"This is *not* a mood swing," I counter. "This is an *I have the flu, feel like crap, and you keep going on with all this* you're pregnant *bullshit* mood."

"Rubber band," she tells me.

I take the rubber band off my wrist and fling it at her. "Fuck that."

Yes, I know.

She's my friend, and she's being very helpful and organizing my pantry, but I don't feel good!

I can't handle this harassment.

She gives me a glare. I pathetically look at her. She huffs and goes back to organizing my pantry.

This is why we're friends. We both know when to back down.

Phillip takes pity on me. He picks me up, carries me over to the couch, and snuggles up with me.

"Sorry," he says quietly. "I just had to tell someone. I felt like I could burst."

"Please tell me you haven't told anyone else."

"Um, I, uh …"

"Phillip!"

"So, my mom called this morning and asked how the move was going, and I told her you were sick yesterday and then again this morning. You know she has baby on the brain, and she asked if you could be pregnant. I told her no. That I thought it was just the flu. But she sorta acted like she didn't believe me."

"Phillip, I have a fever. I don't think that's a pregnancy sign."

Lori, who apparently has been listening, butts in, "I had a slight fever and thought I was coming down with the flu when I found out."

I shake my head at her. I'm pretty sure I could tell her that my toenails hurt and the trees outside swayed in the breeze, and she would tell me it's a pregnancy symptom.

"Phillip, please pray that we're not. We aren't ready for this. We need to be a couple first. Have some fun together. Babies are hard on marriages."

"I don't think I can do that. I can't lie. I would be pretty excited if you were. I can't wait to have an adorable, spunky daughter with a cute, curly ponytail and little freckles across her nose, just like her mommy." His finger grazes my freckles. "I'll give her piggyback rides and teach her how to ride a bike, climb a tree, and punch any boy who tries to kiss her. I can't wait to start a family with you."

Okay, so I don't want a baby right now, but the way he talks about his future daughter is really sweet. And it must be contagious because it makes me think that maybe it wouldn't be that bad.

But I am still on Team Not Pregnant.

Please, not yet.

"Just in case you want to find out for sure, he bought you a home pregnancy test," Lori butts in again.

"I'm not taking that. I'll get my period. I just have the flu."

As the day goes on, my nausea subsides, but it might be because all I've eaten is crackers and 7Up.

I get nothing moving-related done because Phillip makes me lie on the couch and relax while he organizes our home.

That means, I'll never be able to find anything.

I hate you right now.

JANUARY 25TH

I GET UP, feel a little better, and am hungry—well, starved—so I splurge on a muffin and a glass of chocolate milk.

Thirty minutes later, I'm puking it back up, and Phillip is looking like he found the end of a rainbow.

"Phillip, you aren't supposed to smile about someone being sick. It's annoying."

"Princess, why don't you just take the pregnancy test? Then, if it says no, you will know it's just the flu, and if it says yes, well, you can freak, and I can celebrate."

"I hate you right now." I hide my head under the blanket.

Of course, he can't leave me alone, so he snuggles up to me and starts talking through the blanket.

"Tell me why you wouldn't be excited about this? It would be kind of like a surprise gift."

"No, it would not. Having a child is a big responsibility. It's time-consuming, and it takes lots of energy. I don't have the time or the energy right now. Plus, I want to spend time with you. I want us to be a couple before we become a family. Why can't you get that?"

"Princess, sometimes, things happen for a reason. If you're pregnant, it's because God thinks we're ready for this."

"Oh, no, you don't!" I whip the covers off my head and point at him. "Don't you go blaming God for this. If there's a reason this happened, it would be because I was stupid to believe you when you said, *Don't worry about the antibiotics*. This would be God *laughing* at me for my stupidity."

I throw the covers back over my head.

"Jadyn …"

Oh. He's mad at me.

"Don't use that tone of voice with me. I'm sick."

He uncovers me. Kisses my face, my neck, and my forehead. Sweet kisses that make me love him even more.

"All I'm saying is that, if you are, I would be thrilled. I love you. I want to have a family with you, and I don't care when it happens. If you want to wait—I mean, if you aren't already—then we'll wait. But you have to admit, it would be fun to be pregnant the same time as Lori. To have our kids close in age, like you and I were. Just think, we could take naked pictures of them together as babies to torture them with when they were older."

I can't help it. I laugh at that.

"See, whatever it is, you and I love each other. You will be an amazing mom, and I plan on being the best dad ever, but the reason I want a baby is just because I am so in love with you."

He kisses me on the lips.

And I am thinking this boy must really love me because I just puked and did not brush my teeth, and he didn't even cringe.

I still hope I'm not pregnant, but I guess, if I was, it wouldn't be the end of the world.

I look like crap.

JANUARY 26TH

I WAKE UP, stilling feeling crappy, but I don't puke! I'm thinking, *Thank you, God,* but where is Mother Nature when you need her?

Still no period, and I'm starting to think I might be pregnant.

As I watch Phillip unpack, the thought actually crosses my mind that it might be cool if I was pregnant. I know the timing is not right, but Phillip is so amazing, so sweet, and so good to me. It seems kind of selfish of me to want to hog all that love and keep it for myself. He's going to be a great dad, and he's a wonderful husband—of that, I have no doubt.

And, at lunchtime, when he drives twenty-two miles to get me what Danny dubs as the best chicken noodle soup in Kansas City, I almost want to cry because I feel so lucky and loved.

WE SIT AT the kitchen island, eating soft dinner rolls and the amazing chicken soup together.

I know I look like crap. I haven't showered or brushed my hair in two days, but Phillip doesn't seem to care. He still looks at me like I'm the most beautiful girl in the world.

I'm seriously so lucky.

I also seriously have to pee.

It is at this point in my life that I realize Mother Nature has a very warped sense of humor.

My period has arrived.

And I should be relieved. I should be jumping-with-joy happy.

I should go out screaming, *Phillip, it's okay! My period is here! Let's celebrate!*

But that's not how I'm feeling.

I feel … well, I'm still trying to wrap my head around how I'm feeling. Because the way I'm feeling is a shock, even to myself. I'm feeling, um, well, I'm feeling quite sad actually.

I'm feeling let down.

And I have no idea why.

I walk back out to the living room and tell Phillip quietly, "I just got my period."

He looks kind of crushed, and I just start bawling.

I can't believe it, but I think I'm sad that I'm not pregnant.

And I can see disappointment written all over Phillip's face. He looks like he could cry.

I start blubbering, "I'm sorry, Phillip. I know you wanted me to be, and I wasn't sure, and now, I'm, like, so sad that I'm not, and I love you, and *blabber, blabber, blabber.*" I don't even know what I'm saying.

Phillip holds me tight and just listens. When I'm done blathering on, he says, "It's okay, but I will admit, I got a little excited about the possibility. Maybe we've learned something?"

"Like what?" I sob.

"That maybe we don't need to wait? Like maybe we're ready?"

"Yeah, maybe we are."

"So, no more pill?"

I kiss that sweet boy and say, "Deal. We're not trying, but if it happens, we'll be excited."

"Deal." Phillip holds my chin in his hand and adoringly looks at me.

Lori and Danny choose this exact moment to walk in our front door.

Phillip backs away from me, slightly in surprise.

And, really, you've got to love our friends. They don't hold anything back.

Danny's first words are, "You look like crap. Do you feel any better?"

"I'm feeling a little better. Danny, you were right; the chicken soup was amazing. Phillip even thought it was worth the drive."

Lori blurts out, "So, did you take the pregnancy test yet or what?"

"No." I get the stupid tears in my eyes again and bite my lower lip. I'm unable to look her in the eye when I tell her, "I didn't need to. I got my period."

She looks at me and gets tears in her own eyes as realization hits her. "Jade, are you *sad* you got it?"

"Yeah, kinda." I nod my head as little tears start falling out of my eyes.

She runs over and hugs me. She doesn't need to say anything. Her tight hug says it all.

I'm really going to start watching my language for her.

LATER, WHEN PHILLIP and Danny work out, Lori and I go to her house, so she can show me the nursery that was painted while we were on our honeymoon.

"So, are you going to start trying to get pregnant?" she asks.

"I guess. I mean, I'm still kinda getting over the shock that I was sad I wasn't. What do I need to know? How do you go about getting pregnant? All I've ever thought about was how not to."

"Well, first thing is, going off the pill. And they say you shouldn't have sex very often."

"I would think, if you were trying to get pregnant, you'd want to do it all the time, which should make it easy because we already do."

"Do what?"

"Have a lot of sex."

"But you shouldn't do that."

"Why not?"

"You need to chart your ovulation cycle," she explains. "Then, when you are most likely to be fertile, you'll want to do it. If you haven't done it as much, he'll have stored-up sperm and be more potent."

"That sounds sort of gross. Wouldn't I be better off just getting him drunk? Have some wild, carefree sex? I thought, if you tried too hard, it put pressure on you, which then had the opposite effect?"

She rolls her eyes at me. "Jadyn, you want your baby to be conceived in the best possible environment. That means, you shouldn't be drinking. You should be taking vitamins and eating healthy. You should have sex regularly, but not too often."

"What's too often?"

"During ovulation, you'll want to have sex once a day."

"Just once? And I thought trying would be fun."

"It is fun. You get to have sex every day."

"We just got back from our honeymoon, Lori. Once a day would be a bit of a letdown."

She laughs. "Danny and I had a lot of sex on our honeymoon, too." She rubs her belly.

"How far along are you now?"

"Twenty-seven weeks."

"Are you happy you're pregnant?"

"Of course I am!"

"No, I just mean, are you happy you got pregnant when you did? So soon after you got married?"

She frowns. "Like, if I could do it again, would I so soon?"

"Yeah."

"I think so. Maybe. I don't know. Being pregnant can be, um, challenging. Your body is changing. Your hormones are changing. You have the strangest thoughts."

"Like what?"

"When I was throwing up all the time, I sort of blamed Danny."

"Because he got you pregnant?"

"Yes. They say it's normal though. To sort of hate your husband."

"You hate him?"

"No! Gosh, it's hard to explain. And don't you dare breathe a word of this to him."

"I won't."

"It's just that, sometimes, you don't feel good. And it doesn't seem fair that *you* are having *his* baby, and he doesn't have to go through any of it. He can do anything he wants, and you have all these restrictions. It's a weird combination of precious time and worst nightmare."

"Your morning sickness is subsiding though, right?"

"Yes, that helps. During the second trimester, most women feel pretty good."

"Do you?"

She sighs. "I feel better. I wouldn't say great." She pats her belly again. "The baby is kicking a lot, which is both amazing and slightly terrifying. I'd say that's how pregnancy has been for me. Conflicting opposites. It's like you're overwhelmed with joy that a baby is growing inside you. You feel an incredible sense of wonder. But then you also feel out of control. You look down and wonder how you have a baby growing inside you. You're shocked at how much your stomach can stretch. It's the most natural thing and also weird as can be."

"In a few more months, you'll be holding your baby in your arms."

"And it will all have been worth it," she says. "So, back to getting pregnant. They say, if you want a girl, you should be on top, and if you want a boy, the man should be. But that contradicts other things they tell you. Some say, after sex, you should put a pillow under your butt. This tilts your pelvis in a way that gravity helps the sperm swim toward the egg."

"I don't think I'm ready for all that yet. We'll just continue to have fun, and if it happens, it happens."

"Speaking of happens, you never did tell me what happened before the wedding. When you and Phillip broke up."

"When my parents died, I locked up my feelings and put them away. Granted, my personality tends to be of the act-first, think-later side, but I told myself that being reckless and having the *you only live once* mindset would make my parents proud. But it was an excuse to do whatever I wanted. I'm lucky I lived with Phillip and Danny in college. Otherwise, I think I would have been wilder. I kissed a lot of guys, but I didn't sleep with very many because I didn't want to bring them home."

"The boys aren't around. Who all did you sleep with anyway? You've never told me."

"Well, Matt Fuller was my first. Freshman year in college. Then, after he broke up with me, I revenge-dated his best friend. Then, Bradley."

"The smoking-hot bartender," Lori adds.

"Who I was supposed to have my first one-night stand with. But I guess I'm lucky I met Bradley, too. Instead of a bunch of random one-night stands, he became *all* my one-night stands. I went home with him a lot, but that's all it ever was. Just hot sex."

"And a shot named in your honor." She smirks.

"I'm not very proud of that night."

"We thought you should postpone the wedding," she admits.

"You did. Why?"

"Because of what happened at the bar. We only heard about it from Nick, but it was obvious that things were unraveling."

"They were."

"What made you give Phillip the ring back? I was afraid to ask before."

"I thought we failed couples counseling. I almost drove down here that day. Thought you and I could drink margaritas and bash boys."

"Except I can't drink."

"Ha. I forgot about that!"

"Was that the *tick, tick, boom*?" she asks gently.

"Danny tells you everything, huh?"

She nods. "So, where did you go? Phillip was really worried because he couldn't find you."

"I went to our old elementary school. Sat in the car for a long time, just staring at the swings."

"That's where it all started," Danny says, interrupting us.

"Where's Phillip?" I ask.

"He went home to shower."

"Where what started?" Lori wants to know.

"Don't you remember when we got engaged and I told the story of how Phillip kissed me on the swings in fourth grade and told me that he wanted to marry me someday? I think I was just getting through life, waiting for that day. Waiting until the time was right. After Richie Rich—guy number four, if you're still keeping track—I thought maybe. Phillip and I had gone to two formals together, but we never kissed. Then, there was the disaster known as your wedding."

"Hey." Lori slaps me on the arm. "Our wedding was perfect."

"For you. Not for me."

"So then, the drummer," they both say.

"*Guitar player*. Number five. And then Phillip. My number six and hopefully last."

"So, the swings?" Lori says.

"I hooked my charm bracelet to the swing and left it there. It felt like the right place to bury our relationship." I look at Danny. "Then, I went to visit my parents' grave."

Danny's eyes get big. "You said you'd never go there."

"I know, but I went anyway. Lay in the snow and cried. I felt really ashamed. Here all I wanted to do was make them proud by being strong, but ..." Tears threaten, so I shake my head.

"It's okay," Danny says. "They're proud of you now."

"I know. It just took me a while to get here. And then I was remembering how Phillip was with me when they died. I went to touch the cross charm on my bracelet, and I freaked when it was gone. When I went back to get it, Phillip was there. So, I told him everything—how I've always loved him being the most important thing. He told me his original plan was to propose at the swings. Then, he said that he was going to do it right. He dropped to one knee and proposed. I said yes. Then, I was fine."

"So, the honeymoon was fun?" Danny asks with a smirk.

"It was amazing."

"Did you like our XXX honeymoon gift?"

I laugh. "Your gift. Yes. Although we didn't know what to do with half of it."

"Phillip said the same thing," Danny says. "I'm gonna go shower." He kisses Lori and heads toward their bedroom.

"And I think I'll go home and see if I can catch a peek of my husband in the shower," I tell Lori.

Symptoms.

JANUARY 27TH

I'M HALF-ASLEEP WHEN I roll out of bed to pee.

I stop mid-pee, stand up, and look into the toilet.

That can't be right.

I shut the door, lock it, flip on the light, and peer into the bowl. The tampon that has been in all night is pure white.

How could that be?

Now that I think about it, yesterday was way lighter than my normal period.

Weird.

I finish peeing, flush, and go back to bed.

Phillip pulls me into his arms and kisses my neck.

"Morning, Princess. You feeling good enough to go for a jog?"

"It's so cold. I think we should go back to sleep. Or back to the Caribbean until spring."

"You know, once I wake up, I can't go back to sleep. That's why you always wake up to fresh coffee."

"Maybe you should jog by a doughnut shop," I suggest.

He laughs into my neck. "You must be feeling better if you're hungry."

"A chocolate-frosted cake doughnut sounds really good. And some hot chocolate. I think I am feeling better."

"Danny said, if you were up to it, you should go over to their house this morning. The designer is going to be there shortly to go over the final choices for their kitchen remodel."

"Oh, fun! Why didn't Lori tell me?"

"She didn't want to ask when she knew you weren't feeling well and with our disappointment yesterday—"

"Are you disappointed, Phillip, really? Or do you think it's for the best?"

"I have to say, I'm a bit disappointed. But you're going off the pill now, so it will happen soon. I'm sure of it."

I jump up out of bed. "I think I will go over there."

I QUICKLY GET ready and head over just as the interior designer is pulling in the driveway.

I greet her and help her carry samples into the house.

"Jade! You made it!" Lori squeals with excitement, giving me a hug and leading us into the kitchen.

The designer is sorting through samples.

I push my shoulder into Danny's when I see him yawn. Lori is super excited about her kitchen remodel. He needs to at least pretend to be interested.

He leans down and rests his chin on his palm as he tries to focus his blurry eyes while the designer shows them cabinet, counter, floor, tile, and fabric samples.

"What do you think, Jade?" Lori asks.

"I thought you wanted a six-burner stove. The drawing shows it's sized for only four."

"Oh, good catch," she says as the designer corrects the plans. "What do you think, Danny?"

Danny wraps an arm around her. "Whatever makes you happy makes me happy."

She sighs. And not in a good way. "I want you to love it, too."

"I love the white cabinets. The flooring. The stainless steel appliances. I'm not sure about gray tiles for the backsplash though. They remind me of a bathroom."

"Subway tiles are very popular right now," the designer states.

"I thought we agreed on something classic, not trendy?" Danny asks.

"Maybe you should go with tumbled marble. Something softer?" I offer.

The designer digs in her bag. "These are the other options I brought for counters. Why don't you decide what countertop you want first?"

Lori and Danny both point to the white marble. I point to the thick white quartz.

"Isn't the marble more classic?" Lori asks.

"It is, but it also stains. You're getting ready to have kids. Kids spill. Juices, tomato sauce, and especially wine will stain this. Some people like a patina, but I think it would bother you."

"You can seal it, but it's something you have to do regularly," the designer informs.

"I'd hate the maintenance," Lori decides. "Let's go with the quartz."

"Then, I would suggest these for the backsplash," the designer says, pulling out a gorgeous pale blue glass subway tile. "We can do this tile in different shapes, but I like this the best."

"I like it, too!" Lori says. I can tell she's getting really excited.

"And it goes perfectly with these fabrics."

AFTER THE DESIGNER leaves, Danny offers to make breakfast, saying it will be the last time in their old kitchen.

"Phillip went for a run," I tell them. "But he's bringing back doughnuts."

"I'm hungry for an omelet," Lori says, "with grilled onions and peppers. I even have some leftover fajita chicken we could put in it."

"Sounds awesome," Danny says. "You cut. I'll cook."

"Is there anything I can do?" I ask.

"Sure. I'll do the peppers, and you do the onions." Lori hands me a knife as Danny starts grilling bacon.

And it smells so ... gross.

All of a sudden, I'm hit with a wave of nausea.

"Uh, excuse me," I say, running to the bathroom and throwing up the little bit of water I've had this morning. "I'm sorry," I say, coming back out. "I'm still not feeling well."

"If I didn't know you'd gotten your period, I'd think you were pregnant," she says. "Why don't you sit down while we cook?"

I plop down on the couch, grabbing a magazine off the end table. Under it is what Danny calls the pregnancy bible.

Wait.

Could I be pregnant?

Was the little bit of spotting I had yesterday technically a period?

I think back to all the periods I've ever had in my life. The shortest since I went on the pill lasted two days. Yesterday, when I got it, it was really light. But I was so surprised by how sad I felt that I didn't notice.

I pick up the pregnancy book and thumb through it, looking for any shred of information on this subject.

The first chapter is about what to do *before* you conceive.

"What are you looking at?" Lori says, startling me.

"Oh, I was just curious about some things."

"Like what?"

"You know, like, after you go off the pill, when can you start trying?" I lie. What I'm really doing is frantically trying to see if you can sort of get your period and be pregnant. "I see there's a whole bunch of stuff you're supposed to do before you conceive. Um, Lori, could you give me your doctor's name? I think I should go see him. Get started on the right foot." I quickly put the book down and pick up the magazine.

"Sure, let me get my phone. I'll text you his contact info."

Phillip strolls in with a box of doughnuts.

"Jay got sick again," is the first thing out of Danny's mouth.

"Yeah, I think I'm going to go home and lie down," I say.

Phillip kisses me and gives me a smirk. "Care if I stay for breakfast?"

"No, go ahead."

I'm throwing my shoes on when Lori hands me the book. "Why don't you take this home and look over it? There's more than a chapter on what to do before you get pregnant."

"So, there are a bunch of chapters about sex?" Phillip asks with a grin on his face. "Maybe we should read that together."

Danny punches him in the shoulder. "You never should have said that, dude."

I grab the book and the doughnuts. Then, I run home and read the list of pregnancy symptoms.

Tender boobs? No.

Peeing a lot? No.

Really tired? Yes, but could be the flu.

Nausea? Yes, but could be the flu.

Heightened sense of smell? Yes.

Bloating? Doesn't everyone get bloated before their period?

Spotting? That's probably more what my so-called period was.

Missed period? Hmm.

I RUN IN the bathroom to check things out.

Still nothing.

I'm eating another doughnut and rummaging through the kitchen, looking for the pregnancy test, when Phillip sneaks up behind me.

"What are you doing?"

"Um, I was looking for that pregnancy-test thingy. You had it in the kitchen, and, uh, you know, with your parents coming for the Super Bowl party, I didn't want them to see it and get any ideas."

"Oh, good point." He reaches into the pantry, moves a box of protein shake mixes, and hands me the test. "Why don't you put this in our bathroom? Hopefully, it won't be long until we need it."

Holy shit.

JANUARY 29TH

I PRETEND TO be asleep while Phillip gets ready for work, but the second I hear the garage door shut, I jump out of bed, peek out the bathroom window to watch him drive down the street, and then run to the closet, get the test out, and read the instructions.

Remove the stick. Take off the cap. Then, either pee on the stick for five seconds or pee into the cup.

Which do I want to do?

Cup.

I sit on the toilet.

And then start crying.

I don't know what I want.

I run through the living room, grab the pregnancy book, bring it in the bathroom, and reread the part about how you shouldn't drink when trying to conceive.

I mentally calculate the number of alcoholic drinks I had on our honeymoon. The martinis, champagne, and beer consumed at the wedding.

I don't know what I want.

But, now, I really have to pee, so I go in the cup.

Then, I put the stick in and start counting.

One.

Two.
Three.
Four.
Five.

I take the stick out, put the cap back on, and lay it down on the counter.

Now, I have to wait for three long minutes.

I flush.

Wash my hands and set the timer on my phone.

Reread the instructions two more times.

One pink line = Not pregnant.
Two pink lines = Pregnant.
One dark pink line + one light pink line = Pregnant.

I'm not even going to think about looking at it until the three minutes are up.

I stare at the seconds counting down on my phone's timer.

Two minutes left.

Shit.

I peek.

There are two faint pink lines.

I look at the instructions again, wondering if they turn pink first but then the second one disappears.

But the two lines just seem to be getting darker.

Holy shit.

I think I might be pregnant.

I smile and then start crying again.

THE DOCTOR'S OFFICE opens at nine, so I start calling at eight forty-five. I call every minute until finally someone answers at eight fifty-seven. I tell them I just moved to town, am best friends with Lori and *Danny Diamond*—yes, I used his name on purpose—might be pregnant but might not be depending on if these ninety-nine percent accurate tests are really that accurate, and that I need to be seen today.

Like, now.

Preferably right now.

This very second.

She squeezes me in at two o'clock.

I hop in the shower to get ready for work, place my hand across my stomach, peek out of the shower to make sure the two pink lines are still there, and wonder if it could be true.

Could I really be pregnant?

I LIE TO Phillip and tell him I have to go to some showroom to look at bathroom fixtures for the new building. Truth is, I've had them picked out since before the wedding.

In the OB-GYN's waiting room, I'm surrounded by women with big pregnant bellies, and by the time I fill out all the paperwork, pee in another cup, give some blood, and get in to see the doctor, I've convinced myself the home pregnancy test must have been faulty. I can't be pregnant.

"So, I understand the lines turned pink," the doctor says after introducing himself.

"Yes."

"And what was the date of the first day of your last period?"

"Um, Christmas Day. December twenty-fifth."

He picks up a little chart and spins it around. "That means you're due October the first."

"*Due?* As in *I'm pregnant?*"

He squints his eyes at me. "Yes, home pregnancy tests are quite accurate. You're definitely pregnant. Five weeks along today."

"But I'm on the pill."

"Did you take it regularly?"

"Yes, but I took antibiotics last month."

"Well, there you have it. They can sometimes lessen the pill's effectiveness."

"I'm a few days late, but I had some spotting the other night, and I thought it was my period. But then it stopped."

"It's not uncommon to have spotting."

"But I didn't plan on getting pregnant," I mutter.

"You're not happy about your pregnancy?" he asks.

"Not only was I on the pill, but I also just got married two weeks ago. I drank every single day of our honeymoon. What if I've already ruined our baby?" I get tears in my eyes. I don't want our baby to be ruined.

The doctor pats my back. "Being on the pill when you get pregnant does not increase the risk of birth defects. And it's also not uncommon for women to have alcohol before they realize they are pregnant. Back when my mom was pregnant with me, women would smoke and drink alcohol while pregnant. I turned out fine."

"But, now, we know better, right?" I say. "That can lead to low-birth-weight babies."

"You've been doing some reading," he says with a smile.

"A little."

"So, while it's hard to tell for sure, you probably conceived around the eighth of January."

"Oh my God. That was the night ... "

"Did something bad happen?"

"Yes. No." I start to cry again. "It started out bad, but then it ended up good. Like, it was a really special night. I fell asleep and dreamed of fireworks. Could I have known?"

"Some women say they know when they conceive."

"Except I don't have many symptoms. Only two."

"Which two?"

"I'm tired and nauseous."

"Just like no two people are alike, no two pregnancies are alike."

"So, I'm really, truly, honestly, actually pregnant? Like, for real?"

"Yes, Jadyn, you are," he says, making a note in my file. Probably something about my mental stability.

"Wow," is all I can say.

I LEAVE THE doctor's office, planning to go straight home. I can't go back to work because I'm dying to tell someone, and I'm afraid I'll blurt it out to the first person I see.

I have to tell someone.

Or I'm going to burst!

But I don't want to blurt it out to anyone but Phillip.

But how should I tell him? I remember Lori calling me after the lines turned pink. How she told us before she told Danny. I don't want to do that. I want Phillip to be the first person to know.

And I want to do something special.

I go home and search the internet for ways to tell your husband you're pregnant. What I find is thousands of videos.

I watch a bunch of them. The reactions of the husbands are varied, ranging from tears to disbelief to jumping with joy to a whole lot of, *Are you serious?*

I try to imagine Phillip's reaction. He's going to be shocked. I'm still in total shock, and I've had a few hours to let it sink in.

I consider the different ways to tell him. Lots of the videos involve things like signs, cakes, dinners, the positive pregnancy test, baby bottles, booties, and rattles. One told the soon-to-be father on his birthday.

We are having a Super Bowl party this weekend. Could I tell him before everyone arrived?

No, that's six days away.

Six very long days.

No way I can wait.

When a text from Phillip flashes on my phone, I jump, feeling like I've been caught. That he could somehow know.

I read his text.

Mac Daddy Loves You: *Did you get ahold of Lori's doctor?*

Me: *Yes. They had an opening today, so I went.*

Mac Daddy Loves You: *Awesome. Did we get the green light?*

Me: *You could say that.*

I notice he changed his name in my phone from *Phillip Baby* to *Mac Daddy Loves You.*

Ohmigawd. That's it.

I call Danny.

"Hey, is there a place where I can get a couple of custom football jerseys made?"

"Yeah, I drive by a shop on the way to training. Let me look it up, and I'll text you the address."

"Thanks."

"What are you doing?"

"Oh, just getting shirts made for the Super Bowl," I lie.

"I heard the parents invited themselves."

"I heard that, too. And Chelsea and Joey are coming down."

"Did you know they hooked up at your wedding?" he asks me.

"I kinda assumed. What do you know?"

"They danced in Vegas at the bachelor/bachelorette party."

"I remember that. But she had a boyfriend."

"Who she brought to the New Year's Eve couple's shower," Danny says. "But whom she did *not* kiss at midnight."

"Ohmigawd, Danny. Did she kiss Joey?"

"Well, Joey kissed her. I guess he grabbed her right before the countdown, pulled her into the bathroom, and told her that, at midnight, she should kiss the guy she was going to be with all year."

"That's so romantic. I can't believe she didn't tell me!"

"She showed up at the rehearsal dinner single. He tried to sleep with her that night, but she shut him down."

"But not the night of the wedding?"

"Definitely not the night of the wedding. Their first time was in a hotel bathroom. Now, they're dating."

"What do you think of them together?"

"You know I think Chelsea is a cutie. I told him he'd better not just be telling her all that stuff if he didn't mean it."

"And what did he say?" I ask.

"He says she's the one."

"They caught the garter and the bouquet. I never thought that really worked. Do you think they will be the next ones to get married?"

"I wouldn't marry them off just yet. They've been dating for all of two weeks now. That'd be crazy."

I cough.

Danny chuckles. "You and Phillip were different."

"I'm just giving you a hard time. You know, Joey and Chelsea made out a couple of years ago at a party, and then he never called her."

"Sounds like he's calling her now. He's hot for her."

"Okay, I gotta go," I say, knowing I need to get off the phone before I accidentally blurt out that I'm freaking pregnant. "Talk to you soon. Thanks for the address."

"You know we're coming over for dinner tonight."

"You are?"

"Yeah, you told us we could use your kitchen, remember? Demolition started this morning, and we'll be over pretty much every day until it's done. Pray it's finished before the baby gets here."

I think about how I was going to surprise Phillip with the shirts tonight.

Naked.

"Um, I'm still not feeling well. I'm not sure Lori should be around me when I'm sick."

"She was already around you when you were sick."

"Fine. I have a little surprise planned for Phillip tonight. A naked kind of surprise."

"You have your period. Couldn't be that good of a surprise." He laughs. "I'm stopping to pick up ribs."

"But, Danny, we're newlyweds. We're supposed to eat naked."

"Hey, I'm cool with naked. Whatever."

"*Danny.*"

"Tell you what. We'll leave right after dinner, so you can have your newlywed fun. I'll even get you some extra barbecue sauce to take to bed."

"Don't mention that in front of Lori," I tease. "You know how she's been craving barbecue."

"She has? Scratch that. I'm keeping the sauce for myself."

AT DINNER, I can't stop smiling. I'm so afraid one of them is going to notice and ask me why. And I don't think I'd be able to lie about it.

Thankfully, Danny is true to his word and herds Lori out the door after dinner.

I run into the closet, strip down to my underwear, and pull on the football jersey I bought.

Then, I grab the present I wrapped for Phillip and set it on the bed.

"Hey, Phillip," I yell over the TV. "Will you come in here?"

I position myself on the bed. The jersey is riding up and exposing my long legs. The V-neck is pulled down as far as it can go.

"What are you wearing?" he asks as he comes through the

door.

"A football jersey. The Super Bowl is this weekend, you know." I thrust the present at him. "Here, open this."

He picks the box up and shakes it. But then he tosses it aside and slides his hand under my jersey. "I think I'd like to open this first."

I wrap my arms around his neck and kiss him on the cheek. "I'd like that, too, but not until you open your present."

His hand sneaks further up. "You don't have a bra on. You gonna wear it like this to the party?"

"I'm going to cancel the party if you don't open your present."

Oh my God.

Please!

Open. The. Present.

I'm going to burst!

He kisses me instead.

The boy has a one-track mind.

I push him away. "Phillip, please! Stop! I need you to open the present! It's important!"

He's a little taken aback. "Uh, okay. Sorry. You're just so sexy; I can't keep my hands off you."

I feel bad for yelling at him, but I can't take it any longer.

I grab his hand. "Phillip, before you open it, I just want to tell you that I love you. And that ..." Tears pool in my eyes and fall onto my cheeks when I blink. "Um, just that I love you."

He tilts his head, trying to understand why I'm crying. "I love you, too, Princess. What's wrong?"

"I'm just excited for you to see what I got you. It's something pretty special."

I laugh to myself, thinking how everyone kept using the word *special* on the night Phillip surprised me by proposing.

He leans back, grabs the present, sets it on my lap, and removes the bright blue-and-fuchsia-polka-dot bow.

"Really colorful," he says as he rips into the yellow wrap and opens the box. "Sweet! You got us matching jerseys. You know Danny's gonna give us crap though. He sent me some hilarious video showing married couples dressed the same—"

"Our shirts aren't exactly the same," I interrupt.

"They're not?"

"Well, as you can see, mine has black glitter letters. Yours has black embroidery with white trim. And look at the back."

He holds up his shirt.

"*Mac Daddy*. Nice." He sets it down and kisses my neck. "Your Mac Daddy wants to take your jersey off."

"Don't you want to see the back of mine?"

"Can I see it when it's lying on the floor?" He grabs the hem of my shirt, ready to strip it off me.

"No!"

"Fine," he says, picking me up, flipping me over, and pinning me on the bed. "Mac Mommy? Oh, I get it, like I'm the daddy, and you're the mommy." Then, after a few beats, he goes, "Uh, wait. Actually, no, I don't get it."

I smile at him over my shoulder, hoping it will sink in, while taking the opportunity to sit back up. I cross my legs in front of me and stare at him, a wide smile on my face.

He squints his eyes. "Wait. You went to the doctor today about us having kids."

I pull another item out of the box and hand it to him. "I did. Because this happened."

He looks down at the pregnancy test, the two pink lines still clearly visible. "What is this?"

"It's the pregnancy test I took this morning. I'm pregnant, Phillip."

"But you got your period!"

"I thought I did. I saw blood and assumed that's what it was. But the next morning, it was gone."

"Why didn't you tell me?"

"Because I didn't want to get your hopes up again. That's why I borrowed Lori's pregnancy book."

He puts both hands on his head. "I can't even believe this. You're sure?"

"Yes. Did you notice the numbers on our shirts?"

"I'm ten. You're one."

"That's our due date. October the first. Can you even believe it?"

He shakes his head. "No, I really can't."

I panic. "Did you change your mind? Do you not want me to be pregnant now?"

"No! I'm thrilled!" He grabs me and kisses me hard. "I think I'm in shock."

"I cried at the doctor's office. I was pretty shocked, too."

"Good shock though. Really good shock." He wraps me in his arms and hugs me tight. "Holy smokes. We're going to have a baby."

I start crying again.

"I'm so happy you're happy," I blubber.

"Princess, I thought our wedding day was the happiest day of my life."

"You told me that afternoon we spent in bed on our honeymoon topped it."

"You just topped them all. God, I love you." He kisses my face again. "We're really going to have a baby?"

"I love you, too, Phillip. And apparently so."

"I'm going to spoil you rotten. The baby, too." He gently lifts up my jersey and places his palm across my belly. "Wow. So, how far along are you?"

"Five weeks."

"Already?"

"Yeah. And get this. Based on some magic chart the doctor

had, he said we probably conceived on January eighth."

"That was the day you called off the wedding," he slowly states.

"And the day you asked me to marry you again."

"And then we went home."

"Yeah … and then we went home."

"To an incredible night filled with love," he says.

"It was the first time we really made love."

"It's perfect. You're perfect. Have you told anyone else? Is that why Danny and Lori left so early?"

"I told Danny I had something naked planned to get them to leave early."

"No wonder he punched my shoulder and told me to have a good night."

"Phillip, nothing ever seems real until I tell you. I had to tell you first."

not that hungry.

JANUARY 31ST

I SPEND ALL day running around to different showrooms, choosing specific items, so the builder can finalize our costs. The excavation of the land started while we were on our honeymoon, and we're pushing to get the plans finalized and approved, so we can start construction right away.

I'm exhausted and sitting on the couch when Phillip comes home.

He thrusts a gift bag at me and smiles. "A little something to celebrate your pregnancy. I'm still just in awe of the fact that we're having a baby. So, I was thinking you could open this present, and then we could have a bottle of wine, eat dinner in bed, and make love all night long."

I stare blankly at him.

"Oh, shoot. That's right. Well, I'll find you something bubbly to drink, I can have the wine, and we'll still make love all night long."

"Phillip, I haven't made anything for dinner. I've been running around all day, and I'm exhausted."

"Oh, that's right. Women are really tired when they're first pregnant, right? Do you feel like going out?"

"Can I take a nap first?"

He sits down next to me, puts my feet on his lap, and massages them.

"Do I get this kind of treatment every night?" I ask with a content sigh.

He leans over and kisses me. "You can have anything you want, Princess."

"Then, I want a foot massage and—don't laugh—fried chicken."

"Your wish is my command," he says.

"You're being so sweet."

"I was crazy in love with you before, but knowing that you're having our baby … it's just incredible. I love you so much."

"I love you, too. What's in the bag?"

"Oh, I almost forgot. Look inside."

I pull out a beautiful journal. The cover is a rugged leather, but it's wrapped shut with dainty pale blue and green ribbons.

"It's beautiful, Phillip."

"Open it," he says.

I carefully untie it and see that the inside is just as beautiful as the outside. There is a wide array of papers inside—blue and green to match the ribbons, metallic, thin, thick card stock, watercolor, patterned, and plain.

"This is the coolest journal I've ever seen, Phillip. I love it."

"I thought you might want to start a journal."

"For the baby?"

"Yeah, like something she could read when she got older."

"She?"

"I kind of think it's a girl," he says with a beaming grin.

"Why's that?"

"Father's intuition?"

"You're cute."

"Actually, I have no idea, but I don't want to call the baby *it*."

"So, we should name it now?"

"Not a real name yet. Maybe a nickname. But we're not gonna call it a little monkey like Danny does."

"Well, if you are Mac Daddy and I'm Mac Mommy ..."

"We should call it Mac Baby?"

"Hmm. How about Baby Mac?"

He kisses me again. "Baby Mac it is. Now, let's go get you some fried chicken."

I pull him back toward my lips as I slide my hand down the front of his pants. "Maybe I've decided I'm not that hungry anymore."

He strips off my clothes and then pulls me back on the couch.

Very quickly, he's holding my hips, guiding me up.

I toss my head back and start to breathe deeply. It feels so good.

He feels so good.

The front door bangs open, someone gasps, and I turn to see Danny and Lori standing in the foyer.

I throw my arm across my chest and duck down behind the sofa.

I'm mortified.

So mortified.

"Oh, sweet. We get dinner and a show," Danny quips.

"Danny," Lori chides, smacking his arm. "Um, Jade, call us, when you're, uh, ready for dinner," she calls out as they back out of the door.

"Shoot! I forgot they were coming over. That was awkward," I say to Phillip.

He unwraps my arm, kisses my cleavage, and mutters, "I'm not done yet."

Then, I forget all about Danny seeing my boobs.

OF COURSE, I know that Danny will never let me forget it.

When Phillip calls and tells him we're going out for fried

chicken and asks if they'd like to join us, he says something that causes Phillip to blush.

"What did he say to you?" I ask Phillip as we're getting in the car.

"Nothing," he says with a smirk. "Guy talk."

"No, that's wife talk. I'm not just some girl you got caught having sex with."

"Princess ..."

"Don't Princess me."

He leans over and kisses me. If he doesn't watch it, I might throw up on him. I'm suddenly ravenously hungry, and if I don't get food quickly, I think I'm going to be sick.

Pregnancy has turned me into a teenage boy. I'm either hungry or horny.

"He didn't see anything, really. Said, once he realized what was happening, you were already covered up."

"And what else? I know he said something dirty, Phillip. You blushed."

"Do you really want to know?"

"Probably not."

He kisses my hand. "Smart girl. Let's go get you some chicken."

I start giggling.

"What?" he says.

"He said something about deboning the chicken, didn't he?"

Phillip laughs and then coughs. "I haven't heard that term in a while. Danny mentioned something about chicken head."

"Chicken head? What's that?"

"Think about it. How do chickens eat?"

I bob my head up and down, pretending I'm a chicken picking grain off the ground, trying to figure it out.

Phillip is laughing so hard; he's almost crying.

It's then I realize what it looks like I'm doing and start laughing, too. "Oh, I get it."

THE GOOD NEWS is, when we get to the restaurant, the teasing about our couch sex keeps my mind off wanting to scream to the world that I'm pregnant.

When I get home, I'll make the first entry in my journal. Maybe that will help me keep our little secret.

5 WEEKS

Dear Baby Mac,

Phillip, your dad, bought me this journal, so I could record our pregnancy. He thinks you might like to read it someday when you are older. That I will have some words of wisdom for you.

I should start by telling you how excited he is. We both are.

I'm still in shock, honestly.

My first words of wisdom: antibiotics really can cause birth control to be ineffective. So, if you are ever in that situation and don't want to get pregnant, be sure to use a condom.

Maybe I should make you read this before you go to college. LOL.

Honestly, I'll probably never let you read this—because, knowing me, I'll write about something inappropriate—but it will be a fun way for me to track my pregnancy, how I'm feeling, and your growth.

Speaking of tracking your growth, your dad is obsessed with it. In fact, he's already started a growth chart on the wall in your room. Right now, you are the size of an apple seed.

Isn't that crazy?

5.5 WEEKS

Dear Baby Mac,
I almost forgot …

The doctor told me that, if you drink alcohol when you are pregnant but don't know it, your baby will still turn out normal.

So, thank God you have that to look forward to.

They seem bigger to me.

FEBRUARY 2ND

I WAKE UP to find Phillip staring at me.

"What are you doing?"

He gives me the sweetest grin. "Just looking at you."

"I know that. But why?"

He skims his hand across my chest, which is hanging out of the tank top I wore to bed.

I roll my eyes at him. "So, in other words, you were looking at my boobs, not me."

He chuckles. "Sorta. Maybe. They seem bigger. Do they hurt?"

"Um, not really."

"Danny said that Lori's killed her during the first trimester. He said he could look but not touch. I felt sorry for him."

"Why?"

"Because it's like getting a new toy and not being able to play with it."

I playfully smack him. "You're goofy."

He presses his body fully against mine in what I'm supposed to think is a sweet hug, but it's really a plea for morning sex. And I have to admit, Phillip is so sexy in the morning; I can never resist him.

I nuzzle his neck and kiss the side of it.

He quickly responds by sliding his hand up my shirt.

But then he breathes out morning breath.

"Oh gosh!" I jump out of bed and run to the bathroom.

And puke.

Sorta.

It's really more of a gagging than a puking. I sit on the bathroom floor and hold my face in my hands and breathe out in an attempt to calm myself down. But then I realize my breath is a culprit, too. I stand up, gag again, and then quickly brush my teeth, which makes me gag some more.

Phillip wanders into the bathroom, his boxers leading the way.

I burst into tears.

"What's wrong?" he asks, pulling me into his arms.

"Brush your teeth," I sob.

He brushes his teeth and then pulls me back into bed with him. He runs his hand across my face. "Why are you crying?"

"Is this what pregnancy is going to be like? You're going to make me gag? What did we get ourselves into? I don't know if this is a good idea, Phillip."

"Well, it's a little late for that," he says. "Unless something unfortunate happens."

I suck in a big breath as my heart takes residence in my throat. "I didn't mean that! I don't know what I mean. I don't know what I'm saying. I don't want something unfortunate to happen!"

"I read that miscarriages are really common in the first few weeks. In the first trimester really. It sucks, but it's reality."

"That's not going to happen to us, Phillip! Don't say that! Don't even think it! It can't happen to us!" I'm in a bit of a panic now. "We named it Baby Mac. I've already written in the journal!"

"Princess, calm down."

"Don't talk to me about reality and then tell me to calm down. You sound like you expect it to happen! Did you lie to me?

Are you really not excited? Do you want me to have a miscarriage?"

"Of course not. I was sad when I thought you weren't. You know that. I'll admit, I am still in shock. But that brings up a question. When do you think we should tell our family and friends?"

"I don't know. Before this morning, I would have said right away."

"That surprises me," he says, sliding his hand through my hair to calm me. "You usually want to keep stuff a secret."

"I think your parents will be excited." I stop and consider something I don't want to consider. "But, if you're right about the miscarriage thing, I guess I feel two different ways. Part of me doesn't want to tell them until we know the baby is okay. The other part of me thinks, if something bad happened, I'd need them to know."

Phillip gently kisses across my forehead. "I swear, everyone will take one look at you and know."

"How?"

"You're glowing."

"I am not. I was just puking."

He kisses me again. "It was just gagging, and you don't look sick. You look beautiful. What if we tell them at the Super Bowl party? We could wear the shirts, see if anyone guesses."

"That sounds fun."

BEFORE I GO to work, I stop by Lori's house to see how the kitchen remodel is going.

I look around at the mostly empty shell. The room is in shambles.

"Well, it's coming right along! You could come to work with me sometime, if you want to get out of here. Or go hang out at my house anytime you want. You shouldn't be around all this dust."

She raises an eyebrow at me. "I'll make sure to ring the doorbell first."

"After the other night, that's probably wise." I laugh.

She pulls me away from the construction zone and into the den. "You know, if you want to get pregnant, what you were doing won't work."

"Having sex won't get me pregnant?"

She does a little cough. "Are you serious about wanting to be pregnant, Jade?"

"Uh, yes."

"Didn't you listen to all the stuff I told you the other day?"

"Of course I did."

"No, you didn't. Your eyes glazed over. Wait a minute. You were doing it on your couch! Don't you have your period?"

"Oh, uh, it was really light this month. The pill, you know."

She narrows her eyes at me.

She's going to kill me when I tell her on Sunday that I'm already pregnant. But this conversation is cracking me up, so I let her keep going. And who knows? Maybe I'll need to know this for our next baby.

Oh my God. Did I really just think that?

I think back to the marriage test we took. How Phillip said he wanted four kids close together, and I was thinking one sounded good. But I can so see us with a house full of kids.

Or maybe that's the pregnancy hormones talking.

I resist the urge to put my hand across my belly.

She's still going on about how I should put a pillow underneath me and not get up for at least ten minutes.

"How far along are you now?" I ask her, hoping to change the subject even though she just told me a few days ago.

"Twenty-eight weeks."

"You look great," I say even though she's looking a bit disheveled.

She runs her hand through her hair. "I'm still tired, and the workers are here at the crack of dawn. I'm not sure why we decided to do this now."

"Because you wanted it done before the baby comes."

"That's right. I need to keep reminding myself."

"Do you have to be here the whole time they're working?"

"Um, well, no."

"Why don't you go over to my house, take a long shower, take your time getting ready, and then meet me for a late lunch? Then, we could go look at nursery furniture. I know you've been wanting to do that."

And, honestly, I kind of want to go look myself. I'm dying to design our baby's nursery.

"Oh, that sounds fun. I can't believe you're offering to go shopping. Am I going to have to buy you drinks first?"

"No. I'm starting to like shopping more and more. I've been having a lot of fun, choosing all the fixtures and furniture for the office building."

"Well, I'll take it. I have a list of four stores that are supposed to have the best stuff. We'll start with that. Are you sure you can take off the whole afternoon?"

"Yeah, I need to swing by the job site and meet the engineer this morning and then go to the office, but I'll meet you at one. Just text me where."

"That sounds good."

"All right, I'd better get going."

She gives me a tight hug, her plump belly hitting my still-flat one. "Thank you. You know Danny hates to shop."

I get tears in my eyes, thinking about how our stomachs just touched.

"What's with the tears?" she asks, her own eyes quickly filling up.

"I was just thinking how our kids will grow up to be best friends."

"Awww. Wouldn't that be amazing?"

ON MY DRIVE to the job site, Danny calls me.

"Sounds like I owe you a thank-you."

"Why's that?"

"Because you're going nursery shopping with my lovely bride. Not to mention, the show the other night."

"I wondered when you were going to bring that up. You've been way too quiet about it."

"I think it's awesome. Enjoy it while you can."

"What's that supposed to mean?"

"Pregnancy changes things."

"And Lori hates change."

"Yes, she does because she can't control it."

"So, your second pregnancy will go smoother."

"Let's just see if we can make it through the first one. I feel like I'm dancing in a minefield, and I never know when I'm going to make a wrong step and blow up."

"I've heard pregnant women are emotional," I say, thinking about how my emotions are already everywhere.

Danny chuckles. "That's an understatement. You ready for the Super Bowl party? My parents want to stay with you since our house is a disaster zone."

"That's fine. I should be cleaning, but instead, I'll be shopping with your wife. Maybe, since I'm doing that, you should go over to my house and dust."

"Maybe you should hire someone."

"You know how Phillip is with money and now that we're p—"

"Now that you're what?"

"Uh, preparing to have children."

"Preparing, huh? Looked more like *doing* something about it the other night."

"Shut up, Danny," I say, hanging up on him.

5.75 WEEKS

Dear Baby Mac,

I went nursery shopping with my friend Lori today. I've decided that going into a baby boutique the first time you are pregnant is similar to seeing a mythical creature. It's an amazing experience. Everything was so teeny, soft, and perfectly wonderful. I wanted to buy it all and bring it home for you. But, if I had done that, it wouldn't all match, so I started thinking up possible designs for your room.

There are lots of different decor options that are popular right now. And different rules of thought. Some believe a nursery should be bright and stimulating to the baby. Others believe it should be soft and calming. Others go the organic route. And others just want to be on trend. Some of the trends we saw were metallic gold, tribal, rustic, neutral colors, soft colors, bold graphics, vintage, and French-inspired.

So, basically, anything goes.

I'm also currently obsessing over a rose-gold chandelier. Your father would die if he saw what it cost, but if they can get it in a smaller—and cheaper—size, I might have to have it.

I also saw a photo of a room that had teeny twinkle lights in the ceiling, similar to what they sometimes do in movie rooms. Considering your dad and I love to look at the stars, it seems perfect. Now, I have to find the perfect everything to go with it. I'm leaning toward calming colors.

Do you think you'd like that?

Constant worry.

FEBRUARY 3RD

"PHILLIP, WE HAVE so much to do. Go to the store. Clean the house. Get the food ready."

"Why don't you go to the store, and I'll clean?" he suggests.

"Really? You're offering to clean?"

"Yeah, no problem. I'll take care of it."

"Phillip, your mom is coming. Her house is always spotless. I've been sick, and we haven't cleaned since we moved in."

He kisses me. "You're not sick; you're pregnant. And don't worry. I'll do the upstairs bathrooms and vacuum the guest bedrooms. It'll all be good."

I know Phillip is meticulous, and I really don't want to clean, so I take him up on his offer.

Today, for the first time in weeks, I haven't felt sick.

And, although I should be rejoicing, I'm worried. Worried it might mean something is wrong with our baby.

Is this what being a parent is going to be like? Constant worry?

Now, I see why my parents would freak out when I was ten minutes late for curfew.

ON THE WAY to the store, I get nauseous again, which is oddly comforting, and it causes me to stop for a doughnut. I sit in the parking lot, slowly savoring it. Lately, a very slowly eaten plain white cake doughnut has some sort of magical stomach-calming power.

Already behind schedule, I know I'm going to have to rush through the grocery store.

But, when I arrive, the parking lot is packed.

Apparently, everyone and their mother are shopping for their Super Bowl parties.

At the store by my condo in Nebraska, I knew where everything was and could quickly whip through. This store has a completely different setup.

I think there should be some kind of law that forces all grocery stores to be set up in the same basic order. Instead of running through the store and getting all I need, I'm constantly backtracking.

I get sidetracked in the bakery, buying multiple loaves of bread, muffins, and a couple of cakes. But, when I round the corner, the smell of raw fish makes me gag.

And, even though I didn't smell it before, now, it doesn't matter where I go in the store; the scent is overwhelming. I decide I have enough stuff, stand in line forever to pay, and then get the heck out of the store.

WHEN I GET home, Phillip helps me unload the groceries.

"Didn't you get any tortilla chips?" he asks when all the sacks are empty.

I plop onto a barstool and start crying.

"Why are you crying?"

"I don't know!"

He kisses the top of my head. "It's not a big deal. I can run and get some or ask my mom to stop."

"I didn't get everything on the list, Phillip. I was all excited because I didn't feel sick this morning. Well, I was worried but excited."

"Why were you worried?"

"Because, if I'm not sick, couldn't that mean I'm not pregnant anymore? Or that I'm going to lose the baby? But, on the way to the store, I got nauseous, which made me feel better. So, I was fine shopping—even though I couldn't find anything—but then I went by the seafood. After that, no matter where I went in the store, I could still smell it. I had to get out of there."

He pushes my chin up. "You got the beer."

"That's all our friends care about. But it's my first party in our home, Phillip. I want it to be perfect. And that's not like me."

"You never stress over parties. You seem to effortlessly throw them."

"That's because I always get the beer." I laugh. "You're right. The party will be fun because of who is here. It doesn't matter if the house is perfectly done yet or if there's a little dust. It's our friends and family who matter."

"Exactly right, Princess. Why don't you stay where you are, tell me what to do, and I'll make everything?"

"I love you, Phillip," I say gratefully, knowing I probably won't be able to cook the hamburger or the cheese dip without gagging.

"Are you excited to open all our wedding presents tonight?" he asks.

"I am. It's fun that we have room to put everything. I'm so glad that your mom made me keep my parents' dining room set. It fits the room nicely."

"Still looks a little bare though."

"Well, we can't do everything at once. We spent most of our budget on furnishing our very own sports bar in the basement."

"Worth every penny," he says. "It's an awesome room."

"It is. I figure we can save up. Do a room at a time. We still need a kitchen table, too. I looked a little online, but I want something special."

"Special how?"

"I want pieces that mean something to us, not just pretty stuff to fill up the space, if that makes sense. Like my mom's favorite painting was one she and my dad bought on their honeymoon. I think, when we see what's right, we'll know it."

"The Plaza has an art fair every year. Maybe we could find something there," he suggests.

"I love that, Phillip. Maybe even a painting of the Plaza itself. Or our fountain. Wouldn't that be amazing?"

He wipes his hands on a towel and takes mine. "You did all those sketches of what the inside of the offices would look like. Could you do that for our house? Our dream-house book?"

"That's a great idea, Phillip. I'll make drawings for each room. And it would be a great way for me to save paint and fabric swatches, decor ideas. In fact, I found a really cool chandelier for the nursery, and I saved a photo from one of the house magazines I was looking at on our flight home from the honeymoon." I dig through my purse and show Phillip the photo. "See how they did contemporary wingbacks at the heads of the table? I thought that would be so cool, and it'd give the table a more modern look. Hang on." I grab an empty sketchpad from my office, sit back down at the bar, tape in the photo, and then use a metallic marker to write on the front of the book.

Dream House.

I look at Phillip—really look at him—and my heart swells with love. "You're pretty smart, Phillip. You're going to make a great dad."

I am immediately rewarded with a long, sweet kiss.

I TAKE A nap while Phillip makes a trip to the store.

When he gets back, he gently runs his hand across my face to wake me.

I sigh, feeling blissfully happy. I'm so lucky to be married to Phillip.

"I suppose I'd better get ready. Everyone will be here soon, and I can't wait to see what we got."

"We registered for some really cool stuff," he agrees.

"Phillip, I was thinking we could use some of the money we get to decorate the nursery. Would you be okay with that?"

"I think that's an awesome idea."

"I'm excited to decorate the nursery."

"Do you know what you want?"

"Not yet. Looking at the nursery stores with Lori was both amazing and completely overwhelming. So many directions you can go with decor. Do you have anything in mind?"

"Most nurseries I've seen have had bright colors, but it seems counterproductive to me. Don't we want the baby to sleep in there? Shouldn't it be calm and serene, like our bedroom?"

"I think that's a good idea, Phillip. I suppose I should get up and help you put the groceries away."

"I suppose you should," he says, surprising me—and not in a good way.

I thought he'd already have it done and maybe want to slip into bed with me.

But, when I get to the kitchen, I see why he wanted me to come out here.

On the island is a beautiful bouquet of flowers.

"What are those for?" I ask.

"No reason really. Although, technically, you've been my wife for two weeks now." He kisses me. "Happy anniversary."

"Happy anniversary, Phillip. Thank you! They are so pretty. I need to get them in some water. Although I don't have a vase."

Phillip runs downstairs and comes up with a pitcher-sized beer mug called *Das Boot*, which must be German for, *Let's get drunk.*

He fills it with water while I cut the ends of the stems then arrange them in the glass.

"It looks good," I say.

"Hopefully, we registered for a vase." He chuckles.

"Yes, this is looking pretty classy," I say with a laugh.

He grabs my ass with one hand and kisses my neck.

I raise an eyebrow at him. "Phillip, you didn't buy flowers for no reason. You want sex, and you're hoping the flowers will get it for you."

"Really, going back to the store for you should have been enough, don't you think?"

"Yes, that was sweet. Did you know you have a sexual tell? Whenever you do this"—I grab his butt and kiss his neck—"it means you want it."

He gives me a sexy smile but ignores my comment. "And how is my beautiful wife feeling right now?" he asks, picking me up and carrying me into the bedroom.

"Perfect," I say as he lays me on the bed.

I'M FEELING DREAMY after our late afternoon romp.

After showering together and getting ready, he checks his phone. "The parents should be here any minute."

A few minutes later, the doorbell rings, announcing the arrival of the Macs and the Diamonds. After hugs and kisses and questions about the honeymoon, the dads and Phillip are sent out to unload their cars. Very quickly, my hall is filled with bags, and my kitchen island and fridge are filled with more food.

I peek at the roast I put in the oven earlier and see that it's looking and smelling perfect. I toss in carrots and onions and throw some tinfoil loosely over the top. Then, I get everyone set up with a drink and a chair in the dining room. Lori and Danny join us as well.

Mr. and Mrs. Diamond look at each other and then say at the

same time, "We have some news."

Chuck says, "Mary, why don't you tell them?"

Mary smiles. "Chuck decided to go into semi-retirement. We want to travel a lot and decided to start by touring the south of France—Monaco, Nice, and the French Riviera. Then, we're going on a cruise of the Greek Islands. Since Danny is off-season and the baby isn't due for a few months, we decided it would be the perfect time."

Mrs. Mac adds, "And I thought I'd travel down here with Doug while he's on business. Maybe I can help you with the building, JJ."

"Uh, we have most everything picked out already, but I'm sure Phillip could find you something to do at the office," I say in a diplomatic way.

PHILLIP'S SISTER, ASHLEY, and her husband, Cooper, arrive midway through the gift opening. This past fall, I was really worried about their marriage.

But, as we open more gifts, I notice that they are sitting very close to each other, the way they did when they were first dating. His hand is on her knee, and she's beaming.

When we take a break to refill drinks, I pull her aside. "You and Cooper seem so happy. Things going better?"

"Things are going great," she says. "He was really stressed this fall, trying to finish his master's degree and studying for his Series Seven license. He graduated, passed the tests, and is back to doing what he loves—selling financial services. He also got a big raise when he got his license, and he's earning more commission, so he's taking me on an amazing anniversary trip this spring. We're going to buy a house soon, and we're even talking about when we might start a family."

I give her a hug. "I'm so happy for you, Ash. How's your job going?"

"It's good, and it looks like I'll get to transfer to the school of my choice this fall. I might not be able to teach first grade, but I'll be in the elementary school in the area where we want to buy a house, so I'm hoping it all works out. What about you? Sounds like the honeymoon was amazing, and I heard you're breaking ground this week."

"We are. As soon as we get all the building permits, construction will start."

"My dad is really excited. Did you hear that he and Mom are going to be staying with you?"

"Like tonight?"

"Yes, tonight, but also while Dad is traveling down here for business. Phillip told him it'd be silly for him to stay in a hotel. While the Diamonds are out of the country, Mom's going to travel with him. You're going to have to find some way to keep her busy at the office, or she's going to be all up in your business."

"You think?"

"I know. I love my mother, but I wouldn't want her living with me. You know how she is. Everything has to be done her way. Look," Ashley says, "it's already started. See what she just did?"

"Did she just rearrange my water goblets?"

"Yep," Ashley says, giving me a pat on the back. "You won't know where anything is in your own house. And imagine what having her here will do to your sex life."

I wander nonchalantly over to the kitchen cabinet she just rearranged and take a peek. She has all the goblets lined up like little soldiers. She moved the basic ones I use every day to a higher shelf and put the prettier ones on the first shelf.

I shrug off Ashley's comment because, really, I should use the prettier ones more often. And, once we open presents, I'll have to rearrange them again anyway.

I'm sure she's just exaggerating.

THEY SAY EVERY couple gets at least one memorable wedding gift. Sometimes, it is good, and sometimes, it is bad, and sometimes, it's downright ugly.

What we got doesn't fall into any of these categories. Sure, we got many amazing and thoughtful gifts. Gorgeous sets of china and stemware, everyday dishes, serveware, Christmas items, gourmet cookware, garage essentials, candlesticks, gadgets, table linens, sheets, and towels.

But our memorable thing is a Nebraska garden gnome. He's small and dressed in our team colors with a cute hat, but I'm pretty sure this gnome is up to no good.

I privately tell Phillip, "I'm not sure about the gnome. Did you see his shifty eyes? He's looking up at you like he's good, yet he still looks evil. I think he has a plan to take over the world. Can you imagine trying to bow to a gnome?"

"You're being silly. I think it's kinda cute. And, besides, it's a *Nebraska* gnome."

BY THE TIME we get all the presents opened, the moms have drunk a fair amount of wine. They help me do the dinner dishes and quickly retire. Lori goes home. Ashley and Cooper can't seem to wait to get to their hotel, and Danny, Phillip, and the dads are smoking cigars in the hot tub.

I'm puttering around, putting a few of the gifts away.

I decide to tackle the china, proudly opening Mom's cabinet while imagining her doing the very same thing after she and my dad were married.

I'm emotional, and I might have a few tears in my eyes as I reach for a vegetable bowl.

"Ahh!" I scream because there, behind the bowl, stands the gnome.

Oh my gosh! The gnome moved!

Don't laugh. I'm serious.

After the gnome was opened and passed around the room, I set the gnome on the buffet table with some other home decor items—beautiful picture frames, crystal candlesticks, and some cool hurricane lanterns.

I judge the distance from the buffet to the table and wonder how he got there.

It's then that I realize the gnome is smirking at me.

And I know his expression has changed because I clearly remember pointing out his creepy smile.

I walk out to the deck and ask Phillip, "Hey, you know that Nebraska garden gnome? Do you remember it's facial expression?"

"What?" Mr. Mac says, scotch sloshing.

"I do," Danny says with a naughty smirk of his own. "It has an O-shaped mouth, like he'd just been pleasured by a girl gnome."

They all laugh like it's the funniest thing they have ever heard.

I go back and look at the gnome. He's wearing the creepy smile again, and he might have just winked at me.

I ignore the stupid gnome, grab the adorable football-shaped chip and dip bowl and a set of stacked stainless steel bowls, and take them to the kitchen to use for the party tomorrow. Then, I grab the mugs that will be perfect for Bloody Marys and put them in the dishwasher.

Time for bed.

But, as I'm brushing my teeth, I can't stop thinking about the gnome.

I run back to the dining room and look the gnome in the eye. He responds with a blank stare—the kind of stare people give you when they are trying to pretend they don't care about something very important.

I throw some gift wrap over his head and go to bed.

Like each other.

FEBRUARY 4TH

I'M GETTING READY for the party when Phillip's mom asks me to grab our new Crock-Pot.

When I get to the dining room, I do a double take.

The wrapping paper is off the gnome's head, and it's smooshed down next to his little round-toed boot—like all he's been doing since I covered him up is stomp on the paper.

I imagine the gnome moving around at night.

I realize I'm being ridiculous. Even if he did smash the paper, he didn't move very far.

I carefully pick him up, turning him over to study his legs. There's no space between them, just a line appearing to separate them. Really, it's just one big stub going into a large black mono-boot. More inspection shows that he has no knees. If he could walk, it would be more of a wobble.

This is crazy. There's no way the gnome could move on its own. Someone must have moved it.

But, just to be sure, I put the gnome in the china cabinet and lock it for good measure. I reconsider his placement as I have visions of him doing the mono-legged stomp all over my new china pattern. I unlock the door, grab him, and shove him faceup into the top drawer of the hutch—like he's in a little coffin—with

71

my new formal flatware.

Then, I grab the Crock-Pot and go back to making cheese dip for the game.

Phillip's mom, who has been taking food down to the bar, comes back up and says, "JJ, do you have a dust rag? The bar, well, the basement is pretty dusty."

"Uh, sure," I say, handing her a dish towel.

"Dusting only takes a minute," she tells me. "I'll have it cleaned up quick."

I instantly feel like a failure as a wife. My face gets hot, and tears threaten. "Phillip was supposed to dust," I say to myself.

Mrs. D's hand touches mine. "You're barely settled."

I know what she's saying is true, but it feels like an excuse.

"Thanks. I'm gonna go change. Everyone should be here soon."

I'm on the way to our bedroom when Phillip comes up the stairs.

"You didn't dust the basement?"

"No, it wasn't that bad. Besides, why get it spotless when it's just going to get messed up at the party? So, are you ready to put on our shirts?"

"You need to tell your mom that you were in charge of dusting."

"No way! I don't want to get chewed out. Besides, this is our house, and today is not about dusting. It's about telling everyone we love that we're expecting."

"You're right, Phillip. You're always right."

He laughs. "Except when you are."

"You're still right," I tease.

I strip off my sweats, throw on a pair of comfy ripped jeans, my Mac Mommy jersey, and then put a cardigan over the top of it.

"You look sexy," Phillip tells me, grabbing my ass.

"Are you going to say that when I have a stomach the size of a watermelon?"

"Absolutely," he says with such sincerity that I actually believe him.

I'M RUNNING AROUND, finishing getting everyone settled with drinks. Our friends Joey and Chelsea arrived just a few minutes ago along with Danny's teammate Marcus and his wife, Madison.

Phillip hands me a bubbly drink in a wine glass.

I give him a *duh* look.

"It's sparkling water and lime. Why don't you sit, relax, and enjoy the game?" he says.

"I'd rather sit on your lap, snuggled up with you."

"I think I can make that happen," he says, sitting in his favorite spot and pulling me onto his lap.

"They're newlyweds," Danny says. "They still like each other."

"What's that supposed to mean?" Lori asks.

"I just meant it's new," Danny replies. "I wasn't referring to our relationship. I still like you, too."

She looks down at her growing baby bump and frowns. "You didn't ask me to sit on your lap."

Danny says in a patronizing tone, "Why don't we *all* sit on each other's laps? Save some space."

Tears threaten Lori's face as she stomps out of the room.

"Oh, jeez," he says. "She's so freaking sensitive. Now, she's going to accuse me of saying we needed to save space because she's fat. I can't say anything right."

Mr. Diamond says, "But you're going after her, aren't you, son? To apologize."

"But I didn't do anything wrong!" Danny protests.

"You got her pregnant," his dad replies.

Danny takes a long drag of beer and looks longingly at the opening ceremony playing on TV, and then he sets the beer down with a sigh. As he's walking away, he leans down and whispers to us, "Be glad you're not pregnant."

My mouth drops open in surprise.

Phillip slides his hand down my arm and gives me a reassuring squeeze. "We'll get through it just fine. I promise. I can deal with your little moods."

"I have *little* moods?" The TV is turned up to Mach 4, so no one can hear me.

"Of course. Everyone does."

"You're sure we should tell everyone so soon? Now, I'm nervous."

"I can't wait to tell everyone. Although I keep expecting someone to guess. I can tell just by looking at you."

"No, you can't. You were shocked when I told you."

He kisses the side of my face. "Oh, that's right."

I snuggle up closer and pretend to watch the game as I whisper to him, "I think you're the one who looks all sneaky and adorable."

"I'm adorable?"

"Yes. I love you, Phillip. You're the sweetest boy ever. Always have been."

His finger trails along the bottom of my jersey, just brushing my abdomen. "Lori has really popped out. Hard to believe, in a few months, you'll be that way."

"My body won't look the same."

"Does that worry you?" he asks.

"A little. Especially after seeing how pregnancy seems to have affected Lori's confidence."

"You shouldn't be worried. I'm going to spoil you rotten."

I smile. I like being spoiled.

SOMETIME DURING THE first quarter, Lori and Danny rejoin the group, and when Phillip gets up to grab another beer, Danny asks me, "Is that the jersey you had made?"

"Yeah. It's cute, huh?"

"Yours is cute, too," Lori says. "I like the sparkle."

I'm waiting—hoping—that someone will ask me what mine says, but there's an interception, and everyone is glued to the TV.

AT HALFTIME, I take my cardigan off and wait for the fireworks to start. For someone to notice what the back of my shirt says.

But no one does.

BY THE THIRD quarter, I can't take it any longer. I stand directly in front of the TV so that everyone can see my back.

Mrs. Diamond looks from me to Phillip and says, "Mac Mommy?"

I smile. "Cute, huh?"

But she still doesn't seem to get it, and Mrs. Mac is deep in conversation with Ashley.

"So, he's the Mac Daddy, and you're the Mac Mommy?" Mrs. Diamond asks.

I nod again, an even wider grin taking over my face.

"Are you pregnant?"

Phillip bounds across the couch—possibly the fastest I've ever seen him move—and places his hand across my stomach. "We *are* pregnant."

Somewhere along the way, his mom must have overheard part of the conversation because she makes a torturous sound, shakes her head, and says, "No! What? You're pregnant! No way!" She stands up, her hands in front of her face, and starts scream-crying, which turns into an ugly cry as she continues to screech, "No! Really? Is this a joke?"

Phillip shakes his head. "It's not a joke, Mom. You're really going to be a grandma."

"Ohmigawd, I don't believe it!" she yells, flailing her hands in the air.

"Believe it," Phillip tells her, laughing so hard at her reaction that he's practically crying. "We're six weeks along."

She covers her face with her hands, overcome with emotion.

Then, she starts running in place while waving her hands in the air and screaming. She grabs Mrs. D and jumps around her. "Did you hear that? I'm gonna be a grandma! I can't believe it. We'll be grandmas together!"

She's clapping now and still crying.

Phillip's dad is smiling big. He gives me a hug and congratulates his son with a slap on the back. Then, I notice tears well up in his eyes as he glances toward the ceiling. I know he's thinking about my dad missing this moment.

That makes me wonder how my parents would have reacted to the news.

I can't believe they have to miss out on this. It was bad enough they missed my wedding, but this is so much more.

My mom would have cried but in a more dignified way. My dad would have been the more emotional one.

I have to admit, I'm happily surprised by everyone's reactions. The kid in me was kind of worried they'd say we were too young, that it was too soon. All the things I thought at first.

But all I see is joy in their expressions.

Lori mutters to me, "You have some explaining to do." But then she goes on to say something about our babies being future best friends.

Danny rolls his eyes and teases, "Poor Phillip."

Finally, Mrs. Mac rushes over, fanning her face, and hugs us both.

Everyone gives us hugs.

Well, everyone but Chelsea.

I notice she's sitting on the couch, motionless, and then she looks me in the eye, stands up, and cries out, "I'm pregnant, too!"

She bursts into tears and runs upstairs.

Lori and I rush after her, finding her sobbing on the couch.

"I'm like a public service announcement for drunken hookups," she cries. "Don't have sex in the bathroom at a wedding without a condom, boys and girls, or you'll be walking down the aisle at your own wedding in a maternity dress. If he doesn't ditch you."

I sit down next to her and smile. "You got pregnant at my wedding? That's awesome."

She laughs through her tears.

Lori asks gently, "Did Joey already know?"

"Yes, he's been amazing. But I'm so afraid to tell our families. I want them to freak out like Mrs. Mac did, not question it."

"Chelsea," I say, "if you and Joey are excited about it, your families will be, too."

"And I'm sorry I yelled in the middle of your news. I'm so embarrassed."

"Seriously, it's okay. Just think of how fun it will be to be pregnant together."

"It will be nice," she says.

"Come on. Let's go downstairs."

WE GO BACK down to the family room where everyone congratulates us both.

Once the excitement dies down and everyone starts watching the game again, I notice Joey fidgeting. Chelsea isn't sitting by him; she's over by Lori with her knees pulled up on the couch. She almost looks scared.

I can understand why. This pregnancy business is scary stuff.

Emotions. Body changes.

When another round of commercials starts to play, Joey stands up in front of the TV, blocking everyone's view.

"This isn't how I planned to do it," he says. "I was going to do it later tonight, all romantic-like. Candles. Hotel suite. But I think you need to hear me say this in front of everyone." He holds his hand out. "Chelsea, please, come here."

Lori half-pushes her up off the couch.

When Chelsea joins him in front of the TV, she says, "What are you doing?"

Joey takes both her hands in his. "We've had a long history of almosts. *Almost* kissed. *Almost* dated. *Almost* were single at the same time. When I pulled you in the bathroom this past New Year's Eve, I told you I didn't want *almost* anymore. That you needed to kiss the guy you should be with for the rest of the year. What I should have said was, *for the rest of your life*, right then because that's how I felt. And I don't want you to feel like we're almost pregnant just because it happened so fast. I want to tell everyone that you're having my baby. There are going to be no more almosts for us. Chelsea, sweetie, I want you to marry me. Almost as much as I love you."

Chelsea is crying, and so am I because Joey—my goofy, perpetually horny childhood friend—looks sincerely happy.

He bends down on one knee and pulls out a ring box. "Chelsea, will you marry me?"

"You got a ring?" she asks, shocked.

"Yes," he says.

As he opens it, Chelsea starts shaking. "It's beautiful. You picked this out by yourself?"

He smiles at Danny and Phillip. "I got a little advice from a few friends, but yeah."

When he slides the ring on her finger, I notice that he's starting to sweat.

"You haven't answered me yet," he says nervously.

She throws herself at him, wrapping her arms around his neck. "Yes, Joey! Yes!"

I playfully smack Phillip. "You knew?"

"I thought he was going to propose tonight at the hotel. Been a pretty exciting Super Bowl, huh?"

After Joey and Chelsea stop kissing, Lori asks, "So, when are you due, Chelsea? You and Jade have to be due about the same time."

"October the fourth," she says.

"And I'm due on the first. In case you all didn't notice, the numbers on our shirts are our due date."

Chelsea runs over to me. "I'm sorry I ruined your announcement. The way you told everyone was so adorable." She stares at her sparkly new ring and gets tears in her eyes again.

I glance at the close game on the TV and decide it's just not that important.

"You need to come with Lori and me," I say, dragging her upstairs.

"What are we doing?" Lori asks.

"We need to do something, and she needs the practice."

"Practice for what?" Chelsea asks.

I grab a taper candle off my mom's dining room hutch and hand it to her. "Practice passing your candle. I'm your sorority big sister, and there's no way I'm missing out completely."

She grins. "Is there an *I'm engaged and knocked up* version of this?"

"No," Lori says. "You'll announce the engagement first. The rest of it is no one's business."

"He just told me he wants to get married soon," Chelsea says. "I'm throwing up every morning. I have a full load of classes. Sorority. How am I going to plan a wedding?"

"We'll help you," Lori says, lighting the candle and humming. "Pinned," she says, passing it to me.

It doesn't take long for us to pass the candle three times and for Chelsea to blow it out.

"Now, show us the pose," I tease.

"What pose?" she asks, looking confused.

Lori and I dramatically put our rings out to be admired, causing Chelsea to giggle.

"The pose of the happy, newly engaged girl. What else?" I tell her.

She mimics us, laughing, as Lori says, "This will be the question you will hear over and over; so, Chelsea, have you set a date?"

Chelsea laughs again. "No, but I was thinking my parents have that beach house in Florida."

"Spring break heaven," I say. "We had fun, didn't we? What an epic road trip. Then, the guys showed up."

"That was one of our *almosts*," Chelsea admits. "We were alone on the beach, both a bit drunk. But he had a girlfriend. Even though I was kinda mad at the time, looking back, it's good to know he didn't cheat on her. He's a good guy, right?"

"Yeah." I hug her. "He's a really good guy."

"So, what do you think? The beach in Florida? A few good friends?"

"Have you told your families?" Lori asks.

"Not yet. I've been too busy freaking out. Can I tell you both a secret?"

"Yeah," Lori and I reply.

"When I was in high school, I got pregnant and had a D and C. I know it was the right choice for me then, but I've always felt guilty, and I've been so afraid that, when it came time for me to want a baby, I wouldn't get pregnant. Like I would be punished or something. So, even though I was shocked, I am happy it happened."

Phillip wanders upstairs, looking for me. "What's going on up here?" He sees the candle and smiles. "Looks like I need to serenade you," he says and then launches into one of their frat songs.

His deep, sexy voice makes me melt.

I know that I'm so incredibly lucky.

And I say a little prayer that I won't be moody or emotional during my pregnancy.

WHEN WE CLEAN up after the game, Mrs. D and Mrs. Mac tell us, "The pregnant women get to go sit down and put up their feet. We've got this."

"This is crazy," I say, perching on the living room sofa. "All of us pregnant at the same time."

"So exciting though," Lori says, seemingly happy we are now in the pregnancy boat with her. Not only that, but she's also an expert compared to us. "So, how are you feeling?"

"I feel permanently hungover," I admit.

"Ohmigosh," Chelsea squeals, "me, too!"

"I wish I could tell you it goes away in a few months," Lori says, "and for some women, it does. Hasn't for me though. I'm still sick most of the time. Although, now, it's all day instead of just in the morning."

"They say one in five pregnancies ends in miscarriage. Right now, even though it was a shock that I got pregnant, that's what I've been worrying about the most," Chelsea says quietly. "Every time I have a little cramp, I'm so scared."

"Isn't it weird, how protective we are of the pregnancy? Even though mine wasn't planned. Even though I feel crappy. It's like the most important thing ever," I tell them.

"Speaking of that, Jade," Lori says. "Just last week you were crying because you got your period. How are you pregnant? Did you go to the doctor?"

"It's kind of crazy. When I was sick, I was freaking out because I didn't want to be pregnant. But then I got what I thought was my period and was super sad. That's when we decided we'd start trying. But, the next day, my period was gone, and I didn't know why. Then, when Danny was cooking bacon and I got sick again, I started wondering. As soon as Phillip left for work on Monday, I took a pregnancy test and couldn't even believe that it'd turned positive. I saw your OB/GYN that day. Turns out, I just had some spotting."

"That's crazy," she says. "How did you tell Phillip?"

"With the shirts. I wrapped his up and gave it to him and then showed him mine. He was pretty shocked. He just kept smiling and saying, 'Really?' What about you, Chels?"

"I told Joey I was late, so we did the test together. I was too afraid to look, so I watched him. First, his eyes got huge, and then this wide grin took over his face. He turned the stick toward me, picked me up, hugged me, and said, 'We're pregnant.' I don't know, but the fact that he said *we're* instead of *you're* just made me so happy that I started bawling. I'm hoping my mom will be excited when she hears the news."

"Joey's family will be excited," Mrs. Diamond says, sitting next to us. "Just the other day, his mother was telling me how much she likes you."

"Really? So, you don't think they will be mad?"

"Although I didn't scream and jump around like my friend over there," she says, pointing to Mrs. Mac, who is wiping down the kitchen counters, "my heart felt exactly the same. Your parents will be surprised, but they'll be thrilled."

ASHLEY AND COOPER went back to their hotel as soon as the game was over. Now, Marcus and Madison come upstairs to leave, so I walk them to the door and say good-bye. As they're pulling out of the driveway, I notice Danny sneaking back from his house.

"What are you doing?"

"Nothing. Just ran home to use the bathroom."

"We have bathrooms here."

"Had to take a crap," he says, but I know he's lying.

The dads are outside on the deck, smoking a cigar even

though it's fairly cold out.

Lori takes Chelsea and the moms over to see the nursery. The furniture she ordered the other day isn't in yet, but the room has been painted a gorgeous shade of pale yellow, and it has crisp white trim and murals of zoo animals hand-painted across the walls. It's adorable, and I'm in love with the tall giraffes that will peek over the crib.

I creep down the stairs, knowing Danny is up to something.

I stop halfway down and hear the guys discussing their lists of nevers.

"I'll never own a minivan," Joey says.

"And I'll never allow my kids to scream in a restaurant," Phillip says.

"Or on an airplane," Danny adds.

"I won't go crazy, buying stuff for a baby, like my sister did," Joey says. "All it needs is somewhere to sleep and some diapers."

"And I won't let a baby rule our lives. We'll still be able to do everything we enjoy now; we'll just be taking a baby along for the ride," Danny says. "Lori is freaking out, but it's just a baby. How hard can it be?"

"I know I'll never say, *When I was your age*," Phillip says. "Like my parents did."

"Oh, I know," Joey says. "I'll never make them listen to oldies. I'll stay up-to-date on music. I'll never get a beer gut because there's always time for working out, which serves a dual purpose. I'll always be able to whoop my son's ass. Keep him in line."

They all laugh wholeheartedly.

"We'll never stop doing Jell-O shots or Fireball."

"No Dad clothes."

"We'll go to all the coolest concerts."

"And find time to hit happy hour with our buddies."

"It won't ruin my golf game."

"I know one that is absolutely nonnegotiable," Phillip says.

"No child will *ever* eat in my car. Can you imagine French fries on the floor, little dirty fingerprints everywhere? No way. And we won't allow toys sprawled across the house. They will stay in their rooms."

"So, to recap," Danny says. "We will always be cool. We won't let them ruin our stuff. We'll still be spontaneous, and they won't affect our sex lives. And I vote for no curfews. They never made sense to me."

"What if you have a daughter?" Phillip asks.

"Easy. She won't have to worry about a curfew because I'll never let her out of the house at night."

"Because we know what happens at night." Joey laughs.

"Yeah, you get drunk, hook up at weddings, and next thing you know, you're in a basement, talking about how a baby isn't going to change your life," I tease, having slipped down the stairs without them noticing.

Danny jumps. "Ahh! You scared me. Lori didn't hear what we said, did she?"

"No, she's showing everyone the nursery."

He sighs with relief. "Boys," he says seriously, "you have to be careful about what you say all the time. No matter what you say, she'll give you that look. That look where she's blaming you for getting her pregnant because whatever is ailing her is all your fault even though she swears she's happy she's pregnant and happy you are the baby's father."

"Chelsea's such a cool chick; she won't be all emotional and needy."

Phillip coughs. "Except for running out of the room in tears when we announced our pregnancy."

"Ha. They are so emotional," Danny says. "And beware of questions where she asks if she looks bigger. It's a double-edged sword, and you will never answer it correctly. If you say what you think would be the right answer—*No, darling, I can hardly tell you're pregnant*—she will start crying because she'll worry the baby isn't growing properly. And, if you say that it looks like the baby bump has grown, she will cry because she thinks you think she's getting fat, and you won't love her anymore. Pregnancy is like boot camp. Or two-a-day practices. You just have to get through it without getting hurt. Things will be much easier once the baby is born."

"Two-a-days only lasted a few weeks. Pregnancy lasts nine months," Joey counters.

"Although there are a few perks. One of which is the world's best excuse for getting out of doing things you don't want to do. *My wife's pregnant and not feeling well; otherwise, we'd definitely be there.*"

"I'm sure there are a lot of other perks," Phillip says sweetly, pulling me onto his lap and kissing me.

That causes Danny to laugh. "Imagine sex when your wife has a stomach the size of a basketball."

"Chelsea's been very in the mood," Joey admits as Phillip smirks.

"And we know Jay has been, too, based on some things I've witnessed," Danny teases.

I toss a pillow at his face.

"You do realize you all had a similar conversation about girls in college?" I remind them.

"What are you talking about?" Danny, the biggest offender, asks.

I roll my eyes. "*I'm never losing my man card. I won't ever watch chick flicks. I'll never go shopping with her. I'll never change my hairstyle for a girl. I'll never miss a game for a date.* Shall I go on?"

"No need. We get it. We mellowed a little in the name of love."

"Or for regular sex," Joey teases.

"Enjoy that while you can, boys," Danny says, "because this is in your future."

He smirks again and then tosses something white at Joey.

Joey pulls it off his head and holds it out in front of him. "What is this? A tire cover?"

Phillip twists his head to the side and studies it. "No, it has two holes in it. Something goes through it. Is it to cover your golf clubs?"

"Your wife's *legs* go through it. Those are maternity underwear. Something to look forward to, huh?"

Joey is holding them up, trying to fathom Chelsea's skinny ass fitting in something that looks like it could cover the hood of a Mini Cooper. Honestly, I'm trying to imagine myself ever fitting in something that size. I glance down at my stomach. There is no way possible that I could ever fill those things out.

Lori and Chelsea choose this moment to rejoin us.

"Danny!" Lori screeches, horrified. "How could you?"

She turns around and marches up the stairs, Chelsea following her.

"Oh, boy," Danny mutters.

"Rubber band," I tease.

He stops at the bar, pours three shots, and hands them to the guys. "Here's to surviving pregnancy."

"'I'll never chase after a girl. They can chase me,'" Joey hoots. "I very clearly remember Danny saying that. Don't you, Phillip?"

Phillip takes a pull off his beer and smiles at Danny. "I think I do."

Danny runs up the stairs, flipping them off.

"I'm mostly worried about how we're going to afford it," Joey says. "I read that raising a baby costs like a half million dollars, not including college."

"Wow, that's a lot," Phillip says. He's tipsy and squinting his eyes more than normal.

"But it's over a span of, like, twenty years," I say gently. Because, if there's one thing he'll freak out about, it's money.

"Yeah, but it's still twenty-five thousand a year."

"No way a baby is going to cost that much at first. Maybe once they go to school and play sports and stuff," I counter.

"Whatever," Joey says. "We have to get a place to live. She still has to graduate and find a job, which is going to be tough when she's pregnant. I have a job, but it's not in my field. I thought, when I stayed in college to get the extra certification for nonprofit businesses, that it would make it super easy to find something. It's not looking that way."

"Nonprofit," I say. "I forgot that you did that."

"Don't you remember all the volunteer hours I had to do?"

"Yeah, but I just put it together. Did you know Danny is starting a nonprofit and looking for someone he can trust to run it?"

"No. What kind of nonprofit?"

"It hasn't been announced yet, but it's called Diamonds in the Rough," Phillip tells him. "It's a program where former and current college and professional players will go into schools and talk about sports and how getting a college scholarship helped better their lives. Mostly talking to kids about keeping out of trouble," Phillip says.

I add, "They will also eventually have their own scholarships and money to help with after-school programs for grade-school kids."

"That would be a dream job, if it pays decent," Joey says. "I wouldn't mind moving to Kansas City since Chelsea's sister lives here, and it's closer to her parents in Missouri."

"You should definitely talk to him," Phillip says. "And, if not, we're going to have some openings due to our expansion. If you'd be interested in the transportation industry."

Joey gets up and shakes Phillip's hand. "I'll think about that. Thanks, man. I'd better go get Chelsea and get to the hotel. We have some celebrating to do."

I give him a hug. "Congrats, Joey. On the engagement and the baby. I'm really happy for you."

"She loved that you did a little candle passing ceremony for her. Thank you for that. And congrats to you both."

I'M FINISHING UP writing in my journal when Phillip gets into bed with me.

"What a night," he says. "I bet you're exhausted."

"I don't think I'll have any trouble falling asleep."

He wraps his arms around me as I snuggle into my favorite spot in the world.

"Mmm, your neck smells good."

"You always say that," he teases.

"Yeah, well, trust me; it's a good thing because a lot of things that normally smell good are making me sick. Your neck doesn't make me sick."

He laughs and kisses me. "I'm glad I don't make you sick."

6 WEEKS

Dear Baby Mac,
We told your grandma and grandpa and some of our closest friends about you at our Super Bowl party today. I had football jerseys made that said Mac Daddy and Mac Mommy on the back as a way to announce our pregnancy to your daddy. We wore them today, but I kept my cardigan on, so no one would see what the back of mine said.

Everyone loved the Mac Daddy jersey. Mac Daddy actually came from your dad's old high school nickname, Pimp Daddy Mac. Your dad, he was, um, popular with the ladies.

I kept my sweater on, hoping someone would ask what the back of mine said. But no one did!

I was going CRAZY, waiting!

But your grandma was too busy noticing that my house was dusty, I guess.

We just moved, and I've been sick!

And trust me; her son—your father—knows how to pick up a dust rag! Actually, he promised to clean everything, and I'm kinda mad at him.

But whatever.

Except I'm not really mad. He's been spoiling me.

So, anyway …

During the third quarter, I stood in front of the TV, so everyone could see my back. Even then, it took a while before Mrs. Diamond caught on. Then, your grandma made a noise that sounded like a tortured cat.

Then, there was a frenzy of excitement.

Well, except for my friend Chelsea. We found out that she's pregnant, too. And their baby wasn't exactly planned. I mean, technically, I didn't plan for you either. And I feel kind of bad about it. The baby handbook has a few chapters on things you're supposed to do BEFORE you get pregnant. It's like I missed the first few weeks of class.

But I swear, I'll catch up.

It might help if you could stop whatever it is you're doing that's making me feel like I have a permanent hangover.

I have to say though, you sometimes don't seem real.

My stomach is still flat.

But then I guess that shouldn't be a shock since your dad tells me you are the size of a pea.

Sexy French maid.

FEBRUARY 5TH

I DRIVE TO the job site to check in with the survey crew and then go back to the office and make a million calls.

"Whatcha doing?" Phillip asks, standing in the doorway.

I point to the phone and finish my conversation while he stalks toward me with a smirk on his face.

"What's the smirk about?"

He pulls me into his arms and grabs my ass. "Just thinking you look really sexy today."

"I wish I felt sexy," I tell him. "Morning sickness seems to be stretching into the afternoon. Peggy, your new assistant—who I am in love with, by the way—dropped off a piece of her home-made carrot cake, and I thought I was going to puke all over it. That's not the impression I want to make on someone who can bake the way she can."

He grins. "Maybe you need cupcakes instead."

"Are you referring to *actual* cupcakes or cupcake sex?"

"Hmm," he murmurs, kissing my neck. "Maybe both."

"This weekend was sort of lacking in that department with our visitors. Speaking of that, did you hear your mother going on and on about how the house was dusty?"

"Uh, no."

"Well, I did. And it was embarrassing. You told me you were going to clean."

"I told you that I cleaned their rooms and their bathroom. Seemed stupid to clean the basement when it was going to get dirty again."

I roll my eyes. "That's not the point, and you know it."

His gaze lingers on the front of my shirt.

"Tonight, we're going to clean when we get home. No matter how tired I am. We need to get it done, okay?"

"Okay," he says with a sigh. "Cupcake sex sounds a lot more fun though."

"Maybe we should hire a cleaning lady. Just every other week."

"Sounds expensive," he says.

"Somehow, I knew you were going to say that. I guess it's something we have to decide if it's worth the expense."

"How are we going to do that?" He grins and squeezes my ass again.

I remove his hands from my backside and tease, "I'm practically being sexually assaulted by my boss."

"Oh, you haven't seen anything yet," he insinuates.

"Don't you have some work to do?"

He gives me a kiss. "Yes. Was just missing my bride."

"You know you've started calling me your bride when you're trying to be romantic?"

"I'm trying to be sexy, not romantic. We need steaming-hot, raunchy sex tonight. I'm just saying. Even if it means I have to do all the cleaning. How about I take off a little early? Meet you at home around four?" He gives my ass yet another squeeze, kisses me, and heads back to his office.

I MAKE A few more phone calls, but my mind is preoccupied. I'm wondering if cleaning could be both utilitarian and raunchy.

So, I call Danny.

"Sup," he says. "So, are you freaking out about being pregnant? You seem really excited."

"I was a little freaked out about feeling sad about not being pregnant. Then, I freaked when I realized I might be pregnant. Then, I nervously freaked when the lines turned pink. Then, I was shocked and freaked when the doctor confirmed it. Now, I'm just freaking happy. It was fun to tell everyone. Although I'm a little nervous we told everyone so soon. Hopefully, everything will go okay. Other than some nausea and fatigue, I feel mostly okay."

"Your boobs look bigger."

"Phillip said that, too. I think it's wishful thinking on his part. And, speaking of freaking, the look on Joey's and Phillip's faces when you showed them maternity underwear was priceless."

"More like a sad reality."

"Since I'm not quite there yet, I was thinking …"

"Uh-oh. You know we're coming over for dinner tonight."

"I know. Just don't come over until six thirty. Phillip and I are going to be cleaning."

"I don't get it."

"Never mind. The reason I called is, I want to know the name of the place where you bought our XXX honeymoon gifts."

"Looking to purchase a few new trinkets? Maybe I should join you."

"I think I'd like to go myself. And no sex toys. Just something, uh, just something."

"You can't go in there all embarrassed-like."

"I won't. I just don't need to give you details."

"I like details."

"Too bad. Can you tell me the name of it, so I can look up their website and see if they have what I need?"

"I'd rather take you there. Come on. Let's go have some fun."

I glance at the clock. "Fine. Text me the address and be there in thirty minutes. I don't have a lot of time."

I HEAR THE garage door open and run to the laundry room that's just off the door from the garage.

As Phillip walks in, I stop him with a feather duster. "*Bonjour, monsieur.*"

Phillip gives me a surprised grin, but then his dad runs into the back of him.

His dad eyes my skimpy French maid outfit, and I want to die of embarrassment. I run back into the laundry room and slam the door.

Phillip comes into the room, grabs my hand, and pulls me down the hall and into our bedroom. He gives me a steamy look, lust all over his face.

"Can I get a rain check on this?" he asks. "Dad got tied up at work today, and now, Omaha is getting an ice storm, so my parents are spending the night again."

"It might have been nice for you to tell me that. You told me to meet you at home for cupcake sex! What if I had been naked and surrounded by frosting, Phillip?"

He grabs the feather duster and runs it across my chest.

"Stop that!"

But he doesn't. He peeks down the front of the French maid costume.

"A very hot, sexy rain check."

"I don't know, Phillip. This maid is very busy."

He drops the duster and pulls me against him. He slides his hands up my skirt, clearly insinuating that he'd be up for a quickie.

"Your parents are out there," I say, trying without much resolve to fend him off.

"Are you sure we can't?" he says, teasing me by moving his fingers inside my thong.

"Of course we can't. You need to stop that, and I need to change."

"I'll help you," he says, stripping the costume off in one fluid motion and hungrily staring at me.

"That's not exactly helpful," I tell him as he licks his lips. "You need to go out there since you have clothes on, so they don't think we are in here, doing exactly what you're thinking about."

"What do you think I'm thinking about? Because I was thinking about ..." He whispers something naughty into my ear.

"You have a dirty mind."

"Isn't that why you were dressed like that? Because I'm a dirty boy?" he asks, lowering his lips to my chest.

I push him away, grab the outfit I had on today, and quickly put it on. "Please go out there, so we don't go together. I'm embarrassed enough as it is."

"I want to know why you dressed up."

"Because I thought we could make cleaning fun."

"We wouldn't have done any cleaning, and you know it," he says, flipping my skirt. "Although I think you're right. I'd rather have sex than clean. And, with work and you being pregnant, I think a cleaning lady makes sense."

"Really?"

He kisses my nose. "You dress like that, and you are probably going to get anything you want," he states.

BECAUSE I WORKED all day and had sexy times planned for dinner, when we were at the XXX store, buying the outfit, I told Danny to plan on going out for dinner tonight. I quickly call him.

"Please tell me you haven't left for dinner yet."

"We haven't," Lori says, answering his phone. "Danny worked out late and is in the shower."

"Thank God. Please tell me that we can go to dinner together."

"Danny told me you were being the sexy maid tonight."

"I was all dressed up, ready to go, and pushed the feather duster into Phillip's chest, just like we'd planned, but then ..."

"Then, what?"

"His dad ran into the back of him and saw me. Mom was still in the garage, thankfully."

"Oh crap."

"Tell me about it. Now, I'm hiding in my room. The surprising thing is, Phillip wanted to do it while his parents were in the house!"

"And that's bad?"

"It is when they saw how I was dressed. It's one thing to sneak off when no one knows, but when you're dressed in a cheap French maid costume with your boobs and ass hanging out, I'm pretty sure they know."

"True."

"I didn't make dinner because I thought we'd be in bed. Now, I have to go out and face them. Please don't make me do it alone. Come over. Now. Tell Danny to meet us when he's done."

She giggles.

"Why are you giggling? Wait. Don't say it. Don't even bring up the couch incident, and tell your husband that you will give him no sex—like ever—if he breathes a word of it to anyone, especially to Phillip's parents."

"I'm on my way."

"Thank you!"

I PUT ON my boots and then run out of my room and straight out of the house.

"Where are you go—" I hear Phillip say as I shut the front door behind me.

Lori is just coming up the driveway.

"I should have had you bring something, so it looks like I'm helping you. Now, I just look like a lunatic."

"You are a lunatic," Danny says, running up behind us. He gives me a smirk. "Is Phillip a dirty boy?"

"Ohmigawd, Lori! Did you not tell him what just happened?"

"What just happened?" he asks, looking dumbfounded. "And why are you already done?"

I give him a quick replay.

He's still laughing as we head in the house.

An ungrateful brat.

FEBRUARY 8TH

PHILLIP MADE ME ride with him to work today because we were supposed to have a blizzard.

We didn't.

And his parents are still here.

We have lots of food at home, but I'm thinking about a cheeseburger and fries from our local sports bar.

"Phillip, what do you think about going to The Lake Bar for dinner tonight?"

"Um, that sounds really good, but I think my mom is cooking something."

"We could eat it tomorrow. I'm dying for one of their bacon burgers and cheese fries dipped in ranch dressing. Doesn't that sound so good?"

"But she cooked."

"What is she making?"

"I'm not sure."

"Danny and Lori will eat it. She and your dad can eat it. Like, we don't have to eat with them every night just because they're staying with us, do we?"

"No, I guess not. You're right."

BUT PHILLIP'S FACE lights up when he walks into our house. "Oh, I'm in heaven," he says. "Doesn't that freshly baked bread smell amazing?"

I don't say anything because all I smell is the overwhelming stench of cooked broccoli.

I make a beeline for our bathroom, hoping if I smell the gingerbread candle in there, it will keep me from getting sick.

Phillip strolls into the bathroom a few minutes later, where he finds me with my nose inside the candle jar.

"What are you doing?"

"Trying not to puke," I reply, the glass causing my voice to have a deeper, echoing tone.

"I'll be glad when this morning-sickness stuff is over," he says.

"You're not the only one."

"And I know you wanted a burger, but Mom made my favorite dinner. Her homemade garlic rolls, white chicken pasta, and broccoli. You know how I love that."

"Yeah, I know."

"Tell you what," he says. "We'll go there tomorrow for lunch."

"Okay." I pout. Well, pout as much as possible when your face is stuck in a candle.

"Don't give me that look," he says sweetly, sliding his arms around my waist. "I love you, and I want to make you happy."

I suck in one more deep breath and set the candle down. "I know you do, Phillip."

"And you love garlic rolls."

"Yeah, I'm sure dinner will be great," I lie. "Phillip, um, does it bother you that your mom is sort of taking over our kitchen? Shouldn't she have to ask first? See if we have plans?"

"She's just doing something nice for us."

"Yeah, I know. It's just … never mind. Let's go eat."

WE'RE IN OUR dining room, eating. Not only has she cooked

Phillip's favorite meal, but also, somehow, all of our wedding gifts have disappeared.

When I mentioned it to Phillip's mom, she said, "Oh, I thought I'd help you out by putting them away."

And, while that's a nice thing to do—help someone—the truth is, I didn't ask for her help. I didn't want her to put them away. I wanted to do it myself, so I could put things where I wanted them to go.

But I can't say that because I'd sound like an ungrateful brat.

She continues, "And, since you don't have a kitchen table, we had to have somewhere to eat."

That sounds like a slam, directed at me. Like my house isn't good enough. I almost suggest that we go eat at the sports bar like I wanted, but that would probably come off as bitchy.

Danny and Phillip are going on and on about how amazing her dinner is. It's all I can do not to roll my eyes.

Or throw up.

The sauce that I usually love seems too rich, the bread too garlicky, and the broccoli is just gross.

Mrs. Mac is beaming with pride because the boys have eaten about forty rolls apiece.

Danny pats his stomach and says to Phillip, "I wish our wives could cook like this. Although I'm gonna have to work out longer tomorrow to burn these calories off."

Lori and I share a glance.

LATER, SHE DISCREETLY asks me to come see her kitchen progress and sneaks me out the front door.

The kitchen is still a disaster.

"It's coming together," I say but then sigh. "I can't compete with homemade rolls."

"Me either," she says. "I don't have a kitchen."

"Would you make homemade rolls if you did?"

"I don't know," she says. "Maybe if I had time. Maybe I should. But I'm different. I'm mostly home all day. You work."

"Yeah, but you're busy. Your house has been in some form of remodeling since you moved in. I'm sure you don't feel settled yet."

"No, not yet. It's been chaotic. Thankfully, our master bedroom is done. And, in a few more days, we'll have the home gym to beat all gyms. The sauna is going to be nice, although I can't use it while I'm pregnant, but I'm super excited for the area where I can do yoga."

"You're going to do yoga? But you're so—"

"Were you going to say huge?" she screeches, holding her large bump, which is really too large now to be classified as such.

"Uh, no. I was going to say high strung." Really, I was.

"That's why I want to do yoga—to center myself. I'm taking a prenatal yoga class, and I really like it. And inner calmness is good for the baby and me. Did you notice how I was breathing calmly while Danny was going on and on about how good dinner was? What I really wanted to do was take those garlic rolls and shove them up his ass."

"Hmm, maybe I do need yoga."

"You should come to class with me. It's at six a.m., just down the street."

"Six a.m.? Are you freaking kidding me? If you can go around eight, maybe. But back to my problem. What am I going to do about Phillip's mom?"

"I don't know," she says. "There's not much you can do, is there?"

"I don't know either, but I do know I still want a freaking cheeseburger. Wanna go get one?"

"Ooh," she says. "I'd love to. The meal was too garlicky for me. I would have been burping it up all night. Should we take the boys?"

"They might never leave the dining room," I joke.

7 WEEKS

Dear Baby Mac,
You are growing like crazy. You've more than doubled in size. Your dad talks to you at night before we go to sleep. It reminds me of when we were young, and he would call me every night on the phone. I hope you like the sound of his voice as much as I do. He's amazing. You're really lucky.

Me, on the other hand, we're going on three weeks of this permanently hungover feeling.

Except I can't drink.

So far, we're not getting started off on the right foot here.

A naked picnic.

FEBRUARY 10TH

"I THINK I'LL go jogging with you this morning, Phillip," I say as he rolls out of bed.

"Really? Are you sure you're feeling up to it?"

"Yeah, I didn't feel as sick yesterday, and I want to try to stay in shape. They say it makes both your delivery and recovery easier. Plus, I miss running."

He pulls me up. "I've missed running with you. Dress warm though; it's pretty chilly."

I put on my winter running gear and follow Phillip out the front door.

"Whew, it is pretty cold!" I say, practically seeing my breath crystalize before me.

"It's not bad once you get going."

As we're jogging around the lake, Phillip says, "So, our one-month anniversary is the day before Valentine's Day. I think we should do something special since it's our first Valentine's Day as a couple."

"You've given me flowers for as long as I can remember."

"That's because I had a big crush on you. Do you have anything you want to do, or should I plan something?"

"Let's plan it together. Our anniversary is Tuesday, and Valentine's Day is Wednesday."

"Yeah, it's during the week. I was thinking we could take a couple of days off. Maybe spend one day looking at baby stuff. I know you've been looking at ideas on how to decorate the nursery. Are you excited to buy all that?"

"I am, Phillip, but I don't want to get anything yet."

"Why not?"

"I'd like to wait until after our ultrasound. Make sure everything is okay."

He solemnly nods his head. "I've been flipping through the pregnancy book. There is a lot that can go wrong, isn't there?"

"Phillip, you're not reading worst-case scenarios for the first trimester, are you?"

He shrugs. "You know I like to be prepared for the worst."

"I don't even want to consider the worst."

"That's fine. You let me worry about all that."

"Is it freaking you out a little?"

"No, not at all. So, back to our anniversary, I was thinking maybe we could go shopping. Maybe get a couple's massage. Come back to our house for some fun."

"Do you remember when we first got together—how we did it in every room in my condo?"

He grins. "Oh, I remember that well. It was like the Around the World basketball game we used to play. Only I was scoring in every room."

"We have a lot more rooms in our new house," I suggest.

"And that's how you want to spend our two days?"

I give a casual shoulder shrug. "It's just a thought. Depends on if we can be alone."

"I'll make sure we are."

"I love the idea of sleeping in, shopping, having a long and leisurely lunch, shopping a little more, and then coming home and relaxing. Maybe a picnic in front of our fireplace."

"A naked picnic?"

"I was thinking you might like to go shopping for some lingerie, too."

"Oh, I like that idea. It's a date."

All about that lace.

FEBRUARY 13TH

"HEY, PRINCESS," PHILLIP says, gently waking me. "I've got to run to the office for just a bit. Minor crisis to deal with, but I'll be back in two hours with whatever you want me to bring."

"A chocolate chip muffin and some orange juice sound really good," I suggest.

"Your wish is my command. I can't wait to spend the day with you." He kisses my forehead. "Go back to sleep."

I try but can't get back to sleep. I'm too excited for today. Instead, I get up, take a long shower, and prepare myself for our two-day celebration. I shave, paint my nails, blow out my hair and curl it, do my makeup, and then put on a cute dress, tights, and boots.

I go stand in the room that will be the baby's nursery and stare at it. Imagine it with a soft color on the wall. Imagine different furniture arrangements.

We got a large basket as a wedding gift that I thought I would put throws in, but its soft blue color would look really cute in the nursery. I run downstairs, looking for the basket.

"Ahh!" I scream as I catch a glimpse of the Nebraska gnome, who is staring at me from atop the living room mantel.

What the heck?

How did he get up there?

I grab my phone, run into our bedroom—so the gnome won't hear me—and call Phillip.

"Are you on your way home?"

"Yeah, should be there in a few minutes. Why? You just wake up? I was hoping to join you in bed."

"Did you move the gnome?"

"The what?"

"You know, that ugly little gnome we got as a wedding gift."

"The Nebraska one? Uh, no. I honestly haven't seen it since we unwrapped it."

"Or there's another explanation."

"Like, my mom moved it?"

"That, or it's possessed, and it comes alive at night. He moved once before. I just didn't tell you about it."

Phillip laughs.

"Don't you laugh. I'm serious. He was on the dining room table and was creeping me out, so I covered his face with wrapping paper. The next day, the paper was off his head and crunched into a little wad by his boot. So then, I shut him in a drawer with the cutlery. How did he get out of the drawer, Phillip?"

"I'm sure there's a logical explanation," he says. Phillip is nothing if not logical.

"Like what?"

"My mom cleaned up the dining room. She must have moved it."

"I'm going to check the drawer."

"For what?"

"To see if she put anything in it."

I run into the dining room, checking on the way to see if the gnome is still on the mantel.

Thankfully, he is.

And he's not holding a little knife or anything—that I can see.

I whip open the drawer and see that it's exactly the way I left it—minus the gnome.

"Phillip, it's the same!"

"I'm pulling in the garage," he says.

I rush to the door, opening it and throwing a dish towel at him.

He snatches it out of the air. "What's this for?"

"For you to cover the gnome with."

He laughs again. "You've got to be kidding me."

As I grab his hand and drag him to the mantel, he's still chuckling—until he looks the gnome in the eye.

"He does kind of look like trouble," Phillip says seriously, tossing the towel over the gnome's head. "Where do you want him?"

"Back in the drawer," I say, leading him to the dining room and opening the top drawer of the hutch.

Phillip lays the gnome faceup, like I did before, and quickly shuts the drawer. Then, he grabs my ass. "You look pretty. You ready to go, or you wanna go back to bed?"

"Did you forget my breakfast?"

"It's in the car. I figured I needed to rescue you from the evil gnome first. I learned my lesson with the spider and got here as fast as I could," he says with a smirk. "I didn't want to find you on the ground, being stomped on by his little black boot."

I smack his shoulder. "You'd better not be making fun of me."

"Never," he says, giving me a deep kiss. Then, he picks me up and carries me to the bedroom.

NOW, I'M SITTING in the car, eating my muffin, while we drive to the Plaza.

We wander through a bunch of shops, looking at clothes, shoes, and stuff for the house when Phillip stumbles upon something incredible.

"Look at this table," he says, running his hand across the soft wooden top. "People have carved their names in it."

"That's so amazing."

"Can you imagine how cool it would be for our kids to carve their names in it? All their friends. All our friends."

"It'd be a lifetime of memories," I agree. "Just the thought of that—us with a houseful of kids—makes me feel so emotional. That's what I want our house to be—a place where everyone feels comfortable. Where, if you spill juice or some beer, no one's going to freak out. Where you feel love. Happiness."

"I love how excited you are about our future," he says, his hands settling on my stomach. "You changed your mind, didn't you? You want a house full of kids."

"Yeah, I think I do."

"And I think we need a kitchen table like this."

"It looks expensive," I say, hoping my dreams aren't dashed.

Phillip whistles when he sees the price.

"It's one of a kind," I justify, reading the tag and cringing. "Custom-designed to fit your space. You even have a choice of woods."

"I like it just like it is," he says. "Do you think it would go with our cabinets?"

"The rustic, industrial vibe it has would pair so well with our kitchen design. And, my gosh, this wood is so thick." I bend down to examine it.

"It's a single slab," a salesman tells us. "The designer makes only a few pieces a year. If you're interested, you'd put twenty-five percent down as a deposit. That gets you a place in line. When it's time for him to work on your table, we get another twenty-five percent, and then the balance is due upon delivery."

"And how long would it take for delivery?"

"He's running about six to eight months out."

"That's okay," Phillip says, shocking me. "We have the dining room table, and we sit at the kitchen island most of the time anyway. We're going to have lunch and discuss it. I think we'll be back."

"Are you serious about the table?" I ask as we're headed into my favorite Italian restaurant.

Phillip takes my hand in his. "At our wedding, I promised to support your wild ideas. This one's easy to support because I think it's really cool. I especially loved the steel edges. And it's pretty good timing really. We'd get it right after the baby was born."

"It'll be a while before the baby can carve its name."

"That's true, but our first carving could be the baby's name and birthdate. Speaking of names, we haven't talked about them yet. Should we?" he asks as we're seated.

"Um, no, I don't think so yet."

"Why not?"

"The same reason I don't want to buy stuff for the nursery."

"What if we talked about names we like in general for all our possible future children? The kind of names you'd like to see carved in our table."

"Are you really going to order it?"

"If you want it, yes."

"Do you want it?"

"I think it's cool, but it's more than that. It's the way you reacted to it. I want our home to have things that are special to us."

"Me, too, Phillip. You sure you're okay with the price?"

"It's more than I ever thought I'd spend on a table, but it's massive and custom-made, and it will last us forever. I didn't tell you, but I'm getting a bonus. A really nice bonus."

"When? What for?"

"Well, I won't get it for another month, but it's for hitting my goals. My division is up by thirty percent. Considering it was down when I took it over after graduation, that's pretty darn good."

"I'm proud of you, Phillip."

He gives me a grin. "And I want us to have that table."

"Then, I think we should definitely go back after lunch and order it."

"SO, WHAT'S NEXT?" he asks after we've had lunch and put our deposit down on the table.

"Well, if we're doing our picnic by the fireplace tonight, we'll need supplies."

"Like lingerie?"

"And food."

He grabs my hand and leads me across the street to the lingerie store.

"Are you going to be embarrassed to go in here with me?" I tease.

"No way. And you're modeling everything for me."

"I'm not sure boys are allowed in the dressing room area."

"Then, I'm going in the room with you."

"YOUR HUSBAND IS so cute," the too-sexy-for-her-own-good salesgirl says. "He told me to bring you this. Says it's your anniversary."

"Yes, it is." I laugh. "And, apparently, the one-month anniversary is all about lace."

"Oh, you're newlyweds. Did you date for long?"

"We got engaged on our first real date and got married four months later."

"Was it, like, an arranged marriage?"

"No, we'd been friends for a long time."

"So, is it hard, living with a guy who looks like that?" she asks.

"Looks like what?"

"He's so hot," she gushes. "But he doesn't seem like an asshole."

"Yeah, he's not."

"Every hot guy I date is. And the dreamy way he talks about you is so adorable. Where did you find him?"

"Next door," I say with a laugh. "Um, would you send him back here? I want to show him this one."

"Sure," she says, leaving me with more silk and lace.

Phillip comes strolling back, looking sexy as ever.

"Are you out there, flirting with the salesgirls?"

"Me? No. I was telling them all about you. About our anniversary."

"They're all drooling over you; it's the scruff. It's practically devastating," I tease.

"You're silly. Are you going to let me see what you have on?"

I open the door.

"Wow. Now, *that* is devastating. We might need one in every color," he says, feasting his eyes on my body.

"I'm glad you like it." I close the door because I only want him to see a peek, but his hand stops the door from shutting, and he eases his way into the dressing room.

"You're not supposed to be in here."

"The girls out front said it was okay."

"I'm sure they did, but I don't care. I don't want you to see everything. I want you to be surprised tonight."

He leans back, supposedly taking in the lingerie, but his hands are sliding across my hip and toward my thigh.

"I think I'd rather see it all now," he says. "Anticipation is half the fun."

His lips cover mine.

"Um," I say.

"I have a sexy wife," he whispers into my neck as he's kissing down it.

"Are you sure, Phillip? My stomach isn't as flat anymore."

"All I know is, I can't wait to get you home and f—"

"How are we doing on sizes?" the salesgirl interrupts from outside the door.

"Can I try this chemise in a bigger size?" I ask, pulling it off and flipping it over the door.

"Of course," she says. "Be right back."

Phillip takes a step back and grins. "Naked is better." He picks up a bra and dangles it in front of me. "I'd like to see this on though."

I slip the bra on along with the matching teeny briefs.

"Dang," he says. "Your boobs look amazing." He slides his hand across the top of my cleavage. "So sexy. So gorgeous. I can't believe you're my wife."

I giggle. "You're just talking all pretty because you're hoping to get lucky tonight."

"There's no hope involved. I am lucky. You married me."

"Hmm. Totally cheesy line but cute."

I reward him with a kiss.

Which turns hot.

"Here's the other size," the girl says, slinging it over the door.

"Thanks!" I say, ripping my lips away from Phillip's. "All right. I don't want you to see this. Why don't you head over to the gourmet food store and buy food for our picnic tonight?"

He stays put, tightly wraps his arms around me, and slides his tongue in my mouth.

I almost forget we're in a public dressing room.

"Um, Phillip ..." I pull away, knowing if I keep kissing him, we'll be celebrating early.

Right here.

"Later," he says with a sexy smirk.

WHEN WE'RE DRIVING home, I call Nick.

"Nick! How is the combine going?"

"Well, it's the first day."

"Actually, you don't need to answer that. Technically, I know how it's going since Danny has been texting us updates. But I would like to hear if you're having fun. Your forty-yard dash was screaming."

"I've been working out hard since the first of the year to get ready. Added muscle, speed, and we all know my kicking accuracy has always been good."

"I heard the psychological testing is tomorrow. I'm worried for you," I tease.

"Shut up. It will be fine. Danny still talking me up to Kansas City?"

"Of course. He wants you on his team again. So, how are you?"

"All right, Jay. What do you want?"

"Phillip and I were wondering when you might be coming to visit us."

"Why?"

"Phillip met a girl he wants to set you up with."

"And how did he meet this girl?"

"He was crushing on her, but since he can't have her, he thought of you."

Phillip pokes my side, causing me to scream, and then takes my phone.

"Dude," he says to Nick, "she's perfect for you. She works in a lingerie store." Phillip says to me, "Ha. He says that's all he needs to hear."

Phillip puts us on speaker and continues talking to Nick, "But she's not just a hottie. She's getting her master's in criminal justice. And I'm pretty sure she could kick both our asses."

"Hmm," Nick says noncommittally.

"Are you dating anyone?" I ask.

"She means, are you hooking up with anyone on a regular

basis?" Phillip says loudly.

"What's this chick's name?" Nick asks.

"Does it matter?" I say.

"It does to me."

"It's Natalie," Phillip says.

Nick goes, "Hmm. I don't know."

"What were you hoping for? Gigi or Kiki? You know, shoving dollar bills down their thong is not the best way to meet women."

"Shut up," Nick says. "Or we'll talk about Sex on the Stairs."

"The drink?" Phillip asks.

"Yep," Nick says.

"I'm pregnant!" I yell out to change the subject.

"What? Seriously? Did you know that Joey got Chelsea pregnant at your wedding? Does that mean you got pregnant there, too? Jeez, thank God that's not catching."

"Nick! Did you hook up with someone at our wedding?"

"My lips are sealed," he says. "But yes."

"Who?"

"It might have been one of the bridesmaids."

"One of the bridesmaids? Lisa was there with her boyfriend. Katie was definitely with Neil. Oh my God. You didn't sleep with Phillip's sister, did you? She's married!"

"For goodness' sake, Jay. If I'd slept with Ashley, I'm pretty sure I would never speak of it to Phillip."

"That's right," Phillip grunts.

"Wait. Lisa was pretty drunk. You like drunk girls."

"Lisa was practically passed out. I don't like them *that* drunk."

"Wait, so were you. You were sleeping on the couch when we left."

"Just a little catnap," Nick says. "I rallied."

"Well, that only leaves Chelsea and—oh, no! Nicky! Macy is *engaged*! Her wedding is this summer!"

"Yeah, about that ..."

"What about it?"

"Have you talked to her since you got back from the honeymoon?"

"Uh, we've texted some. Wait. Is that why she stayed in Kansas City for the rest of the week?"

"Uh, maybe."

"Nick, I went with her to pick out her wedding dress. Do you know how much she spent on it?"

"Eleven thousand dollars," Nick says flatly, like he's heard it many times.

"I remember you two dancing, but I didn't think anything of it since you walked up together. Was she drunk?"

"Jadyn," Phillip says, giving my knee a little slap, "Nick doesn't have any problem picking up women. And I doubt she was drunk all week."

"I know that, but I'm just so shocked. Why didn't she tell me?"

"Probably because she knew you'd react like you just did," Nick says.

"Are you two still talking? Or worse, *doing*? Is she still engaged?"

"It's complicated," Nick says.

"Oh, boy," I say, sucking in a breath. "What does that mean?"

"It means, she's trying to figure out what she wants."

"What do you want, Nick?"

"It wasn't the first time we'd hooked up," he admits.

"Really? When did you?"

"In the hot tub at our place," Phillip says. "I remember that."

"Where was I?" I ask.

"At the bar probably," Nick says, once again warning me he knows way more than he should.

I'm not a fan of Macy's fiancé. He can be kind of an asshole. So, I ask, "Do you like Macy? Love her? What's she going to do?"

"It's too soon to say, but we both think there's something there. But she's feeling a lot of pressure. Her parents have put down deposits. She doesn't want to upset them. She jokingly asked if I'd want to get married this summer—at least, I think she was joking. What should I do?"

I raise an eyebrow at Phillip, silently asking for his advice.

He purses his lips and thinks. Finally, he says, "Don't sleep with her again until she decides."

"Ah, man. I knew you were going to say that."

"That's because you know it's the right thing to do," Phillip says sincerely, and I swear, I fall a little more in love with him.

I squeeze his hand. He always knows the right thing to do.

"Yeah, I know," Nick sighs. "All right, I've gotta get to dinner. Talk to you later."

"Good luck with the rest of the combine, Nicky," I tell him. "Everything else will work out if it's meant to be."

WHEN WE GET home, Phillip sets up the picnic in front of the fire while I go change into my first lingerie look, a sexy coral silk chemise with sheer insets.

Phillip is lying on a blanket, wearing just a pair of silky boxers.

And, even though I was just thinking I was hungry, I suddenly couldn't care less if I ever ate again. I slide onto his lap, straddling him.

"I didn't see this one in the store," he says. "You holding out on me?"

"You were probably too busy flirting with the lingerie sales-girls to notice," I tease.

"I wasn't flirting."

"But you knew her name. Her major."

"I was just being polite and making conversation while you were trying stuff on."

"She was crushing on you."

"I can't help it."

"Were you crushing back? She was pretty, and she did have the kind of bombshell body I'll never have."

His fingers trail across my chest. "I don't know; you're looking pretty bombshell to me right now."

"I don't have curvy hips, Phillip."

He grips my hips in his hands while I slide off his boxers.

"Listen closely," he says. "I love you. I think you're sexy as all get out, but that's not all that makes you sexy. It's your confidence, your sense of humor, and your willingness to try anything that I love. I hope, while you're pregnant, you don't ever doubt my love. I want you to try to enjoy the way your body changes. And know that I think you having our baby might just be the sexiest thing ever."

8 WEEKS

Dear Baby Mac,

You are growing super fast right now. And your heart is beating super fast, too. One hundred fifty beats a minute! That's about double mine.

You have arms and legs, and you can move them. Your dad says you're waving at him when he talks to you, but I can't feel it because you are only the size of a raspberry.

I've gained three pounds though, which seems kind of excessive for a raspberry. Although, I'm pretty sure, it's gone straight to my boobs, which are now bigger than normal, and your father is obsessing over them.

I am also craving Milk Duds and am considering buying stock in them.

Things are super busy at work. Our plans for the new building were approved, we had a groundbreaking ceremony, and construction has officially commenced. If all goes as planned, we'll move in well before you're born.

I'm also officially addicted to searching nursery designs on the internet, and I have been compiling ideas. I'm not sure what I want it to look like yet, but I'm pretty sure it will be a bluish gray.

And, just so you know, there are about a thousand blue-gray paint colors available, but I promise to find the perfect shade.

Your grandmother is very excited about you. She and your grandpa have been staying here a lot. It's been sort of challenging, if I'm being honest.

Your dad and Danny have been enjoying her cooking. And I'll admit, it is nice sometimes to come home to a warm, home-cooked meal.

It's been sweet of her to cook for us.

It was also sweet when she put all my wedding gifts away.

And it was even sweeter today when she reorganized all my kitchen cabinets.

But ...

It's sort of pissing me off.

It shouldn't be because she's doing it to be nice.

But it is.

Take out a hit.

FEBRUARY 24TH

PHILLIP IS LYING across the couch, watching a college basketball game.

I stand directly in front of the TV, arms crossed and foot tapping in irritation.

"What?" he asks, trying to look around me.

"Don't *what* me," I say. "It's not funny."

"What's not funny?"

Phillip looks confused. I really thought he'd smile.

"You moved the gnome to freak me out."

"The gnome? No, I didn't."

"Phillip, do you promise—swear—you didn't move it?"

"I swear. What is your obsession with this gnome?"

"He's moving of his own accord, Phillip. You're the man of this house. Doesn't that concern you?"

"Can you move over just a little?" Phillip asks, still trying to see the game.

I grab the remote and threaten to turn it off.

Phillip leaps off the couch and then pins me to the chaise. "You're being a bad girl."

"Phillip! Stop thinking about sex. I mean, don't stop thinking about sex, just don't think about it right this second. I need you to come upstairs and deal with this."

He laughs. "Deal with the gnome? What do you want me to do with it? Shall I bring in a gnome from a rival school? Take out a hit on it?"

"You're not taking this seriously." I pout.

He gets off me and pulls me up. "Fine. Show me the gnome."

I tiptoe upstairs and point toward the living room where the gnome has now taken up residence on the back of the sofa table.

"How did he get there?"

"I have no idea."

"This is silly."

"I know!"

"Let's wrap him up tight and put him back in the hutch," Phillip says, going out to the garage. He gets a ball of twine and wraps the gnome's legs with it. "There, he won't be able to walk now."

"You think he's walking?"

He rolls his eyes at me. "*You* think he's walking; that's all that matters."

"But he has a mono leg. I think he hops, so I don't think the string will stop him, Phillip."

"Fine," he says, anxious to get back to the game. "I'll tie him into the hutch."

He opens the top drawer and ties string around my heavy cutlery tray. Then, he lays the gnome down faceup and ties those strings around his legs.

"He's not going anywhere now," Phillip says, shutting the drawer and heading back downstairs.

10 WEEKS

Dear Baby Mac,
Your dad is obsessed with reading my pregnancy books. And not in a good way.

He's starting to read all the horror stories. Ectopic pregnancies. Blighted ovums. Miscarriages.

Please, promise that you won't do that to me.

I know it's only been ten weeks, and you're only the size of a prune, but I can't wait to meet you.

Your dad is convinced you're a girl.

Later in the pregnancy, we can find out what sex you are, but I don't think I want to know, so, hopefully, you're okay with a gender-neutral nursery.

Although, just in case, I bought a really adorable dress with a pale pink tutu and a butterfly appliqué. Oh, and matching sparkly pink booties that my mom would have gone crazy over.

But, shhh … don't tell Daddy.

And guess what.

Next week, you're getting your first picture taken!

We're having an ultrasound. And I'm nervously excited!

So, be good, be there, have a nice strong heartbeat, and show off your itty-bitty self!

Get my hopes up.

MARCH 12TH

"I'M SO NERVOUS," I tell Phillip as we enter the doctor's office.

"I'm excited," he says. "This is going to be so incredible. We're going to see our baby for the first time."

"I know. I'm so excited, too, but I'm scared. Afraid to get my hopes up. Especially after you were talking about all the different types of miscarriages. With the blighted ovum one, you can feel pregnant, even start to show, but there's no baby. Just an empty sac. That would be so sad. And what about the other one you read about, where they couldn't find a heartbeat? I don't know what I'll do if that happens, Phillip."

He grabs my hand and squeezes it. "Everything is going to be just fine. I'm sure of it."

I nod. "You're right. It will be fine," I say, but I'm still a nervous wreck. It's weird. I know I'm pregnant. I know my body is changing, but sometimes, I don't feel pregnant, which makes me question if everything is okay.

"Do you care if I record the ultrasound?" he asks me. "Danny said we should even though they will print us out a picture."

"Yeah, I think we should."

"Did you drink enough water?"

"My teeth are floating."

Phillip laughs, and it helps break the tension. "That ought to be good enough then."

We get set up in the ultrasound room—me on the table with my shirt pulled up and Phillip sitting next to me, his phone ready to record.

Our ultrasound tech comes in. She puts gel on my stomach and rubs the wand across it. Grayness moves across the screen in front of us. She frowns at the screen.

I squeeze Phillip's hand tighter, worried there's no baby to find.

But then she slides the wand to the other side of my abdomen and says, "There we go."

On the screen is a little black oval, and inside of it, at the bottom, is—

"Is that it? Is that our baby?"

"Yes, it is. See there? That's the baby's head," she says, directing us with the pointer on the screen. "And there are the facial bones. You can see the cord coming out of the belly here, and there's its bottom. How far along are you?"

"Eleven weeks."

"It's moving," Phillip says, sounding a little worried.

I want to look at him, but my eyes are glued to the screen.

"It is very active," she says. "The last baby I had was quiet and napping. This one is bouncing all over the place."

"Look at his little arms move. And his legs are kicking. It's amazing."

"The baby is moving a lot. Is that normal?" Phillip asks.

"It's completely normal. Let's see if the baby will hold still long enough for me to get some measurements." She makes a few clicks and then says, "Your baby is measuring at eleven weeks and two days, so its size is as expected. Your due date should be accurate."

"Look at the baby! It's going crazy. Is it because I'm nervous?"

"No," she says. "Your baby's putting on a show for you. Oh, look, there's its hand. It just waved at you. Hello, baby."

"Ohmigawd! Hi," I say.

"Hello, Baby Mac," Phillip says.

I turn to look at him. There's joy written all over his face, and he's practically vibrating; he's so excited. He pulls my hand to his lips and kisses it.

"Can you believe that's our baby?" he says to me.

"I can't believe I can't feel the baby moving. It's all over the place."

"Well, the baby's not very big yet," the tech says. "In a few more weeks, you'll feel all of this. At first, like a flutter, and then later, you'll feel hard kicks and elbows to the ribs. Look at him showing off. That was a somersault."

"Did you see that?" Phillip says. "The baby just opened its mouth."

"And swallowed," the tech says.

"That's amazing. This is all so breathtaking."

"Let's hear the baby's heartbeat."

The room fills with the kind of sound you would expect to hear in a submarine. An odd, sonar-like whooshing sound.

"That's your baby's heartbeat," the tech says.

"That's crazy. I can't even believe this. I'm sorry. It's just such—" I get choked up.

"A beautiful sound, isn't it?" she says. "I never get tired of hearing it."

"The heartbeat seems fast," Phillip says.

"It is. About one hundred and sixty beats per minute. Your baby has a nice strong and normal heartbeat. Everything looks great."

Phillip puts his lips across my knuckles again, only this time, he keeps his head down. When he finally looks up at me, his eyes are glistening with tears. "This is really happening."

Seeing Phillip get emotional causes tears to flood my face.

I nod at him. "We're really doing this. We're really having a baby."

We walk hand in hand to the car, not saying much. I think we're still both in awe.

"I could have stayed all day and watched that. Have you ever seen anything so amazing?" he asks me.

"I haven't. Could you believe how much it was moving? It was crazy."

We go get lunch, but neither of us eats much. We're too busy watching the ultrasound video over and over.

LATER THAT EVENING, Phillip strolls in from work as I'm getting ready to run over to see the progress on Lori's kitchen. His tie is slightly loosened, and he looks delectable.

"Hey," he says, putting one hand on my ass and kissing my neck. "Where are you going in such a hurry?"

"I was just running over to see the kitchen progress before you got home."

"My parents won't be here until late tonight. They have a benefit dinner."

"Yeah, I saw your mom was all dressed up. She looked really pretty."

"Did you show her the ultrasound video?"

"No, I wanted to wait for you," I tell him, giving him a kiss and running out the door. "I'll be right back."

When I'm standing in Lori's kitchen, looking at a newly framed wall, I realize that I just missed out on an opportunity. "Lori, does Danny have a sexual tell?"

"What do you mean?"

"Like, in poker, a tell is how you can tell what kind of hand they have."

"I don't know. I've never thought of it. What does Phillip

do?"

I walk up to her, put one hand on her ass, and pretend to kiss her neck just as Danny breezes in.

"Can I play, too?" he asks. "I knew you were gonna be a good neighbor."

Lori and I look at each other and laugh. Danny struts across the kitchen and pulls Lori's waist in tight to his but gives her just a sweet kiss on the cheek.

"Oh my God!" She bursts out laughing. Danny looks confused, but Lori points at me and screeches, "That was just it!"

"What was what?" he asks.

"Nothing," she says to him.

"Well, on that note," I say, "I'd better leave you two alone."

"Good idea," she says, not even bothering to walk me to the door.

WHEN THEY'RE FINISHED with whatever they were doing, they come over for dinner. Since Phillip's mom isn't here, we eat delivery pizza at the kitchen island.

Phillip and Danny both stand and eat. Something she would not approve of.

And that makes me happy in a sadistic way.

"So, Mac," Danny says, "did you know our wives have started hooking up behind our backs? I mean, the least they could do is let us watch if we can't play along."

Phillip squints at me as I'm setting down a plate of brownies.

Lori giggles in a way that makes her look guilty.

"What are you talking about?" Phillip asks.

"When I walked in tonight, your wife's hand was on Lori's ass, and she was kissing her neck. It was pretty hot, I'll admit. Been a while since the days of two girls kissing."

"We weren't kissing, Danny," I say.

Danny waves his hand at me and goes, "Whatever."

"Did you do that in college?" Lori asks him. "Like, two girls at once? A threesome?"

Phillip and I remove all expression from our faces. I'm pretty sure this is not something Lori wants to hear about right now.

I say to her, "Of course not." Then, I turn to Phillip. "I wasn't kissing Lori. I was demonstrating your sexual tell."

"My sexual tell?"

"Yeah, what you do when you want sex. You grab my ass and kiss right here on my neck. And Danny pulls Lori's hips in tight to his, but then he just gives her a sweet little kiss on the cheek."

"I do, do that." Danny laughs. "Lori has one, too, though. She rubs her hand up under my shirt."

"So, we had the ultrasound today," Phillip says with a beaming smile.

"Really?" Lori says. "Why didn't you tell us?"

"JJ was nervous," Phillip says. "We wanted to be sure everything was okay."

"And?" Danny asks.

"We have a video," Phillip says proudly.

11 WEEKS

Dear Baby Mac,

Congratulations! You are real!

And we have the proof on video! The ultrasound tech said you were showing off for us, and I think she was right. You were moving all over, kicking and punching, and you even stopped to wave at us! It was seriously the most amazing thing I'd ever seen.

You have a really big head, but the tech said that's normal right now, that your brain is super important because it's helping you grow and develop!

And, although I couldn't see it, the baby book says that, as of this week, you have hair! And I'm dying to know if it will be blonde like mine or brown like your daddy's. Your dad has amazing brown eyes with golden flecks. I have blue eyes, but when I was little, I wished I had pretty brown ones like his.

I've known him since I was born. Crazy, huh? There are photos of my mom holding him when she was pregnant with me.

Considering how fully formed you appeared, it's hard to believe you're still so small—although we're moving up to the bigger fruits.

You are now the size of a lime.

Sorry, I just let out a little sigh.

Mommy might have, on very rare occasions, liked to do something called a tequila shooter. It's a tasty adult beverage that you have with salt and lime.

Mommy misses it.

And caffeine and soda and alcohol and—oh my gosh, what I wouldn't do for a beer. It's not fair that Daddy still gets to drink them when Mommy is pregnant. Oh, and I didn't want you to feel bad if you are a boy, so today, I bought you a cute blue onesie with a baseball on it. And little striped booties. When I showed your daddy, he said they reminded him of something called Naughty Dream Week.

Speaking of that, Daddy just took his shirt off and is getting in bed. I should probably go, uh, rock him to sleep or something.

12 WEEKS

Dear Baby Mac,

Daddy says you're the size of a plum.

And, now, I'm hungry.

Oh, and thanks for easing up on the hangover thing. I'm starting to feel more normal. Although I can't button my skinny jeans even though I've been jogging almost every day.

Right now, I want to go to the movie theater, so I can put Milk Duds on top of some warm, buttery popcorn.

And, you know, maybe see a movie.

Contractions

MARCH 22ND

PHILLIP WAKES ME up by rubbing my face.

"Morning," I sigh. "Are you leaving for work now?"

When I sit up, he hands me a cup of hot chocolate. "We got some ice last night, and it's kinda slick, so I was thinking you could either ride to work with me or just work from home."

"Can't you work from home today, too?"

"Normally, I would, but we have clients in town, so I have to be there. Dad was supposed to drive down this morning, but they got snow up north, and he's not going to make it. And, since it's predicted for them to get more, he's going to stay up there this week."

"Oh boy! A week with the house to ourselves. Whatever will we do?"

He kisses my forehead. "How about, tonight, we have a romantic dinner in front of the fire?"

"Naked?" I ask, but then I look down at my bloated-looking stomach. "Or not."

Phillip puts his hand on top of my teeny bump. "Naked sounds perfect. Are you going back to sleep?"

"No, I think I'll lie in bed, reply to emails, and drink my hot chocolate. Thanks for making it."

"You're welcome. Have a good day."

I REPLY TO some emails and then get up. I get dressed and head to the kitchen and make myself an omelet.

I'm just finishing up when Lori calls me.

"Jade, are you still home?"

"Yeah, what's up?"

Her voice is shaky. "Is there any way you could drive me to the hospital?"

"The hospital?"

"Yes, I've been having contractions. The doctor wants me to come now."

I throw my partially eaten omelet into the sink, grab my purse and coat, and throw on a pair of snow boots. "I'm on my way."

"I'm scared, Jade," she says.

"It'll be fine," I tell her, trying to stay calm myself. We all know how I feel about hospitals. "Go down and open your garage door, so I can pull in. It's icy, and I don't want you to fall."

I get in my car, crank up the heat, quickly back out of my driveway, and pull into hers. Then, I get out and help her into my car.

She clings to me with one arm while the other is clutching her abdomen.

"Are you in pain?" I ask her as I pull out of her driveway.

"Not right now, but they hurt when I have them."

"Did you call Danny?"

"I left him a voicemail."

Danny had meetings about endorsement deals in Los Angeles yesterday.

"But shouldn't he be getting on a plane and coming home immediately if you're in labor?"

"I looked it up in the pregnancy book. There's something called Braxton Hicks contractions. They're contractions that don't do anything. Don't cause you to dilate. Apparently, they are sort of your body practicing for the real thing. They started last night, about four in the morning. The book said to start timing them and see how far apart they are. Right now, they're about every ten minutes—oh, hang on." She stops speaking, holds her stomach again, and fans her face with her other hand. "Can you turn down the heat?"

"Oh, yeah." I flick the heat off, being mindful not to take my eyes off the road.

The good news is, there isn't much traffic. The bad news is, the roads are bad, and I'm practically crawling through the neighborhood.

I creep down a hill, putting the car in neutral, and gently apply the brakes, praying the car will stop at the intersection.

"It's really slick, isn't it?" Lori asks. She glances at the clock. "Make that every eight minutes."

"So, do you think it's the Braxton Hicks thing or real labor?"

"I thought they were just the pretend ones; that's why I didn't call Danny earlier. But, now, I'm thinking it's real. The doctor said that Braxton Hicks are usually not painful, don't happen at regular intervals, and don't get closer together like mine have. But I'm really nervous, Jade. I'm only thirty-four weeks. The baby isn't ready to be born yet."

"Do you want me to call Danny?"

She seems incredibly calm, and I'm freaking out but trying not to show it. Danny would be so upset if he missed the birth of their baby.

"I called after I talked to the doctor, but he was already on his flight home, so I had to leave him a voicemail."

She doesn't say much after that. She seems to flip between being lost in thought to being in pain.

And I try to focus on getting us to the hospital safely.

Fortunately, under normal circumstances, we're only about

seven minutes away. I know this because Lori timed it as part of her birthing plan.

WHEN WE FINALLY pull into the emergency area, a stressful twenty minutes later, Lori is visibly upset. Tears stream down her face, and I can't tell if it's because of the pain, because of Danny not being here, or because she's worried about the baby.

Her doctor called ahead, so they put her in a wheelchair and take her straight to the maternity ward. And all this is starting to seem very real.

The nurse gets a urine sample, gets her into bed, takes her vitals, and puts a monitor on her belly that shows her contractions. Then, she checks to see if she's dilated.

"Well, you're at a one," she says.

"So, I'm going to have the baby now?"

"We're going to monitor you and the baby for a bit. Then, we'll let your doctor know what's going on. Have you felt the baby kick?"

Lori starts crying. "No. And I'm so worried."

"Stay calm," the nurse says. "Baby could be asleep, or it could be that you're so worried about the contractions that you just haven't noticed. I'll be back shortly."

The second she leaves, Lori grabs my hand. "I'm so scared, Jade. What if the baby died?"

"I'm sure the baby is fine," I say, trying to be reassuring.

"If it's born now, it will be premature. That's not good. Oh—" Another contraction causes her to stop mid-sentence and squeeze my hand. "I haven't even finished our class. I don't know what to do!"

"Breathe. Like when you work out. Breathing increases your oxygen and will make it easier," I offer, knowing full well I'm bullshitting. I don't know what I'm even talking about. I just want to keep her from breaking my hand off.

The nurse comes back in and points to the monitor. "See this line? It shows that you are experiencing a contraction right now."

Lori rolls her eyes at me because we don't need a monitor to tell us that.

"And this line on the bottom shows your baby's nice strong heartbeat," she says, causing Lori and me to sigh with relief. She taps some information into the monitoring machine and then says, "Your contractions are pretty steady at seven minutes apart. How are you tolerating the pain?"

"She's doing awesome!" I say, trying to be encouraging. I know her birth plan consists of no drugs.

The nurse ignores me and directly asks the question again to Lori.

She replies, "I'm hanging in there. So, what's next?"

"We wait and see what the doctor has to say. He'll be here shortly."

As soon as she's out of the room, Lori says, "Thank God the baby's heartbeat is okay. Please look up what risks there are for a preterm baby."

I do a search.

"It says here that, from thirty-five weeks on, they are called late-preterm infants."

"I know how you are, Jade. I need to know the good and the bad. Start with the bad."

"Um, okay. Well, it says that they can be at a greater risk for respiratory disease because their lungs aren't fully developed. Or maybe they are developed, just not as strong as a full-term baby. Um, it says they weigh less, have less body fat, and have a hard time controlling their body temperature. But it just says they need to dress a little warmer. It says they have a higher risk of developing jaundice."

"Want to hear a funny story?" she says. "Last night, I dreamed that my baby came out a full-sized child, who was wearing a baseball hat backward and break dancing."

"That's funny." I laugh.

"Yeah, Danny showed me some video of a break-dancing three-year-old. I'm sure that's what caused it."

"Hey, I just thought of something. If Danny has Wi-Fi on the plane, you should be able to message him."

She grabs her phone off the bedside table and starts typing, but then she stops and looks at me. "Do you think I should tell him?"

"Why wouldn't you tell him?"

"He's on a plane, and he can't do anything right now."

"He'll feel even worse if you're in labor and you don't answer your phone when he gets off the plane."

She shakes her head. "You know what? Why don't you message him?"

"Why me?"

She clutches her abdomen again. "Because I'm in freaking pain!" she yells as she squeezes the life out of my hand.

"If you give me my hand back, I'll text him."

She lets go and whimpers, "Oh, these hurt."

I decide now is probably not the right time to mention that the baby can hear her.

I grab my phone out of my bag and see a text from Phillip.

Mac Daddy Loves You: Took me forever to get to work. Roads are bad. Don't go out.

Mac Daddy Loves You: Did you go back to sleep?

Me: Lori is in labor. I'm at the hospital with her. Baby's heartbeat is fine. Danny's on a plane back from LA but doesn't know we're here. About to try to message him.

Mac Daddy Loves You: Do you want me to come?

Me: The doctor is supposed to be here soon. I'll let you know what he says.

I send Danny a message.

Me: *Hey, it's me. Just wondering if you've got Wi-Fi on the plane and can talk.*

Danny: *I'm here. What's up?*

Me: *Thank God. Lori and I are at the hospital. She's in labor. She was really nervous that she hadn't felt the baby kick in a while, but they just checked, and the baby's heartbeat is perfectly normal. We're waiting for the doctor.*

Danny: *Are you messing with me?*

Me: *I wouldn't joke about something like this, Danny.*

Danny: *Why didn't she message me?*

Me: *She left you a voicemail earlier. I drove her to the hospital in the middle of an ice storm, and every time she squeezes my hand during a contraction, I'm pretty sure she's going to break it. Don't give me a hard time right now.*

"Lori, I'm texting Danny. Is it okay if I take a picture of you, so he knows you're okay?"

"Sure," she says. "Is he freaking out?"

"He thinks I'm messing with him."

"You wouldn't joke about something like this, would you?" she asks.

"Duh."

"Okay, take my picture."

I forward it to him.

"Maybe you should talk to him," I suggest. "It might make you feel better."

"I really don't want to talk to him," she says, almost spitting at me. "This is his own fault. I begged him not to travel when I'm this far along, but he said we had plenty of time. Obviously, he was wrong, and now, I'm probably going to have this baby all by myself."

She's mad, but there are tears in her eyes.

"Are you scared?" I ask her.

"Of course I'm scared. I didn't intend on doing this alone."

"You're not alone," I say, giving her hand a squeeze as the doctor comes into the room.

> **Danny:** Is she pissed at me? I told her nothing would happen. What if she has the baby without me? I'm so dumb. She was right. Nothing is more important than being there. I land in an hour and a half. Tell her to message me.
>
> **Me:** Um, she said she didn't want to talk to you. But then she started crying. She's scared, Danny. And, honestly, so am I.
>
> **Danny:** What did the doctor say?
>
> **Me:** He just got here.

The doctor looks at Lori's chart and then smiles at her. "So, these aren't Braxton Hicks contractions. You're definitely in labor."

Lori wipes tears from her face and nods, bracing for the worst.

The doctor sits down next to her. "Where's Danny?"

"He's on a plane home from LA," she says. "Even though I'm mad at him, I don't want to have the baby until he gets here."

"I'm thinking it's a little early to have the baby, but let's take a look." He examines her, studies the monitor, and consults her chart again. "You're having what we call preterm labor. There's no bleeding, which is good. There's no sugar in your urine, which is good. You don't have a urinary tract infection. You're dehydrated though, so I want to get you started on an IV. We're going to do an ultrasound, and then I suspect we'll give you a shot to stop your labor."

"Stop it?"

"Yes, it will relax your uterus. We want to keep your baby inside for as long as we can."

"Will I have to stay here, or will I get to go home?"

"I suspect you'll get to go home later today, but I can't say for sure."

"Did I do something wrong?" she asks.

"No, you didn't. About ten percent of women suffer from preterm labor. No one knows for sure what causes it. They suspect that dehydration, infections, stress, and gum disease are possibly related. You're a little dehydrated, so we'll give you the IV, just in case that triggered it." He smiles at us. "Now, for the big question. We're going to do an ultrasound next. Do you want to find out the sex?"

"I don't know!" Lori exclaims.

"Why don't you think about it, and you can let me know when I get back?"

Lori turns to me. "What would you do?"

"I wouldn't find out."

"But I want to find out."

"But you and Danny decided you wanted to be surprised."

"I know we did. But, if he hadn't been stupid and left me, he would have been here, finding out."

"Could you keep it a secret, or would you tell him?"

"Lots of people are doing those cool gender reveal parties and announcements. That might be fun."

I nod.

"But I don't think I could keep it a secret. I'd start buying clothes. No. No. I don't want to know. We agreed."

"I think that's a good decision."

"Are you going to find out what you're having when you can?" she asks me.

"I know finding out is more practical, but we want to be surprised."

Phillip: *Do you know anything? Danny just messaged me and asked.*

Me: *The doctor was just here. He's going to do an ultrasound and give her an IV, but it sounds like they might be able to give her something to stop the contractions. She'll probably be able to go home later today.*

Phillip: *That's good news. I love you.*

Me: *I love you, too. They are getting ready to do the ultrasound.*

Danny: *What did the doctor say?*

Me: *We're getting ready to do an ultrasound. We'll know more then, but she's fine, Danny. The baby's heartbeat is good. They think they can stop the labor with some medicine. Everything is fine.*

Danny: *Everything is not fine because I'm not there. I'm an idiot.*

Me: *Danny, it's well over a month before she's due. You couldn't have known this would happen.*

Danny: *Still …*

The doctor does the ultrasound, and we get to see the baby. This ultrasound looks so different from mine. The baby is big.

"Oh my gosh," Lori says, "it's sucking its thumb."

"That's so adorable," I say.

"Did you decide if you want to know the sex?" the doctor asks.

"I don't," she says confidently.

And, even though she says she doesn't want to know, I do. So, I'm scanning the screen to see if I can see any boy or girl parts.

But, just when I think I might have seen a little boy part, the baby flips over, and all we can see is its butt. So much for getting an advantage in the pool that I'm sure our friends will have to guess the sex and birthdate.

The doctor tells us everything looks good.

Lori gets an IV and a shot to stop the contractions, and a couple of hours later, Danny arrives.

He's got a big bouquet of flowers and a tentative look on his face. He's expecting her to be mad at him, but instead, she just bursts into tears.

I give them each a hug and tell them to call me when they're on their way home.

The roads aren't as slick as they were this morning, so I stop at the store on the way home and get the ingredients to make lasagna. I figure the least I can do is have something ready for when they come home.

WHEN LORI AND Danny get back from the hospital, I take the food over to them on a tray, and they eat dinner together in bed.

"Do you have to be on bed rest?" I ask her.

"No. I don't have any restrictions other than to take the medicine they gave me. They expect I will carry the baby full-term now."

I brighten. "That's such good news!"

"We thought so, too," Danny says, squeezing Lori's hand. "But I made her get in bed when we got home. She's exhausted. And, going forward, I'm going to make sure she stays hydrated. In fact, while you're here, Jay, I'm going to run to the pharmacy. We dropped off the prescription on the way home, and I just got a text saying it's ready."

After he leaves, I ask Lori, "Are you still going to be able to travel up to Omaha for your baby shower?"

"Yeah, the doctor said it was fine."

"Awesome. I think a girls' weekend is just what you need."

"I think you're right," she says with a sigh.

"Are things okay with you two?"

"Yeah, Danny felt really bad. And then I felt really bad for being mad at him."

"You were just scared," I tell her.

"I was so afraid I was going to have the baby alone. I was equally afraid that he'd miss his baby's birth. Thank you for being there for me, Jade. I'm lucky to have a friend like you."

"I think I'm the lucky one," I tell her.

THE
SECOND
TRIMESTER

13 WEEKS

Dear Baby Mac,
You are now the size of a peach, and you have your very own fingerprints.

Lori gave me some stretch-mark cream to rub on my stomach, so you don't ruin me for a swimsuit.

I keep looking at the ultrasound photo and touching my stomach. Honestly, it's hard to even believe I have a baby growing inside me. Like, it's totally surreal.

Your daddy is telling everyone he knows—and even everyone we don't—that we are expecting. He is so excited.

Even though I saw you in the ultrasound, I'm hoping I'll feel you kick soon. Then, I think it will seem more real.

Dripping wet.

MARCH 27TH

I WAKE UP early and stretch my arms out. I feel good. I'm super excited to say that I think—hope/pray—that my morning sickness is officially over. I haven't dared to say it to anyone who asks how I'm feeling, for fear I'll jinx myself and it will come back.

I hear that Phillip is taking a shower, so I decide to surprise him by getting up and making him breakfast.

I open the pantry to get the pancake mix out.

"Ahh!" I say.

Okay, maybe I screamed really loud because Phillip comes rushing out, towel wrapped around his waist and dripping wet.

"What's wrong?"

"Um," I say, feeling ridiculous for screaming. "I, uh, thought I saw something."

"Like what?"

I let out a big sigh and then open the pantry and show him.

He jumps back. "What the hell is the gnome doing in there? And why is he holding a noose?"

"He's threatening us!" I say, slamming the door shut. "He scared the shit out of me! How does he keep moving?"

Phillip narrows his eyes. "Danny was in our dining room last night after dinner. He said he was looking at our wedding photos."

"The ones your mom decided to put into all the frames we got as wedding gifts and display all over the dining room?"

He glazes right over my irritation with his mother. "Yes, exactly. And he was looking sneaky."

"Do you think he's the one who's been moving it?"

"It would make sense," Phillip says.

"And it's a whole lot more comforting than the alternative."

"What's the alternative?"

"That the gnome is slowly working its way into the kitchen, so it can find a knife to kill us in our sleep."

"You've watched too many scary movies."

"You and Danny used to make me watch them. I hate them!"

Phillip wraps his wet arms around me. "I loved them because, when you were scared, you always snuggled up next to me."

"That's because Danny was just as scared as I was. If I recall, he was snuggled up to you, too. Although I'm sure he would deny it."

"So, what do you think?" He smirks, holding the gnome in front of me. "Time for some payback?"

"Definitely," I say, my hand sliding under his towel.

"Let's put the gnome back in the drawer, so Danny doesn't know we know he's moving it."

PHILLIP'S BRUSHING HIS teeth while I curl my hair.

"I don't know, Phillip. I'm not sure it was Danny. How would he even know to do it?"

Phillip has a mouthful of toothpaste and is talking through it, "I maybe told him you thought it stomped on the wrapping paper."

"Were you making fun of me, Phillip?"

"I was maybe laughing a little."

"A little?"

"Fine, I thought it was pretty darn funny. Danny was laughing his ass off."

"Then, it was definitely him. We need to get back at him by putting the gnome somewhere only he would find it."

"His workout room," Phillip says. "It's going to be done in a couple of days."

"Yeah, but Lori is going to do yoga and work out there, too."

"Hmm," Phillip says.

"Oh! I know! The sauna. Lori said Danny is all excited for it, but she's bummed she can't go in it while she's pregnant due to the heat."

"That's perfect," Phillip says. "You're brilliant."

Batshit crazy.

MARCH 28TH

Nicky: *Will you please text Macy?*

Me: *Uh, sure. Any reason?*

Nicky: *Did Phillip tell you that she won't see me or talk to me?*

Me: *No, he didn't. He's out of town today, visiting a client.*

Nicky: *I'm dying.*

Me: *Did she choose Peter?*

Nicky: *Not yet. Supposedly, she's not seeing or talking to either one of us until she makes up her mind. She wants to see who she misses.*

Me: *And how long is that expected to take?*

Nicky: *I have no freaking idea. Honestly, I don't think she does either.*

Me: *Remember the advice Phillip gave you?*

Nicky: *About not sleeping with her until she decided?*

Me: *Yeah. Did you?*

Nicky: *I might have slipped a few times. Well, quite a few times. Okay, so I could only resist once. Look, I'm not this kind of guy. I've never screwed around with a girl who has* *a boyfriend. Let alone someone who's engaged.*

Me: *What about Karly?*

Nicky: *She told me she didn't have a boyfriend.*

Me: *And Madeline?*

Nicky: *They were sort of broken up. So, fine, I have but not on purpose.*

Me: *Accidental cheating, Nicky. That's why I love you.*

Nicky: *Shut up. I don't run a background check on every girl I meet. We're getting off topic here. YOU NEED TO TEXT HER AND FIND OUT WHAT THE HELL SHE'S THINKING BEFORE I GO BATSHIT CRAZY! I'm seriously ready to do something crazy here!*

Me: *Sometimes, crazy is good. But hang on. I'll text her.*

I glance at the clock, noting it's nearly three. I can picture my bridesmaid sitting on her bed in the sorority house, her bubblegum-pink toes dangling off the bed and her dark brown waves pushed over one shoulder as she studies. With her piercing blue eyes and great body, she bears an uncanny resemblance to a young Megan Fox, only she has an adorable Southern twang.

Me: *Hey, Macy! What's up? I haven't talked to you in forever! Do I get to see you at Lori's shower?*

Macy: *Did Nick ask you to text me?*

Me: *Would it be a good thing if he did?*

Macy: *I miss him.*

Me: *He misses you. He's going crazy. Actually, he said he's going BATSHIT CRAZY.*

Macy: *Aw. :(I hate that I'm doing this to him. Peter, too. He's such a sweetheart. He just …*

Me: *Isn't doing it for you?*

Macy: Kind of. Everything is so hot with Nick. We have this amazing, incredible chemistry.

Me: And Peter?

Macy: He's my best friend.

Me: Chemistry?

Macy: Not through the roof like with Nick. That's why I'm so confused. Peter is a good guy. He'd be a good husband and a great dad. I know exactly what I'm getting with him. With Nick, I don't even know if we'd end up married. Do I risk giving up my engagement to a great guy for a possible relationship with Nick?

Me: Nick said you aren't supposed to talk to either of them. Have you?

Macy: Peter isn't abiding by the rule. Does that mean he loves me more?

Me: It means, he doesn't want to lose you. He's fighting for you.

Macy: But Nick isn't?

Me: Nick is trying to play by the rules you set. He's being respectful, if you ask me.

Macy: OMG!

Me: What?

Macy: Some guy is outside the house with a big, glittery I LOVE YOU sign. It's so adorable. And he's blaring music. I can't quite make out the song.

Me: Who is the sign for?

Macy: I don't know. Let me take a closer look.

Macy: OMG! OMG!!! OH MY GOD!!! IT'S HIM!

Me: Which him?

Macy: NICKY!!! Holy shit! I've gotta go!

153

14 WEEKS

Dear Baby Mac,

Now, you are the size of a lemon, and apparently, you are sucking your thumb in there. We aren't going to find out what sex you are, but get this. I just read that, if you are super hungry when you're pregnant—as in hungry like your dad and Danny used to be when they were teenagers—that research shows you could be expecting a boy.

I'd be happy with either a boy or a girl. I just pray that you're healthy.

But ... I kinda think you are a boy.

Well, I did. Until Lori started telling me about different ways you can tell what you are having. These ways are called old wives' tales, which means they are like a fairy tale and you don't really know if they are true or not. But, if you are a boy, you failed.

First, she set a key in front of me and told me to pick it up. I picked it up by the narrow part, meaning you are a girl.

Then, I had to take off my wedding ring, tie it to a piece of string, and hang it over my belly. It swung back and forth, meaning you are a girl.

She also said, because I had morning sickness, that I'm having a girl. That means she is, too. It would be fun if you were both girls.

But I still think you are a boy.

Over the next few months, your dad and I are going to have to come up with some awesome baby names. A girl's name is going to be hard. It's a tradition in my family that the firstborn girls have the middle name James, which was my great-great-grandmother's maiden name. My great-grandma was named Darlene James, my grandma was Elizabeth James, my mother was Veronica James, and I am Jadyn James. And although, when I was younger, I hated my name and swore I'd never give my daughter that middle name, now, I want to—in honor of the women who came before me.

poetic promises.

APRIL 4TH

AS I'M DRIVING to my meeting this morning, I'm smiling and feeling like I'm driving under the influence. They talk about influencers on social media, people with social clout who can make you buy a product or watch a video. Phillip is my influencer. He affects my moods. He's an integral part of my soul. The beauty of his love is purely in that love's existence. The power of our hearts to find our match and the profound impact on our life when we do.

I almost sound poetic.

Ha!

Which is fitting, I guess. Poetic promises of love are murmured into ears on top of pillows and behind closed doors. But I know that real love isn't just a bunch of pretty words.

Real love is when you are running way late for a meeting, and as you are rushing out the door, you realize you drove home on fumes last night because you were too tired to stop for gas and put it off until the next morning. You get in your car, expecting to have to coast halfway to the gas station, but then in front of you is what appears to be a miracle. The gas needle is not buried below empty but is sitting on the other side of the energy rainbow—straight-up full. And, as you look through a shiny, clean windshield, you realize that, when the man you're married to ran to the store last night to buy you Oreos and milk, he took your car, and not only did he fill it up with gas, but he ran it through the car wash, too.

When people asked my grandmother how she and Grandpa stayed married for so long, she would say, "It's the little things that matter, not just the big gestures."

Like every girl who grew up listening to fairy tales, I thought love was all about big gestures. But, now, I understand exactly what Grandma meant.

It's the heart he drew in the sand on our honeymoon, driving miles to get me the best chicken noodle soup when I was sick, making me coffee every morning.

Getting me gas.

AFTER MY MEETING with the construction team, I peek into Phillip's office.

"There's my gorgeous wife," he says, looking up from his computer. "How was your meeting this morning? We on track?"

"I really like the general contractor and the foreman who's overseeing the job site. They say we'll finish on schedule."

"Helps that Dad offered a bonus if they do."

"I was running late this morning," I confess.

"Shocker," Phillip teases.

"And I still needed to get gas."

He gives me a proud grin. "I got you gas last night."

"And washed my car. You didn't tell me. What made you do that?"

"When I went into the garage to go to the store, I noticed your car was all salty, so I thought I'd run it through the car wash. I didn't have much choice on the fuel."

"It was sweet. I love you."

"I'm sweet on you."

"I have a surprise for you tonight," I say as he pulls me into his arms.

"I love your surprises, but don't forget, my parents are back in town today."

"Crap, I forgot. I think my bra is still lying by the couch. But I wasn't referring to sex."

"Damn."

"Phillip, do you like being repaid with sex?"

"I didn't do it to get repaid. I did it to be nice. But, yes, I like it when you're nice back."

I LEAVE WORK before Phillip does, stopping on the way home to pick up his surprise.

As I'm pulling into our subdivision, I get a text.

Macy: I did it. Broke off my engagement with Peter. Told my parents. I thought they would be so mad, but they didn't want me to marry him if I wasn't sure. I can't even tell you the weight that's been lifted off my shoulders. And it sounds crazy, but Nick and I are officially dating!

Me: I'm happy for you!

When I bought my condo in Omaha, I had to buy a new refrigerator. Our new house came with a built-in fridge, so Phillip put the one from my condo in the garage, dubbing it his *beer fridge*. But, as of yet, it's only had a few random Coronas and some Miller Lite cans in it.

I pull into the garage and get to work, readjusting the refrigerator shelves to allow for three rows of bottles. I then organize the fourteen different types of beer I bought into perfectly neat rows. The cans get put into the produce drawers, and the door shelves are filled with back stock.

I stand back and admire my work.

I can't wait for him to get home! He's going to be so excited!

I grab my purse and tote out of the car and head into the house. Phillip's mom is in the kitchen, surrounded by flour, and has my new mixer—which I've yet to use myself—running.

"Oh, hey," she says, wiping her hands. "I have a surprise for you!"

She gestures toward the breakfast room where, in front of the bay window overlooking the lake, a white wooden kitchen table sits with six shaker-style chairs surrounding it.

"What's that for?" I ask. I can't say much else. I can't even begin to describe all the ways in which this table is completely wrong for the room.

I want to cry.

She's ruined my kitchen—my beautiful, modern kitchen. Even though I don't want to get closer to it, I'm drawn toward the offensive table and realize it's even worse than I thought. Not only has she ruined my kitchen aesthetically, but she's also added insult to injury by choosing a table made of pressed wood.

"It's similar to the table at our house," she says, "but I got white, so it would match your house better. Surprise! Now, you don't have to sit at the bar."

I tear my eyes away from the train-wreck table to look at her.

She's smiling, happy, and still speaking, "Phillip has always loved our table. I have so many good memories of him and Ashley and often you eating around it."

"Your table is solid oak," I manage to mutter, my mind a blur of worry. "It was really nice of you …" I start with a compliment, hoping to ease the blow. "But Phillip and I have already picked out a table."

"Well, now, you don't need it," she says firmly.

I RUSH INTO my bedroom. I can't look at the table. I can't pretend to be excited about it. *How do I ask her to take it back? To get the hideous thing out of my house?*

I hear a car, rush to the window, and see Phillip pulling into the driveway.

Thank goodness he's home. Maybe he can tell his mother we will not be keeping the table. He's her son. Even if she gets mad at him or gets her feelings hurt, she'll get over it because she loves him.

I don't want her to hate me, especially now. Lately, she's made me feel like I'm not good enough for Phillip. My house is dusty. I don't cook five-course meals every night.

I don't have a kitchen table.

I hear Phillip's heavy footsteps coming down the hall, so I rush in my closet and rip off my clothes, so he'll think I'm just changing out of my work clothes and not hiding in the bathroom, freaking out.

"Hey," he says, peeking around the corner as I'm pulling on a pair of yoga pants. He comes into my closet and gives me a kiss.

I expect him to say something about the table, but he doesn't.

Maybe he already handled it, and she's moving it to the garage as we speak.

That's probably wishful thinking.

"So, uh, did you see what your mom bought?" I ask.

"Yeah. What do you think of it?"

"Um, what do you think of it?"

"It reminds me of when we were kids. Mom suggested we cancel the table we ordered. It'd definitely save us some money."

My mouth falls open, and my eyes widen. I'm holding back tears and unable to comment.

Phillip twists his mouth. "You still love the table we ordered, right?"

"Yeah, it's the perfect table for our future family."

He frowns. "My mom made me think you'd decided against it. I was surprised by that."

"No, Phillip," I say, letting the tears fall. "We love that table.

It's what we want. You have to tell her she needs to take her table back."

"I'm not telling her that. It will hurt her feelings, and she's all excited about it."

"Phillip, it's hideous."

He gives me a look.

"Okay, so it's not hideous on its own. It just looks hideous in our modern house. I wanted to cry the second I saw it."

"What did you tell her?"

"That it was sweet of her to get but that we'd found a table."

"What did she say?"

"That we didn't need it now. Phillip, you have to do something."

He mutters something unintelligible as he goes to change out of his suit.

I consider refusing to even sit at the table, but when I go out to the kitchen, Phillip's dad is sitting at it, and dinner is spread across it.

AFTER DINNER, I'M hiding in my office, sketching in my dreamhouse book. I found out today that not only is Phillip getting a bonus, but I am, too. Part of a company-wide profit-sharing plan. And I know exactly how I'd like to spend it. I want to work toward finishing our dining room. Because we already have the expensive furniture pieces, it won't take much. All it really needs is two wingback chairs, curtains, fabric to reupholster the dining chairs, and a great piece of artwork.

I want to get Phillip on board, so I'm doing a rendering of how the room will look. And I'm really excited by how it's turning out.

I print off a photo of the glossy pale gray-metallic leather wingback chairs—which are highlighted by silver nailheads that accentuate its modern lines—and glue it to the page along with a swatch for the menswear-like gray velvet pinstriped fabric for the curtain panels and dining chairs. I add to that a traditional wool rug in muted tones and a funky silver and crystal chandelier.

It's surprising really that someone who always hated to shop for clothes found out during a college interior design class that she was good at putting rooms together. Interior design is like a puzzle to me. A fusing of elements to create the perfect feel, the perfect look. I actually considered switching majors during my junior year, but my advisor suggested that having the ability to do both structural and interior plans would enhance my résumé. That it would allow my aesthetic ideas to be incorporated into the elemental design of a building. That's part of why designing the Mackenzies' new building was so fun. It had to incorporate the modern, luxe feel Phillip's dad wanted with the required space, functionality, logistics, and security needed for transportation, warehousing, offices, and their call center.

Phillip strolls in with a beer in his hand and a big grin on his face. "I like what you did with my beer fridge. Are you working on more plans for our house or doing work?"

"House. I just finished with the dining room. Want to see it?"

"I'd love to," he says, sitting on the floor across from my drafting table.

I sit next to him and spread the book across our laps.

"So, I found—"

Phillip stops me with a kiss.

"You taste like beer," I tell him after a steamy make-out session.

"You've been craving beer," he says with a grin.

"I miss it. I hope Baby Mac appreciates my sacrifice."

Phillip laughs, but then he cradles my face in his hands. "I know I do. You're being incredible with everything. Seriously, you amaze me. After all that Danny has been going through with Lori's pregnancy, I've been expecting the worst. But I should have known pregnancy wouldn't change you."

"It is changing me though, Phillip. I can cry at the drop of a hat. I'm hungry all the freaking time." I look down at my stomach. "And I'm starting to show."

"You seem happy."

"I am happy."

"I'm about to ask you to do something that won't make you happy."

"What?"

"I can't tell my mom to take the table back. She's so excited about it. What if we keep it until ours comes in and then move it somewhere else?"

"Phillip, it looks awful."

"Please?"

"I want to be proud when our friends see our house. That table doesn't make me proud. And I don't want them to think I chose it."

"Then, you tell her. I'm not."

I cross my arms in front of my chest and pout. "I'm giving away all the micro-brewed beer in your fridge and filling it with wine coolers and off-brand cans."

Phillip kisses me again. "You play rough. Why don't you show me your dining room plans and maybe we can negotiate?"

I WAKE WITH a start, quickly realizing I was dreaming. A glance at the clock tells me it's nearly five a.m.

I can't remember what I was dreaming about. I just know it was bad.

And, when I close my eyes and try to go back to sleep, all I see is the red from my dream, running like a current.

a little more fun.

APRIL 5TH

LAST NIGHT, PHILLIP approved my plans for the dining room, so this afternoon, I'm online, ordering everything, when Danny calls.

"Whatcha doing?"

"Working."

"Phillip told me you are ordering stuff for your dining room."

"And working," I say.

"So, this baby shower thing."

"Yeah?"

"Lori said you're getting up early, driving the three hours up there, having the shower, and then driving home that night."

"That's the plan."

"Any chance you could change the plan? Spend the night?"

"That's what I wanted to do, but Lori was adamant."

"I need a night out, Jay. I thought Phillip and I could invite a couple of the guys over. Hang out. Play pool."

"Phillip doesn't want me driving back at night. Plus, it would be fun to go out with our friends after the shower. I think Lori could use a night out, too."

"That's the spirit," he says. "I'll leave it up to you to convince her."

"You're a chicken, Danny."

"Bawk, bawk," he says and then hangs up.

I start a group text, figuring Lori won't be as likely to argue this way.

> **Me:** Hey, everyone! I thought it would be fun if we all went out after the baby shower on Saturday. You up for a fun night?

Lori doesn't respond, but I get a lot of, *Hell yeah*, from our sorority sisters.

Chelsea sends me a private text.

> **Chelsea:** How are you feeling?

> **Me:** Really good. You?

> **Chelsea:** I had to leave a class to throw up this morning. My clothes don't fit. I moved out of the sorority house and into Joey's apartment. Am planning a quickie wedding. Have two tests and a paper due this week. But whatever. So, here's the big question; are you free the weekend of May 11th?

> **Me:** Is that your wedding date? I'll make sure we are.

> **Chelsea:** I was going to ask you this weekend, but I know Lori will be with us the whole time, and I didn't want it to be awkward.

> **Me:** What to be awkward?

> **Chelsea:** Will you be my maid of honor?

> **Me:** OMG! YES!!!

> **Chelsea:** Joey's going to ask Phillip to be his best man. It's because of the two of you that we're together. Can you believe we caught the bouquet and garter at your wedding, and a few months later, we are getting married? When have you ever heard of that happening in real life?

Me: *Pretty much, like, never.*

Chelsea: *He's been really amazing, Jade. He took me shopping this weekend. Bought me a cute dress to wear to the shower.*

Me: *That's so sweet.*

Chelsea: *Another favor. I saw your group text. Since I assume you're spending the night, is there any way I could get you to come dress shopping with me on Sunday morning? That nice wedding shop here is having a big sample sale. It's probably going to be a free-for-all, but the deals are supposed to be amazing. Joey and I are going to use some of the money my dad gave us for the wedding for the down payment on our house, so I'm trying to be really frugal.*

Me: *I'd love to help. Okay if Lori comes, too, if she doesn't have any other plans?*

Chelsea: *Of course. What kind of dress do you think I should get? I don't know what I want.*

Me: *I think, for us to find you a dress at the sale, you're going to need to know what you want. Go this week and try on a dress of every silhouette. The big, poofy ballgown. The softer version, like mine. A-line. Drop-waist. Mermaid. Ask Alyssa to go with you. She's good with fashion.*

Chelsea: *Good idea. Is it bad I want something super sexy?*

Me: *My mom used to say to flaunt it while you got it.*

Chelsea: *I'm not gonna have it much longer. Got to go to class.*

Danny's dad, Mr. D's, name pops up on my cell phone.
"Hey, Mr. D. How's Europe?"
"Wonderful. Quick question. I know you're coming for the

baby shower this weekend. I have something for you. Can you swing by the house before you leave town, like on Sunday afternoon?"

"Yeah. When are you getting back home?"

"Not until early Sunday morning. We got our dates mixed up when we booked the flights. Tried to get it changed to come back on Friday, but it was sold out. Mary won't be able to make the shower." He lowers his voice. "And she's not very happy about it."

"I'm sure Lori won't mind. This shower is mostly sorority girls. Her mom couldn't make it either. So, uh, what do you have for me? Like, paperwork or something?"

Mr. Diamond is the executor of my trust fund.

"Something a little more fun than that," he says mysteriously. "See you Sunday."

15 WEEKS

Dear Baby Mac,

You are orange-sized, and even though I still can't feel you, they say you are moving around like crazy, which isn't really a surprise since you were very active during the ultrasound.

Your dad read something about keeping a pregnant woman comfortable on the job. He told me I should stop wearing heels to work. I told him that, since I wasn't on my feet all day, I could wear whatever shoes I wanted to.

And I need to wear the shoes. They are about the only things that fit. I've been wearing my skirts and jeans unbuttoned, and I have to wear flowy shirts.

So, anyway, your daddy put a water cooler in my office, so I will drink enough water daily. He brought in an ottoman, so I can put my feet up. He makes his assistant bring me in snacks every few hours because he read that I should be eating five small meals a day.

Since he's started this, I've gained four pounds.

Could be all the Milk Duds though.

Truth: Sometimes, I give away the healthy snacks and just eat Milk Duds. But that will be our little secret.

And, for goodness' sake, would you freaking kick me already? Like, hard enough for me to actually feel it?

Lori says she first felt her baby kick at fifteen weeks. She says it felt like a flutter.

I want to feel the flutter.

However many shades.

APRIL 9TH

MY EYES ARE shut, and I'm half-asleep as I rub the back of my hand across my nose. Something keeps itching it.

I squint my eyes open.

"Ahhh!" I scream. "What the fu—" I jump off the bed when I realize the thing touching my nose is the gnome.

I find Phillip lying on the floor next to the bed, laughing.

"What the hell are you doing?"

He gives me a devious grin. "Danny's workout room is done, so I'm meeting him over there this morning. Thought I'd take our little friend. I wanted to give you the chance to say good-bye."

"Hopefully, good riddance. What the heck did you do to him?"

Phillip holds the gnome up even with my face. He's drilled a little hole through the gnome's fist, stuck one of my new cocktail forks through it, and wrapped a red ribbon around his eyes.

"I gave him a pitchfork. Like the devil."

"You're crazy. Are you going to put him in the sauna?" I ask as I hop back into bed.

"Yep." He leans down and gives me a kiss. "Wish us luck."

"WHAT'S WITH THE Fifty Shades gnome?" Danny says when I

answer my ringing phone.

"What are you talking about?"

"Don't play coy. I know you hid it in my sauna."

"You just woke me up, Danny."

"Scared the shit out of me, honestly. Cheeky little bastard. Get dressed. I'm on my way over."

I get up quickly—shocked to see it's almost ten—brush my teeth and hair, and throw on some clothes. I planned to work from home this morning, not sleep in late.

As I'm heading to the kitchen, Danny comes through the front door with the gnome.

"So, did you know we watched that movie, and she bought that stuff?"

"Danny, you woke me up during the middle of a very involved dream. I have no idea what the heck you're talking about."

"Lori and I watched that *Fifty Shades of Grey* movie. She bought some sexual aids similar to those used in the story to spice up things in the bedroom."

"Do things need spicing up?"

He lets out a big sigh. "Since she's been pregnant, our sex life has definitely taken a hit."

"How so? Not that long ago, you were talking about how horny pregnant women are."

"That was a long time ago. And you know how Lori's been. Sick, crabby, moody. *You're* pregnant and tired. Has your sex life taken a hit?"

"Uh, no. Although having Phillip's parents here has contained it to the bedroom."

"How often do you do it?"

"Every day usually. Sometimes, every other day."

"It's been two weeks. I'm horny. I don't need a freaking red room. I just need for her to be in the mood."

"Sounds like she's trying if she bought stuff."

"Yes, and that was a flipping disaster. Last night ... no, I can't even say it."

"She wanted to, and you didn't?"

"*Couldn't.*"

"Couldn't? Why not?"

"Because she's gone all however many shades on me. I'm sorry, but have you seen her? Her stomach is huge. I can't do that to her now. Not with my child inside her. It just feels wrong."

"Are you not attracted to her because her stomach is huge?"

"That's not it at all. I very much want to have sex with her. I just can't do the kinky stuff."

"Maybe you can save it all for after the baby is born and just go for the romance angle."

"I don't know about romance, but *angle* is the right word. It's like freaking geometry class, just trying to get close to her."

"She only has a few weeks left."

"Did you know that you're not supposed to have sex for six weeks after the baby is born?"

"Uh, no. That seems like a really long time. Why is that? Does it hurt?"

"At first, probably. But it's got something to do with infection." He points to the gnome. "When I saw the gnome with the fork and the red blindfold, I thought, somehow, you knew."

I laugh. "This looks like a devil gnome to me, not a XXX gnome."

"I guess I'm just sensitive. So, who did it—you or Phillip?"

"Neither of us. The gnome keeps moving on its own," I lie, hoping he'll fess up. "The other morning, it scared the crap out of me. I found it in the pantry, holding a noose. I've been locking the bedroom door, just in case."

"Did you hear Chelsea and Joey set a date?"

"I did. Will you be able to go?"

"He asked me to stand up with him. Of course I am."

"But the baby will be just a few weeks old."

"Perfect time to take the little monkey with us, right? It will sleep the whole time."

"Uh, yeah. That's true," I say, but I babysat an infant one summer and know it's a little more complicated than that.

My dream life.

APRIL 11TH

JUST AFTER MIDNIGHT, Phillip wakes me up like he has for as long as I can remember. When we were young, he'd sneak out of his house and come bounce on my bed. He's thrown confetti at me. Water balloons. Silk butterflies. Skittles. Rubber ducks. Every year is something different.

"Happy birthday, Princess," he yells, flipping on the light as baby booties shower over me.

"Ohmigosh! Look at all these!" I screech, holding a little pink crocheted bootie with a fluffy white pom-pom in one hand and a furry leopard one in the other. Our bed is full of booties of every size and color. I hold up each one and imagine putting them on our baby. Tears well up in my eyes. "They're so adorable, Phillip. So teeny. I love them."

He sits down next to me, wraps his arm around me, and asks me the same old question, "So, do you feel older?"

"Should I answer that the way I used to or how I feel now?"

"Hmm, how you feel now."

"I'll always be younger than you."

"Oh, meanie," he says, giving me another kiss. "When we were younger, you always told me you did."

"I was lying. I never really felt older. I will admit though, this year feels different."

"How so?"

"I'm so happy, Phillip. I don't think I've ever been happier in my whole life. It's because of you."

His smile is genuine. "Why me?"

"I'm living my dream life. I'm married to my sexy best friend. We bought an amazing house. I got to design a building, and now, I'm watching it be built from the ground up. And I'm having your baby. Really, the only thing that is missing from this perfect picture is my parents, but I guess I've come to terms with it. They'd want me to be happy. Sometimes, it scares me though, like our life is too good to be true."

He flops across the bed, half on top of me, and brushes the hair off my face. "You shouldn't be scared. You and I can face whatever life throws at us. As long as we're together."

I wrap my arms around his neck and kiss him.

And kiss him.

"Hang on," he says. "I have something else for you."

"I can wait to open the rest of my presents until morning."

"I think you're going to want this now." He hops off the bed, grabs my hand, and leads me into our bathroom, which is glowing with candlelight.

"It's so pretty, Phillip."

"Close your eyes," he says.

I shut my eyes and try not to peek.

"Okay, open!"

When I open my eyes, Phillip is standing in front of me with a plate of cupcakes, each with a birthday candle blazing atop it.

"Cupcakes, huh?" I say.

"You should make a wish," he replies, taking a little chocolate frosting, smudging it across my neck, and then licking it off.

"I wish you'd do more than that," I say, blowing out the candles.

"IS CUPCAKE SEX really what you wished for?" he asks me later.

"No, I was pretty sure that was already going to happen."

"So, what did you wish for?"

"That you and I would always be together."

15.5 WEEKS

Dear Baby Mac,

So, here's the deal.

Today's my birthday! Yay!!!

And, since it's a special day, I think that you should kick me hard enough so that I can feel it. Pretend you're kicking a soccer ball with all your might.

Hmm. You probably don't know what that is yet, but kick! Wave those feet! Punch those little arms around.

Make your mommy's day!

Your dad got me a bunch of baby booties. Every year since we were little, he's woken me up at midnight and thrown a whole bunch of stuff at me. Confetti. Candy. Jacks—those kind of hurt. You get the idea.

You don't really think about stuff like this when you're younger, but I realize now that your dad started a tradition I can't wait to pass on to our kids. We will always celebrate your birthday at midnight. And we'll always make you feel special.

He took me to one of my favorite restaurants for lunch today and then gave me pennies to throw in our fountain, so I could make a bunch of wishes.

What I wished for:

That you would be healthy.

That we would be happy.

That we'd all stay safe.

That your dad would always love me.

That we'd get the building done before you were born.

That you would kick me. (Hint, hint.)

He also gave me a super-cool present.

I don't think I told you this, but your dad's family owns a transportation business. It's a high-end, white-glove service. They'll move anything safely, like the furniture you ordered online, the classic car you bought at an auto auction, your baby grand piano, your grandmother's hutch. Stuff like that.

I majored in engineering, and it was my dream to someday design a building from scratch. When your grandpa Mackenzie needed to expand their company with offices here in Kansas City, he let me do just that. Right now, the site has been excavated, the foundation has been poured, and the steel and concrete are going up. That means, I'm at a muddy job site most every day. And I kinda have a thing for shoes. Heels mostly.

The guys at the job site gave me my very own hard hat and have been giving me crap about wearing my heels there. And, apparently, they told your dad that he needed to buy me some work boots.

But he did so much better than that. He got me adorable Hunter rain boots in a glossy teal color.

They are so cute!

Your dad is probably the sweetest boy I've ever met.

Something kinda odd about today though. All my friends called and texted to wish me a happy birthday, but my best friend, Lori, didn't.

And I'm not sure why.

A right of passage.

APRIL 12TH

I GLANCE AT my phone, knowing I've missed most of my meetings today because of a problem here at the job site. When the contractor and I met with the inspector, he decided one of the beams in the two-story entrance wasn't hefty enough and wanted us to replace it due to the length of the span. I called my old boss, the engineer who'd approved my structural design so that this wouldn't happen. He said the inspector was going for overkill but suggested we do what he'd asked. Told me it was better to be on their good side than risk more arguments. So, I listened even though it's going to put us behind at least two weeks while we wait for the new steel beam to be constructed and delivered.

When I get to the office, Phillip's assistant, who has been handling all my appointments, asks me if everything is okay. While we were meeting with the inspector, I couldn't very well call and chat.

"Yeah, it's fine. We had an issue with a beam. Can you call Brenda at the office furniture company and ask if she can reschedule for tomorrow?"

"Sure thing," she says. "There are some notes on your desk, and Phillip wants to see you as soon as you get in."

"Tell him to come to my office when he's free. I've got to

rework these timelines."

"Cute boots," she says.

"Thank you!"

I quickly make my way to my office, knowing that she could chat with me all day and somehow still manage to keep the office running.

When I get the timeline reworked, I see that the building is scheduled to be finished just five weeks before my due date. Add another week to move in all the furniture, and I'm down to a month.

I pray there are no more setbacks.

"Danny Diamond on line four," Peggy says over my speaker-phone.

"Hey, Danny," I say.

"So, how were the cupcakes?" he asks, his deep voice barely above a whisper.

I whisper back, "The cupcakes were fun."

"Phillip monopolized all your time yesterday. I need to give you my present."

"Why are you whispering?" I ask him.

"So, my wife doesn't hear me."

"Why don't you want Lori to hear you?"

"Because I'm supposed to be putting the crib together."

"Who are you talking to?" I hear Lori say from somewhere in the background.

"No one, honey. Just singing," he lies.

"Are you not allowed to be on the phone?"

"I just don't want to upset her."

"Have you thought of hiring someone to do it?"

"Oh, I've thought of it, but Lori seems to think it's something I should do. Like a rite of passage."

"Can I ask you something?"

"Sure."

"Is Lori mad at me?"

"I don't think so. Why?"

"Yesterday was my birthday."

"I know. I sent a bunch of doughnuts to your office."

"Did Lori help you with that?"

"No. Why?"

"She didn't say anything. Didn't text me. It's just unusual."

"She's scatterbrained right now. They say it happens in the last trimester. Who knows? Shit, she's coming. I've gotta go."

WHEN LORI AND Danny come over for dinner, she still doesn't say anything. Phillip grabs Danny and himself a couple of beers, and I get Lori a bottle of water.

"You're not having one?" she asks me.

"No," I say as I grab a Diet Coke out of the fridge, pour it over ice, and take a big gulp.

"You're drinking that?" she asks with horror, like I just poured poison down my throat.

"Yeah. My doctor—who is also your doctor—told me, everything in moderation. He said I could have a pop occasionally. This is the first one I've had since I found out I was pregnant."

"How's it taste?" Phillip asks, setting plates and silverware on the table next to the bags of takeout.

"Freaking amazing. And I love Diet Coke with Chinese food. It smells incredible, doesn't it?"

"You seem like you're feeling awfully chipper," Lori states flatly.

"I am. No more morning sickness."

"I wouldn't call what you had morning sickness," she counters. "You gagged a few times."

"I was nauseous and didn't feel good. The doctor called it morning sickness, so I'm assuming that's what it was."

"Of course she had morning sickness," Danny says, shaking

his head at her. "Enough of the pregnancy talk. I have something more exciting."

"What's that?" Phillip asks, digging into the fried rice and dishing it onto our plates.

I can't wait to dig in.

Danny pulls an envelope out of his back pocket and hands it to me.

I open what I assume will be a birthday card. One that probably has some hilarious and inappropriate joke that will make Phillip and me laugh.

But, as I open it, I see a university seal instead. Inside the card are photos of what appears to be a skybox.

"What's this?" I ask.

"I got you a skybox. Well, I got *us* a skybox."

My eyes widen in shock. I glance at Phillip; he looks the same way.

"Are you serious? You got a skybox for the Nebraska games? Ohmigawd! That's amazing, Danny! Thank you! What an incredible gift!"

"When did you do that?" Lori asks.

"It's something I've been working on."

I jump up from the table and throw my arms around him in a big hug. "I love you," I tell him.

"I love you, too," he says. "Happy birthday!"

"I'm pretty sure I'm in love with you as well," Phillip jokes.

"Well, technically, it's mine. But you will have seats for any game you want. And, with my schedule, you'll probably use it more than I will."

"We're gonna have fun," Phillip says.

He and Danny fist-bump across the table as I sit back down.

"I can't believe you bought that and didn't tell me!" Lori yells at Danny.

"We talked about it before. I just didn't want to tell everyone until it was a done deal."

"It's a lot of money," she states.

"And I can afford it."

"*We* can afford it, you mean," she says in a really bitchy tone.

"No," Danny says back. "I meant what I said. *I* can afford it since *I* earned the sign-on bonus that paid for it. It also bought our house and is paying for the remodel. I don't have to ask your permission to spend money I earned before we got married."

"I've decided I'm not hungry anymore," she says, slamming her chopsticks on the table, getting up, and walking out the door.

"You should probably—" I start to say.

Danny holds his hand up. "Don't say it. I'm not chasing after her. She's being a ridiculous bitch, and I'm sick of her blaming it on the pregnancy. You're pregnant, and you aren't behaving like that. Besides, months ago, I told her it was something I wanted to do, and she was all for it. She knows it's been my dream since I was a kid. My parents are thrilled, and I knew you guys would love it. I'm not going to let her ruin our excitement."

"And you shouldn't," Phillip says, "because a skybox is pretty exciting."

The cutest little bump.

APRIL 13TH

PHILLIP KISSES ME as he's leaving for work.

"Happy anniversary to my sexy husband," I say.

"Happy anniversary, Princess. Can you believe we've been married for three whole months?"

"I have to be honest, when we were going through marriage counseling, I thought marriage was going to be hard. Everyone says the first year is so hard."

Phillip laughs. "Parts of our first three months *have* been hard."

"Which parts?"

Phillip grins.

I roll my eyes at him. "Always thinking about sex."

"I told you, we've got a lot of catching up to do."

"Phillip, I don't want to fight with you."

"Did I do something wrong?"

"No, I mean, in general, I don't want to fight with you. And I would never make a scene and stomp out like Lori did. I respect you too much to do that in front of our friends. She really was bitchy to him. I didn't like it."

"I'm glad he didn't go chasing after her this time. Lately, she seems to think that she can say anything and get away with it. It pissed me off how she acted like your morning sickness wasn't real because hers was worse."

"Do you think she's mad at me because my pregnancy has been pretty easy?"

"It hasn't been easy for you. You've been tired. You've felt sick. And you work all day and never complain. She doesn't have a job. What the heck does she do all day?"

"Sometimes, I complain."

"You've yet to be a bitch."

"That's because you bring me cupcakes."

He kisses my nose. "I'm taking you out tonight."

"What are we going to do?"

"Dinner and a movie?" he suggests.

"Oh, popcorn sounds so good."

"Actually, scratch that. Movie first. If you're still hungry after you've eaten the theater out of buttered popcorn and Milk Duds, then we'll get dinner."

"Sounds like the perfect night," I tease.

He lays his hand across my stomach. "I want to start taking pictures of this."

"Of me waking up?"

"No, of your stomach. So, we can see how you're growing."

"I saw a super-cute thing online where you write how many weeks along you are on a chalkboard and take a picture with it."

"We should do that. You have the cutest little bump." He gives me another kiss. "I love you."

After Phillip leaves for work, I grab my phone off my nightstand and text his mom.

Me: Would it be okay if Lori and I spent the night on Saturday? We're coming up for the shower and then going out after. We probably won't get there until later.

Mrs. Mac: Of course! I'll give you an extra key at the shower. What are your plans for Sunday?

Me: *Going wedding dress shopping with Chelsea, and then I'm supposed to stop at the Diamonds' before we leave town.*

Mrs. Mac: *I'll make lunch for when you get back from shopping. And, yes, I heard about the surprise.*

Me: *Got any hints for me?*

Mrs. Mac: *My lips are sealed.*

I throw my robe on, grab a breakfast bar, go into my home office, and check my emails. Nothing too pressing, which is good because I have to finish getting everything ready for the shower. I rented a great event space, one I found when we were looking for our wedding reception. I loved the historic location, the brick-floored courtyard, and the palladium windows overlooking a small garden.

And the staff has been great to work with on the catering. We're having a popcorn bar, fruit kabobs, tea sandwiches, pastel macarons, and a stacked lemon cake. There will be a bar set up with decanters full of juices that you can mix with fresh berries or champagne. The table centerpieces are baby bottles filled with yellow flowers.

I decided against your typical sit-down-in-a-circle-and-play-games baby shower. We've done that enough lately. I want this shower to be more about mingling and fun. So, instead of games, I'm having activity stations.

I asked all the shower guests to bring a baby photo of themselves. When they arrive, they will hang it, clothesline-style, on a piece of twine from mini clothespins. Behind each photo will be a piece of pastel paper in different colors, so the game of guessing which shower guest is which baby will become part of the decor.

The second station is the advice area. I covered a paint can with fabric to match Lori's nursery and then hand-drew a giraffe design, which I then printed on plain notecards. Everyone will write their best piece of baby or parenting advice on a card and put it in the can.

The third station is for decorating a baby onesie. I bought a whole bunch of snap-bottom T-shirts in different colors. Each guest can use paint, fabric markers, or iron-on decals to decorate one, and Lori will get to take them all home.

All the shower gifts are going on one table in the center of the room. This becomes the present station. Lori will be opening presents throughout the party and displaying them on another table for all the guests to see. Guests can sit in a small circle of chairs to watch her open gifts when they want, but they won't be forced to sit the entire time.

Can I just take a brief moment to say thank God for Pinterest? It's made doing things like this so much easier. Sometimes, when I can't sleep, I pull up the app on my phone and pin stuff, like amazing food I hope to make someday, decor for our house, holiday decorating, cool architecture, DIY, crafts, travel spots, clothing boards, gardening, bucket lists, and party ideas. Considering my mom used to do this by cutting stuff out of magazines and gluing them into a notebook, this is pretty incredible.

I've been working on all the details since I got back from our honeymoon, and even though I'm irritated with the way Lori acted last night, I hope she loves it.

I'm also looking forward to having three hours alone in the car with her. Maybe she'll tell me what's going on.

I decide to text her.

Me: *Are you excited for the shower?*
Lori: *Yeah.*

One-worded text = not good.

Lori: *I forgot your birthday. Luckily, my husband didn't.*

That's quite the present.

Passive-aggressive. Shit.

Me: *It is. Thanks to you both.*

Lori: *Obviously, I had nothing to do with it.*

Me: *Lori, what's going on? Why are you not excited about this? Think ahead. You don't love football that much. This is a way for you to go to the games, take the baby, socialize, and not have to sit out in the weather. It's the best of both worlds. Like having your friends over for a party at your house, yet you get the excitement of the crowd.*

Lori: *Do you know how much it cost?*

Me: *Actually, I do. Danny's dad is very conservative. He helped Danny with the decision.*

Lori: *He just wants the box, too.*

Me: *You just don't get it, Lori. Doing this for his family and friends is like a dream come true for Danny. I really wish you were more supportive of him.*

Lori: *Of course you would take his side on this. You want the box, too. I don't want people using him. I have his best interests at heart. That's what pisses me off.*

Me: *How could I be using him when I didn't know about it until he'd done it? You're being ridiculous. And I'm saying that as your best friend.*

Danny texts me.

Danny: *Want to go get lunch in a little bit?*

Me: *Are you at home? I'm texting Lori. I thought she would apologize. For forgetting my birthday. For her outburst last night. Instead, she's trying to defend herself.*

Danny: *That's why I want to go to lunch. I need to get* *away from her before I say something I'm going to regret.*

Me: *What happened when you went home last night?*

Danny: *Are you at work?*

Me: *No, I'm working from home today. Although, technically, I'm not doing much work. I'm finishing up getting everything ready for the shower tomorrow.*

Danny: *I'm coming over.*

Me: *I'm in my office. Front door is unlocked.*

A few minutes later, he strolls in my office. He looks like he didn't sleep last night.

"Are you okay?"

He plops down on the floor and runs his hands through his hair. "I'm not sure I can live like this."

My eyes get big. "What are you saying?"

"I'm saying, right now, I want a divorce. And, if it wasn't for her being pregnant and due soon, I'd be getting one." His voice is angry, but I can see the hurt in his eyes. Danny never quits or gives up at anything he does, so this is serious.

I stop what I'm doing and go sit on the floor next to him.

"Why are you still in your robe? It's almost noon."

"I'd wear my robe all day if I could."

"Are you naked under there?"

"We're all naked under our clothes, Danny," I say with a laugh.

He laughs, leans his head on my shoulder, and smiles. "You always know how to make me laugh."

"That's because my answer has been the same ever since you started asking me that question ten years ago. Or whenever it was that you went through puberty. Danny, you and Lori have only been together for a couple of years. She's not going to know all the stuff I know about. She has been acting differently lately though.

Her not remembering my birthday just glares at me. It's not that big of a deal. We forget sometimes, no biggie. But she's the girl in our sorority who never forgot a birthday and gave everyone an adorable hand-made birthday card. It's not like her."

"It's the preterm labor. She's been pissed at me since then. Although it's weird; she didn't seem pissed when I got to the hospital. She was happy and relieved. It wasn't until a few days after that she started acting crazy."

"Danny, they put her on medicine to stop the contractions."

"Yeah."

"Does the medicine have side effects?"

"I don't know. Jesus, I hope that's all it is."

I grab my computer and set it on my lap. "I know they gave her a shot of something that started with a T at the hospital. Is that what she's taking now?"

"No, she's on progest-something."

"Progesterone?"

"Yeah, I think so."

"But that's a hormone."

"Yeah, that's it. It's a hormone."

"Well, no wonder. Hang on; let me look this up to be sure." I do a quick search and then turn the computer toward him.

He reads. "*Side effects can include upset stomach, appetite changes, weight gain, fluid retention and swelling, fatigue, and PMS-like symptoms.* Oh my God. Why didn't the doctor tell me this? That's what it's like. She's in constant PMS bitch-mode."

He puts his hands on his face and rubs it.

"At least you know it's temporary. Danny, you love her."

"I do. Now, I feel bad."

"Why?"

"Because she's pregnant with my baby, and I'm telling you I want a divorce because she's being either an irrational bitch or sobbing lunatic, and it turns out it's probably not her fault. She's taking the medicine to keep our baby inside her longer, so it can grow and be healthy. I'm an asshole."

"Danny, you aren't an asshole. You just didn't understand. The doctor should have told you to expect this. Why don't you go see if she wants to go out for lunch?"

"Yeah," he says, getting up. "Thanks, Jay, for just listening."

"You know Phillip and I are always here for you."

"I tried talking to Phillip about it this morning. He said I should suck it up, be a man, and take care of my pregnant wife."

I melt. "Ahh, he's so sweet."

"I told him we'd revisit that conversation when you're a few weeks away from giving birth." Danny laughs. "See ya."

Glimmers of us.

APRIL 14TH

ON SATURDAY, AS we're driving up to Omaha, Lori says, "I'm sorry I forgot your birthday. I don't know what's been wrong with me lately."

"You're pregnant," I say. "It's okay. I know you've had a really hard time with it."

"I'm sorry I stomped out of your house, too."

"It's okay. Just relax and enjoy the baby shower today. You get to see all your friends."

She smiles and pats her belly. "That will be nice. I'm so huge though."

"Of course you are. You're due in a few weeks. But you're wearing a cute dress, and you're glowing with impending motherhood."

She nods. "Thanks, Jade."

THE SHOWER IS so much fun and a huge success. Everyone loved the location and setup, and Lori got some adorable keepsakes from it—not to mention, a boatload of gifts.

I arranged for Mrs. Mac to take Lori back to her house, saying that I had to run an errand.

I drive to the cemetery, stopping to get flowers on the way.

As I round the corner leading to their plot, I see there is a funeral just finishing up. People in black are wandering back to their cars, looking a little lost.

That makes me sad. Sad other people have died. Sad another family had to bury ones they loved. I say a silent prayer for them. A prayer hoping they will come to terms with it and find peace. A prayer hoping they don't wait as long as I did to come back to the grave of their loved one.

I park as close as I can, grab the flowers and the other items I brought with me, and walk to their headstone.

Reading their names engraved in marble stops me in my tracks.

It probably always will. Maybe because it doesn't seem like it could possibly be real.

It makes sense why they make headstones out of marble. It's cold. Hard. Like death.

I didn't tell Lori why I chose this date for her shower. I didn't want to ruin her big day with the fact that today is my dad's birthday, and I wanted to visit his grave.

But, now that I'm pregnant, it seems like the perfect day to tell them.

Like, in case they don't already know.

I run my hand across the marker, my fingers tracing their names and then my dad's birthdate.

"So, I know me coming here is unusual," I say to the stone. "But today is a special day." I set the flowers in the grass in front of the marker. "Happy birthday, Dad. And, although I can't really give you a gift, I want to tell you something. Something I wish with all my heart that you and Mom were here for. Something I know you would be so excited about. I mean, you probably wouldn't have jumped up and down like Mrs. Mac did, but I know you would have been super excited. I hope that, somehow, you still know what's going on in my life. Know how often I think

of you. Hear me when I talk to you. But, just in case you don't"—
I set the adorable pink-fuchsia-and-teal-striped rattle down next to
the flowers—"I'm pregnant. Due on October the first. A fall
football baby, who I'm going to teach how to hold its arms up in
the air for *TOUCHDOWN*, just like you taught me."

The tears that have been slowly trickling down my cheeks
become more pronounced as I kneel on the ground.

"I have—I have a picture. I brought you a picture of the baby," I sob, setting the ultrasound photo down next to the flowers.

A voice says, "Jadyn?"

I turn to see Pastor John dressed in a dark suit.

"Oh, hey, Pastor."

He reads the stone. "Today would have been your dad's birthday."

"Yeah," I say with a smile, standing up and wiping my tears.
"Were you just at the funeral over there?"

"Yes, I officiated. It was a car accident. Father of three young
children. Tragic."

"Pastor, why does God let bad stuff happen? I know we all
make choices, and I get freewill, but then that doesn't make sense
either. My parents didn't choose to die. Bad things happen to
good people. I don't understand. I'm sure the people at the funeral
you just did don't understand either because it doesn't make sense.
And, honestly, it's affected my faith."

"Do you believe in an afterlife? Do you believe your parents
are still with you?"

"Yes. But is that just because it's comforting to me?"

"I thought you said you'd never come here. Is this your first
time visiting?"

"No, I came here the night before Phillip and I had our last
counseling session. Had a little meltdown."

"I heard about the meltdown. Your mother-in-law thought
you'd call off the wedding."

"What did you think?"

"Honestly, I didn't think you would. It's pretty obvious that you and Phillip respect and love each other."

"Do you think my parents know what's going on with me? Like, if there is something special going on in my life, would they know?"

"I believe they see glimmers of us. I picture heaven like a veil. They can't completely see the picture, but sometimes, they can make out images. I think love affects it."

"I'm torn about the whole grave thing. I feel like they aren't here, yet I still came to tell them the news."

"And what news is that?"

"I'm pregnant."

Pastor John beams. "Congratulations. How are you doing with that? I thought, during couples counseling, you'd mentioned wanting to wait for a few years."

"Yeah, well, sometimes, our brain and our heart aren't always on the same wavelength. Logically, there are a lot of reasons waiting would have been more practical."

"And your heart?"

"It's thrilled. We had an ultrasound. Would you like to see the picture?"

"Of course."

I pull the photo out from under the flowers and hand it to him.

"Isn't the creation of life a miracle?" Pastor John says, studying the ultrasound. "How far along are you?"

"I'll be sixteen weeks on Monday."

Pastor John smiles. "I bet Phillip is over the moon about it."

"He is super excited."

"How's married life?"

"Mostly good."

"What's not good?"

"What's the best way to deal with your mother-in-law?" I ask.

He chuckles. "I wish I knew the answer to that. I've been married for thirty years and given my mother-in-law three beautiful grandchildren, but I'm still convinced she doesn't like me that much."

"I love Phillip's mother; don't get me wrong. She's made me feel like part of their family. But, lately, she's said and done a few things that have made me feel like she thinks I'm not a good wife."

"What does Phillip think? Does he think you're a good wife?"

"Yes," I answer, not saying any more because I think Mrs. Mac's version of an ideal wife and Phillip's are very different.

"Is she excited about the baby?"

"You should have seen when she found out. She was screaming and crying. But I'm worried I won't do things right. Or the way she thinks I should."

"Just remember, Jadyn, when she had her first baby, she didn't know any more than you. My advice would be to respectfully listen to what she has to say, but ultimately, it's up to you and Phillip how you raise your children. Things have changed since you were born. Lots of new technology. New theories on discipline. I have a parenting book that I highly recommend. I'll send you a copy. It's about raising confident children."

"That would be nice. Does it have advice for dealing with in-laws, too?"

"It does. I use many of its techniques in dealing with everyone in my life."

"What does it say to do when she buys you a gift that you hate?"

"In our household, gifts like that are prominently displayed *only* when my mother-in-law visits."

"Interesting. One more question, and I'll let you get going. What's your take on gnomes?"

"They scare me."

I laugh. "Yeah, me, too."

As the pastor heads to his car, I slide the ultrasound photo back under the flowers, kiss my hand, and touch the headstone. "I love you guys."

I stay there, watch the sun set, and then leave when it gets dark.

WHEN I GET to the Mackenzie house, I haul my tote bag up to Phillip's room and then plop across his bed.

Me: *I'm lying in your room. It's weird, being here without you.*

Mac Daddy Loves You: *I miss you. Danny and Joey say they miss you, too.*

Me: *What are you guys doing?*

Mac Daddy Loves You: *We're at the bar.*

Me: *I miss the bar.*

Mac Daddy Loves You: *Are you mad I'm out? We were supposed to just hang out at our house.*

Me: *No. Why should I be? Wait. Are you at a bar or a club? Oh gosh. You're with Danny, and Lori is out of town. Tell me you're not going to the strip club. Lori will be pissed!*

Mac Daddy Loves You: *Will you be pissed?*

Me: *No.*

Mac Daddy Loves You: *Lori is. But why? She's never cared before.*

Me: *It's different because she's pregnant. She's emotional, and she needs Danny's support even if she's acting a little crazy.*

Mac Daddy Loves You: *To be honest, I'm worried about their marriage.*

Me: I am, too. Maybe it will be better once they have the baby. But, somehow, I don't think the strip club is going to help the situation. I'm sort of surprised you'd take him.

Mac Daddy Loves You: I'm not so sure about that. Everything I've read says that a new baby is stressful on your marriage. If pregnancy is this bad, what's that going to be like for them?

Me: I don't know. Just be there for him.

Mac Daddy Loves You: Why do you think I'm going to the strip club? We were in the basement, playing pool, having a couple of beers, and next thing I know, Danny had ordered a party bus, invited a bunch of guys from the team, and made reservations at the strip club. We're at a bar pre-partying, waiting for everyone to get here.

Me: You're a good friend, Phillip. I stopped at my parents' grave today. It was my dad's birthday.

Mac Daddy Loves You: I totally forgot about that. I'm sorry.

Me: It's okay. Can you believe, in a few days, it will be the fifth anniversary of their deaths?

Mac Daddy Loves You: No, I can't. You doing okay?

Me: Yeah, I took some flowers and a copy of the ultrasound picture. I wanted them to know. Like, in case they don't already.

Mac Daddy Loves You: I think they already know. I love you. What are you doing tonight?

Me: Supposed to meet everyone at the bar.

Mac Daddy Loves You: Is Lori going to the bar?

Me: I assume.

Mac Daddy Loves You: Just keep her busy, so she won't text Danny.

I change into some stretchy jeans that still fit and a black V-neck tee and touch up my makeup.

When I hear the garage door open, I run downstairs. Chelsea and Lori come inside with Mrs. Mac.

"Hey, guys! Did you have a nice dinner?"

"You're awfully chipper," Lori says to me, looking irritated.

"I take it, you heard about the strip club." I realize that going to the bar is probably the last thing she needs. She'll obsess over how skinny everyone is. She'll start thinking about Danny being at a bar where everyone looks like this. "I am chipper," I say, "because I'm excited for us. I thought, instead of going out, we could have a slumber party. Make popcorn. Eat cake. Watch girlie movies. We haven't done that in forever. Just us girls."

"That sounds fun," Chelsea says.

"Did you come up with that before or after you heard about the strip club?" Lori asks bitchily.

"You know what, Lori? Why don't you decide what you want to do? We can go to the bar and meet everyone, or we can do the slumber-party thing. Either is fine with me. Just let me know," I say as calmly as I can.

I swear, I'm about ready to blow. Not only did she forget my birthday, but I also worked really hard on the shower that everyone loved, and she hasn't even said *thank you*. We all know that I'd rather go to the bar. I don't even care that I can't drink. I just want to see everyone.

I remind myself of the medication she's on, calm myself down, and then turn toward Mrs. Mac. "You wouldn't happen to have any leftovers, would you?"

"I have some chicken enchiladas and rice."

"That sounds perfect," I say, following her to the kitchen.

"You sit," she says as she takes a pan out of the fridge and dishes me out food. "You did an amazing job with the shower today, JJ. I'd never been at one quite like that. It was really fun.

And all your sorority sisters are just so delightful."

"Thanks." I beam.

I take a seat at the kitchen table, thinking about all the times I've sat at it. Eating peanut butter and crackers after school. Cake every year on Phillip's birthday. Family dinners. Pizza parties with our friends. The table has been here for as long as I can remember.

But I notice it's shinier than usual, and the long scratch from Phillip's backpack is gone.

"Your table looks different," I say.

"I had it refinished."

I look at the table some more, feeling sad. It used to have character and memories, which have all been wiped away.

And, even though I know the table we ordered will look new when we get it, I can't wait to have our friends carve their names in it. I can't wait for my kids to eat sandwiches on it. I can't wait for the first scratch. For the table to be a history of our time together.

Somehow, I have to figure out a way to get her to return the table she bought us without hurting her feelings.

She's smiling and happily chatting to Lori about the baby shower. I'm nodding where it's appropriate, but my mind is thinking about how appreciative she was when I let her help plan some of the wedding. Maybe that's the solution. Maybe I should take her to see the table we ordered. Or let her help me pick something out for the house.

I managed to convince both her and Mrs. Diamond that seeing the groom before the wedding wasn't bad luck. That it would be a special moment. Maybe I need to do something like that again.

Chelsea interrupts my thoughts as she slides into a chair next to me. "Decorating the onesies was such a cute idea. Everyone loved it. I'd love to do that for my shower. I'm also dying to read the advice. Are you going to share them, Lori?"

"Maybe," she says. "I thought I would save them until after the baby is born."

Mrs. Mackenzie takes a plate out of the microwave and sets it in front of me. "Where did you go after the shower today?"

"I visited my parents' grave. Today was my dad's birthday."

"April fourteenth," she says, shaking her head. "That's right. I can't believe it's been almost five years since they passed. How are you doing?"

"I'm okay," I tell her. "Pastor John was there. I told him about our pregnancy."

"I bet he wasn't as excited as I was." She chuckles.

I feel my phone vibrate and peek down at my lap.

Phillip: *Just so you know, I confiscated Danny's phone. Lori is being a HUGE bitch. I didn't realize how bad it was. It's not often I do this, but I'm feeding him shots. He needs them. Love you, Princess.*

"So, what did you girls decide?" Mrs. Mac asks. "If you're staying here, I'll make you some mocktails. Maybe mudslides and strawberry daiquiris?"

Lori looks down at her phone and sighs. "That sounds good. Let's stay here."

I decide to do what I can to make Lori have fun and forget where Danny is.

We watch as Mrs. Mac throws stuff in the blender, and then she sets pitchers on the table while I get glasses.

Chelsea pours us each a drink, and I say, "Okay. We're setting some ground rules for this slumber party. All pregnancy, birth, and baby words and topics are off-limits, starting now. Tonight, we're just girls."

"That's good," Mrs. Mac says. "You need to just be a girl sometimes, especially once you become a mother—"

"Drink!" I yell out, pointing at her. "Uh, sorry, old habit. But you just committed a party foul."

Mrs. Mac is taken aback. "Oh, well, I was just going to say that, no matter what your, uh, *role* is in life, you should always remember to take care of yourself. You are first and foremost a woman. Wife and mother—"

"Uh …" I say while chanting, *Drink mothereffer in my head,* but feeling proud of myself for not yelling it out.

"All come later," she finishes.

"I got a whole lot of advice about that *role* today," Lori says. "And what's the deal? Do women take pleasure in scaring us by describing their deliveries?"

"Uh, drink," I say to Lori as Mrs. Mac places a delicious-looking slab of chocolate ganache cake and three forks in front of us.

"Damn," Lori says, automatically taking a chug of her mudslide. Old habits die hard.

"You cussed, too," I remind her.

She takes another drink, laughing.

"I haven't had this much fun in a while," she says as a hunk of cake makes its way toward her mouth, barely hanging on to the dainty dessert fork.

But her question has me thinking. "Um, Mrs. Mac, I was talking to Pastor John today, and he was telling me about his mother-in-law. Did Mr. Mac's mom like you?"

"You said *mom* and *mother,*" Chelsea points out.

I happily take a slug of mudslide.

Mrs. Mac frowns. "She didn't really approve of me."

"Why?" I ask.

"Even though we'd been dating for quite some time, getting—" She stops before she says pregnant. "Um, *Ashley* was a surprise. We eloped, which really upset her. But you have to do what's right for you as a couple. And eloping helped us avoid the drama. Well, sort of."

"What do you mean?"

"I was still in college while carrying, um, *our surprise*."

I squint at Lori, and we agree to let the *carrying* slide.

"This one time, she came to our apartment and complained because it was a mess. Said something about how her son wasn't raised that way."

"What did you do?" Lori asks her.

"I told her it was her son's mess. *That* didn't go over well. Doug's family was fairly well off. My family was just pretty normal. She thought I'd tricked him into marrying me for his money. They really weren't that well off," she says under her breath. "Sure, they owned the business that he eventually took over, but it was struggling. He made it what it is today. Anyway, I'm headed to bed. You girls enjoy your night. There's more leftover chicken enchiladas and homemade salsa in the fridge if you get hungry later."

"Thanks," we say in unison.

Once she's out of earshot, Chelsea levels her gaze at me. "How did Phillip's mom go from a newlywed with a messy apartment to Martha freaking Stewart?"

I shrug. I was wondering the same thing myself.

"Do you think that will be us someday?" Chelsea asks. "Like when we have, um, *houses* of our own. Will we get better at that stuff?"

"I think so. Did you hear Danny's cousin talking?" I ask.

Lori says, "Yeah. She made it sound like she was in, uh, *pain* for three days straight before she gave, uh, before the *event*."

"You can say it," I tease. "You'll just have to drink."

"This mudslide is so good. I feel like I'm drinking, but I'm not. And, fine, I'll say it. Does anyone really have three days of labor?" She automatically chugs her drink.

"She mentioned that she had a huge, um, that *she required numerous stitches* afterward as well," Chelsea says. "Just thinking about that makes my nether regions hurt."

"She was exaggerating," Lori says. "No one takes three days for the event."

"My point though is that she said all her two-year-old eats are apples, chicken fingers, and strawberry Pop-Tarts."

"Sounds like my college diet." Lori laughs.

"Exactly!" I say. "Meaning we can handle it."

Lori smiles. "Yeah, you're right. We *can* handle it."

I get brave and ask her what has really been on my mind, "Lori, are you and Danny doing okay?"

"Yes. Why do you ask?"

"I heard you were mad they were going out. That kind of stuff never bothered you before."

She plays with the ends of her hair and then pats her baby bump. "Does it bother you?" She turns to Chelsea. "What about you? Joey is with them. You're starting to show. You're a few weeks behind Jade, and your stomach is way bigger."

"What's that got to do with anything?" Chelsea says. "It's not like I'm fat. I'm pregnant. Besides, Jade is taller than me. My mom said she popped out right away, too. Different body types carry babies different ways. And, no, it doesn't bother me at all. I trust Joey."

"It doesn't bother me either," I say. "They're being guys, having fun. It's not like they go very often. The last time was Phillip's bachelor party."

"I know it was," Lori says. "And bachelor parties are usually the only time he goes."

"Why don't I heat up some more enchiladas, and we watch a movie?" I suggest. I don't want her dwelling on the club. I shouldn't have even brought it up, but I wanted to make sure they're okay.

"I can't wait to put my feet up," Lori says. "They're swollen for some reason."

"You go do that. I'll heat up the food."

Chelsea plops on the couch while Lori perches on the edge of it, moving pillows around before leaning back and getting comfortable.

I throw the enchiladas in the microwave and make up a tray of chips and salsa.

Lori says, "Jade, do you think Danny would ever cheat on me? Honestly."

"I honestly don't, Lori," I say, setting the food on the coffee table.

"He cheats at board games," she counters.

"Yeah, he openly cheats. That's different."

Chelsea chooses a movie we've seen a million times.

WHEN I GO into the kitchen to get more chips, I send Phillip a quick text.

Me: *How's the party?*

Mac Daddy Loves You: *Danny is buying rounds of lap dances.*

Me: *Are they better than the one I gave you at your bachelor party?*

Mac Daddy Loves You: *Yours was by far the sexiest.*

Me: *I can't dance.*

Mac Daddy Loves You: *You gave it a good shot. And you earned shoe money.*

Me: *I gave the money back to Danny.*

Mac Daddy Loves You: *Hmm, well ... wanna earn some more when you get home?*

Me: *I love you. Have fun. Be good. Don't get arrested. And don't let Danny drink too much.*

Mac Daddy Loves You: *I have all but the last one covered.*

Me: *Then, don't let him do anything stupid.*

Mac Daddy Loves You: *Have I ever?*

Me: *Well, you have tried. Doesn't always work. It needs to work tonight. I think his marriage is at stake. Seriously.*

Mac Daddy Loves You: *Got it. But we both know he's not going to cheat. Is he having fun? Yes. Is he a cheater? No. Never has been.*

Me: *True. Okay, I've gotta go. Have fun.*

Me: *But, like, not too much fun.*

"So, the guys were doing their list of nevers at the Super Bowl party," I say, setting the chips down. "Do you have anything you swear you won't do when you're a parent?"

"My kids will never eat fast food," Lori says.

"I think it's easy to say you'll never do something," Chelsea says to her, "but when I took my nephews to their hockey practices while my sister went Christmas shopping a few months ago, I got them fast food. I know my sister doesn't let them eat that stuff—hell, I won't even eat it unless I'm drunk. I know it's bad for you, but they were whining, crabby, and hungry, and when I asked if they wanted to get some food, they casually suggested a drive-through because we didn't have much time. It wasn't until later, when they were happily munching down fries and drinking Mountain Dew like it was the nectar of the gods, did I remember my sister had a no-fast-food rule."

"Well, sometimes, when you're traveling or in a hurry, you need to stop for something quick," I sympathize.

"No, wait," she says. "There's more. And, if it wasn't bad enough that I'd broken that rule, I told them not to tell their mother. I taught them how to lie! I don't know how she does it. Whenever they go somewhere, it takes her forever because she has to pack a freaking cooler—like just to go for a drive because the boys get hungry. She always has a healthy array of snacks."

"Although I disapprove of fast food as well," Lori says, "you weren't prepared. Your sister should have packed you a cooler."

"You're right," Chelsea says. "See, it wasn't my fault. Except maybe for the lying. But she would have been mad at me. Although I thought she did all her Christmas shopping online, but she said she and her husband were going together. Maybe they just needed some time alone."

"I read an article that says it's important to still have a date night with your husband, even when your kids are little and you don't want to leave them," I say.

"Her boys are seven and nine. They actually have a really good babysitter. That's one thing that will be awesome if Joey and I move here after I graduate. Like, if one of the jobs works out."

Lori smiles at me. I know Danny has already decided to hire Joey and is putting together a sweet package for him.

"I'm sure one of them will," I say.

"My sister owes me. I babysat those kids when they went on vacation. Three years in a row."

"How's the wedding planning going?" Lori asks Chelsea.

"How did your parents take the news?" I ask, knowing her parents are very driven.

"They were freaking out a little at first. Worried I wouldn't graduate. Worried we'd only been dating for a few months, but then I told them about how long I'd known him—the almosts. I also mentioned that my big sis, Jadyn, has known Joey since, like, birth."

"First grade," I correct, "but close enough."

"See. And they like Phillip. They're relieved Joey has already graduated. I told them about the job possibilities. Kind of insinuated one was a done deal, but that was just to put their minds at ease that we won't starve or anything.

"His parents, on the other hand, were very excited and supportive. They seem to like me. My dad kinda growled at Joey when we told them. And I'm happy. Once I got over the shock. I mean, it's not like I expected to be pregnant now, but I'm so amazingly happy. I was emotional and was nauseous for the first couple of weeks, but that's about it. I feel pretty good now."

"I hate you," Lori says. "You and Jade are going to be, like, pregnancy unicorns, wearing high heels and looking gorgeous, and I'll be the dumpy one in her husband's sweatpants."

"Lori," I say, "you never look dumpy."

She sighs. "At least people can finally see that I'm pregnant and not just fat."

"Is it really that bad?" Chelsea wonders. "Because I can't wait to have my stomach look like that. It will mean my baby's growing and healthy."

Lori's eyes get huge. "I didn't mean that I don't want a healthy baby, and I know it's worth it. Ah, shit. I don't know what the fuck I want. Danny is driving me nuts. Hell, I'm driving myself nuts."

"And you said three curse words," I say gently.

She ignores me.

"I'm emotional. I cry for no reason. I'm sensitive. It's like some sulking, insecure, PMSing fifteen-year-old is living inside me, controlling my emotions. Danny is so sweet and so good to me, but he can't do anything right. In my mind, I know I'm being ridiculous with the way I'm acting, but it's how I feel. Like, my emotions are on my sleeve. I'll be lucky if he doesn't divorce me before the baby comes. I'd deserve it. See? I suck. I made him rub my feet before I forgave him for showing the guys my pregnancy underwear. They don't even fit me, but the girls at the store said I would need them eventually."

"Joey thought they were a tire cover." I laugh.

She laughs, too. "If Danny had told me that, I would have been hurt."

"He says you blame him for how you feel."

"I do!"

"So, maybe you need to flip your attitude. Maybe think of your pregnancy as an amazing gift."

"Are you sending me to Babyville?" She rolls her eyes. "I love him, but there are days I look at him and want to hurt him. I'm crazy. And, to make matters worse, I got invited to lunch with Mitzi Nathaniel."

"Dirk Nathaniel's wife?" I ask.

"Yeah, he's one of the team captains, and she's sort of the goddess of the football wives. Goes to games all decked out in designer clothes. Heels. Fur. Has four kids and looks perfect. All. The. Time."

"I read an article about her while I was waiting at the doctor's office. She has a nanny, fitness instructor, and a chef. That's why she looks perfect all the time," I tell her. "So, what do you think? Do you have some nevers?"

"I do!" Chelsea offers. "I will always get up, shower, and get dressed even if the baby hasn't slept much that night. I won't wear my pajamas all day."

"I will never get a minivan," Lori says. "Maybe an SUV but no minivans."

"That was on the boys' list," I say with a laugh.

"I have a birthing plan," Lori admits. "I don't want them to give me pain medication."

"My sister says the only words you need to remember when you give birth are, *I'll have the epidural, please.* She had one kid with pain medicine and one without. She says the one with was a much nicer experience. I'm the girl who had to do tequila shooters when she twisted her ankle. No way I'll survive that kind of pain without help," Chelsea says. "Plus, as my sister says, *Why would you want to?*"

"I've read that it slows down labor," Lori says.

"To which my sister would counter, *So I had two extra hours of pain-free labor. So what?*"

"What about you, Jade?" Lori puts me on the spot. "Do you have a birthing plan?"

"Not yet. I'm just hoping there is a birth."

"What do you mean?"

"I had kind of a bad dream the other night," I admit. "I was bleeding."

"It's normal for pregnant women to have bad dreams. It doesn't mean anything," Lori tells me, obsessively smoothing out her napkin.

"Have *you* been having bad dreams?" I ask pointedly.

She sighs. "Yes. But they haven't been about the baby. They've been about Danny."

"What about him?"

"He's cheating on me, but who could blame him? In my dreams, I'm the size of a moose, and I haven't washed my hair in weeks. I wake up, bawling. He's such an idiot in them. It's like nothing I say affects him. That's almost scarier than finding out he cheated. And, in the dreams, I witness the cheating, I call him out on it, and he acts like I'm being ridiculous. And I'm thinking he can't be that dumb. But then I do think he's dumb. I want him to swear to me it's not true, but he just sits there with that smirk of his and doesn't really say anything."

"I had a lot of crazy dreams before the wedding. You told me it was because it was on my mind."

"I can see that about something pertaining to—wait, are we still playing?"

"We haven't been, but we should be," Chelsea says. "Be right back. I have to pee."

"Okay. Uh, pertaining to the *little monkey* but not Danny. Did you know I signed a prenuptial agreement?"

"It doesn't surprise me. Mr. D had Phillip sign one. He says anyone who comes to a marriage with a significant amount of assets should."

"I know. And he told us that he hoped our marriage would never end, but that it's better to set the terms while you're in love than when you aren't on good terms. It all makes sense. And this is going to sound bad no matter how I say it, so please don't take it wrong."

"Uh, okay."

"But when you're, uh, *with a little monkey*, you come to the realization that you are stuck with your husband. No matter what you do, once you bring a, uh, *monkey* into the equation, he will always be a part of your life."

"Well, yeah," I say. "Common sense tells you that."

She sighs. "I think, in the back of my mind, I always felt like, if we didn't work out, that I could get out of the marriage. No harm. No foul. We go our separate ways. And, now, if he leaves me, I'll be a twenty-three-year-old single mom. I think that's why I'm having dreams about him cheating. Because, for the first time, I've realized that I need him. I don't think I can do this by myself. And that makes me feel helpless and unconfident. Combine that with the fact that I'm a super-sized version of myself, you can see why I am a bit of a wreck and why my husband being at a strip club makes me want to simultaneously scream and cry. And, if I'm being really honest, I know the things he loves most about me— my confidence, my intelligence—are gone. I don't know if I can handle a ba—uh, shoot, *a monkey*. And I'm afraid, if I don't know everything, he won't love me anymore. It's a vicious circle."

"It's just a night out with the boys, Lori. Don't make it more than that. You were pregnant—"

"Ha!" she yells, pointing at me. "Drink!"

I take a drink and then finish my sentence, "You were pregnant during Phillip's bachelor party, and Danny didn't cheat on you. So, you don't have to worry now."

She tilts her head. "That's the most sense you've made all night."

"Remember my wedding disaster dreams? None of them happened. And Phillip told me that you could change your dreams. If he's cheating on you in your dream, whip off your ugly costume, reveal the gorgeous slinky, skinny dress you're wearing, and know that he wouldn't because you're beautiful to him, pregnant."

"Did he tell you that?"

"He did. Before the wedding. Don't be so hard on yourself."

"Back to the nevers," Chelsea says, joining us back on the couch. "I'm never going to be too tired for sex."

To which Lori chuckles but doesn't say anything.

So, I tell them, "I was in the grocery store the other day, and this kid was lying on the floor in the cereal aisle, screaming bloody murder. Her little body was flailing in ways that seemed anatomically impossible. I felt bad for the mother, but what did she do to set the poor child off? I would have been horrified, but she was ignoring it. She was talking to the cereal instead. Saying something about how only the strongest, healthiest cereals could come home with them. I'm pretty sure she had gone batshit crazy. My child will never have a tantrum in a store."

It's Chelsea's turn to laugh. "My nephew had one once while we were at his brother's hockey practice. Everything was going great. He was happily running his little cars across the bleachers. I was texting some hot guy when he tried to grab my phone and said he wanted to play with it. I calmly replied that it wasn't a toy; therefore, he couldn't play with it. He let out this screech like a hot poker had gotten shoved through his arm. Then, he rolled down two stairs, fell on the ground, and started pounding his head on the bottom bleacher. I was horrified!"

"What did you do?"

"I gave him my phone. He texted the hot guy the words *snot and pussy.* Deleted half of my apps and then started playing an explicit song. The whole room filled with lyrics about eating dick for breakfast. I think having kids must be a humbling experience."

"Particularly when you give birth," Lori says. "When we toured a birthing room, they told us there are sometimes up to five strangers—all medical professionals, mind you—watching you give birth!"

"My sister says you go into some sort of birthing zone and don't give a shit who sees your vagina. You just want the baby out of you."

"I'm going to heat up some more enchiladas," I say, getting up to do so and then bringing them back on a pretty platter.

"Wait!" Chelsea says as I'm getting ready to serve them. "I have to take a picture of this. Line up our drinks, too."

I artfully arrange our food and beverages.

"Perfect," she says, snapping away.

"Does your sister take pictures of her food?" I ask.

Chelsea laughs. "I think all she makes is macaroni and cheese. Although she uses gluten-free pasta and coconut milk."

"I'm considering making my own baby food," Lori tells us. "I've heard it's much healthier."

"Lately, I'm lucky if I have time to pick up the phone to call and order delivery," I say. "And it doesn't help that, when Phillip's mom is there, she makes the most amazing meals."

"She is such a good cook," Lori agrees. "These enchiladas are so good."

"But I had visions of my husband coming home from work to find me in sexy lingerie with an amazing dinner waiting for him, spread out in our perfectly decorated, candlelit dining room."

"I think that's what is funny about the nevers." Chelsea laughs. "You know even though we say we won't do that stuff, we totally will."

A surprise.

APRIL 15TH

WE GO SHOPPING and find Chelsea a dress that is perfect for a beach wedding, have lunch with the Macs, and then head over to the Diamonds'.

Lori knocks on the front door.

"Oh my goodness," Mrs. Diamond says, looking at Lori. "You've dropped."

"Do you think?" Lori asks.

"What's that mean?" I ask.

"When you drop, it means you're carrying the baby lower. It's usually a sign of impending birth."

"Oh, cool. So, that's good!" I say.

"Yes! I'm so excited!" Lori smiles.

"WHY DON'T YOU two go sit in the study?" she says.

Mr. Diamond comes in and gives us each hugs. Then, he and Mrs. D give Lori and me souvenirs from their trip. Gorgeous, soft intricately woven shawls from Greece.

"What are those scratching noises?" I ask.

Mr. Diamond smiles at me. "I have a housewarming present for you." He turns to his wife. "Go get her."

"Her?" I ask as a black blur tears into the room, jumps onto my lap, and licks my face. "You got a puppy? She's so cute!" I say, petting the little black Labrador retriever. "Oh my gosh, look at her face!"

"She's yours," Mr. Diamond says.

"What do you mean?"

"I bought her for you. I went out to a client's farm before we left on our trip, and I was remembering how I used to shoot skeet there with your dad. So, he takes me inside and shows me his new puppies. All the puppies in the litter were male, except for her. The others were running around, biting each other, playing. She was looking at me with those big, adorable eyes. My client was sharing all their names, and when he told me hers was Angel, I just knew you had to have her." He looks somber as he adds, "Yesterday was your dad's birthday. I can't believe it's been almost five years."

Tears fill my eyes. "Her name is really Angel?"

Mr. Diamond gives me a hug. "Yes. So, what do you think? Do you want to keep her? Mary had a fit when I brought the puppy home today. Told me that I should have asked you first. It's peed on our carpet more times than it's gone outside. I told her we needed new carpet anyway. Doesn't matter now though; she's in love with the puppy, too. Angel can come stay at Grandpa's anytime."

The puppy runs around in a circle, chasing a little ball. She's so adorable. I pick her up to snuggle her again and notice her pretty pink rhinestone collar.

"What a pretty collar."

"Did you see her name is on it?"

I look under her pudgy little neck and see a princess crown dog tag with Angel engraved on it.

It reminds me of the princess charm on my bracelet.

"Does Phillip know about the dog? He's always wanted one."

"Nope. I wanted to surprise you both."

I set the puppy down to hug Mr. Diamond. "Thank you."

"I went today and got everything you need. Kennel, food, leashes, collars, toys."

"I don't know how all this is going to fit in my car," I say. "It's packed full of baby shower gifts."

"Why don't you take my SUV?" Mr. D offers. "We'll be coming down to KC when the baby is born. We can switch back then."

Mr. Diamond's SUV is a gorgeous black Mercedes.

"Uh, sure," I say. "That's really nice of you."

"Why don't you play with Angel while I load everything?" he suggests.

I sit back down on the floor. Angel bounds onto my lap and covers my face with rough tongue kisses.

"You are so cute," I tell her, rubbing her ears.

She jumps off me and runs across the room like a rocket, grabs a chew toy, and barrels back to me, her feet slipping on the hardwood.

"She's going to be a bit of a handful," Mrs. D says.

"Uh, yeah, but she's so darn cute. And I'm sure he named her Angel for a reason. She's probably a super-good little puppy."

Angel drops her chew toy in my lap, so I toss it down the hall for her. She takes off running again.

"I'd recommend crate-training her. That's what she's used to," Mrs. D explains. "And we've got a whole binder with all her shots and medical information. She's AKC breed, and her parents are both Field Champions."

"Awesome. Thank you," I say. "What do you think, Lori?" I ask, trying to involve her.

She hasn't said anything about the puppy.

"Cute," she says, but I get the feeling she doesn't really mean it.

The puppy comes running back toward me with a different

toy in her mouth. She jumps up on my lap, curls up in a ball, and goes to sleep.

"She's so freaking adorable. I just love her."

"All loaded up," Mr. D says. "Let's take Angel out back and run her around for a while, and hopefully, she will sleep the whole way home."

WHEN LORI AND I are almost home, she finally says, "I just don't understand why they would get you a dog but not their own son one. He was telling them at the Super Bowl party how much he wanted a puppy."

"I'm sure they *would* have gotten Danny a puppy if it wasn't for the fact that his wife said, 'No way in hell.' She also said that a baby would be enough to manage. They wouldn't want to upset his wife or cause trouble in his marriage."

"Maybe I wouldn't have trouble if you weren't Little Miss Perfect."

This pisses me off. It takes a lot to get me mad, but I've about had it. And, if it wasn't for the fact that I don't want to cause her to go into labor, I'd let her have it.

"I have nothing to do with the state of your marriage, Lori. That's between you and Danny."

"He's been acting all secretive lately. Barely talks to me. I haven't spoken to him since last night."

"Well, he probably barely talks because, no matter what he says, you think he's either wrong or dumb. And he probably doesn't want to hear you bitch about him having a little fun last night. You want your husband to be faithful and love you, then you have to treat him with love, trust, and respect back. It's not his fault you don't feel good. It's not your fault either. It's just the pregnancy you were dealt. Why don't you try dealing with it together instead of letting it tear you apart?"

She doesn't reply.

As I pull into our neighborhood, I call Phillip. "Hey, what are you doing right now?"

"Waiting for my gorgeous wife to get home."

"Is Danny there, too?" I ask.

"He is. We're watching ESPN and having a beer."

"Awesome. You're not going to believe the surprise I'm bringing home."

He lowers his voice. "Do I need to get rid of Danny?"

"No, this is something he'll want to see, too."

"Baby stuff?"

"Not exactly. See you in a few."

AFTER I CAREFULLY maneuver Mr. D's car into the garage, I tell Lori, "Danny and Phillip are in the basement, watching TV. I'm going to let Angel go potty in the backyard and then take her in the basement door. Go on in. We can have the boys unpack the car later. They'll be so excited to meet Angel."

"That's kind of a dumb name for a dog," she says, cutting me to the bone. "I don't understand why Danny's dad thought it was so cute that he had to get it."

"Because *Angel* was my dad's nickname for me."

"Oh," she says. "Um, I'm just going to head home. Night."

I don't bother to try to convince her to stay. If she wants to go home, she can go. I don't care right now.

I let Angel run around the backyard. She's bounding through the grass, chasing her tail, sniffing the fence, and running up to give me kisses. After she finally decides to go to the bathroom, I pick her up and knock on the basement door.

Phillip lets me in.

"What the heck? Whose dog is that?" He grabs Angel out of my arms. "Look at this, Danny. Have you ever seen such an adorable face?"

Danny pets the puppy and lets her lick his cheek. "Well,

aren't you the cutest thing ever?" he says to her.

"Look at her pretty little pink collar," Phillip says as the puppy chews on his hand. "I want to keep her."

"That's good," I say. "Because she's ours. Boys, meet Angel."

"*Ours?*" Phillip asks excitedly. "Where did you get her?"

"She's a gift from Danny's dad. I have a carload of baby gifts and puppy gifts."

Danny looks around. "Where's Lori?"

"Uh, she went home." I try not to purse my lips.

"What's wrong?"

"I'm not sure, but I think she's mad that your dad gave me a dog and didn't get one for you."

"Well, no shit. When I mentioned a dog, she said something like, 'Over my dead body.'"

"Yeah, she did," Phillip says. "I remember thinking the way she said it was really rude."

Danny sighs. "Two more weeks, people. Two more weeks. Then, we'll have the baby, and everything can go back to normal." He rubs the puppy's ears and says to her, "I'll be back to see you tomorrow morning. You're a cutie." Then, to me, he says, "Do I need to unload your car tonight, or can it wait until morning?"

"It can wait until morning." I study him. "Are you still hungover?"

He points to Phillip and laughs. "It's all his fault."

Phillip laughs, too. "We had fun though."

"Yeah," Danny agrees. "It was a good night."

PHILLIP AND I play with the puppy until she collapses in my lap and goes to sleep.

"So, we have a new addition to the family," he says with a grin. He hasn't stopped smiling. "Did you choose the name Angel for her?"

"No. Remember how our dads used to go out to that farm

and shoot skeet?"

"Yeah, I went with them sometimes."

"That's where she was born. They had already named her Angel."

"Your dad always called you Angel."

"Mr. D said, as soon as he heard her name, he knew he had to get her for us. Do you think it'll be okay if we take her to work with us?"

"Of course. Everyone will love her," he says, softly petting her.

"She's going to get all your attention now, isn't she?" I fake pout.

Phillip laughs. "You just might have some competition."

16 WEEKS

Dear Baby Mac,
Your muscles are getting stronger, and you have eyes, eyebrows, and eyelashes!

And, now, you are being measured in inches instead of being compared to a fruit. You're about five inches long!

And I think maybe, possibly I felt a little flutter.

Honestly though, it was probably all the Mexican food I ate for lunch.

I've been thinking a lot about your nursery. It will be in a pretty room with a big palladium window that overlooks the backyard and the lake. I think you will love it.

We also started taking weekly pictures of my stomach, so we can chart both our growth. Right now, my stomach just looks kinda bloated, except I can't suck it in anymore.

And, in some super-exciting news, you have a sister.

Well, a furry sister.

We got a puppy!

She's so cute! Her name is Angel, and I know the two of you will be best friends someday.

Knows it all.

APRIL 18TH

DANNY COMES OVER after he and Lori get home from their birthing class.

It's been four days since the shower, and I haven't heard a word from Lori.

And I'll be damned if I'm calling her.

"Learn anything new?" Phillip asks Danny as they sit on the couch with their beers.

Angel immediately jumps on Danny's lap and chews on his hand.

"Not really. We discussed birthing plans. Apparently, you're supposed to decide how you want the birthing process to go before you go into labor. Lori was premed, so she thinks she knows it all."

"She didn't know how to breathe through her contractions when she had the preterm labor," I mention.

"Maybe that's why her birthing plan is so detailed. She has a list of stuff to pack for the hospital. She's bringing in soothing music. I'm supposed to give her back massages. She wants to do it all natural—ouch! This little puppy has sharp teeth!"

"Oh, here." I hand him a chew toy. "She likes this."

"Anyway, she read her plan—and I totally just condensed it

for you guys—to the class. Afterward, this guy takes me aside. He said they are on their second baby and that, although I'm called the coach, the second the doctor comes in, I'll become a nobody. He told me women worship their OB/GYN. He said that I should remember three things: don't look below her elbow, don't faint, and to keep a couple hundred-dollar bills on me at all times. He said Lori's birth plan reminded him of his wife's first one. Apparently, she wanted a natural childbirth and waited too long to get an epidural. By the time she decided she wanted one, it was too late, and she had to deliver naturally. He is convinced that, if he could've slipped the anesthesiologist a couple hundred bucks, he would have gotten it done—shit, Angel." He quickly pulls his hand back. "She keeps biting on both my hand and the toy. I think she likes my hand better."

"Come here, Angel," Phillip says. "Let's go outside."

He takes the dog out, and just as they're coming back in, Lori comes stomping down the stairs.

"Hey," Danny says to her. "I was just telling them about—"

Lori's face is red with anger as she thrusts a piece of black fabric at Danny. "What is this?" she yells.

"I don't know. Stop waving it around, so I can see it."

"It's a freaking thong, Danny!"

"Uh, okay."

"It was in your jacket pocket. Did you really cheat on me when I'm just a week away from having your baby?" She's hysterical. Crying. Screaming. "I can't believe you slept with a stripper! I knew this would happen!"

"I didn't cheat on you!" Danny says, defending himself. "Seriously, Lori, you need to calm down."

"Don't you dare tell me to calm down! I knew you were acting weird!" She throws the fabric at his head.

Angel leaps up, snatches the thong out of the air, and takes off running.

"Ohmigawd!" I yell. "Don't let her chew on that! Phillip! Get her!"

While Phillip and I are chasing Angel, Danny yells at Lori, "You need to calm down."

Angel is fast. Just when I think I have her cornered behind the bar, she darts through my hands.

"Phillip! Get her, please. That's so nasty. I don't want that in her mouth!"

Phillip dives across the floor and misses her.

Lori screeches, "I want a divorce! I'll raise this baby on my own, and you will never get to see it. Do you hear me? Never. Ever. You're not fit to be a husband or a father!"

"Got her," Phillip yells, cornering Angel by the television.

He grabs the dog and then attempts to get her to give up the thong. But Angel isn't having it. She's got her jaw clenched, and she is playing tug-of-war with him.

"Angel. Give!" he says in a deep, stern voice.

The puppy looks up at him, spits the thong onto the floor, and starts doing victory laps around the couch.

"I didn't do anything! Some chick at the club put them in my pocket. I was drunk and forgot to take them out. Phillip, you remember that chick with the red hair and the silver glitter stars over her boobs?"

"Uh, I think so," Phillip says.

Lori waves her finger at Phillip. "I don't believe anything you say. Of course you're going to lie for him."

"I wouldn't lie about something like that, Lori," Phillip says. "The girl was suggestive, but nothing happened. We were sitting next to each other all night. *All night.*"

"Maybe you cheated, too," she accuses. "And you're both covering for each other. Really, I don't care anymore. Don't come home, Danny."

"I'll come home if I want to. Lucky for you, I *don't* want to.

You're being ridiculous. I'd never cheat on you."

I pick Angel up and hug her. "Lori, you need to calm down."

"Shut up, Jadyn. Just shut up!"

Angel starts barking at Lori. I don't blame her. I want to bare my teeth and growl, too.

But I don't get the chance.

She lumbers up the stairs and slams the door on her way out.

Danny plops his head back on the couch. "Fuck. Do you really think she'd take my child from me?"

Phillip sits down next to him. "You have rights if it comes to that. Hopefully, she will calm down, and you can apologize."

Angel jumps out of my arms, flies up onto the couch, and covers Danny's face with kisses, somehow knowing he needs them.

Danny grins and halfheartedly attempts to stop her. "I can't believe you grabbed the underwear," he says to her and then starts laughing. "You should have seen the look on your face, Jay."

"I was horrified! I can see why Lori freaked out, Danny. You need to go apologize."

He rubs his face. "Yeah, you're right. Shit. I would have been pissed, too." He pats Angel on the head and says to us, "I'll see you later."

A Hail Mary.

APRIL 20TH

PHILLIP, ANGEL, AND I went for a run this morning. Then, Phillip took Angel with him to work, so I can actually get something done today. I'm working through emails when I get a call from Danny.

"I need your help," he says. "What am I supposed to do?"

"Did she finally calm down?"

"Calmed down, yes. Forgave me, no. I slept on the couch."

"Oh, Danny, I'm sorry. But, look, you're in the home stretch. This is like the end of a game. You're down with a few seconds remaining, and only a touchdown can win it for you."

"Are you saying I need to throw a Hail Mary pass?"

"Yeah. A big gesture to make her feel better. So that she knows you love her."

"I was stupid. I shouldn't have gone out."

"Danny, it's okay to go out with your friends. The underwear was the bad move."

"So, what are you thinking?"

"You never did go on that babymoon. What if you got a hotel room for tonight? Scheduled a couple's massage or something."

"Pamper her, order room service. That kind of thing?" he asks.

"Yeah, reconnect."

"You mean, suck up."

"Basically, yes."

"I had a necklace made for her."

"You did?"

"Yeah, it's pretty spectacular. I was going to give it to her after the baby was born, but maybe I should do it tonight instead."

"I think that's a good idea, Danny. Having a necklace made was sweet of you."

"Okay, so if we're going to surprise her, we need to work fast. She's getting her nails done right now. Can you go over to the house, pack up a bag with whatever she would need, and meet me at the Plaza for lunch? I'll book a room and schedule massages. Should I get some candles or something, too?"

"That would be nice. Why don't you get some votives? But don't get any that are too strong. You know how she is with certain scents."

"Got it. See you in a little bit."

I let myself into their house, expecting to find a whole construction crew working. But no one is. They are a week away from her due date, and it's still far from done. No wonder she's so freaking stressed. I wouldn't want to bring a baby home to this mess either.

I breeze through the kitchen and pack up the duffel I brought with a pretty maternity nightgown, a soft robe, her nightly bedtime products, and a toothbrush. Then, I find a cute maternity dress with the tags still on it and carefully fold it into the bag.

DANNY GREETS ME with a hug at the restaurant, and we talk and joke through lunch, followed by a cheesecake dessert. Well, I order cheesecake because he's on some sort of no-sugar diet to help him build more muscle. I shove a piece in his mouth anyway.

When we've demolished the cheesecake, he says, "Let's walk over to the jewelry store and pick up the necklace."

A HEAVYSET WOMAN goes to the back and brings up a black velvet box.

When she opens it, I suck in my breath and then go, "Wow! Danny, that's so beautiful!"

"One hundred marquise and round brilliant-cut diamonds, totaling a little over nine carats."

"It's really exquisite." My eyes are huge, and there's a big smile on my face.

Lori is going to D.I.E when she sees this.

"Just the reaction I told you your wife would have," the saleswoman says to Danny.

"Oh, I'm not his wife. Just a friend," I tell her.

She pats my hand. "That's okay, darling. It can be our little secret. Would you like to try it on?"

"Uh, no, that's okay."

"Put it on, Jay. I'd like to see it."

The woman puts the necklace on me and points to a mirror.

"What do you really think?" Danny quietly asks. "Is it too much?"

"Give me a few minutes to get over the shock of seeing all the sparkle first." I look in the mirror, gently running my hand across the necklace. "I love how it fits, how it molds to your skin. Lori will love its classic style. When it was in the box, I thought she could only wear it with a ballgown, but, now that it's on, I think she could wear it every day, and it wouldn't look out of place."

He lets out a big sigh. "I'm so glad you think so. I was worried it was too much. It also fits you way better than it did her." He nods toward the woman. "Her neck is so thick."

"It will lay perfectly on Lori. And this little piece here will fall down into her cleavage. I think it will make her feel sexy."

Danny smirks. "I like her cleavage."

"I know you do, goofball."

He takes the necklace off me and hands it to the saleslady.

As she's packaging it up, Danny looks at his watch and says to me with a grin, "We'd better get to the hotel."

I STAND IN the lobby with our bags while Danny gets checked in. He's walking toward me, holding up his key, when I clutch my stomach in surprise.

"Ohmigawd, Danny! I think I just felt the baby kick!"

"Is it the first time?"

"Yes! Ohmigawd, I'm so happy!"

Danny wraps me in a hug. "Congrats, Jay. That's so exciting. Wait until it kicks so hard that Phillip can feel it, too. He'll freak out."

"He hasn't freaked out about anything so far."

"Did you know he's looking into college funds?"

"Ha! No. Is he really?"

Danny laughs and nods. "He really is. One thing about Phillip, he's always prepared. Come on, let's hurry and get everything set up, so you can go home and tell him."

I'M DRIVING HOME when Phillip calls me.

"Where are you?" he asks.

"Just headed home."

"Where have you been?"

"At the Plaza. I met Danny for lunch—"

"But, this morning, you told me that you were working from home all day. Needed a day without having to deal with the dog."

"Yeah, change of plans."

"Lori called me. She's very, very upset. Says there are photos of you and Danny spending the afternoon together, having an intimate lunch, shopping at a jewelry store, and hugging in a hotel lobby. An anonymous source reported that Danny bought diamonds for someone who isn't his wife and was taking her to a hotel for an afternoon tryst. What was really going on?"

"I was helping him plan a special night for Lori."

"Well, she thinks the two of you are having an affair. She's packed, and she says she's going to her parents' house."

"Where are you?"

"I'm home now. She called me at work and was hysterical."

"Don't let her go anywhere. Um, Phillip, you don't believe it, do you?"

"No, I don't. But the pictures along with the accompanying story make it seem believable."

"Were we kissing in any of the pictures?"

"Nope."

"If he really bought me that necklace, I totally would have kissed him."

"Is it pretty?"

"Yes, it's amazing. Like ten carats. Lori will die when she sees it."

"I hate that the press jumped to that conclusion," Phillip says.

"It's a steamy story. Readers like that, but Lori should know better. Let me talk to her."

"She says no—wait, she says yes."

"Why couldn't you just be happy with Phillip?" she yells. "How long has this been going on? Since we were dating? Since we've been married? Whose baby are you carrying—Phillip's or Danny's? Or do you even know?"

"Lori, I am *not* having an affair with Danny. And to suggest that Phillip's not the father of my baby is just ridiculous."

"Are you with Danny now?" she asks.

"No, he's in his car. I'm following him home."

We're lined up, stopped at a stoplight, Danny in front of me. I can see him on the phone, talking to someone. A few seconds later, I get a text from him.

Danny: *Just got a call from my publicist. There are pictures on the internet of you feeding me cheesecake. Of us* *at the jewelry store. Hugging at the hotel. They're suggesting we're having an affair. If Lori sees that, she will freak.*

Me: *She already has. Phillip, too.*

Danny: *Does she believe it?*

Me: *Yes.*

Danny: *Does Phillip?*

Me: *Not at all.*

Lori continues screaming into my ear, "You can tell your lover that there is no more home for him."

"Lori, there's a logical explanation for this. Will you please calm down?"

"Don't think you can lie your way out of this," she says. "I know how you are."

"I'm not a liar! There is a reason we were where we were, and it has to do with you!"

"Yeah, because I'm a pregnant bitch! What were you doing, sitting around, laughing at me?"

Laughing at her? Is she even sane? If I thought my husband was having an affair, sitting around and laughing at me would be the last thing I'd worry he was doing.

"Lori, Danny is pulling in the driveway. Please, listen to him."

I watch Danny jump out of the car, and Lori and Phillip come out of our house. Danny marches over to them as I get out of the car.

"You can't believe what you read," Danny says calmly to Lori. "Jay was just helping me—"

"No!" she screams, covering her ears and bawling. "Bullshit! I'm not listening to your lies! I knew something was going on! You're always sneaking over here!"

"Lori, you need to calm down," I say.

She storms up to me and points her finger in my face. "I want the truth. How long has this been going on? Since college, right? I should have known! You're a horrible person, and I never want to see you again! How could you? How could you betray our friendship?"

Danny steps between us. "Lori, stop it! You're being ridiculous! Don't yell at her like that! She doesn't deserve it!"

"Oh, sure! Stick up for her! Take her side! I don't know why that doesn't surprise me. I know what I saw!"

"If you'd just stop screaming and let me explain!" Danny yells back.

Lori's hair is a mess, rivers of black mascara are running down her face, and she's hysterical.

I can't blame her. I'd be hysterical if I thought Phillip was cheating on me. But, if I saw a photo of her and Phillip hugging, I would never think they were cheating. I'd have to see photos of them literally in the act to ever believe it.

I realize that we're not as good of friends as I thought. Because, if we were, she'd never believe it. Never in a million years.

The only way to convince her is to show her.

"What are you gonna say? That you didn't mean to? That it just happened? It's all bullshit. Bullshit! Bullshit! Bullshit!" she cries.

"You know what? Fuck it!" Danny yells, throwing his hands up in the air. "I give up! I try to do something nice—"

"Nice? *Nice?*" she screeches.

"You know what, Lori?" I say coldly. "You're right. Danny and I were up to something that we didn't want you to know about."

"I knew it!" she yells. "You bitch! I hate you!"

"Danny, can I have the room key, please?"

He gives me a puzzled look but fishes it out of his pocket.

I grab it and hand it to Lori. "Here. Take this. It's the key to the hotel room that Danny rented for the night. You should go see for yourself what we were up to. Phillip, take Lori, so she can see the messed up sheets, the discarded champagne bottles, and the condoms in the trash. All the details of our lurid affair are still there, waiting to be seen."

She shudders and stops crying. "Why in the world would I want to do that?"

"Because I want you to see it," I tell her in the bitchiest tone I can muster up, knowing it's the only way to get her to go.

She shakes her head and glares at me. "Fine! I'm taking photos, too. That way, I'll have proof of your infidelity. I'll sue you for everything, Danny. Just wait! I'll make your life a living hell! And you'll never, ever see your baby!" She grabs Phillip's arm and marches him to my car.

"The keys are still in it," I tell Phillip. "Go."

He tries to help Lori in the car, but she yells at him, "I can do it myself!" and slams the door shut.

As he runs around to the driver's side, I'm in tears.

He pulls me into a hug and kisses the top of my head. "It'll be okay," he says reassuringly. "I love you."

"I love you, too."

ONCE THEY LEAVE, Danny and I plop down on the sidewalk. He puts his arm around me, and I sob on his shoulder.

"I can't believe she could ever think I would do something like that!"

He rubs his face. It's red. Like it used to get during two-a-days or after a hot practice when he was hungover.

"It'll be okay, Jay," he says, although he really isn't very convincing.

"I keep going over it in my head, Danny. Have I ever flirted with you? Have I ever given her any reason to doubt our friendship?"

Danny slumps down. He looks defeated, and Danny Diamond never looks defeated, no matter how bad the odds.

"I can't think of anything. I mean, I know she's been having dreams where I cheat on her. And the panties were not a good move. So, I can see—"

"Those were *not* my underwear!"

"Do you think I've ever given her any reason not to trust me? I come home every night. I'm with her all the time. I've gone on two business trips by myself since she's been pregnant. I was gone one night and talked to her from my hotel room for most of it. I can't believe any of it. Then again, everything about this pregnancy has been a surprise."

"What do you think she'll do when she sees everything we set up? You wrote her that sweet note, told her about the massages, that you had a gift for her. Do you think you should go to the hotel, Danny? Once she sees it, she's going to feel horrible. You should be there. You could still get your massages and salvage the night."

"No freaking way," he says. "Let's go inside. I need a drink, and you need to stop crying."

Once we're inside, Danny heads to the beer fridge while I sit at the island.

"Get me one, too."

He comes back in with two bottles, sets them on the counter, opens them, and hands me one.

"Nothing to cheers about with this one," he says, clinking my bottle with his. Then, he looks at me. "You're a mess."

I rub under my eyes and then take a drink of beer. "Ohmigawd, this tastes good."

"Should you be drinking it, Jay? Lori says—"

"I really don't care what your wife says, Danny. I'm sick of her judgmental bullshit. This is the first sip of alcohol I've had in three months. Our doctor said it's fine to have an occasional glass of beer or wine."

"I know. Jay, I'm really sorry. I can't believe she acted that way."

"I can't either. I don't think I've ever been so hurt. I've been dumped by a lot of boys, but this hurts worse. Way worse. I just can't fathom how she could even think it." I swirl the beer in my bottle. "I have to be honest with you, Danny. I'm not sure I'll ever be able to get over her accusing me like that. Of how she looked at me. Of the horrible things that were spewing from her mouth."

"Me either," he mutters. "She threatened to take away my baby."

I hear Angel whimpering in her kennel. I leave Danny in the kitchen to ponder his life and go get my adorable Angel puppy. I hug her, let her give me a million kisses, and start crying again.

"Let me take her out for you," Danny says, pulling her out of my arms. "You sit down."

When he comes back in, I hand him my beer. "You want the rest?"

"Can't do it, huh?"

"I feel sorta sick to my stomach, to be honest."

He sets Angel down, and we watch as she run circles around the island, growling at a tennis ball.

"I'm gonna sit on the couch," I tell him and move to the living room. Angel bounds onto the couch with me, nips my nose, and then bounds down again.

"She's so freaking cute," he says, picking her up and hugging her before she squirms out of his arms. He plops down in the chair across from me. "And, now, we wait."

"Today is the anniversary of my mom's death," I mutter.

"Oh, Jay, I'm sorry," he says.

AN HOUR LATER, Angel barks when she hears my car pull into the driveway.

Phillip and Lori come into the house. Danny stands up and walks into the dining room.

Lori moves slowly toward him. "I'm sorry," she says softly. "Can we go home?"

"I'd say you owe Jay an apology first. Do you have any idea how much you hurt her?"

Lori just stands there, motionless.

"I love you. I chose you. I'm having a baby with you, but none of it is enough. I don't think I'm ever going to make you happy. And that pisses me off because I don't deserve to be treated like this. You said some really hurtful things." He looks at me. "To both of us."

But Lori won't look at me.

"I just want to go home," she says again.

"What happened to you? One of the things I love about you is your confidence in me. That confidence is gone. Jay helped me plan this. She was doing something nice for you. And this is how you repay her? And, not only that, but before you even give me a call, so I can set the record straight, you call Phillip and tell him that the girl he has loved most of his life is cheating on him. I looked at the pictures, Lori. We hugged at the hotel because something cool happened to Jay." He says to Phillip, "She felt the baby kick for the first time." He turns back toward Lori and continues, "But that's all that was in the photo. Two friends hugging. The photo of us at the restaurant? For gosh sake, I told her I wasn't eating sugar, and she shoved cheesecake in my mouth. None of us deserves the way you treated us."

He pulls the black velvet box out of his pocket, opens the lid, and sets it in front of her.

"Here's the necklace I had custom-made for you. I was going to surprise you with it tonight. I know pregnancy hasn't been easy on you or easy on us, but I wanted to get you something so spectacular that you would know how much I love you and appreciate what you've gone through. I made Jay try it on because I wanted to make sure it would lay properly, and the lady at the store had a fat neck. So, you enjoy. I'm out of here." He heads toward the door.

"Danny! Wait!"

"No, I'm sorry. You being pregnant and the hormones you're taking can excuse some things, but not this. You figure out what you want. You let me know. I'll be sleeping at the hotel tonight."

When the door shuts behind him, Lori drops to a dining room chair, studies the necklace, and starts crying.

"You should probably go now," Phillip tells her.

She leaves the necklace on the table and walks out the door.

Phillip locks the door behind her and then rushes to me. "Did you really feel the baby kick?"

Made up.

APRIL 21ST

"LET'S TAKE ANGEL for a walk," Phillip says, pulling me into his arms. "You've been moping around the house all morning."

"I just still can't believe Lori. Have you heard from Danny?"

"Yeah, he texted me early this morning. Apologized again for everything. Wanted to check on you."

"What about Lori?"

"She went to the hotel late last night. Sounds like they made up."

I sigh. "Well, that's good, I guess."

"Give her some time," Phillip says. "Come on, Angel. Wanna go for a walk?"

The puppy comes tearing around the corner with one of my shoes in her mouth. The corner of the heel is chewed to pieces.

"Are you kidding me? Angel, bad girl. Give me my shoe!"

The dog sprints down the hall, so I run after her.

"Princess, stop chasing her. She thinks you're playing with her."

I stop and sit down. Angel peeks at me from under the ugly kitchen table that is still (un)gracing my house. She prances over, drops the shoe in my lap, and licks me.

I inspect the damage to the shoe. "We're going to have to find her something to chew on besides toys. She's destroying them faster than I can buy them and then she goes after my shoes."

"Let's take her for a walk and wear her out," he offers.

LATER IN THE day, I get a text from Lori.

Lori: *I was being stupid. I'm just a stupid girl.*

I can't disagree with that, and since she didn't apologize, I don't bother replying.

17 WEEKS

YOU KICKED!
YOU KICKED!
YOU KICKED!
(Thank you!)

I'm able to feel you kick now. Not all the time, but once in a while. At least every day since the first one I felt. It's weird. But very, very cool.

You are now the size of my palm, and you are practicing sucking and swallowing, which will be super important soon!

It's been a rough week, if I'm being honest. My best friend and I aren't talking.

And it hurts.

Last week was also the five-year anniversary of my parents' deaths. I mentioned earlier that you have grandparents in heaven. They died in a car accident when I was a senior in high school.

It's weird how certain memories are ingrained in your mind. To this day, I can close my eyes and smell the popcorn in the hospital waiting room.

I really don't love hospitals, to be honest.

But I went twice for Lori. Once when they thought she was having a miscarriage and again when she was in labor.

And I'm going for you.

I hope that my experience in having you turns my view of hospitals around. That I'll start thinking of them as a place where miracles happen. Where babies are born. Where people get better.

You know, sometimes, people you think were your friends

turn out not to be as good of friends as you thought they were. But, when you find ones who are true, cherish them.

And here's a life lesson for you: If you screw up—and you will—own up to it. Tell the people you care about that you made a mistake and apologize.

Because making excuses for your bad behavior is not okay. And it devalues your friendship.

So, even though Danny has forgiven Lori, I just can't. I could if she apologized. But she hasn't. Instead, I just hear excuses. She was stupid. It was her hormones. She was dumb.

And, even though I'm being nice and saying it's okay, it's not okay.

And neither am I.

The little monkey.

APRIL 26TH

SINCE DANNY HIRED Joey to run his nonprofit, he and Chelsea are in town, looking for a place to live. Phillip and I worked until noon and then spent the rest of the day taking them on a tour of some of the neighborhoods they are going to look at tomorrow with a realtor.

"I'm starved!" Chelsea says, grabbing a menu as we all slide into a booth at our favorite sports bar.

"She's not kidding," Joey teases. "Stand back when the food comes, or you might get your hand bitten off."

"Not funny," she says, but she's laughing along with him.

"We need appetizers, stat," Phillip says to the waitress. "We have two hungry, pregnant women here."

The waitress chuckles and takes our order.

"So, did you have any favorite areas?" I ask.

"We really like this area," Joey says. "Lots of restaurants. Close to everything. Good schools. Even though that might not matter to us now, my dad says it's important for your resale value to buy in a good school district."

"The one I like best online is near the park, too. I hope we like it as much in person."

A text flashes on my phone.

Danny: *Lori is in labor. We're at the hospital. This is it! It's time!*

Me: *Are you sure?*

Danny: *Yep. Her water broke, so we'll be meeting the little monkey within the next twenty-four hours.*

Me: *That's amazing, Danny! Are you nervous?*

Danny: *The weird thing is that Lori was on medicine to stop her labor, and now that her water broke and she should be in labor, she's not. They have her walking the halls, trying to get it started. If it doesn't progress on its own, then they will give her something to start the contractions. But I have a problem.*

Me: *What's that?*

Danny: *We don't have the bag we packed for the hospital. When her water broke, we were out. We called the doctor, and he told us to go straight to the hospital. Lori is sorta freaking out about not being able to follow her birth plan. Is there any way you could bring it here?*

Me: *Of course we can.*

Danny: *Thank you. It's by the front door. We're in room 320.*

Me: *Good luck, Danny.*

I announce to the table, "Danny and Lori are at the hospital. Her water broke."

"That's awesome!" Chelsea says, but then she looks at the table and does a little frown.

I told her most of what had happened with Lori in confidence because I truly needed a girlfriend to talk to about it. She feels the same way I do. Lori owes me an apology, not excuses.

"He needs me to pick up their hospital bag and take it to them."

"You guys stay here and eat," Phillip says. "I'll run home, grab the bag, let Angel pee, drop the bag off, and meet you back here. Sound good?"

I let out a sigh. I didn't realize I'd been holding my breath. "I *am* hungry."

He leans over, gives me a kiss, and heads out.

Actually, I'm really not that hungry. I just sorta didn't want to take Lori anything.

But then I internally chastise myself for being a shitty friend.

WHEN PHILLIP GETS back, Joey's had enough beers for all of us, and Chelsea and I are stuffed.

"Their kitchen is never going to be done before they get home. It's too bad," Phillip says. "I wouldn't want to have to take a baby home to that mess."

"I wonder if we can make it happen," I say, a plan slowly forming in my head.

"Make what happen?" Chelsea asks as she's perusing the dessert menu.

"I'm going to step outside for a minute. Make a couple of phone calls."

The first person I call is the contractor who's working on our building.

"Hey, Mike. It's Jadyn. Big favor. Do you think you could get a crew together to finish a kitchen remodel?"

"Maybe. How soon are we talking?"

"It needs to be done in the next thirty-six hours."

"Wow, that's fast! What is there to do?"

"Well, the flooring and cabinets are in, but the door fronts aren't on. The countertop is in but not the backsplash. Electrical and plumbing are complete, but the appliances are sitting in the garage, and the light fixtures aren't hung. Then, there are the finishing touches, like putting on the cabinet pulls, hanging curtains, decorating."

"What's the rush?"

"It's my friend Danny Diamond's kitchen, and he—"

"*The* Danny Diamond?"

"Yeah. His wife just went into labor. This remodel was supposed to have been done last week, but they had some electrical issues that set them back. I just can't have them coming home to a mess with their new baby. I'll get ahold of the designer. Do you think we could all meet at their house, like, in an hour? Will that work?"

"I can do it, but it's gonna cost you."

"I figured. Offer them double overtime."

I know Danny would gladly pay anything to have it done, but I don't plan on asking him. I know Mr. Diamond will let me take it out of my trust. Surely, he wouldn't want his grandchild to go home to that.

"That will help get them there," he says.

I give him the address. "See you soon."

Next, I call their interior designer, who calls her construction crew. They all agree to meet me and seem up for the challenge.

Then, I call the one woman who I know could probably pull this off single-handedly. "Hey, it's JJ."

"Did you hear the good news? Lori is in labor," Phillip's mom says.

"Any chance you'd like to come visit me tomorrow?"

"What do you need?" she asks, so I tell her.

Designated hitter.

APRIL 27TH

I WAKE UP super early because I have to pee. Then, I can't go back to sleep, so I grab my phone, thinking I'll read for a little while when I notice I have a group text.

> **Danny:** ***IT'S A GIRL!!!*** *Baby Diamond was born via emergency C-section at 3:07 this morning. Both mother and baby are doing fine. Labor was rough. She pushed for two hours before they tried forceps. (Don't ask.) Then, they decided baby was just too big and did a C-section. Baby weighed in at a whopping 9 pounds, 2 ounces and is 17 inches long. And she's perfect.*

"Phillip!" I screech. "It's a girl!"

"Uh, what?" he says groggily.

"Danny and Lori had their baby. It's a girl!"

"Aww. That's awesome. Everything go okay?"

I read him the text.

"Did they say what they named her?"

"No. At least, not yet. I'm not sure if they had decided on a name."

"We need to start thinking of baby names. What do you think of Otto?"

"Otto? Are you serious?"

"Sure, it's cool. Two Ts and two Os. Easy to learn to spell. And it's a palindrome."

"Is it short for ottoman?" I tease.

"Very funny. Fine. Let's hear your ideas." He rolls over and faces me, propping himself on his elbow.

"For boys, Owen is kinda cute. Carter. Liam, um—"

"I thought you weren't thinking of baby names yet."

"I don't want to choose one yet, but if I hear a cute name, I try to remember it. Although my favorite boy name right now is Chase. Chase Mackenzie just sounds like a little stud. Like a boy I would have had a crush on in school."

"I'm surprised. I thought you would like funkier names."

"Well, for a girl, I do. I like Harley and Aria. I also like Addison, Landon, and Emerson, but I want to spell them with a Y at the end, like mine, instead of an O. And we know her middle name has to be James."

"Of course," Phillip says. "Those are all pretty. When do you think we should decide for sure?"

"Well, we have plenty of time. But I suppose we should make a firm decision a few weeks before we are due. Naming a child is hard. You have to think of all the potential bad nicknames kids could come up with."

"I think you can rule out Aria. That reminds me of that word for nipple. I never know how exactly to say it."

"Areola?"

"Yeah, that's it. And Airhead. Hairy, Scary, Airy. Short names are tough. They rhyme with a lot."

"You're cute," I tell him, ruffling his hair and giving him a good-morning kiss.

Which leads to some other morning fun.

BEFORE WE GO to the hospital to see baby Diamond, we check in on the kitchen progress. I made a cute pink *It's a Girl* banner to hang in the entryway. The crew has been working nonstop in shifts since last night. I'm shocked at all they have accomplished. The backsplash is in, and the cabinet doors are being installed.

"Can you believe how much they've gotten done already?" I ask Phillip as we're walking down the hall at the hospital.

"Yeah, it's starting to look like a real kitchen. Mom said she's headed down."

"I thought we could go shopping and stock their fridge. Your mom's going to whip up some dinners and put them in the freezer along with an assortment of baked goods. Danny's parents are on their way, too, and have offered up their help. I think we'll have it done. Especially since she had a C-section. I think that means she'll be in the hospital for a day longer."

"So, does all this mean that you and Lori are okay now? You still haven't talked to her much, have you?"

"No, just some awkward texting."

"And are you doing okay with being here at the hospital?" he asks, giving me a little squeeze.

"As long as you hold my hand, Phillip, I'll be fine."

"I can tell you're pregnant today. Your shirt's tight around your tummy. It's cute."

I look down. "No denying it anymore."

"What you're doing for Danny and Lori is really nice. Are we going to tell them today?"

"No. I want them to be surprised when they walk in the door."

"Will you tell them it was you who made it happen?"

"Probably not, Phillip. I'll let the designer take the credit. I don't ... like, it's not about that. I don't know if she'll ever be my friend again. But, regardless, I want both of them to be happy when they bring their baby home. Maybe it will help them, too. I know they made up, but Danny said things are still a bit strained."

"I saw her wearing the necklace the other day," Phillip states dryly.

"Well, she must not be as traumatized as she claims."

He flattens me against the wall, his strong body firmly against mine, holding me in place. "Are we good?"

"We seemed pretty good this morning."

"Okay, let me rephrase that. Are you good? Do you feel good about us?"

"I feel great about us, Phillip. I can't wait until people are coming to the hospital to visit our new baby."

He kisses me. "I can't wait either. Let's go see this new little girl."

PHILLIP KNOCKS GENTLY on the door, and Danny tells us to come in.

Lori is lying in the bed, holding a little pink bundle.

"Congratulations!" we both say. "Are you so excited it's a girl?"

Danny takes the baby out of Lori's arms and holds her out for us to see.

"She's beautiful," I say sincerely.

"Thanks," she says.

"She has a little bit of a cone head," Danny says with a laugh. "Stuck in the birth canal for a few hours does that to them, I guess. And I was surprised. I thought she was going to be a boy."

"So, the birth sounds like it was a little crazy," Phillip says.

"Oh, yeah. You should have seen it. Miss I Want A Natural Birth here was like, 'Get me the epidural now!' And I was like, 'Honey, but you told me, no matter what you said, I was supposed to follow the birthing plan.' I told her she should focus on her breathing more, like in yoga. Then, she grabbed me by the shirt, like a scene out of *The Exorcist*, and said in a voice that sounded like the devil himself, 'Get me the fucking epidural. NOW!' So, I did. Thank goodness, too. They were able to do the C-section quickly when they needed to, and it was amazing. They pulled this sweet little monkey out of her lickety-split, and I cut the cord, and she was crying, and I was crying. It was the most beautiful thing I've ever seen in my life." He sits on the bed next to Lori, and they share a sweet look.

I hope that means they are going to be okay.

"So, the text didn't mention a name. Have you chosen one yet?" Phillip asks.

"We have," Lori says. "Meet Devaney Alayna Diamond."

"Devaney?" Phillip says. "Like the great Nebraska coach, Bob Devaney?"

"Yep," Danny says. "Isn't it the coolest name ever?"

"I really like it," I say. "It's very pretty. I've heard of the name Delaney before but never Devaney."

"That's why we like it," Lori says. "It's different and pretty. We'll probably call her Devan for short."

"That's really cute, too," I say directly to Lori. "I'm glad everything worked out so well."

"Do you want to hold her?" Danny asks me.

"I'd love to. Can I wash my hands first?"

"There's some antibacterial soap in the bathroom."

After washing my hands, I am rewarded with a beautiful baby girl lying in my arms. She looks up at me and moves her lips, like she's doing a fish face.

"She's ready for selfies." I laugh, mimicking her.

Danny talks to Phillip while I stare in wonder at Devaney.

"So, one thing you should know about childbirth is your doctor, who your wife has spent months getting to know, only shows up the second it's time for delivery. You think he's going to be with you the whole time. Like through labor and all that. No. He's like a designated hitter, only shows up when he's at bat."

The baby looks like she's going to cry.

I gently pat her back and hand her to Lori. "I think she wants her mommy."

Lori smiles at the baby. "I think I'm going to like being a mommy," she says, snuggling Devaney into her chest.

18 WEEKS

OMG!!!

Danny and Lori had their baby this week.

It's a girl, and her name is Devaney Alayna Diamond.

Devaney is a super-cool name because Bob Devaney was a legendary football coach at Nebraska. Devaney is known for starting what is now known as the Blackshirts, which is what our defense is called. The story goes like this: One of the coaches got sent to the local sporting goods store because they needed some jerseys to distinguish the offense from the defense during practice. The black jerseys were on sale, so he bought those. The black shirts were given out each day and taken back at the end of practice. So, every single day, starters had to earn their shirts. Pretty much from then on, the Nebraska defense has been called the Blackshirts.

Pretty cool, huh?

And it's official.

I have a baby bump.

Time to shop for some new clothes.

(And praying I will never need big white maternity undies.)

A relative term.

APRIL 30TH

"PUT THE FLOWERS in the vase on the island," the designer yells at me.

I scurry over and set the big bouquet of tulips where I was told while the designer takes a moment to look around.

"Wow. This really looks great. Thank you, everyone, for all your help." She gives me a hug. "And for finding the crew to make this happen. When we had to redo their electrical work, it really put us behind schedule. I didn't think this was possible."

Mrs. Diamond yells out, "They are leaving the hospital now!"

"Okay, everyone out!" I say to the crew that has been helping us put the finishing touches on the remodel.

Everyone quickly clears out, and I give Mrs. Diamond and Mrs. Mac hugs. "Thank you for doing all this."

"I can't wait to tell Danny and Lori how you put this all together," Mrs. D says.

"Um, I, uh, don't really want them to know."

"Why not?"

"I just don't. I didn't do it to get a thank-you or any praise. I just wanted them to come home and be able to relax with their baby."

Mrs. D gives me another hug. "If that's what you want, dear," she says, "my lips are sealed."

"Come on, Mrs. Mac. Let's get out of here."

On the walk across the yard to my house, Mrs. Mac questions me, "Why wouldn't you want them to know what you did for them? I mean, what an amazing gift."

"Lori and I haven't been as close as we once were," I confide.

"I noticed that when you were up for her shower. Was she mad at you then?"

"I think she's just been upset in general. She and Danny have had a rough time. Both with the pregnancy and their marriage."

"Oh, that's too bad. Pregnancy can be tough on a relationship. Doug and I were married for a very short time before we had Ashley, and it wasn't easy. Sadly, it gets worse once the baby is born."

"It does? Danny thinks things will go back to normal now that the baby is here."

Mrs. Mac lets out a full-on belly laugh. "Oh, wow. That's funny. Danny is in for a rude awakening. Normal is now a relative term. It won't be anything like when you were dating or first married. Those days are over."

And this worries me.

Growls at it.

MAY 5TH

WHEN DANNY COMES through the back door, Angel barks happily and spins around in a circle, wagging her tail. She loves Danny but hasn't seen much of him lately. None of us have seen him much since the baby was born. And Phillip and I haven't wanted to intrude. Danny's mom was here the first week, and Lori's mom has been here ever since. We were thrilled when he called earlier to ask if he could come over for a beer and watch the fourth round of the draft.

"Aww, how's my Angel?" Danny says, greeting the dog first and giving her a brown stick from a package.

"What's that?" I ask him.

"It's called a bully stick. Marcus was telling me he gives them to his dogs." He hands me the rest of the package. "Says they have kept Madison from divorcing him because his dogs chew on these and not on her expensive shoes."

We watch as Angel lays the stick on the ground, sniffs it, races around the couch, nudges it with her nose, picks it up, and flips the stick in the air. Then, she takes another lap around the couch, stick in her mouth.

"Should she be running with a stick?" I ask.

"It's so big; I don't think she could choke on it," Danny says, laughing at the puppy, who has finally decided to nibble on the corner of it for a second.

She drops it at Danny's feet, growls at it, and then takes off running in circles around the couch again.

"So, how's Devaney doing?" Phillip asks as we all plop down on the sofa and flip on the TV.

"She cries a lot and is a lot more work than I ever imagined. But she's precious."

"Is there anything we can do to help? You look tired," I say.

"No, Lori and her mother have it covered. They would really prefer I didn't help. Her mom acts like I don't know what I'm doing. I mean, technically, I don't. But, if I don't practice, how am I supposed to get better? Although her mother got mad at me because the trash in the kitchen was half-full, so I guess I'm supposed to help with that. It's like she thinks I'm the hired hand instead of the dad."

"Danny, you should talk to Lori if something is bothering you," I suggest.

"You're one to talk," Phillip says to me.

I bug my eyes out at him.

"What?" Danny says, looking from me to Phillip.

"It's nothing," I say.

"It's *not* nothing," Phillip counters, turning toward Danny. "Was Lori surprised the kitchen was done when she got home?"

"Are you kidding me? She was thrilled. I don't know how the designer pulled it off. Just the day before, she said it could be three more weeks."

"Did she ask who made all the food? Or did she wonder how it all got done?"

"Uh, I assume the designer. My mom said she and your mom did the food."

"Has Lori thanked anyone?"

"She was crying and hugging the designer, thanking her."

"The designer had help," Phillip says.

"*Phillip*, you promised."

"Promised what? What aren't you telling me?" Danny asks.

Phillip shakes his head at me and says to Danny, "Jadyn is the reason it got done. She said she didn't want you to have to come home to that, so she called the contractor who is doing our office building and got him to get a crew together. They worked for thirty-six hours straight. Jadyn, the moms, and the designer worked another twelve hours after that getting the decor and food done."

Danny slumps against the back of the couch and shakes his head. "Why didn't you tell us?"

I run my hand through my hair, stalling.

"Because Jadyn did it for you, Danny. And for Lori even though she'd accused her of cheating. Even though she's never apologized. And even though she's barely spoken to her since. I just thought you should know."

"I don't want her to know," I say, barely holding back tears.

"Why not?" Danny asks.

"Because."

"She really hasn't apologized?" Danny says, shocked.

I shake my head. "No."

"But she said she texted you."

I hand him my phone. Show him what she said, which is pretty much just that she wasn't perfect and she was a stupid girl.

"After the way she treated me, the way she accused me, it just isn't enough. All she's done is make excuses for her behavior. But what I don't think she realizes is that, with every accusation and point of her finger, she eroded away our friendship."

Danny lowers his head. "I'm sorry, Jay. I haven't told you that either."

"You didn't do anything, Danny. Did she apologize to you?"

He shakes his head. "Mostly, she just cried until I couldn't stand it anymore and told her to stop."

"Does that bother you? That she would automatically assume the worst?"

"Yeah, it does. She used to trust me. Now … I'm really hoping it was just pregnancy hormones combined with the bad dreams she'd been having. That she'll get back to being herself. But, honestly, the things she said have stuck with me. So, why don't you want her to know what you did?"

"Because I'm not over it, and I don't want her to think I am. I want you to be happy, Danny, and I knew, if you both came home to a finished home, it would be one less thing for her to be stressed about and would make your life easier."

"Are you and Lori doing okay now?" Phillip asks Danny.

"The birth experience definitely bonded us. But, since then, we haven't really slept much. We're tired and stressed. Nursing isn't really going well. Devaney cries a lot. Lori is trying to keep her on a schedule. But I don't know. It's like we finally get her to sleep, and then Lori wakes her up, so she can nurse again."

"She's waking the baby up? Isn't there some rule about letting a sleeping baby lie?"

"Yeah, but she read that babies need routine."

"And we know Lori likes routine," Phillip says. "Maybe it helps her feel in control."

"How are you doing on a schedule?" I ask Danny.

"I can barely keep myself on a schedule. You really think I could do it for someone else?"

"Well, she's your child, too," Phillip says. "You have a say in how she's raised. If you want to try something different, it's okay for you to suggest it."

Danny laughs. "Uh, no. It's not. That'd be like committing mutiny. Thanks, but I think I'd rather go down with the ship."

We turn our attention toward the TV when we hear Nick's name being called in the draft.

"Dang," Danny says. "I was hoping we'd get him."

"His parents are probably thrilled though," I say. "St. Louis is the closest NFL team to where they live."

Angel stops throwing the stick around and plops down to nibble on it. I guess she's decided it's pretty good to chew on.

I take a moment to text Nick.

Me: *Kicky Nicky! Congrats!!! You were the first kicker chosen in the draft! Go YOU! And go ST. LOUIS! I bet your parents are so thrilled. Heart you!*

24 WEEKS

Dear Baby Mac,

I haven't written in here for, like, six weeks, but work and life have been kinda crazy. I won't bore you with the work details, but I will say that I've been putting in some really long hours.

It's interesting though, how you're growing inside me as the building I designed is taking shape. It's almost metaphorical, sorta. Honestly, I'm not sure that's even the right word. I just mean, your growth is sort of paralleling the building's growth.

Speaking of growth! We had another ultrasound a couple of weeks ago. You've grown a lot since we first saw you!

You are now weighing in at about a pound and a half and are measuring nine inches long. You're developing senses, like touch, sight, hearing, and taste.

Your daddy still talks to you every night before we go to sleep. It's so sweet. And it's exciting, knowing that you can hear him. That you will recognize our voices after you are born. He also lays his hand on my stomach because he wants to feel you kick.

So far, he hasn't. But you do kick when you hear his voice. When he comes into the room, sometimes, you'll give me a swift kick. I wonder if you're dancing around in there or just excited, like Angel is when she runs around the couch when Daddy comes home.

Speaking of Angel, I told Mr. Diamond that he should sue the breeder for false advertisement. She might look like an angel when she gives you her big puppy-dog eyes, but she is not.

This past weekend, your daddy and I were planting flowers in the backyard. We did one side and then moved on to the other. Angel had been just aimlessly running around, yipping at ducks and geese and chasing the daredevil squirrels. She came running over to me and gave me a muddy kiss. I turned around to pet her and saw that she had dug up all the flowers we had just planted. She ran over to the dug-up mess, grabbed an uprooted flower, then bounded over with it, and dropped it at your dad's feet. She was very proud of herself.

So, after giving her a bath and drying her off, I opened the basement door. She went running inside, jumped on her blankie, and looked up at me with adorable, sleepy eyes. She had her head down and was asleep before I ever went back outside.

I was outside for a total of five minutes, finishing planting the flat of flowers we were working on while your dad cussed up a storm, replanting the dug-up ones. When I came in the house to get him a beer, I was greeted with fluff and feathers.

And not just any cheap fluff.

We're talking down.

Angel had apparently not stayed asleep on the blanket. Instead, she'd decided to chew up/destroy my pillows. And the dog has good taste. She didn't mess with my cheap Target throw pillows. No, she'd chosen the ones that came with the couch. Pillows that cost about two hundred dollars a piece to replace. But we won't tell Daddy that!

Needless to say, Angel is not ready to be alone in the house. She's also nearly chewed up the desk leg in your dad's assistant's office. Angel comes to work with us pretty much all the time now, and Daddy's assistant has a jar of mini dog treats on her desk.

And Angel's smart. She's learning to go from office to office—like she's trick-or-treating or something—whenever she gets a whiff of food.

She's become a junk-food junkie.

I keep telling people not to feed her, but they can't resist her adorable begging.

She also ate four wadded-up pieces of paper from my trash can the other day. Thankfully, paper is biodegradable, and the vet assured us it wouldn't harm her.

We were also busy with Joey and Chelsea's wedding. Daddy was the best man and held a bachelor party in Omaha the week before the wedding. Chelsea opted not to do a traditional bachelorette party since she's pregnant. So, I did a lingerie party for her instead. Everyone got her something pretty to wear—for before and after the baby—and we had a dessert bar and served champagne. It was a lot of fun.

Danny didn't go to Joey's bachelor party, but he did come to the wedding. He couldn't wait to show Devaney off to his friends, but Lori had a fit about the germs, the lack of schedule, being tired, and all that. So, he went by himself. I think it was a good break for him. He slept for fourteen hours straight!

I'm worried about Lori though. She won't take a break. Baby Devaney is so cute, but she seems to cry a lot before she can settle down and go to sleep. It's like she's stressed.

Just so you know, I'm not good with routines, so I hope that you can function well in a sort of go-with-the-flow environment.

Grandma and Grandpa stayed with Angel all week, and after the wedding, your daddy and I checked into a beautiful hotel on the beach and spent four days doing nothing.

Our own little babymoon.

Oh, also, I look and feel great. Like, I don't know what magical mix of hormones and vitamins is happening here, but my skin is clear and glowing, my hair is thick and shiny, and my nails are growing longer.

So thank you for that.

Oh, also, even though I have seen the ultrasounds and know you are a baby, I keep having crazy dreams where I give birth to an alien/dolphin/puppy/hamster/unicorn (that was kinda cool) pizza/ and Channing Tatum wearing a baby bonnet. The only problem is that, no matter what kind of baby comes out, the dream ends with red. Lots and lots of red.

I'm hoping it just means that will be your favorite color.

Go Nebraska, right?

P.S. Lori still hasn't apologized, but she is starting to act like we're okay. And, even though I miss us being okay, I'm not really okay with it. Things just aren't the same. I miss my friend. I miss talking to her every day. She uses being busy with the baby as an excuse, but it's like she's still mad at me.

But shouldn't it be the other way around?

27 WEEKS

Dear Baby Mac,

It's the last week of our second trimester!

Let's talk about you first. Your little lungs are developing now so that you can take your first breath, and sometimes, you get hiccups, and I can feel them! You weigh more than two pounds and are about fifteen inches long.

As for me, I am still feeling pretty awesome. Still jogging. And seem to have more energy. My stomach is more than a bump, and for some reason, people seem to think it's okay to touch it. (P.S. It's not.)

And, hello, I didn't lose brain cells as my stomach grew. I can still actually have a conversation about something other than being pregnant.

I have also heard enough birthing horror stories to last me for the rest of my life, thank you very much.

Now onto the funner stuff! This week is the Fourth of July. I'm super excited for it. We're having a party. Surprise, surprise. Our neighborhood has some cool events, like a kids' parade in the morning. An afternoon picnic in the park. And, at dusk, what I'm most looking forward to, the fireworks over the lake. Because we live on the water, we'll be able to see them from our backyard, so we invited everyone we know.

I have a bit of heartburn. I'm hungry all the time. My stomach itches, and my belly button has popped out.

My only real problem is that you seem to wake up about the

time I'm ready to go to sleep.

It's like, all day, when I'm moving around, you're crashed out. Then, when I lie in bed, you wake up and decide to party.

And I'm pretty sure you are dancing.

Or possibly having your friends over.

A pretty big target.

JULY 2ND

PHILLIP'S PARENTS ARE in town this week for the Fourth of July festivities, although Mr. Mac isn't going to be here tonight. He left for Dallas with one of the guys on their Board of Directors this afternoon after our board meeting. When we walk in our house, Phillip and I are greeted with a wonderful smell.

"Is that fried chicken?" I ask Phillip's mom as I pet Angel and tell her not to jump on me.

"Chicken-fried chicken, corn on the cob, mashed potatoes, gravy, and homemade biscuits," she says.

I'm about to kiss the woman until I see a different kind of chicken.

Not just a chicken, mind you, lots of chickens. A whole coop's worth, staring down at me from the top of my cabinets.

"Uh, is it theme night?" I ask hopefully.

She looks up. "I thought your cabinets looked a little bare, so I decorated them. What do you think?"

Surely, she can tell by the horrified look on my face that I hate them.

I quickly smile. "Uh, thanks. That was sweet of you. I'm gonna go change. I'll be right back."

I walk in on Phillip undressing. He's in the process of loosening his tie, and he is only wearing boxer briefs and his dress shirt. I want to grab a bowl of popcorn and watch.

"You look really sexy," I tell him. "I wish every day was Board day."

He finishes undoing his tie, pulls it from around his neck, tosses it over me like a lasso, and pulls me toward him.

"I'd say that was a cool little trick, but I'm a pretty big target these days," I say as he kisses me.

"You're a beautiful target. Although do you think you should still be wearing heels?"

I look down at the most conservative mid-heel pumps I own. "Uh, these really don't qualify as heels."

"I was reading that your muscles and ligaments are loose right now and that you'll become more clumsy."

"Phillip, my cute shoes are about the only things that still fit me." I hold up my hand. "And don't you dare say yoga pants. They don't count."

Phillip laughs. "So, chickens."

"Yeah, they have to go. But, since my ligaments are stretching and all and I don't want to be clumsy in front of your mom, I'll leave it to you to tell her to take them back."

"Get changed and let's go eat," he says, playfully slapping my butt.

"I INVITED DANNY and Lori over," Phillip's mom says as we return to the kitchen. "They should be here shortly."

Just as soon as she gets the words out of her mouth, the front door opens, and the Diamond family strolls in. And I'm pretty sure they've brought half their house with them.

Danny has Devaney in a baby carrier. Slung over his shoulder is a massive diaper bag, and in his other hand is some sort of pink contraption. Lori has another small bag along with a blanket, a baby radio, and a baby jungle gym.

"Angel, down," Phillip says when Angel jumps up on Danny.

Danny sets the baby carrier on the floor, so he can empty his hands. Angel sniffs Devaney's toes and then licks across the face.

Devaney smiles.

"Ohmigawd!" Lori screeches. "Get the dog away from the baby!"

Angel doesn't like the pitch of Lori's voice because she scurries under the dining room hutch and won't come out. Mrs. Mac finally bribes her with a treat, and Phillip decides to put her in her kennel.

I touch Devaney's little chin and smile. Her eyes are a shade of brilliant blue just like her daddy's.

"You definitely showed up for the party," Phillip says to Danny. "She looks so much like you."

"She has Danny's eyes, but her sweet heart-shaped face is just like her mom's," Mrs. Mac compliments.

"Thanks," Lori says.

"How are you guys getting along?" Mrs. Mac asks as everyone gets situated around the dining room table.

"Some nights are better than others," Lori says. "She's starting to sleep a little more."

"Once we actually get her to sleep," Danny clarifies. "And, although it was wonderful, having our parents here to help, it's nice to have it back to just our family."

Mrs. Mac passes the serving bowls, and we load up our plates.

The second we're ready to dig in, Devaney starts crying.

"I just fed her before we came over," Lori says.

I walk around the table, pick the carrier up off the floor, and put it on the table. "Maybe she doesn't like being away from the action," I offer. "Do you, Devaney?" I say to the baby.

She stops crying and replies by blowing bubbles out of her little pink bow-shaped mouth. I make a face at her, and she coos.

"She's so cute. I bet you just sit around all day, staring at her adorableness."

"You have *no* idea how much work a baby is," Lori states haughtily.

"We have a puppy. We're breaking ourselves in slowly." I laugh.

Everyone laughs, except for Lori.

"You can't put your baby in a kennel," Lori replies. "Big difference."

"No, but she has a crib, doesn't she?" Mrs. Mac asks politely.

Point for Mrs. Mac.

But I'm still not keeping the chickens.

"Of course she has a crib," Lori says. "What's that got to do with it?"

"Do you ever put her in her crib when she's crying?"

"No! I'm a good mother! I could never do that!"

Mrs. Mac shakes her head. "You need to let your baby cry occasionally. How else are you going to teach her how to calm herself down?"

"I, uh, I don't know," Lori says, looking confused.

"I'm not saying you should let her cry for hours or even very many minutes, but letting a baby cry for a bit isn't going to hurt them. And you might even be shocked that she'll cry herself to sleep."

"I don't ever want my child to cry herself to sleep!"

"You're in for a long road then," Mrs. Mac replies. "Sometimes, for your sanity, you have to put a crying baby down. Try doing it for thirty seconds at first. Then, check on her. Pat her back. Say something reassuring. Then, walk back out. Keep doing that for a few minutes, maybe five. If it doesn't work, then at least you tried."

"We should try that," Danny says. As is typical, he's game for trying anything once.

Devaney wails again. This time, she can't be soothed with my voice.

"Put her in the rocker, Danny," Lori orders.

Danny sets his fork down and assembles the ergonomically correct rocker. It's like a mini baby swing that sits on the table. He swaps it for the carrier and gently picks up Devaney. He's so good with her. And his love is apparent from the way he beams at her.

"Watch her neck!" Lori snaps.

"I've got her neck," Danny says calmly. "Besides, it's not so wobbly anymore, is it, little monkey? You've been lifting it up on your own."

"She's nine weeks. Of course she has been. She's very advanced for her age—" Lori replies but stops when there is a loud noise coming from Devaney's diaper area. Lori closes her eyes, sighs, and sets down her fork. She suddenly looks very tired.

"Why don't you let me change her?" Mrs. Mac offers, grabbing the diaper bag and whisking the baby away.

"Always something," Danny says, shoveling food into his mouth. "We haven't sat down and eaten an uninterrupted meal since ..."

"Before she was born," Lori finishes his sentence and pushes her plate away. "I'm going to go check on them."

THE DIAMONDS MAKE their way home quickly after dinner. Phillip and I clean up while his mom lets Angel out, and then she sits at the island. As I'm loading the dishwasher, I wonder if she feels like the chickens above her are out to get her. Because that's kinda how they are making me feel. Like I'm being watched. I think about the Hide the Gnome game we were playing with Danny. How everything has come to a halt.

"They are typical first-time parents," Mrs. Mac says. "I just want to hug them and give them advice, but they have to learn the hard way. I was like that with Ashley. The girl rarely slept in her crib. She always slept in my arms or in a bassinet next to the bed.

I'd rock her to sleep. Couldn't stand the sound of her crying. Crying felt like the sound of failure.

"Fast-forward a few years, and Phillip is a baby. I'm in the nursery, almost done feeding him, when I hear a boom coming from Ashley's room. I took the bottle out of Phillip's mouth, quickly laid him safely in his crib, and ran into her room. When I came back a few minutes later, Phillip was asleep. I stood there and just stared at him in wonder as I thought, *They can do that? They can fall asleep on their own?*

"It's why firstborn children have the characteristics they do. They are coddled. I hope, when you have your baby, that you try to relax. Just because the baby makes a peep doesn't mean you have to go running."

"That's good advice," I say. "Remind us of that when our baby is screaming."

"My MOM MADE some interesting points tonight," Phillip says as we're lying in bed. "But I don't know if I could let our baby cry."

"I don't know if I could either. Maybe if it was at intervals, like she said."

"Even though Lori seemed horrified you compared her baby to our dog, you were right that it's been good prep for us. We're responsible for something besides ourselves."

"Except that, for the most part, Angel hasn't stopped us from doing stuff. We take her along."

"Did you notice all the stuff they brought with them? It was like they were going away for a weekend, not dinner."

"I thought so, too, when they walked in, Phillip, but they used a lot of it. The carrier. The swing. They changed her diaper twice and her outfit twice."

"Was it twice?"

"Yeah, she blew out her diaper all over the first one and spit up all over the second one."

"Hmm, I don't know then."

"So, I've been thinking more about names," I say.

"Have you narrowed them down yet?" he asks. "We agreed we would each choose our two favorites, and then we would choose from one of those."

"Yes, for a girl, I like Landyn and Emersyn the best. What about you?"

"I like Kennedy and Haley."

"Those are both super cute. It's going to be so hard to decide."

"Let's try them with the middle name," Phillip suggests. "So, Landyn James Mackenzie. LJM. LJ. No real possible nickname but Lands' End. Kennedy James Mackenzie. KJ. KJM. Hmm. I love the name Kennedy, but when paired with James and Mackenzie, it sounds like we mixed up the names of a bunch of dead presidents. I'd say that's a pass."

I nod my head, agreeing with him, and take ahold of his hand.

"Next up, Haley James Mackenzie," he announces. "HJM. I think that's pretty cute."

"It is really pretty together."

"I can't come up with any bad nicknames either. We'll leave that one as a contender. Okay, let's try Emersyn James Mackenzie. EJM. We could call her Em. Maybe even Sunny. Definitely not EJ though."

"What's wrong with EJ? I think that's cute."

"Ejaculation," Phillip says seriously. "And no boy better ever think that around my little girl. I'm just saying." He pats his firm stomach. "I've gained ten pounds since you got pregnant."

"Sympathy weight?" I ask.

"Hell no! I'm adding bulk, so I can whip some ass—particularly the ass of any skinny little punk who thinks he'd like to date my daughter."

I laugh. "I think you have a few years before you have to worry about that."

"I know, but I've been thinking about other stuff, too, like college funds."

"Maybe we should focus on a diaper fund instead."

"So, what do you think about Emersyn?"

"It used to be my favorite, but it's not as pretty as Haley James. I think you picked the winner."

"Really?" Phillip asks, practically glowing.

"If you like it the best, I like it the best, too."

He sweetly kisses me. "I love it. It's a beautiful name. I think we need to get cracking on the nursery, too."

"Oh, I meant to tell you about that. I've decided on a color palette. Remember at Chelsea and Joey's wedding, I mentioned the gorgeous colors of the hydrangeas? I was thinking those might be the perfect soft colors for the nursery. A pale green, a soft pink, dusty purple, and that gorgeous blue. It will go well with the blue-gray I want to do on the walls."

"I think that would be nice."

"Awesome. I'm going to draw up some plans for you to see."

"I have some plans for you."

"What kind of plans?"

"I know you've been having trouble falling asleep lately. I was reading that it might help if you had a nighttime routine."

"Phillip, you know I hate routines."

"This routine you might like. It's a bedtime snack, followed by a bath or massage, and then some lovemaking."

"Oh, you might be right," I say, sliding my hand down his lean torso. "What's our snack for tonight?"

He kisses me and then runs to the kitchen, bringing us back cookies and milk.

"This is the best bedtime ritual ever!" I tell him.

"I agree," he says, dunking another Oreo into the milk and stuffing the entire thing in his mouth.

We eat Oreos differently. Always have. I pull the sandwich

apart, scrape the cream off with my teeth, and then dunk the chocolate part in milk.

Phillip sets the empty plate on the nightstand and starts my massage. But my *massage* seems to be focused only on the area between my legs.

"Are we moving on to the lovemaking part already?"

WE'RE IN THE throes of passion, meaning we are getting it on, hot and heavy.

I've already had a few orgasms, but Phillip is still going strong. There's got to be some correlation between pregnancy and orgasms because I can practically have one from just a bumpy car ride.

"Oh God," I say as he thrusts harder, our headboard banging against the wall as Phillip nears the edge of release.

"Phillip dear!" his mother yells from outside our room, causing Phillip to freeze mid-pump. "I think someone might be knocking on the door, but it's so late that I'm afraid to answer it."

"Can she be that oblivious? Don't she and your dad have sex?" I whisper.

"Oh God. I hope not," Phillip says. "What am I supposed to do?" He takes a deep breath, rolls off me, throws on a pair of boxers, and goes to check the door.

When he gets back, he tells me, "Surprise, no one was at the door."

I reach inside his pants.

"*That* is long gone." He laughs, sliding his hand across my stomach. "Maybe we'll try again—oh! What was that? Oh my God! That was it, wasn't it? I felt the baby kick!"

"The baby is kicking like crazy right now. I'm pretty sure he's going to be a gymnast. You really felt it?"

"I did. It was like your whole stomach moved." He snuggles up to me, keeping his hand on my stomach and talking to it. "I just felt you kick, Baby Mac. And, although it was amazing to feel, it's time for Mommy to get some sleep. So, why don't you go to sleep, too?"

"Maybe you should sing us a lullaby," I suggest.

And he does, sending me off to dreamland.

"PRINCESS, WAKE UP," a faraway voice says.

I feel someone shaking me, but I'm screaming in pain as fire shoots across my nerves.

"My leg, my leg," I murmur. "It's broken."

"Jadyn, wake up!" Phillip shakes my shoulder, tearing me away from the scene of the accident.

I reach down and hold my leg, which still hurts.

"What kind of creature did you give birth to this time?" He chuckles. "And how did you break your leg? Or was the baby a shark? No, I guess that would have eaten your leg."

I shake my head. "I was in a car accident. Head-on, just like my parents. Well, not just like my parents. It was during the day, and it was raining. A car lost control and came at me. It all happened so fast. I tried to turn away. I could feel the car crumple around me, crushing me. And my leg hurt so bad, but then I was bleeding. And bleeding. My stomach was cut open, and the baby …" I start to cry. "The baby came out dead." I throw my head into his chest and sob. "It felt so real." I reach down and rub my leg. "And my leg still hurts."

"Shh, it's okay," Phillip whispers. "That's not going to happen. Our baby will be just fine. I promise."

THE
THIRD
TRIMESTER

28 WEEKS

Dear Baby Mac,

Well, you made your dad's life!

You kicked so hard that he felt it. Actually, you probably aren't kicking any harder than you used to, but you've grown, and you are filling out your living quarters. You are two and a half pounds and about sixteen inches long.

The baby books also say that you can dream.

I'm pretty sure that's what you do all day.

You're already like a teenager.

Or possibly a vampire, waking only at night.

But, so far, I haven't craved blood like Bella, so I think we're okay.

Danny and Lori came over for dinner the other night with baby Devaney. Danny was loaded down like a pack mule. I found it hard to believe that a teeny baby could need so much stuff.

But I think they do.

I'm really not nervous about taking care of you physically. I babysat and understand basic baby care, like changing diapers, burping, bathing, and feeding.

But I'm worried about the emotional side of it.

When does the joy of becoming a parent turn you into a stressed-out mess?

Does it happen after a few weeks of not getting enough sleep? Will I start shouting orders at Phillip to get your rocker set up?

And what if your grandma is right about letting a baby cry so that it can learn to calm itself?

I know Lori got mad when we compared her baby to our puppy, but we used to have a hard time getting Angel to settle down at night. She wanted to just run around and play. Now, we give her a bully stick. It almost acts like a pacifier. She chews and chews, and pretty soon, she can't keep her eyes open.

I want to teach you to calm yourself down. I want to teach you everything you need to know how to do in life.

But what if I screw it up?

How do you care for your baby emotionally?

Actually, I think I know the answer. I should do what my parents did.

They loved me.

That's what you need.

Unconditional love.

And, you, Baby Mac, now have a name—if you are a girl.

It's Haley James Mackenzie.

Isn't that pretty?

Blow off steam.

JULY 12TH

P HILLIP SETS OUT on his typical jogging route—down the sidewalk, to the left, and then right onto the trail.

"Let's go a different way today," I suggest.

"But I know exactly how long this route is," he argues.

"It's fun to go different ways, Phillip. Besides, you shouldn't be so predictable. What if a killer were stalking you and watching your habits? Predictability makes you vulnerable."

"You've been reading too many spy novels," he says with a laugh.

"Maybe, but we're still going this way today." I point, heading the opposite direction of where we usually go. "Come on. Who knows what we'll see?"

We take a jogging trail that ends up cutting through a portion of our neighborhood that has multimillion-dollar homes. A lot of Danny's teammates live here. I've always wanted to drive through and gawk at the houses.

Although we enjoy jogging together, we really don't talk much. We listen to our own music, Phillip playing pump-me-up rock while I play a wide assortment from rap to EDM to country. I'm not sure what Phillip thinks about while jogging. He always says it helps clear his mind, that he doesn't want to think. I'm the opposite. When I'm stuck on a design or a project, a jog helps me figure it out.

Phillip turns the corner, and we end up going down a hill into a large park area. There's a big, swirly slide and a bank of swings. I stop running to stare at them. It's been a while since I've been on a swing. My mind flashes back to a few days after my parents' funeral when Phillip took me to swing. Then, it flashes to a time in college when I was having a meltdown over failing a test. It was the beginning of my sophomore year, and I'd never failed a test in my life. I figured I'd go drown my sorrows at a frat party, but Phillip drove me to a park where we swung and drank vodka out of a flask. We stayed there for hours, playing like kids, until the mosquitoes started attacking us. We went back to our townhouse and watched a movie. I must have fallen asleep during it because I woke up the next morning, all tucked in my bed. Phillip's arm was draped across me, and he was snoring softly. If I hadn't known it for sure before then, I knew in that moment that I wanted to wake up with him every day of my life.

Phillip realizes I'm not running anymore because he jogs back to me, pulling out his earbuds and looking at the swings. "Been a while, huh?"

"Yeah, it has," I say.

"Last one there's a rotten egg!"

I race after him, catching up and jumping on his back, but I sort of forget I'm pregnant, and my belly bashes into him.

He falls to the ground, laughing about how he's getting too old for this, and then he rolls on top of me and pins me to the ground.

"If you're too old and out of shape for a piggyback ride now, there's no hope of you whooping your daughter's future boyfriends," I tease.

He leans down and kisses me.

"Your body isn't exactly the same as it used to be," he says gently, pulling me up. "Do you want to swing?"

"I don't know," I tease. "You think I can with a belly like this?"

"You're not that big," he tells me.

"I know. I haven't really popped out yet. But I'm glad. Chelsea was telling me that her back is really bothering her."

"Do you think Baby Mac will like to swing?"

"I don't know. Let's find out," I suggest.

Pretty soon, I'm flying high with my toes pointed toward heaven.

"I want to build our kids a big swing set in the backyard," Phillip says as we're swinging. "We used to play on ours all the time."

"How many kids do you want?"

"I don't know. A lot. Four, maybe five. What about you?"

"I want more than one because I always wished I had brothers and sisters. Maybe we should see how we do with one first though."

Phillip laughs. "We're going to do fine."

"Do you think we will? I wasn't worried about it before, but Danny and Lori seem to be struggling. It makes me nervous."

"I think we have a very different kind of relationship than Danny and Lori."

"How so?"

"Well, we get along."

"But what about when we're under stress? When we're tired and crabby?"

"We survived four years of finals weeks together," he offers.

"That's because we drank a lot in between studying to blow off steam." I laugh.

"Well, there you have it. We'll make sure we don't forget to blow off a little steam together." He grabs my swing, stops it from swinging, and pulls me into his arms. "And, by blowing off steam,

I mean, sex."

"I read that dating is important after a baby. Not just sex. We need to remember to take time to focus on our marriage, too."

"Happy wife, happy life,' is what my dad always says."

"I think that's misleading. In trying to make Lori happy, Danny is making himself miserable. I think it has to be a balance."

He kisses me. "I think you're right. I'll try to keep you happy. You try to keep me happy. And we'll be fine."

I nod. "I love you, Phillip."

"I love you, too. Speaking of that, I wanted to talk to you about something."

"Like what?"

He grabs my hand. "Let's walk home, and we can talk."

"Okay," I say as we head back to the path.

"So, I was thinking about getting you a new car."

"Why? My car is only a few years old."

Phillip looks up at the sky. "Um, I was just thinking a bigger car would be nice. You take the dog everywhere. We'll have a baby seat and all that stuff soon."

"If you're trying to talk me into a minivan, it's not going to happen. I'm only twenty-three. I'm not ready for that."

"I was thinking of an SUV. You seemed to like driving Mr. D's when you had it, didn't you?"

"Are you saying you want to buy me a Mercedes? Um, okay. But what if I got a convertible instead?"

"That sort of defeats the purpose of a bigger car."

"I like my car, Phillip. Maybe you should get an SUV."

"Fine. I looked up the crash ratings on your car. It's not as safe as it could be."

"Is this about my dream the other night?"

"Maybe. Kind of. It just got me thinking. What if it was a premonition, Jadyn?"

His calling me Jadyn stops me in my tracks. "You told me all my wedding-disaster dreams didn't mean anything."

"You weren't pregnant then."

"You're being silly," I tell him. "I'll be fine. It was just a stupid dream."

God forbid I tell him about the river of blood. He'd probably buy me an ark.

"Princess, I'd appreciate it if you didn't argue with me about this. Would you just come look at the Audi and the Mercedes? Surely, you want to keep our baby as safe as possible, don't you?"

"Can we even afford it?"

"Sometimes, it's not about the money, Jadyn."

I guess I can't argue with that.

Kicked out of the neighborhood.

JULY 14TH

TWO DAYS LATER, on Saturday morning, there's a shiny, new black SUV sitting in my driveway.

Danny comes wandering over to check it out. "Nice." He whistles. "You trade in the Beemer?"

"No, Phillip got to keep his sports car. I got the mom car."

"This is hardly a mom car," Danny says. "Horsepower of three twenty-nine. It's got some get up and go."

"And one of the highest crash-test ratings," I tell Danny.

"That's smart," Danny says. "You'll have some precious cargo in there pretty soon."

Phillip comes up behind me, wraps his arms around my shoulders, and kisses the side of my face. "I already have precious cargo."

And, yeah, that makes me melt. I lean my head back into his chest. "I'm teasing about it being a mom car. I think it's beautiful."

"Plus, you look hot, driving it," Phillip whispers. "Course, you'd look hot, driving anything."

"Okay, you two." Danny rolls his eyes. "No sex in the driveway. We don't want you getting kicked out of the neighborhood."

Phillip and I laugh.

"How's Devaney doing today?" I ask.

"She's asleep," Lori says, sneaking up from behind us, baby monitor in hand. "Phillip, did you get a new car?"

"I got this for JJ," he says to her. "I knew it would take something really nice to get her to trade her car in."

"A Mercedes. Well, aren't you a spoiled brat?" Lori says to me. She says it in a way that's supposed to be funny, but there's a bite to her voice.

"I got it because it's one of the safest SUVs on the market," Phillip tells Lori. "Not because of the brand."

"That's so sweet of you," she says. "Danny, have you ever checked the safety rating for my car?"

"Uh …" Danny stutters.

"Your Altima has a good rating," Phillip interjects.

She purses her lips and nods her head. "Lucky me."

"Plus, I just bought a boat," Danny announces.

"You did what?" Lori says. It's obvious she knew nothing about it.

"I bought a boat. I was just coming over here to see if Phillip could go to the dealership with me. Then, I thought I would surprise you with it, Lori. It's a gorgeous day. We can get out and enjoy it."

"You want to take our newborn on a *boat*?" Lori asks incredulously.

"She's almost three months old. The couple up the street has a two-month-old, and they take him on their boat. They say that he sleeps, well, like a baby. I thought it might be a way for us to get out of the house."

"I'll have to do some research on whether or not it's even safe," Lori says.

Devaney makes a little sniffle noise over the monitor, and Lori rushes into the house.

Danny shakes his head. "I can't win."

"Danny, if you make a big purchase, it's probably a good idea to tell your wife about it," Phillip suggests.

"It was supposed to be a fun surprise." He runs his hand across the hood of my car. "You know, she commented the other day about how all the other players' wives have luxury cars. Couldn't you have gotten Jay a nice, safe Toyota or something? Although I'm not getting her one until she starts leaving the house. You know she's started ordering groceries online. She's paranoid the baby will catch a germ."

"Maybe you should take her out on a date," Phillip suggests.

"That's why I bought the boat, people. It was supposed to be the best of both worlds. Baby sleeps. We can relax, talk, and reconnect."

"Maybe we could all go out on it," I suggest. "That would be fun. Or we could watch the baby while you go out."

"Let's all go," Danny says.

DANNY AND PHILLIP pick up the boat and get it pulled up to the dock in front of their house, and by some miracle, Lori has agreed to go out. Devaney is safely strapped into her baby carrier, which is set on the floor of the pontoon in the shade. Danny wrapped a life jacket around the top of the handle, so in the unlikely event that the carrier gets knocked into the water, it won't sink to the bottom.

Danny cruises around in the boat for a bit, and once Devaney is lulled to sleep, he stops in a calm cove, drops the anchor, and pops open a couple of beers, tossing one to Phillip.

I strip off my tee and shorts. "Let's get in the water!"

Phillip grabs my hand, and together, we jump off the swim deck. "Ahhh! That's cold!"

Danny dive-bombs right in between us. "This is awesome," he says. "Come on, Lori. Get in."

"I'll pass," she says. "I'm afraid my body is not swimsuit ready yet."

"Who cares?" Danny says. "It's just us."

"I care, Danny," she says in a snotty tone.

As I GET back into the boat, she looks me up and down. "I never would have worn a bikini when I was pregnant."

"I think she's beautiful," Phillip says, rubbing his hand across my belly.

"I don't mean this in a bad way," Danny says, "but your stomach doesn't seem that big."

Lori rolls her eyes.

"The doctor says, because I'm tall, the baby has more room lengthwise. We just had a third ultrasound, and the baby's right on target."

"I like how you've been posting pictures of your bump with the chalkboard that shows how far along you are," Danny says. "We'll have to do that for the next one, Lori."

"Do you want to wait a while to have another or have them close together?" Phillip asks them.

"I can't even think about that right now," Lori says.

"That makes sense," I say, trying to be nice. "I think I'd like our kids fairly close together, but that's all just a theory at this point. Babies are obviously a lot of work. I can't even believe how much Devaney has grown already though. She's beautiful."

"She's really developing a little personality, too," Danny says. "That's the fun part. When she smiles, she just melts my heart. My new goal in life is to make her laugh."

"When do they start doing that?" I ask.

"Three to four months," Lori says. "And Devaney is very advanced, so I'm sure it will be very soon."

Danny tosses Phillip another beer. "Lori, you want one?"

"I'm nursing," she says, like he's an idiot.

"I thought you could pump and dump?" Danny counters.

"Do we even want to know what that means?" Phillip asks with a laugh.

"It's when you pump breast milk out and throw it away. Lots of women do it when they want to drink, but don't want to pass alcohol along to the baby," Danny replies, holding out a beer for Lori, who declines.

"That's awesome," I say. "I'm totally doing that. I can't wait to drink again."

30 WEEKS

Dear Baby Mac,

You're seventeen inches tall and weighing in at around three pounds. You're not going to grow that much more in length, only a few inches, but as we get closer to your birth, you're going to pack on the pounds at a rate of half a pound per week.

Since your dad can feel you kick all the time now, he's starting to freak out a little.

The good news is, I got a really gorgeous, new car out of the deal. I've been complaining a little about *losing* my two-door sports car, but I freaking love this SUV. It's luxurious and sleek, and it even has heated seats, which I can't wait to use this winter.

Your dad bought us the safest car he could find because he says we are his most precious cargo.

Which is really pretty sweet.

He's also having our home security system redone. We used to have basic door alarms, but he's adding glass break detectors to all the windows and something that detects if they are opened.

Poor child, you'll never be able to sneak out at night.

He also made them add a cellular uplink, so in case someone ever cut our phone lines, the alarm would still go off.

He also has baby-proofed the house.

This is something you typically don't do until your little bundle of joy starts to become mobile.

But we now have covers over all the outlets and annoying little latches on the cabinets. I guess the good news is, when you do start moving around, we'll be ahead of the curve.

Angel is getting bigger and bigger. I can't believe how fast she is growing. She doesn't look like my little baby puppy anymore. She loves to go jogging with us and whines and sits by the garage door when it's time to go to work.

Mostly, she likes to go to work because Peggy brings her Chick-fil-A biscuits every morning. The other day, it was pretty funny. Angel puked the biscuits up all over Peggy's purse. I thought she'd get upset, but she wiped it off, called her a little minx, and then gave her a cookie.

Although Angel isn't allowed to get close to Devaney, when she has, she's been so gentle. Considering how rambunctious she is, that says a lot. I know she's going to love having you around.

She had to go to the groomers the other day after she decided rolling around in goose poop was a fun activity. They sent her home with a hot-pink bandana, and she looks so stinking cute. It fits her spunky personality.

Although I've known it for quite some time now, your dad just realized that Angel isn't really an angel.

While he was in the shower this morning, she shredded the bathroom rug.

I have no idea how he didn't notice she was tearing it into bits when the shower door is glass.

Could be a boy.

JULY 23RD

I COME HOME from work to find Phillip's mother surrounded by bags.

"Looks like someone's been shopping," I observe.

"I have been. I got so many cute little pajamas for the baby. And some toys. I also bought an assortment of diaper sizes. Oh, and look." She grabs my hand and pulls me into the entryway, pointing toward our dining room.

I swallow hard. "You bought us a picture. Of a storefront in Paris."

"Your dining room looks so pretty since you got the new chairs, rug, and curtains, but that wall just looked bare."

"We were waiting to get a painting at the art fair this fall."

"Oh, well, now, you don't have to!"

"Uh—" I start to say, but she pulls me back into the living room and distracts me with adorable baby clothes.

She pulls out a list. "Phillip found this list of baby needs online. I'm working my way through it."

"You don't have to buy all this stuff," I tell her. "It's really nice of you though."

She gives me a beaming smile. "I tell everyone I see that I'm going to be a grandma. I can't wait. I noticed Phillip has been baby-proofing."

"Yes, I suspect he's going to build a plastic bubble over the house soon."

She laughs. "He's pretty excited. I think he'll be a very good father."

"I think he will be, too. Although I'm going to have to hide the pregnancy bible. He keeps reading the worst-case scenario section."

"That's normal for a first-time dad, and I can see it being important to Phillip. He's a Boy Scout. He's always supposed to be prepared."

"That's true." I laugh.

She looks up at the ceiling and then says somberly, "I'm sad your parents aren't here for this."

Her sudden change in conversation catches me off guard, and her words fill me with sadness.

"I am, too."

"I think it's part of the reason I'm going a bit overboard on the clothes and toys. Can you imagine the fun your mom and I would have had shopping together?"

"She did love to shop."

"This is something she would have bought," she says, showing me a pink onesie with an attached tutu, flower ribbons, a matching floral headband, and socks. "She dressed you like this when you were little. All pink, flowers, and glitter."

"Until I learned the word *no*."

"You always wore dresses. In fact, you didn't actually ever crawl. You did this weird handstand thing because when you were on your hands and knees, you would crawl onto your dress and get stuck."

"That's funny. I didn't know that."

"I also bought a bunch of baby hangers. Do you have time to go put this stuff in the nursery?"

"Yeah, let's do it. Hang on though. The baskets I ordered for the changing table came in. We can put all the diapers away, too."

WE'RE ORGANIZING ALL her purchases when my phone rings.

"Hey," Phillip says. "My car won't start. You might have to come pick me up."

"That's fine. I'm at home."

"What are you doing?"

"Your mom and I are folding baby clothes."

"Cool. Hang on; I'm going to pop the hood and check the battery connection." I hear the car door shut and then him opening the hood. "What the heck? You're never going to believe this." He laughs loudly.

"Believe what?"

He chuckles again. "I'll have to send you a picture."

"Uh, okay. So, do you need me to come get you or not?"

"Not," he says. "I'll be home soon."

A few seconds later, a photo pops on the screen.

Lying on top of the engine is the gnome wrapped in a battery cable.

Me: *OMG! That's HILARIOUS!!!*

A short while later, Angel comes tearing into the nursery and drops the gnome in my lap. I notice she's chewed off the top of its hat. She runs over and gives Mrs. Mac a sloppy kiss, and then she steals a baby headband and takes off running down the stairs.

Phillip comes upstairs a few minutes later to return the headband and see all the baby clothes we've amassed.

"You do realize, Mom," he says, "that the baby could be a boy."

"I know." She laughs. "Little girl clothes are just so precious. Have you thought about names yet?"

"Yes," Phillip says. "If it's a girl, we're going to call her Haley

James Mackenzie."

"Oh, I love that. It's just precious!"

"I'm glad you like it," I say.

"It was my choice," Phillip says proudly.

"And what about a boy?" she asks.

"We can't seem to agree on a boy's name," Phillip tells her.

"What are your options?"

"Well, I like the name Otto, and Jadyn likes the name Chase. We had a whole bunch of other names but have rejected them all for various reasons."

"Otto is different," his mom says. "Otto what?"

"Man," I joke.

"Otto Man?" she repeats.

"Yeah, like an ottoman. Although we might go old school and name him Ottoman Empire Mackenzie." I laugh. "We're going to have to come up with a compromise name."

"You guys up there?" We hear Danny's voice wafting up the stairs.

"Yeah, we're in the nursery," I yell back.

Angel sprints out of the room, and I hear Danny talking to her. "Oh, look at you. You're getting so tall, and you've got such big feet."

"We're heading out to the deck," Phillip yells down to Danny. "Grab some beers."

Mrs. Mac looks at the time and rushes out of the nursery. "Oh, I need to go freshen up. Your father and I are going out to dinner with some clients tonight."

Phillip gives me a kiss and says, "Well, the baby will have plenty of clothes."

"Yeah, your mom is having fun. I wish that were all she was buying."

"Uh-oh. What else did she get?"

I lead him down the stairs and point toward the picture on the dining room wall.

"It's not awful," he says.

"Phillip, I chose every single detail of this room. We agreed to get a piece of artwork this fall. Remember?"

"I do."

"And we wanted that artwork to be special, remember?"

"I remember, Princess."

"So, can you please ask her to take it back? Along with the chicken coop?"

Phillip sighs and rubs his temple. "I'll talk to her."

"Yay! Thank you!" I reward him with a kiss.

Angel is scratching at the deck door because Danny is out there, beer in hand.

"What's up?" Phillip asks him as we sit down at the patio table.

"It's a gorgeous day, and it's beer o'clock. Since I can't talk my wife into having a beer, I thought I'd come over here."

"Angel, go get 'em," Phillip says to her, pointing at the geese meandering just outside our iron fence.

Angel tears down the stairs and runs through the grass, barking.

"Those geese drive her nuts."

"She's a hunting dog; they should," Phillip says. "She loves the backyard."

Angel barks again for good measure when the geese fly off. Then, she trots across the fence line with her tail high in the air.

"Look at her strutting around. She looks like Danny on the football field," I tease.

She sees a squirrel and chases it.

Danny rolls his eyes at me and takes a pull of his beer. "The squirrels seem to enjoy teasing her."

"As long as she doesn't catch one. She brought me a dead frog the other day. Came in all bouncy and dropped it on the basement tile. I screamed."

The boys chuckle, and then Phillip says, "So, Danny, you're heading to LA tomorrow?"

"Yeah, meeting with my agent."

"About another endorsement deal?" Phillip asks.

"Yeah. Don't laugh."

"What? Do they want you to model underwear or something?" I wonder.

Danny nods. "Compression shorts. I'll be shirtless."

"That will be hot. Women would all buy them."

"The shoe deal made sense. I don't know about this one."

"Why not? Will Lori be mad?"

"I haven't even told her about it. Probably won't until it's a done deal. I just mean that I thought endorsements would highlight my athletic abilities, not exploit my body."

"Says the man who enjoys strip clubs," I cough.

Danny laughs. "True."

"You know, Danny," I say, "Tom Brady is a good quarterback, but why do you think so many women cheer for him?"

"Because he looks good in his underwear?"

I nod. "Exactly. He's hot."

"He's also married to a supermodel."

"They do make a really pretty couple. My point is, he does ads for more than just sports-related merchandise. He's done underwear, cologne, shoes, watches, clothing labels, and cereal. I read that he makes million a year just off that. And you're younger and better-looking than he is. I know you earn plenty, but why wouldn't you want to make more? You could put it into your charity, set up a trust fund for your kids, or use it as fun money."

"You sound like my agent," Danny says with a grin. "What about you, Phillip? Would you pose in your underwear?"

Phillip looks at Danny like he's nuts. "Uh, in a heartbeat. Are you kidding? All those women drooling over me? I'd love it."

He gives me a little smirk.

Danny says, "Maybe you can be in it with me. Hell, your abs are thicker than mine."

"That's only because you still need to be fast on your feet. Gotta be able to get away from those defenders."

"Yeah," Danny says, nodding. "Hard to believe it's going to be my second season. Training camp starts soon."

"When does it start?"

"August fourth."

"Back to living in a dorm?"

"Yep, it's like freshman year in college. Some of the older guys get their own room, but most of us have a roommate. Honestly, last year, I was so freaking tired; I could barely stay awake to call Lori. I'm really going to miss Devaney."

I notice he doesn't mention missing his wife, but I don't say anything.

Angel comes up the stairs and drops a tennis ball at Phillip's feet.

"I'm gonna grab her a bully stick," he says, running in the house and then giving her one.

Angel furiously wags her tail and then plops down on the deck, chewing contently.

A few minutes later, she's asleep.

"I don't know what's in those things," I say, "but they're like doggy crack. Only they lull her to sleep."

"You do know what those are made out of, right?" Danny asks.

"Mean kids?" I tease.

Danny laughs.

"I'm kidding. I assume they are a beef product. From a bull. Like jerky."

"No, they're—" Danny stops in the middle of his sentence when Phillip bugs his eyes out and makes a shushing sound.

JILLIAN DODD

"Wait. Why don't you want me to know, Phillip?"

"Because they're made out of a bull's penis," Danny says, cracking up.

"Oh, gross! She shouldn't be eating that!"

"No, she should be *sucking* on that!" Danny quips.

I tightly shut my eyes. "Don't make sexual jokes about my baby puppy."

"Couldn't resist." Danny laughs.

"A bull's penis, really?"

Danny and Phillip both nod.

I look down at Angel, still happily nibbling it in her sleep, and decide I'll continue to pretend it's just beef jerky.

On my list.

JULY 27TH

"JAY, I NEED to talk to you. Can I come to your office?"

"I've got a lot going on today, Danny. Can we talk tonight?"

"Please? I really need someone to talk to."

"Is everything okay?"

"Not really."

"Do you want me to reshuffle and meet you for lunch?"

"I'd like to come to your office where no one will overhear what I say."

"Okay, come to my office then. I'll order in some lunch."

A SHORT TIME later, he shows up at my office, looking like a wreck.

"You know how I was in LA for a meeting?"

"Yeah, how'd it go? Did you decide to do the underwear ads?"

"Yeah, I did. But this is about something else. You can't tell anyone."

"Okay."

"Not even Phillip. He won't understand."

"Um—"

"Promise me."

"All right, I promise."

"When I was in LA, I met someone."

"I'm sure you met a ton of people."

"Yeah, I did, but this particular someone is a girl."

"Oh," I say slowly, the implications of what he's trying to tell me sinking in.

"Please talk to me. I have to talk to someone. Tell me what you consider to be cheating."

"What do you mean?"

"Like, I wouldn't consider flirting with someone as cheating, would you?"

"Um, no. I guess not."

"What about kissing? Making out?"

"Well, I certainly wouldn't want Phillip kissing anyone else. But I suppose, on the cheating scale, it's toward the bottom."

"What happened with Bradley that night you were at the bar? Nick told me the two of you went in the back, alone."

"He leaned into me. Pressed his body against mine. Had his hands on my shoulders, and I thought he was going to kiss me."

"How did it feel?" he asks.

"All wrong."

"What would you have done if it had felt right?"

"Probably wouldn't have gotten married. Danny, why don't you just tell me what happened instead of asking me twenty questions?"

He lets out a deep sigh and starts talking. "Okay, so you know my agent, Carter Crawford."

"Yeah."

"His brother is also an agent, but he represents people in the entertainment industry as opposed to sports. He invited me to a party, so I could meet Aiden Arrington."

"Aiden Arrington. He's engaged to that hot Hollywood actress, Keatyn Douglas, right?"

"Yes. And they own a vineyard. One of their wines is called

Moon Wish, which is not-for-profit and raises money for charities."

"I've seen the ads for that wine. Keatyn is in them."

"That's right, and they are getting ready to start a new ad campaign. Carter thought maybe Aiden and I could work together. I could be one of the athletes in their advertisements, and they could donate to Diamonds in the Rough."

"So, you got to meet Keatyn and Aiden?"

"I did. The party was at their home in Malibu."

"Is Keatyn as pretty in real life as she is on the big screen?"

"She's gorgeous, and they seem very much in love. So, that all went great. I think we'll end up working together. You'd like them. They seemed very normal."

"That's really cool, Danny. And it would be great for your charity."

"Yeah, I know. So, that's all good. Anyway, while we're talking, this girl bounds up to us. She's cute as can be and a little tipsy. Keatyn introduces me to—you're never going to believe this either—Jennifer Edwards and Knox Daniels."

"Oh my God! Knox is so hot! That Jennifer is one lucky girl. Not only is she our age and has been in huge blockbuster movies, but she's also dating *the* Knox Daniels, who was voted one of the sexiest men alive!"

"Sounds like you have a crush."

"I do. Even Phillip knows that Knox is on my list. Like, if I ever meet him, I can have sex with him, and Phillip will understand."

"Who does Phillip get to have sex with?"

"No one," I tease. "Actually, I'm pretty sure his list is full of swimsuit models."

"So, are you telling me that I could have slept with Jennifer, and it would have been okay if she were on some sort of celebrity list?"

"Well, theoretically, yes. Uh, but I'm not sure because you're really not ever supposed to meet them. Wait. Is Jennifer the girl who it *felt right* with?"

He nods. "Yes. She's all personality. You would love her. She's so freaking funny."

"You liked her because she was funny?"

"I mean, of course, she's really pretty, but there are a lot of pretty girls in the world."

"So, it was her humor that made her different?"

"Yeah, and she was fun with a capital F. She flirted with me. Made me laugh. And then ..."

"And then what?"

"We went for a walk on the beach."

"She left Knox freaking Daniels to go for a walk with *you*?"

"What?" he says, holding up his hands. "You think I can't get the girl?"

"Were you *trying* to get her, Danny?"

He rubs his face. "I don't know. Kind of. Yes. Definitely yes. I totally turned on the charm. I couldn't help myself."

"Oh, boy. Did you sleep with her?"

"No."

"But you wanted to?"

"Yeah, I did. If I wasn't married, I'd still be in bed with her."

"It's been three days."

"I know. Um, it's been a while since I've felt that kind of passion. We talked all night on the beach. I told her stuff I haven't even told you. Next thing we knew, the sun was coming up, so we watched the sunrise and then got breakfast. Neither one of us wanted the night to end. She drove me to the airport, and when she dropped me off, I wanted to kiss her so bad. There were so many times that night I'd wanted to kiss her. She gave me a couple of air kisses that connected and then slowly backed away, like she was testing my self-control. All I wanted to do was devour that sexy mouth."

"Danny!"

"I know! I know! But I didn't. I kissed her hand, which was almost worse because my lips touched her skin. She told me she wanted to give me something to remember her by." He rolls up his sleeve, showing me his autographed arm. I also notice there is a heart on top of the I in her name. "I feel like a tween who met his favorite pop star. I don't want to wash it off. And we've been texting."

"So, you're going to be just friends?"

He shakes his head. "That's the problem. It doesn't feel like we're *just* friends. Although we didn't sleep together, we were emotionally intimate. I realized that's what is missing from my relationship with Lori. We have—well, *had*—a good physical relationship, but she doesn't seem to get me. She thinks I'm immature. Really, she thinks we both are. She seems to think being an adult means you can't have any fun, like when she yelled at us for the rubber-band war. Would Phillip have yelled at you for that?"

"No. He would've gone and gotten a box of them, Mac-Gyvered together some rubber-band machine gun, and whooped us."

"Exactly. He's smarter than us. He's very organized and responsible, but he still likes to have a good time. And the novelty of learning about football has worn off for Lori. She didn't even attempt to watch the Super Bowl. She talked the whole way through it. She's pissed I'm leaving for camp. If it wasn't for the money football brings in and the bit of status that goes along with it, she would tell me it wasn't a grown-up job."

"I noticed she's wearing the necklace."

"Did you also notice she touches it a lot? Especially when she's mad at me. It's like she's rubbing the necklace to remind herself of what she'd be giving up if she left me. When we got engaged, you said she grounds me. Maybe she did in college, but she doesn't anymore. I'm not sure she still even likes me. All I know is, I want to kiss my father on the lips for making her sign a prenup. And, if it wasn't for Devaney, I'd divorce her tomorrow."

His head is down, and I can tell this is tearing him apart. I put my hand on his leg and give it a little squeeze.

"But I don't want to be that guy. I want to be with my daughter every day. Sometimes, when Lori's asleep, I sneak out of bed and just go sit by Devaney's crib. She's so beautiful and innocent."

"So, what are you going to do?"

He shakes his head. "That's why I'm here, Jay. I've been thinking about it for three long days, and I don't know what to do."

"Danny, I can't tell you what to do. It's obvious that you're not happy in your marriage right now, but I don't think you should be texting Jennifer. Are you still in love with Lori? Do you think things are salvageable?"

"I don't know."

"Well, we know you used to love her."

"Yeah."

"What did you love about her?"

"Honestly, she was a challenge. The fact that she didn't know who I was. The fact that she didn't know anything about football. She was sort of a novelty. The novelty has definitely worn off." He studies me. "Tell me the truth. Are you and Phillip going through any of this? Are you happy?"

I nervously rub my eyebrow.

"What?" he says. "You can tell me. Please tell me the truth."

"Honestly, I'm happier than I've ever been."

"Why didn't you want to tell me that?"

"Because I feel bad about it."

"You shouldn't. Has your pregnancy been that easy, or do you just suck it up?"

"I don't think any pregnancy is easy, Danny. I was kinda sick the first trimester. I wear out easily. Food is at the top of the priority chain right now, possibly above sex." I chuckle. "Okay, maybe not. But close. I have weird aches and pains. My feet get sore. I try not to complain, but Phillip also babies me."

"What do you do for Phillip?"

"I keep his beer fridge stocked," I tease. "I try to give him massages before he goes to sleep. When he's had a stressful day, he lays his head on my shoulder, and I run my fingers through his hair. And this sounds stupid, but he loves when I rub his temples. He says it takes the stress out of his eyes. We go jogging together. I don't know if that's for him or not; we usually don't even talk when we run. But, when we get home, we conserve water by showering together."

"So, even as far along as you are, sexy times are still happening?"

"Pregnancy hasn't really changed our sex life much. We've had to be a little more creative from a timing standpoint. Like, when I was first pregnant, morning sex was out because that's when I felt sick. Can I be honest?"

"Maybe. Yes. What?"

"Lori doesn't respect you. To me, that's the problem in your marriage. She doesn't even speak nicely to you. And, every time she snaps at you, it makes me mad."

"Why does it make you mad?"

"Can I quote Phillip on that?"

He laughs. "Sure."

"It's like you've lost your balls, Danny. Why do you let her talk to you that way? Why aren't you speaking up when she does something with Devaney that you don't agree with? You're a born leader. You can talk just about anyone into anything. Why does she make you back down?"

"I don't know. Phillip chewed my ass for not standing up for you when Lori's been mean."

"You said you would go down with the ship."

He hangs his head. "I just might."

"So, maybe you need to fix the ship instead of letting it sink."

"So, we're back to the same question. What should I do?"

"If it wasn't for Devaney, what would you do?"

"Leave Lori's ass and go screw Jennifer for days. And, if it was as good as I imagine it would be, then I'd probably marry her. On the spot."

"Marry her?" This is serious. "At least I wouldn't have to worry about her marrying you for your money," I joke, trying to make light of it.

"Lori also blames me for her not going to medical school, which pisses me off because I encouraged her to go. She acts like she made this big sacrifice for me. I told her just the other day that she should stop bitching about it and go to school if that's what she wanted.

"And my connection with Jennifer is different. The way we were together reminded me of you and Phillip. I invited her to come to a Nebraska game this fall. You'll get to meet her."

"Danny, I'm not sure ..."

"That it's a good idea?"

"Yeah."

"I can have friends, right?"

"Yes, you can have friends. But the fact that you wanted to be more than friends is the part that makes this tricky. It sounds like you need to reconnect with Lori. What if Phillip and I babysit tomorrow night? You can go out to dinner. Talk. Go home. Have uninterrupted sex. Pick Devaney up late or even let her spend the night."

"That's what Jennifer said I needed to do. So, yes, I'll take you up on that."

"Okay, but can I make another suggestion?"

"Sure."

"I think you need to talk to someone who has been married for a while. Your dad. Mr. Mac. Someone on your team maybe? Someone you can ask if this is normal after having a baby."

"Actually, someone spoke to me about it. Dirk Nathaniel. He and his wife have four kids. He asked how I was doing after mini camp, said I looked exhausted, and it caught me off guard. I sort of spilled my guts to him. Want to know what his advice was? Get a nanny."

"That's actually not a bad idea, Danny. Maybe, if Lori felt like she got a break, she wouldn't be such a bitch."

"That's what he said."

Figured it wouldn't hurt.

JULY 28TH

PHILLIP AND I are watching TV, Angel is upside down, asleep on the couch next to us, and Devaney is sleeping in her swing.

Around midnight, Danny texts that they are home. Phillip saw them pull into their garage a couple of hours ago, so we're hoping that means they had some adult time.

Phillip takes Angel to her kennel in our bedroom and then lets them in.

Danny and Lori come downstairs, holding hands and looking content, which makes me happy. I was pretty worried when he told me how Jennifer had made him feel. He should feel that way about his wife.

"We had a great night," Danny says. "Thank you so much for watching her."

"You look relaxed," I say.

"We are," Lori agrees. "It's been a while since we've had time to just talk."

"And we decided to hire a part-time nanny. That way, Lori can get a break each day even if it's just to go to the grocery store or work out," Danny adds.

"That's awesome. I'm happy for you guys," Phillip says.

"So, how was my little monkey?" Danny peeks at his adorable, sleeping baby. "Do you hate us for leaving you so long when all she does is cry?"

"She really didn't cry that much," Phillip says.

"She didn't?" Danny's eyes widen in surprise.

"No, she was good. We played patty-cake, and she was enthralled with the dog."

Lori sits down and stares at Devaney. "I figured she'd be crying since she usually nurses around this time."

"She actually went to sleep really easily," Phillip tells her.

"She did?" Danny looks perplexed. "What did you do?"

"Um, well, when she started crying, we listened to some music. I figured maybe she was getting sick of baby Beethoven, so we listened to my running playlist. Some rap, dance, pop. We danced around. She's going to be a party girl, I think. She doesn't want to go to sleep and miss out on the fun."

"I still can't believe you got her to go to sleep without eating," Lori says.

"Oh, well, the dancing only kept her happy for about an hour," Phillip says.

"Yeah," I agree. "So, around eleven, I fed her."

"How did you do that?" Lori asks. "I didn't give you enough milk."

"I know, and I didn't want to interrupt your date, so I gave her some of the sample formula the doctor gave me."

"YOU DID WHAT?" Lori yells. "Why would you do that? You know I'm nursing!"

"I know that, so I made Phillip look it up online," I explain. "We read on a nursing site that it's perfectly okay to supplement with formula at her age. It was just a few ounces, and then she conked out."

"How could you do that?" Lori yells at me like I fed her baby tequila.

"Because she was hungry," I say. "She loved it. Sucked it

down, burped, fell right to sleep. It's not a bad thing."

"Are you serious?" Danny asks. "She didn't cry. Not at all?"

"Not one bit," I say. "This is probably a stupid question, but could there be something you're eating that's upsetting her tummy?"

Lori's eyes bug out. "How *dare* you even suggest such a thing! Breast milk is always best!"

Phillip interjects, "She's suggesting it because, after we fed her the breast milk, she cried for an hour. Maybe she was just tired, but she didn't cry after the formula."

"Maybe Jay's onto something here," Danny agrees.

"Oh, sure," Lori spews. "Take her side, like always."

"This isn't about taking sides, Lori. Let's just talk to the doctor about it." He sighs, and I feel his pain. No matter what he says, she thinks it's wrong.

"You should have called me!" Lori snatches the baby carrier, grabs the diaper bag in a huff, marches toward me, and gets in my face. "You're going to be a horrible mother!"

Phillip immediately steps in front of her. I've never seen him look so angry. His body looms over hers. "You need to take that back and apologize to Jadyn."

"No," Lori says, clutching the carrier and shaking her head.

"All we did for the last six hours was take care of your child, so you could go out. Your baby is asleep and safe. Tell Jadyn thank you, or you will never step foot in this house again."

She grits her teeth, turns to me, spits out a, "Thank you," and then marches up the stairs, slamming the door on her way out.

"Go, Phillip," I say with a smile.

Phillip glares at Danny. He's still pissed.

Danny shakes his head in embarrassment and gives me a hug. "I'm sorry for what she said, Jay. For what it's worth, I think you're going to be a great mom. And thanks to both of you for letting us have a night out."

Phillip looks Danny in the eye. "You should have been the one to say something to her. Not me. Time to be a man, Danny."

"Yeah, I know. I'll see you guys later."

Always playing.

JULY 29TH

MY MORNING WAKE-UP consists of getting jumped on and being given sloppy, wet kisses.

"Morning, Angel." I laugh. "You're not supposed to be on the bed. Get down."

"I told her to go find Mommy, and she took off." Phillip chuckles, following her into the room. He snaps his fingers. "Angel, down."

The dog obediently jumps off the bed.

"How'd you do that?" I ask.

"Do what?"

"Make her get off the bed."

"I just told her to get down."

"Yeah, but you snapped and then told her."

"Oh, I don't know," he says. "I was just getting her attention."

"Hmm. She never listens to me."

"That's because your voice is high, and she thinks you're playing."

"So, if I lower my voice, you think she'll mind me?"

"Yeah, maybe," Phillip says.

Angel runs out of the closet with a pair of my underwear in her mouth. She's always stealing dirty clothes out of the hamper.

"Angel, no! Give," I say in the deepest version of my voice.

The dog grins at me, pink lace hanging out of her mouth, and runs around the room, throwing my underwear up in celebration.

"Angel, no. Give," Phillip says.

The dog stops, sits on her butt, and drops the underwear.

"I hate you," I say to Phillip as he picks up my underwear and hands Angel a chew toy in return. "How was your run?"

"It was good," he says, walking into the bathroom and stripping off his sweaty clothes. "Danny joined me."

"You got on his ass last night."

"He deserved it. Not to compare Lori to a dog, but if he doesn't let her know who's boss, she's gonna keep acting like that."

"We offended her, Phillip."

"No, we didn't. We took care of her child as a favor and did a very good job of it. She should have thanked us. And, if she didn't want us to give her baby formula, she should have given us enough breast milk to last. The reason Danny went running with me is because he wanted to know everything we did last night. Apparently, Lori nursed Devaney when they got home, and Devaney was crying again."

"Interesting," I say, getting out of bed to brush my teeth.

"What are you wearing?" he asks.

I look down at the blue skull cotton boy-short undies of Phillip's that I have on. They are all I have on. "I stole your underwear. They're comfortable because the waist is big, and they fit low on my hips, just under my bump. You got them in the white elephant Christmas gift exchange. I didn't think you'd mind."

Phillip leans his sweaty body into mine. "Oh, I don't mind at all. In fact, I think they're pretty sexy."

32 WEEKS

Dear Baby Mac,

We are starting our eighth month! We're on the homestretch here.

Although, from everything I have read, this is when women start to get uncomfortable. I remember Danny telling us how Lori had bought a body pillow about this time.

I didn't get a pillow. I just drape myself over your dad.

So far, he doesn't seem to mind.

You're about four pounds, and while we get everything ready for your arrival—like buying those teeny little diapers and adorable onesies and prepping the nursery—you are getting ready to be born. You're practicing breathing, kicking, sucking, and swallowing.

Chelsea and I have been talking and texting a lot. It's nice to have someone to go through all this with. I was worried about her last week because she'd been having fainting spells. They were concerned about gestational diabetes, but it turns out, her blood sugar was just getting a little low, so she has to make sure she's having snacks in between meals. After a long search, she and Joey found a really cute house about five miles from where we live in one of the neighborhoods they really liked.

We purchased a super-safe—as in your father researched them for days—car seat. So, we're ready for your trip home from the hospital.

I haven't been jogging as much. I was having some shortness of breath, and it freaked your dad out. But the doctor says it's just because my uterus is pushing up against my diaphragm, which is completely normal. He says, once you drop in preparation for birth, it will go away.

Speaking of that, you've been giving me a lot of swift kicks to the ribs. I don't know what all you're doing in there, but you must be having a good time.

I'm a little worried about something though.

I'm afraid, when you're older, that you won't mind me.

Why? you ask.

Because I'm failing as a dog parent.

Angel NEVER listens to me.

All look the same.

AUGUST 6TH

"PHILLIP! YOU'RE FINALLY home!" I say as he steps into the house. I grab his hand and drag him into the nursery. "I need your help!"

"Well, my first piece of advice would be to paint the walls all one color," he jokes, scanning the nine different squares of blue painted on the walls.

"Very funny. Tell me which one is your favorite."

"Uh," he says, his eyes moving from swatch to swatch. "Can I be honest?"

"Yes, I want your honest opinion."

"They all look the same to me."

"Phillip, they aren't the same!" I point to the color closest to me. "Like this one, see how it's more blue? Almost a baby blue?"

"Mmhmm."

"And, this one, see how it's got a more yellow undertone, and it's a little more aqua-colored?"

"Okay," Phillip says. "Which one is your favorite?"

"No, I want you to tell me which one is your favorite."

Phillip starts fidgeting.

"Do they really all look the same to you?"

"They all look blue," he says. "But, okay, this one looks too baby blue, which I don't think we want since it's supposed to be

316

gender neutral, right?"

"Yes! Keep going."

"This one looks really washed out. This one, here," he says, pointing to my favorite, "is more gray. Isn't that what you want?"

"That's my favorite. Do you like it?"

He pulls me toward him, my bump hitting his stomach. "You're my favorite," he says. "I can't believe you picked out all these colors."

"I want the perfect shade, Phillip."

"That's part of why I love you. We're getting close though, and so far, we haven't made much progress in here. All we have is the changing table and a whole lot of clothes. Will it be done in time?"

"I hope so. The painters will be here this week. I've ordered the crib. I've got more swatches coming in for the rocking chair, but I needed to choose the paint color before I made a final decision. I ordered the chandelier, and when the electrician installs it and the twinkle lights, he's going to add a dimmer. I have some curtains picked out, but I am waiting to decide which color pom-poms I want on the edges of it. I still need to find a rug ..."

Phillip laughs. "Okay, I got it. You still have a lot to do."

"Yeah, but even if it's not completely ready in time, that's okay. The first few weeks, the baby will sleep in its bassinet in our room. Trust me, the crib is so gorgeous; it's worth the wait."

"I'm sure it will be. What is that big box in the garage?"

"Oh my gosh, Phillip. Your mom is going crazy, buying stuff for the baby. That is a Little Tikes play kitchen. It's for ages two and up."

"There's more than just a kitchen. I could barely get my car in."

"Yes, we're going to have to find a home for all the toys she's buying. There's a slide and a basketball hoop, too. I'm thinking we're going to need a playroom."

"Where do you want to put it?"

"That's what I've been trying to decide. You want a playroom close to where you're going to be. So, most people want them by their kitchen, so they can cook and stuff while the kids play. Once we have kids, I'm going to want to work from home, so it would make the most sense to have it upstairs by my office. But I don't want to take up another one of the bedrooms, especially if we really do want four or five kids. It'd just be a short-term solution. So, I was thinking, we have that big room down in the basement that we're not doing anything with right now."

"That's supposed to be my future home theater," Phillip says tentatively.

"I know, but what if we eventually finished the storage space under the garage instead? It's got a lower ceiling, and it's all concrete. The acoustics will be amazing. And we spend a ton of time in the basement. So, while we have our friends over to watch football, the kids could be in the next room, playing. There are French doors out to the backyard, so when they are older, they can go outside and play, and I'll still be able to keep an eye on them."

"So, you want to make that room both your office and a playroom?"

"Exactly. It's not something we need to do right away though."

"Actually, I'd prefer to do it now while we're not busy with a baby. What do you want to do with the room? Have you thought about it?"

I can't help but chuckle.

He grins. "Of course you have. Did you draw it up for me?"

I drag him downstairs, get him a beer, sit him at the island, and run to grab my dream-house book.

"Ahh!" I scream. "Oh shit!"

Phillip comes rushing into the laundry room. "What's wrong?"

I point at the gnome, whose head is sticking out of my tote bag.

Phillip's face breaks into a wide grin.

"Why are you smiling?" I glare at him. "Did you put it there? You can't do that! I've heard pregnant women can pee if they get scared!"

"I didn't do it."

"Then, why do you look like that cat who just ate the canary?"

"Danny must have done it before he left for training camp. It's been a while since we've played the gnome game. I think it's a good sign. Like maybe he's getting back to normal."

"Gosh, I sure hope so."

34 WEEKS

Dear Baby Mac,

While you are packing on the pounds, you are also adding to your brain. Making it bigger and getting smarter. They say, anytime now, you will move into a head-down position that will make it easier to start the birthing process.

But, if I were you, I might wait a while before I did that.

Standing on my head for six weeks would give me a massive headache.

Your playroom, my office, and your nursery are coming along nicely. Really, your nursery is completely done, except for two things.

The crib and rocking chair that I ordered are still not in, but we have plenty of time.

I'm starting to have Braxton Hicks contractions.

The doctor calls them practice cramps and says they are my body preparing for the big day.

And I can see why it's preparing.

Even as much as I've enjoyed being pregnant with you, I'm starting to get a bit uncomfortable.

And we still have six weeks left to go.

I'd tell you to stop growing, but that wouldn't be very motherly of me.

But I would like to request that you stop kicking my bladder.

Yesterday, when you kicked me, I thought I was going to pee my pants.

This is me using my stern voice. "Baby Mac, the bladder is off-limits."

You go, girl.

AUGUST 23RD

"NO. JUST STOP!" Phillip says, waking me up.

I wonder who he's talking to but quickly realize he's dreaming. I push on his shoulder. "What are you dreaming about?"

"We got stuck in a snowstorm, and I had to deliver the baby myself, which, impressively, I did."

"Well, that's good, except you were yelling to stop."

"Yeah, that's because, once I delivered the first baby, they just kept coming."

"Kept coming?"

"Yeah, one baby after another. Like when you're in a batting cage and the machine keeps pitching. The babies kept coming and coming."

"You've seen the ultrasounds, Phillip. There's only one baby," I tease.

"I know. It was crazy. Have you packed a bag for the hospital yet?"

"Not yet, but I'm pretty sure we won't have a snowstorm on the first of October."

"Still, I just would feel better if we were prepared. We finished our birthing class a couple of weeks ago, and we don't have that done or a birthing plan."

"My birthing plan is simple. Just six words long. *I'll have the epidural now, please.* Do you need me to write that down, so you'll remember it?"

"Probably not." He laughs. "I'm supposed to go lift with Danny this morning. He's back home from training camp for a couple of days since the second preseason game is tomorrow night. I decided I'm taking the gnome with me."

"Where are you going to hide it this time?"

"I'm not sure, but I'll think of something."

WHEN HE GETS back from working out, he's talking to me from the bathroom while he's shaving. "So, Danny wants us to come over for dinner tonight. He said he's grilling steaks."

"That sounds good. Does Lori know he invited us?"

"I didn't ask."

"Probably for the best. Where did you put the gnome?"

"In his beer fridge on the deck. If we're lucky, we'll get to see him find it."

THE DOG DAYS of summer are officially here. Even Angel doesn't want to be outside for very long.

I've been feeling pretty good, but lately, the heat has been getting to me more than it used to.

Thankfully, as we trod up the stairs to Lori and Danny's deck, the breeze has picked up, giving us a reprieve.

"Hey," Lori says to us.

"I brought some brownies," I tell her, setting them on the patio table, hoping that will ease the tension.

We haven't really talked since the formula incident. And, if it wasn't for the fact that we've only seen Danny once since training camp started a couple of weeks ago, I wouldn't be here.

"I can't eat those," she immediately says. "I'm on a very strict diet."

"How come?"

"So, I can get back to my pre-baby weight," she says, like I'm an idiot.

"I figured. I just read that, when you nurse, you aren't supposed to diet."

"I'm still consuming plenty of food; it's just the right kind of food. Lots of fruits and vegetables. Lots of water. Danny got me a personal trainer and nutritionist."

"That was nice of him," Phillip says, squeezing my hand.

I know what the squeeze means.

More brownies for us.

Lori smiles. It's pretty much the first smile she's thrown my way since ... I can't even remember.

"He comes highly recommended by our team trainer, so hopefully, it's not a waste of money," Danny interjects, joining us on the deck with Devaney in his arms. "Lori, would you mind grabbing me and Phillip a beer?"

Phillip and I look at each other in a panic, suddenly remembering the gnome. We both go, "Wai—"

"Ahhh!" Lori screams. She grabs the gnome and throws it at Phillip. Thankfully, he's quick-handed and catches it. "Why am I the only adult here?"

Danny and I bust out laughing.

"Stop laughing! I'm serious! It's a stupid, ugly gnome that you keep hiding to try to scare each other. It's childish. Are you ever going to grow up?"

Danny can't stop laughing. "Lori, you should've seen the look on your face. Priceless."

"It's not funny!" she yells.

Devaney smiles at Danny and then laughs.

"Ohmigosh! Did you see that? Devaney is laughing, too!" I burst out.

"Even you think the gnome is funny, don't you, little monkey?" Danny says, tickling her chin.

"We're not hiding the gnome, Lori. It's been moving of its own accord," Phillip manages to say with a straight face.

"You're all nuts," she says, stomping into the house.

"That didn't go over so well," Phillip says to Danny.

"Mommy needs to learn to take a joke, doesn't she?" Devaney moves her hands around, touching Danny's face. He grabs her finger in his mouth and shakes it, causing her to squeal with delight. "She loves it when I do that. You think your daddy is hilarious, don't you?" he says, never taking his eyes off his baby girl.

We watch him play with her for a few minutes.

I can't wait until Phillip makes our baby laugh like that.

Chelsea sent me a link to a social media account the other day along with a text that said her ovaries just exploded. The account contains pictures of hot guys holding babies. I'll admit, there is something pretty sexy about seeing a man holding a baby. I can only imagine how sexy it will be when he's holding *our* baby.

Apparently, Lori wasn't too traumatized by the gnome because she brings steaks and corn on the cob out on a platter. Danny hands Devaney to her and puts them on the grill.

"Are you excited for your second preseason game?" I ask him.

"It's good to be playing again, but, like last week, I'll only be in for a little while. My backup needs experience, and they don't want me to get hurt. I saw workers at your house. What are you doing over there?"

"I'm building JJ an office slash playroom," Phillip says proudly.

I love that he's gotten so excited about it. He even helped me pick out cabinets.

"We thought it would be easier for me to work from home once we have kids. Did I tell you I'm working on another building? This is a smaller project, and I'm only doing the interior space planning, but it will be fun."

"You didn't tell us," Danny says, flipping the steaks.

"Phillip's company is expanding again, so they are adding an office in Dallas. I also have another job, working with our contractor. He has a client who is consolidating with a new campus here. It will be a huge project."

"That's awesome," Danny says. "You go, girl."

I smile. "Thanks."

"How in the world are you going to work with kids running around?" Lori snarls.

"Because she's brilliant." Phillip grins. "We split up the big room in the basement that I was going to use as a home theater. The part that's her office has a set of French doors leading into the playroom, and instead of walls, there are half-walls with windows that slide open."

"It makes my office look like a sunroom. There's lots of light, and we had it painted this gorgeous shade of pale pink. The construction is done. Now, they are just installing the cabinets. I did a long run across one wall. It will be cool because, when we want to have parties in the backyard, it can double as a buffet. And my drafting table is like a Murphy bed. I can fold it inside a cabinet when it's not in use. Since it has its own entrance, I'll even be able to have clients over, if need be."

Lori laughs. "That'll look professional. Toys scattered all over."

"The French doors and windows that face the playroom have curtains, so I can hide the clutter. Anything is possible with a little creativity." I give her a tight-lipped smile.

"On that note," Danny says, "time to eat."

35 WEEKS

Dear Baby Mac,

Only five more weeks until we get to meet you!

You have no idea how excited I am about that.

And I'm not just saying that because my stomach feels like it weighs about eight hundred pounds and might explode if it gets any bigger.

In reality, you are only weighing in at about five pounds and feeling cramped, too. You probably can't do all the fun flips and somersaults like you used to.

But come this Saturday, we'll have something to cheer about!

IT'S FOOTBALL SEASON!

This Saturday is the home opener for our alma mater and favorite college team, Nebraska. Our friend Danny, who will be your godfather, is a quarterback in the NFL and used to play there. He got a skybox where we get to watch the games from, which will be really nice.

Even though I'm feeling a little uncomfortable at times, I'm still trying to enjoy every moment of my pregnancy.

I read something around the time that my parents died that said, *When you're stuck in a moment, it can be hard to see past it.*

That all you can see is that moment.

But I'm trying to look ahead.

I know you won't be inside of me for much longer. I know

that you'll grow up fast, and someday, I'll look back and wonder if I appreciated every single moment I had with you.

More than anything, I want that answer to be yes.

Like a movie star.

SEPTEMBER 1ST

PHILLIP AND I are in Lincoln, enjoying the Nebraska home opener in Danny's new skybox.

"Isn't this awesome?" Danny says, looking down at the field.

"It is." I rub my belly. "Especially since it's so hot. I'm not sure I could have taken the heat today. It will be so great to have both air-conditioning and our own bathroom. I swear, this baby's goal in life is to get me to pee my pants. It's got to be a boy."

"Why do you say that?"

"Because a girl wouldn't do that to another woman. A boy would think it's hilarious."

Danny laughs. "You might be right about that." He lowers his voice and leans closer to me. "Get this. Last night, Lori asked me if I might get traded to a different team eventually."

I can't hide my shock. "What? Why did she ask that? I don't want you to get traded. Why would they trade you? You're doing great!"

"That was my initial reaction. I couldn't believe she'd even suggested it. And then she said she wished I had gotten drafted to somewhere more glamorous, like Chicago, New York, or Miami."

"She wants you away from us," I say with a sad sigh.

"I think you might be right," he says grimly as his phone

vibrates. He reads a text. "Holy shit. She's coming. She's here."

"Lori decided to come to the game?"

"No, *Jennifer*."

"Jennifer Edwards? Why?"

"Yesterday, when Lori decided not to come, I invited her. She didn't reply, so I assumed she wasn't coming, but she just texted me and said she's here. That she wanted to surprise me."

"Are you surprised?"

"Holy shit. Yeah, I am. Promise me you won't treat her like a movie star."

"Have I ever treated you like a football star?"

"No."

"Then ..."

"Okay, just make her feel at home." He wipes off his forehead.

"You're sweating. Are you nervous?"

"Ya think? I'm a freaking wreck. I didn't think she'd actually come. Do *not* let me be alone with her." He shakes his head. "Unless I tell you I want to be alone with her. No, no. Not even then. Even if I say I want to be, don't let me."

"Is she still seeing Knox?"

"I think so."

"Is she happy with him?"

"She says it's not serious. That she's always had a crush on him. But he's, like, ten years older than she is. Way too old."

"But you're just the right age?"

"Shut up." He shoves his hand through his hair, causing the front of it to stick up. "Shit."

"Danny, calm down. Your parents just walked in."

"That's about like getting caught with a boner. What am I supposed to tell them? I didn't think this through."

"Have you ever thought anything through?" I can't help but laugh. "Tell them the truth. That you met at a party in LA and invited her to Nebraska, so she could see what the fuss was all about."

"Yeah, that's perfect. I shouldn't be nervous. I mean, we're just friends."

"Yes, you're just friends."

"We're just friends," he repeats.

"Danny, would you like me to go meet her?"

"No. No, I want to go. I'll be right back."

DANNY ESCORTS JENNIFER into the skybox and introduces her to me, then Phillip, Nick, and our friend Blake, who is so cute. His nickname is Blakeness, as in Blake, His Royal Hotness.

"Well, hello," Jennifer says, fanning her face and looking from Danny to Phillip to Nick to Blake. "Who knew this state was so full of hotties? I totally should have come here sooner."

"You should have," Danny whispers to her.

She's gracious to his parents, and she is a ball of energy. She's funny, silly, and cute, just as Danny described.

After she gets introduced to everyone, she plops down next to me. "Danny told me all about you. That you've been friends for a really long time. He also said you introduced him to his *wife*."

I let out a breath. "You get right to the subject, don't you?"

"I wasn't sure how you'd feel about me being here."

"Well," I say slowly, wanting to be tactful but still letting her know how I feel, "Danny says the two of you are friends. I happen to believe that you can never have too many *friends*."

She nods slowly and then breaks out into a beaming grin. "I think I'm going to like you. Oh, sweet, the game's starting. Let's go get a seat."

She sits front row between Phillip and Danny and is animatedly cheering.

She and Danny jabber up a storm about everything and nothing.

Phillip leans over and says to me, "I have a surprise for you.

Why don't you come to the kitchen?"

That probably means he wants to talk to me about Jennifer.

But he walks straight to the fridge, pulls out a beer, and hands it to me.

"What's this?" I ask.

"It's a nonalcoholic beer."

"I didn't know there was such a thing. Who would want that?"

"People who want the taste of beer without alcohol. I figured you'd like having a beer during the game."

"That's sweet of you, Phillip," I say, popping the top and taking a sip. "Not bad."

"So, what's going on down there?" He waves a finger toward Jennifer and Danny.

"The game?" I ask, pretending like I don't know what he's talking about.

He gives me a sigh.

"They're friends."

Phillip shakes his head. "Yeah, that's what they keep saying, so why don't I believe them?"

"Because they have a whole lot of sparks."

"That's what worries me. Is it a coincidence that Lori isn't here, or was it planned?"

"Lori chose not to come last night."

"And when did Danny invite Jennifer?"

"Well, he invited her when they were in LA, but he texted her again last night and told her Lori wasn't coming. She didn't reply, and he was genuinely shocked when she showed up."

"So, did they hook up when he was in LA?"

"They talked all night," I tell him.

Phillip rolls his eyes. "*Talked?*"

"That's what he said."

"Do you believe him?"

"Yeah, I do."

"Interesting," Phillip says but then breaks into a wide smile as Jennifer runs around the box, high-fiving everyone when we score. "Is it bad that I really like her?"

I smack him. "You like her because she said you're hot."

He grabs me around the waist and kisses me. "Are you jealous?"

"Do you want me to be?"

"Do I want you to go all raving bitch like Lori? No. Do I want you to fight for your man by sticking by his side and kissing him all day? Yes."

"Phillip, I loved you before you got so hot."

"Good point. Dang. Guess that means there are no movie-star girlfriends in my future."

"No way."

"What about you? I know you and Lori haven't been close lately, but does her being here bother you?"

"A little, but what happens in their marriage isn't really our business. I just want him to be with whoever makes him happy."

"Yeah, me, too," Phillip says, but a few short minutes later, he pulls Danny aside and talks to him privately.

DANNY MAKES A last-minute decision to spend the night instead of driving home and begs us to join him.

Phillip calls Peggy, who has been watching Angel, to see if she would mind if we spent the night.

She told him that the little hellion ate a loaf of bread, bag and all. But she was sleeping, curled up on the couch next to her, and she'd be happy to.

"So, what's fun to do in this town?" Jennifer asks. "Is there, like, a water tower we can climb or a tractor we can ride? Wait! Can we go cow-tipping? I've never been on a real farm."

"What about a hayrack ride?" Danny suggests with a smirk

that insinuates the only thing he wants to ride is Jennifer.

I've been wondering how I really feel about all this.

Truth is, even though Lori has been a bitch to me lately, I didn't want to like Jennifer, out of some sort of leftover best-friend loyalty.

But I can't help myself. She's fun and down to earth, and seems genuinely nice.

And, from what I can tell, she and Danny haven't crossed any lines. They act like buddies even though their chemistry is palpable.

"We could call the Warren twins," I suggest.

THIRTY MINUTES LATER, we're on a hayrack ride with a bunch of old friends, drinking beer.

Everyone adores Jennifer, and she likes that no one is treating her any differently than we would each other.

"Jennifer is cool," Phillip says, snuggling up with me in the hay.

"Yeah, she is. I really like her. Although I still sort of feel like I'm cheating. Danny told me that he and Jennifer have emotional intimacy."

"Sounds like us before we dated."

"Yeah, I thought the same thing."

"It's interesting," Phillip says for about the tenth time today.

36 WEEKS

Dear Baby Mac,

The work baby pool results are in:

A whopping sixty-two percent think you are a girl.

The most common birthdate is September 29[th.]

They had to also guess your weight as a tiebreaker. If majority rules, you will weigh in around eight pounds.

And, in other good news, construction of the office building is complete!

All that's left now is to watch all the cool finishing touches go into place. The traditional furniture. The modern artwork. The cool smart boards. The funky chairs in the break room.

You should be proud of your mommy. There were times I wasn't sure I could pull off a project of this scale, but I'm so pleased with how it turned out.

I'm also happy to announce that my office/your playroom is done, and this weekend, we're going to move all my stuff down there and hang the curtains.

On the nursery front, I was told your chair and crib had shipped. I think that means they are on a slow boat from China, and I'm pretty sure, if I call and hound the company one more time, I will never, ever see them in my lifetime.

Your dad keeps making me call them. It's driving him nuts that everything isn't done.

I told him to chill. That we still have four weeks.

But he's starting to get a little crazy.

At first, it was sweet.

The car. The outlet covers. The cabinet locks.

The security system.

Now, he's starting to annoy me a little.

Even though my birth plan is really just one simple line, he wants me to write it down.

So, here we go.

JADYN'S BIRTHING PLAN
Step One: Get me an epidural.
Step Two: Pain-free labor.
Step Three: A beautiful, healthy baby.

I've packed a hospital bag for each of us, and they are sitting by the door.

He's also mapped out six different possible routes for our trip to the hospital even though we are only a few miles away from it. He has also mapped out multiple routes depending on where we are when I go into labor, like work, dinner, shopping, etc.

He's also redone our wills.

Upped our life insurance.

And I'm pretty sure he's already chosen your college.

Just kidding.

I think.

you've gotten huge.

SEPTEMBER 7TH

I'M EXHAUSTED AND headed home from work on Friday afternoon.

It's been a long week.

We've moved all the office furniture into the new building and added all the decorative touches.

No one has let me do much because I'm pregnant, but I've been on my feet the whole time, overseeing the process. The company grand-opening party is next Thursday, and I want everything to look perfect.

I'm so incredibly proud of how it has come together, but right now, all I want to do is go home and soak in a warm bath.

Unfortunately, I don't get to do that.

Danny begged me to try to get my friendship with Lori back on track.

I told him she needed to apologize first.

But then he told me that he decided to stop talking to Jennifer. When I asked him why, he said it was because he really liked her, and if he kept talking to her, it would eventually destroy his family.

As I ring their doorbell, I feel torn about his decision. On one hand, I'm proud of him for being responsible, for not giving up on his marriage, and for making his baby a priority. On the other hand, my heart aches because I want him to be crazy happy in love.

Lori answers the door, and upon seeing me, she says, "Wow, you've gotten huge!"

I rub my growing belly. "I know," I say sweetly, trying to kill her bitchiness with kindness. "Isn't it exciting? I only have three and a half weeks left."

"You know, just because you've had an easy pregnancy doesn't mean you'll have an easy birth."

"What do you mean?"

"You've skated through your pregnancy. That means, you'll have a rough delivery. It's just how it works."

My blood starts to boil. "It almost sounds like you're *hoping* my delivery won't be easy. Like it's some kind of sick payback for yours being crappy. And, personally, I think that's a pretty shitty thing to say to a friend. Although I don't know why I'm surprised. You haven't been my friend lately. The only reason I even stopped by is because Danny, who I love, begged me to. And, since you aren't on medication anymore, Lori, what is your excuse for being such a bitch?"

She starts to speak, but I hold up my hand. "Don't bother replying. I already know the answer. You don't have one. And I'm sick of it. Sick of the way you treat me. Sick of the way you treat Danny. He might be stuck with you, but I'm not! Have a great life, Lori."

I'M PISSED OFF when I march into my house.

I'm barely through the front door when Phillip's mom grabs me. "I have a surprise to show you!"

She leads me toward the nursery.

Oh. No. No. No. No. No. No.

Please, God. Please tell me she didn't do anything to the nursery.

But she has.

Phillip's old crib is shoved into the corner where the rocker is supposed to go, and there are ugly cartoon animals stuck to the beautiful paint I spent weeks agonizing over.

And that's when I lose it.

Tears stream down my face as I storm out of the nursery, grab my suitcase out of the hall closet, take it down to my room, and start throwing stuff in it.

"What are you doing?" she asks, following me.

"I'm leaving. I'm leaving my dream house. Because it doesn't even feel like my home any more."

"What do you mean?" she asks as I slam the suitcase shut and wheel it down the hall.

"I didn't have a picture on the dining room wall because Phillip and I were waiting for the Plaza Art Fair where we were going to find the perfect piece of art. Something that would always remind us of the place we went every year as kids and where we got married. Instead, there's some horrible picture of a place in Paris that we've never been to and was"—I can barely get out the words—"mass-produced. And we didn't have a kitchen table because we found a beautiful custom table that our kids and friends would carve their names in. But, because the artist only makes one at a time, we have to wait another month before it will be done. And, in the meantime, I have a table that doesn't match the style of my kitchen at all, and not only that, it's made of"—I start crying harder—"pressed wood!"

I storm by the kitchen.

"And I freaking hate chickens. No one under fifty has chickens in their kitchen. No one! So, you and Phillip can live here because it's not even my house anymore." I grab my portfolio, take out my dream-house sketchbook, and throw it on the counter. "I guess I won't be needing this anymore. And, just for the record, no one knocks on our front door at night. We were having sex because that's what newlyweds are supposed to do!"

I waddle out of the house, slamming the door behind me.

I throw my suitcase in the car and pull out of my driveway.

I have no idea where I'm going.

Once I get a few blocks from my house, I pull over.

I can barely see the road through my tears.

I don't even know where to go.

I pat the top of my belly as the baby gives me a swift kick in the ribs, and I intuitively know that I need to calm myself down.

Stand up for your marriage.

PHILLIP

I COME HOME to find my mother's bags packed and her sitting at the kitchen island.

I also notice something else new. "Is that a *chicken* rug?"

"Yes, Phillip," she says curtly, "it is."

"Did Jadyn buy that?" I ask delicately, already knowing she didn't.

"Your wife is very talented," my mom says. "Have you seen her sketchbook of all the things she wants to do to your house?"

"Of course I've seen it. It's our dream book. When we see something we like, she draws it to help me visualize it. We can't buy everything at once, so we're doing a room at a time."

"Yes, that's what I hear. Your wife packed her suitcase and left. And it's all our fault."

"What do you mean, she left?"

"I brought your old crib and hung some wallpaper in the nursery to surprise her."

I run my hands through my hair. "Oh, Mom ..."

"So, you *do* know," she says.

"Know what?"

"That JJ has been unhappy with what I've been doing around your house."

341

Now, this is awkward. "Um, yes, I know."

My mom points at me, and she's pissed. "Sit down, Phillip!"

I sit.

"JJ is your wife. Wife trumps mother if you are going to have a successful marriage," she lectures.

"I didn't want to hurt your feelings."

"She's your *wife*. She's pregnant with *your* baby. My grandchild. And she left."

"Where did she go?"

"I don't know. I've been calling all around, but no one has seen her. When she left here, she was crying and really upset."

"What happened?"

"She blew up. I guess the nursery was the last straw. Phillip, you and your wife have to be a team against anything and anyone that might affect your marriage. I've been affecting your marriage, haven't I?"

I put my head down and nod. "A little."

"So, why didn't you say something?"

"I knew you being here was temporary. I figured things would be fine once you and Dad got your own place. And I didn't want to hurt your feelings."

"But, in the process, you were hurting JJ's. You know, one time, when your father and I were first married, we got into a wicked fight. I packed my bag and went to my parents' house." She starts crying. "JJ doesn't have anywhere to go. She's all alone, except for you. Except for us. You have to be her rock, Phillip. You have to stand up for your marriage. I'm really worried about her."

"I saw your bags. Are you leaving?"

"Yes, your father will be here shortly. I suggest you find your wife. JJ is pretty outspoken and generally lets people know how she feels. What I want to know is, why didn't she say anything to me?"

I'm quiet.

"Phillip?" she says again, using that tone. "I asked you a question."

"Because I told her I would," I admit.

She puts her hand on my shoulder. "Even if you hurt my feelings, I'll understand. But your wife won't. Your wife will feel like you're choosing your family over her, and it will erode her trust and faith in you. You should have been a man—the man of your dream house, the man I know you can be—and told me. You're going to be a father soon. You have to be a man, Phillip. From now on."

"Yes, ma'am," I say.

Everything my mom says is right. I screwed up big time. How am I supposed to be a father when I can't even be the head of my own house? I think about all the planning I've been doing. I've been pretending we'll be fine, but I've seen the toll it's taken on Danny and Lori's marriage. I'm afraid we've been moving too fast. From first date to married to pregnant in under six months. And I know I'm the one who was excited about her being pregnant so soon.

I just want everything with her.

Right now.

Always right now.

I'm a planner. A doer. A fixer. Jadyn is creative. A dreamer. All the things I love the most about her are the ways in which we're different. And they are also the things that are starting to drive me crazy. We don't even have a crib, for God's sake, and the baby will be here in less than a month.

The doorbell rings as I'm rubbing my temples, hoping to dispel the headache I feel coming on.

"That's probably your father," my mom says, going to answer the door. "Oh, Phillip. It's a truck with a delivery."

I get off the barstool and watch as the deliverymen unload a crib. The crib from Jadyn's sketches.

"Do you know where to put it?" Mom asks.

I grab the sketchbook. "I'll be in the nursery. Send them up."

When I get in the nursery, instead of seeing all that isn't done yet, I see all she's accomplished. The room is a calming shade of the palest blue-gray. The changing table is filled with colored cloth bins, holding diapers, onesies, and other baby essentials. A large gray-and-white-patterned rug is spread over the hardwood floor. I look at the nursery animals my mother stuck on the walls and my old, ugly crib with its gaudy animal bedding and understand why Jadyn flipped out.

I quickly shove the crib across the hall and into the guest bedroom.

I hear my mom directing the movers my way. They bring in and then unwrap a gorgeous crib. It's the kind of crib we could pass on to future generations. The wood is intricately carved and the headboard oversized. I instruct them to place it in the center of the room, as per Jadyn's plans.

Mom says, "I think you should put it on that wall over there. It would look—"

I don't say a word, just raise an eyebrow at her, which shuts her up.

"We have a chair for you, too," the deliveryman says, and they quickly bring in the slipcovered rocking chair.

Jadyn ordered numerous fabric swatches before she found the exact shade of dusty-purple-gray velvet she'd envisioned. I remember thinking it really didn't matter what color the chair was, but now that I see the room coming together, I notice every little detail. The white blackout curtains with gray pom-poms running down the edges. The ceiling she added extra coving to, so she could insert deep navy panels with little lights that look like stars. The pale pink, yellow, green, and blues of the baskets. The mobile hanging above the changing table that she made from pale strips of fabric and ribbons.

"How do we get these stickers off the wall, Mom?"

She's looking around, too. "They don't really go, do they?"

"No, they don't."

"I used wallpaper paste," she says. "I'm not sure we can get them off without damaging the paint."

I grab my phone out of my pocket and Google it. I don't say anything to her, just run and get JJ's hairdryer.

I take it to the nursery, turn it on high, and say a prayer.

AFTER PULLING, CUSSING, and burning my hand, the stickers are gone.

"Let me get some water," my mom says. She comes back with a sponge and wipes off the remaining adhesive.

We both stand back.

"You can't even tell they were there," I say with relief.

My mom hugs herself. "This is the most beautiful nursery I've ever seen. You need to call JJ."

But I'm way ahead of her.

All that really matters.

JADYN

I GET DONE with my massage and am at my locker, getting dressed.

The baby, who must have been sleeping during the massage, has decided to wake up and do some kind of workout. I'm getting kicks to the stomach and elbows to the ribs. I pat my belly, the stress I felt when I got here instantly reappearing.

I still have no idea what I'm going to do.

Or where I'm going to go.

But then I look down at my engagement ring and remember what Phillip told me a few days before our wedding.

"*This ring means one thing. That I love you. Promise me that, no matter what, no matter if we fight, no matter how hopeless things might feel, you will look at this ring and know that, when you love someone, that's all that really matters. That we'll always figure it out together.*"

I promised that I would.

I was a tad overdramatic when I stormed out on Phillip's mom. Honestly, I wasn't really that mad at her. And I'm a big girl. I should've talked to her about it myself instead of waiting for Phillip to say something. I just didn't want to hurt her feelings. She's made me feel like part of their family since my parents died.

I'll just be honest with her. Tell her that we love having her stay with us, but it's our house, and there are a few rules. Make that one rule. *No decorating.*

I'll apologize, tell her the truth, and then tell her what Lori said because that's what upset me the most. That's what set me off. The nursery was just the spark that lit the powder keg.

I still can't believe Lori said that to me. Wished that on me.

How could a friend say something like that?

That brings me back to the same answer I've been avoiding since she accused me of cheating.

A friend wouldn't.

Besides apologizing to Mrs. Mac, I also need to have a serious conversation with Danny. If he wants to stay with Lori, that's his business, but I can't be friends with her unless she gives me a sincere apology. I'm done pretending like things are okay. And I hope and pray it won't affect our relationship with Danny.

My phone vibrates.

"It's your dad," I say to my stomach. "Close your ears. I might say a few bad words. Hello?" I say into the phone.

"Come home," Phillip says.

"No, thanks," I reply even though I want to go home. I just want it to be *my* home when I get there.

"Are you okay? Mom said you were really upset when you left."

"I'm fine, Phillip," I lie.

"I just need to make sure you're okay."

"I just told you, I'm okay, Phillip," I say with a sigh. "Just like I told you that your mother doing stuff to our house was upsetting me. Just like I told Danny I couldn't be friends with Lori anymore."

"I'm sorry about my mom. I kept thinking it was temporary. That we just needed to get through it. Then, we could do things our way as soon as she left. I didn't want to upset her."

"But it was okay to upset me? Why does everyone think it's okay for me to be upset?"

"What happened with Lori?"

"I went over there before I came home. Danny wanted me to make up with her, but I wasn't even through the door before she said something horrible."

"What did she say?"

"That I would have a rough delivery because I've had such an easy pregnancy."

"What a bitch," Phillip says. "You're done being friends with her. I'll talk to Danny about it."

"I came home upset, and when your mom showed me the nursery, I just blew."

"I don't blame you. Mom chewed me out," he says softly.

"Why?"

"Because I didn't stand up for you. She said that I suck at being a husband."

"You're not a bad husband, Phillip. You were in an awkward situation. I get that. I understand why you always took her side. I just didn't like it."

"But I shouldn't have. And I shouldn't have left the burden on you to tell her. It wasn't fair of me. Just like Danny asking you to be friends with Lori again isn't fair. My parents are leaving, just so you know. They will stay in hotels from now on."

"I don't want them to leave. I just don't want her decorating."

"Please come home."

"While we're at it, let's talk about you, Phillip."

"Me? What'd I do?"

"I haven't wanted to say anything, but since I'm getting it all off my chest, I might as well. Your worst-case scenarios, the college funds, the baby-proofing, the planning. You're so far into the future; it's crazy. Are you doing all that out of love or fear?"

"Seeing Lori and Danny's relationship deteriorate so quickly has me nervous."

"We're not going to be like them, Phillip. So what if we don't change the baby's diaper perfectly or if we don't have money saved for college yet? The baby won't know the difference. We'll learn and grow with it. Remember what you told me about my engagement ring? How love is all that matters. I wasn't lying when I said you were going to be an amazing father. You're fun and smart, and you have strong arms. Those are the things I remember most about my dad—that, and I always knew he loved me. And, if something ever happens to me, I know that you'll raise our kids to be strong, confident, and caring."

"Don't even say that. Nothing is going to happen to you."

"You've read all the worst-case scenarios, Phillip, and I've lived my own worst-case scenario when my parents died. Things can and do happen. It's important for me to know, if something ever does happen, that you'll always remember love is the most important thing. Just love."

"I've always known that," he says. "I guess I just lost sight of it. But I learned it again today. From you."

"How so?"

"The crib and the rocking chair came. The nursery looks beautiful and calming, just like you wanted it to. But it's more than that. The room feels like you're being wrapped in a hug because you chose every single little detail for it out of love. So, I get it. Love is all that matters. And I love you desperately."

"I love you, too, Phillip. Does it really look good? Did you put everything where it's supposed to go?"

"It looks perfect. And my mom and I were able to get the stickers off the wall without ruining the paint."

"Ohmigawd! Really? I'm dying to see it. I'm leaving the spa now. I'll be right home."

"I can't wait, Princess. I love you."

"Any chance you can get rid of the chickens, the table, and the bad artwork, too?"

"Already done." He chuckles as we end the call.

I RUSH TO my car and head for home.

I can't wait to see the nursery.

I've obsessed over every single detail that would go into the room, all the way down to selecting over a hundred coordinating fabrics and ribbons for the mobile.

I hope it looks the way I've envisioned it.

"Crap," I say, hitting the brakes as the left-turn arrow changes to red.

I sit patiently and wait for the cars to cross in the other direction.

When the green arrow lights up, I make my turn.

I'm just out into the intersection when I see a car coming toward me. My brain quickly processes our impending crash. I hit the gas hard, hoping to avoid the unavoidable.

The collision is loud and violent.

Brakes screaming.

Metal bending and twisting.

Tires screeching.

Glass breaking.

A motor hissing.

Air bags exploding toward me.

The smell of smoke.

It seems like the noise lasts forever.

But then there's an eerie silence.

I SLOWLY OPEN my eyes and assess myself, wondering if I'm injured but feeling an overwhelming sense of urgency to get out of the car. I remember the salesman telling me that there is a smoky smell when an air bag goes off, but my brain is overriding that knowledge and urging me to get out of the car.

I try to undo my seat belt, but it won't budge.

I grab the tool Phillip bought me, cut my seat belt, pop the air bag, and escape from the car.

I'm stumbling, dazed, my mind trying to comprehend it all.

There are metal pieces tossed across the street.

Teeny squares of broken glass.

The sweet smell of radiator fluid.

A car's hood buried into my passenger side, its motor steaming.

Its driver motionless.

I'm a little woozy, and I feel off-balance as I stagger away from the vehicle.

A big arm slides around my waist. "Jadyn!" Marcus says. "Are you okay?"

"What are you doing here?" I ask him.

"I was heading home. Saw the crash." He grabs my arm. "Jadyn, look at me. Try to focus."

I try to do as he asked, but my brain is on sensory overload.

"Your pupils are huge," he assesses, grabbing my face and holding it still. "Were you wearing your seat belt? Did you hit your head? Does anything hurt?"

"Uh, I'm not really sure," I reply, still looking at the wreckage of the other car and wondering if this is what it was like when my parents crashed. "The other driver isn't moving."

"I'm going to check on him. Are *you* okay?"

"I forgot you studied to be an EMT," I say, wiping the sweat from my face. "And, yes, I think I'm okay."

"What about the baby? Have you felt it kick?"

"Oh my God! No!" I'm suddenly panicked.

Marcus puts his hands on my shoulders. "Take a deep breath, Jadyn. I'm going to check on the driver. Yell if you need me."

He runs over to the other vehicle.

There's a lot of commotion now.

A siren in the distance.

People trying to help the other driver.

Yelling.

Lots of yelling.

People on cell phones, taking photos.

Others gawking as they slowly drive by.

In the midst of the mayhem, the baby kicks me in the ribs, which makes me start crying in relief.

More sirens.

Police cars.

Fire trucks.

Ambulances.

Lots of questions.

Questions I don't know the answers to.

"How fast were you going?"

"Did you see him coming?"

Then, pain ripping through me.

"Ahhh!" I yell out, clutching my abdomen as a sharp, piercing pain brings me to my knees.

Marcus runs over. "What's wrong?"

"I just had this horrible pain. Could I be in labor?"

"An event like this could most definitely trigger labor," he tells me.

I suddenly feel wet.

My first thought is that I've had some kind of peeing incident, but then I realize what it is. "Um, Marcus, I think my water just broke."

"Let's get you over to the ambulance."

He speaks to the paramedics at a rapid pace, "Female Caucasian. Twenty-three years old." He turns to me. "How far along are you?"

"Um, thirty-six weeks."

He continues, "She's thirty-six weeks pregnant. Water just

broke and experiencing severe pain. Let's get her to the hospital."

The paramedic hooks me up to a blood pressure machine.

"Your blood pressure is a little lower than I would expect after an accident. But you're doing great. Just keep breathing through the contractions. On a scale of one to ten, how bad is the pain?"

"Ten, maybe eleven. Can't you stop it? Give me a shot or something? I can't have the baby now. It's too soon."

"Once your water breaks, you need to deliver within twenty-four hours, so get ready. You're going to have a baby today."

"Did the wreck hurt the baby, and that caused me to go into labor?" I'm trying not to panic.

"It's not unusual for emotional or physical trauma to cause a woman to go into labor. Everything will be fine," he says reassuringly.

"Marcus, will you call Phillip and have him meet us at the hospital?"

"Of course I will. It's a little sooner than anticipated, but are you excited?" Phillip must answer because Marcus stops talking to me and goes, "Hey, Phillip. Um, I'm with Jadyn. She was in a car accident." Pause. "Yes, calm down. She's okay, but her water broke, and she's gone into labor."

Another contraction rips through me, and I cry out in pain again.

"Yes," Marcus says to Phillip. "The labor pains are strong and pretty close together. The paramedics are checking her vitals, and then we'll be heading to the hospital. You'll probably get there before we will, so just meet us in Emergency."

"Is he freaking out?" I ask Marcus as the paramedic checks my oxygen levels.

"Every father freaks out a little when his wife goes into labor."

"Would you?"

"I'd like to say that, with my training, probably not as much, but I'm sure I will."

"At our class, we were told that giving birth is the most natural thing in the world. This doesn't feel natural. It hurts."

"Is it just the contractions that hurt?" the paramedic asks. "Or do you hurt anywhere else?"

I point to a spot on my lower right side, near where my leg attaches. "This is where the sharp pain is. I'm having contractions, too, but they hurt all the way across my stomach, like really hellacious cramps."

"You were hit hard from the side. Does your back hurt? Your shoulder? Your neck?"

I shrug my shoulders and then move my neck in a circular motion. "Shoulder and neck seem stiff but not painful."

He puts his hand across my rib cage. "How about here?"

"A little."

He makes a note of it as another piercing pain rips through me.

PHILLIP

MY MOM AND I are disassembling my old crib when I get a call from Marcus.

I listen in disbelief and then run to the garage door, grabbing my wallet off the kitchen counter.

"Phillip, what's wrong?" Mom asks, following me to my car.

"JJ. Wreck. Labor. Hospital." I say something to that effect.

Mom grabs my shoulders. "Is she okay?"

"She's fine, but the wreck caused her water to break, and she's in labor. I don't know much else."

"Okay, you go. I'll wait here for your father, put Angel away, and lock up. We'll be right behind you."

I nod as I open the car door and peel out of the garage.

UPON ARRIVAL AT the hospital, I give them my name and Jadyn's and tell them she's on her way in an ambulance.

"I'm not sure if she'll give birth naturally or if they will want to do a C-section," the maternity nurse says, "but let's go ahead and get you scrubbed in."

JADYN

THE AMBULANCE TAKES off, sirens blaring.

It reminds me of being in the police car the night my parents died. But, that night, the siren's rhythmic sound was sort of soothing. Today, it's not.

The contractions hurt way more than I imagined they would. I thought they were supposed to come in waves. Every few minutes. That you breathed through them, rested, and then breathed through them again until they got closer and closer together. Then, it meant you were ready to have the baby.

But, in between these contractions, I still feel a deep pain coming from my side. I know I've never been in labor before, but something feels off.

I look down and notice blood on the sheet.

"I'm bleeding ..." I say, mostly to myself, coming to the realization that my bad dreams are playing out in front of me.

The paramedic doesn't respond to me.

He yells to the driver, "We have a possible placental abruption. Let the hospital know."

Placental abruption. That's one of those worst-case scenarios. But I can't remember what it means. Common sense tells me the placenta ruptures.

As in stops working?

I have another searing pain.

All I know is, this bleeding is not good.

I yell out again as I try to focus on the words and phrases floating around me and not on the pain.

Bleeding.

Possible placental abruption.

Baby's possible lack of oxygen.

Blood pressure dropping.

ETA.

Blood loss.

Emergency C-section.

"Marcus, is the baby going to be okay?" I ask, squeezing his hand as another contraction rips through me. "And tell me the truth—the worst-case scenario."

"There are a lot of factors. You're obviously bleeding, but we can't know the extent of the abruption. In a full abruption, both the mother and baby are at risk. In a partial abruption, time is of the essence. The placenta feeds your baby oxygen and food and takes away the waste. Those things are key to the baby's viability."

"*Viability?*" I repeat, the word settling in.

Similar words scroll through my head from the night my parents died.

"*Your father suffered severe brain trauma, and his body is shutting down. We've revived him once, but we need to discuss what you want done when it happens again. Does he have a living will?*"

I grab the front of Marcus's shirt and pull him close. "Marcus, this is important. I need to tell the hospital my wishes," I say as another contraction causes me to cry out in pain.

"What wishes?" he asks.

I close my eyes, not wanting to say the words I've been thinking. But there's something inside me that innately knows this is going to end badly.

"If there's a choice to be made, I want the baby saved. Do you understand?" I look at the paramedic. "Do you *both* understand?"

The paramedic nods, but Marcus squeezes my hand. "Jadyn, I don't think—"

I cut him off. "This is important, Marcus. These are my instructions. Please, tell me you understand."

"I understand," he says.

"We need it in writing. We'll have the paramedics give it to the staff as soon as we get there. Do you have some paper?"

PHILLIP

ALTHOUGH IT FEELS like forever, a few minutes later, Jadyn is being wheeled in on a gurney.

All I see is blood.

Why is there blood?

And whose blood is it?

Hers?

The baby's?

Marcus said everything was fine. That her water just broke.

There shouldn't be blood.

She sees me and reaches out for my hand.

"I'm sorry, Phillip," she says, crying, before a contraction causes her to groan and clutch her stomach.

Everyone is moving quickly around us.

"Her water broke, but we're seeing some blood, so there's a possible placental abruption," Marcus tells me.

The nurses rushing about haven't said a word. They are focused on her.

Marcus squeezes JJ's hand. "It'll all be okay."

"Remember what I told you," she says to him.

"What did you tell him?" I ask, but she cries out in pain again.

Placental abruption. That's bad. But I seem to remember that it could vary in severity.

I put my hand on her forehead, trying to keep her calm. Her

eyes are big, and she looks scared to death.

And that scares the shit out of me.

"It'll all be okay," I tell her, praying that it will be.

"Jadyn, we're going to do an emergency C-section," someone says.

Jadyn nods, tears filling her eyes.

"Phillip," she says in a panic, "I wrote it down, but you need to know, too. Make them save the baby. Not me. And please promise me that you'll always remember what we talked about earlier. The love part."

"What? Don't even say that! Don't even *think* that!" I yell, repeating the words she said to me when I was telling her about all the things that could go wrong during early pregnancy.

"Here's the anesthesiologist," someone says as they're wheeling her into an operating room.

I'm following them, holding her hand, and so far, no one has said anything to me, but they are busy prepping her for surgery.

The nurse who scrubbed me in says, "You can be here for the birth, but they're going to have to put your wife under."

We're in the operating room now, and everyone is moving quickly.

The anesthesiologist says, "Jadyn, I'm going to put this mask over your face. Just breathe normally, and you'll be asleep quickly."

I give Jadyn's hand a squeeze, hold it tight, and mouth, *I love you.*

"I love you, too," she says.

She doesn't look as panicked now.

Instead, she has a faraway look in her eyes as the doctor puts the mask into place.

Her abdomen is draped, so I won't see them make the incision. I don't want to see that part.

Instead, I focus on her.

I gaze at her face and realize all the beautiful moments in my life have been with her by my side.

I try to focus on those moments.

Think positive thoughts.

She's here at the hospital. She'll be okay.

But her warning about saving the baby haunts me. Why would she say that? Does she know something we don't? She looked scared when they brought her in, but I'm sure being in an accident and going into labor when you don't expect it would be scary.

But it felt like more.

Then, I remember her dream.

The reason I got crazy and bought her the safest car I could buy.

Oh. My. God.

No.

Please, God, please let her and the baby be okay.

Mostly, let her be okay.

I need her.

My eyes fill with tears as I imagine a life without her.

Something I can't even begin to fathom.

I shut my eyes tightly.

Stop thinking that way.

Positive thoughts. Positive.

Everything will be okay.

I look around the surgical room, wishing I could remember more about emergency C-sections from our birthing classes. All the details I thought I would remember so clearly have vanished from my brain, probably because I thought it would never happen to us.

Everything is happening quickly but methodically around us, the surgical team moving like a well-oiled machine. And that calms me. They are calm. That means things are going to be fine.

In a few minutes, they have her opened up.

"The abruption is much worse than we thought," the doctor says while I'm trying to remember what I read.

What was the worst-case scenario for a placental abruption?

From somewhere in my brain come the words, *While a small abruption can be tolerated, excessive blood loss can result in the death of both mother and child.*

I tightly squeeze Jadyn's hand, praying for the best and trying not to even consider the worst.

"Make them save the baby. Not me."

She did know something. She knew something was wrong.

She knew.

Oh. My. God.

She can't die.

Cannot die.

It'll all be okay. It'll all be okay. I keep trying to tell myself that.

But, now, all I can think about is losing her.

Of losing the baby.

And I know that I can't agree with her wishes.

If there's a choice to be made, I'll pick her.

I could survive the loss of our child, but I couldn't survive losing her.

I'm pretty sure I couldn't exist without her.

I remember her coming home from one of Lori's baby showers. Telling me how someone was telling them about a stillborn baby. How just retelling the story brought tears to her eyes. How she was clutching her growing baby bump like she was afraid to mention the word in front of our child.

The doctor pulls out the baby, who looks bluish, not red and angry like in the childbirth class photos.

My heart sinks.

And Jadyn's hand goes limp in mine.

I turn to look at her, innately knowing that, even though she's under anesthesia, she knows that our baby didn't make it.

She's going to be devastated.

A machine beeps.

Then, another.

"She's crashing!" a nurse yells.

"She's lost too much blood!"

My world spins out of control as I recognize the underlying panic in their once-calm voices.

"Her blood pressure is too low."

"She's coding."

The mood in the room changes in a heartbeat.

Everyone is suddenly very serious.

Grim.

I hear an announcement over the hospital's PA system, "Code blue."

"Code blue?" I ask.

"Get him out of here!" someone yells.

"NO!" I scream. "I'm not going anywhere! Someone needs to tell me what's happening!"

"Sir, you need to leave." A male nurse tightly grabs my shoulder as tears of frustration and rage spill out of my eyes. "We need you to leave now."

"I'm not leaving," I tell him, still holding her hand but standing up taller, so he can take in my size.

No freaking way he's making me leave.

But then two people have ahold of me.

I maneuver away from them, bend down next to Jadyn, and yell in her ear, "Stay with me, Princess! Don't you leave me! Don't you *dare* leave me! I need you!"

"I said, *get him out of here!*" the doctor's voice booms.

They manage to get ahold of the back of my shirt and drag me away, forcing me to let go of her hand. But I still have my hand outstretched toward her. I can't let go.

I can't.

But, as I stare at her lifeless body, the fight is knocked out of me.

They drag me to the door, but I don't want to go. An insurmountable amount of pain courses through me. This can't be happening. This cannot be happening.

I cry out again, "Don't you dare leave me, Princess! Don't you dare!"

I'm thrust outside of the operating room and into the hall where a group of nurses is rushing toward me. I back against the wall to get out of their way but stop one who looks nice.

"What does code blue mean?" I ask as she's opening the door.

"I'm sorry," she says sympathetically, rushing inside and slamming the door on everything important in my world.

I drop to my knees and sob as visions of her dance through my head.

Hair that looks like sunshine blowing in the breeze as she swings upside down from a tree.

That same blonde hair under a veil as she floats down a staircase.

My heart swelling in my chest when she says, "I'm pregnant."

The symphony of her laughter when I tell her that she's always loved me.

Her lips on mine as she straddles me and says what I've been longing to hear.

Her hand squeezing mine seconds before she speaks at the funeral.

Taunting me with giggles when she catches her first fish before I do.

The sound of her voice in my ear every night.

Smooth, soft skin that smells like summer pressed against mine.

Screams as I save her from a garden snake.

Freckles covered with mud, a white T-shirt becoming transparent as we wash off the four-wheeler.

Standing cheek-to-cheek by the swings, her tears making my shirt damp.

A ring sliding on my finger as she recites, "For as long as I'm lucky enough to have you."

Gratitude when she sees the angel wings tattoos on Danny and me.

A grin that completely undoes me.

Tossing her into a pool and then getting chased and letting her catch me.

Being rewarded with a kiss on the cheek as she tells me, "You acted like a prince today."

OUR LIVES ARE like single threads meticulously woven together—the result an exquisite tapestry of past, present, and future. Bound by unflappable trust, our hearts, our desires, her life woven into mine.

"Don't pull on the thread of your sweater when it's unraveling, Phillip. It will come undone."

Her sly grin as she says, "Let's pull it and see if it's true."

Stitch by stitch.

Row by row.

I'm slowly coming undone until there is nothing left of me.

My Princess—my life, my world—is dead.

DANNY

MRS. MACKENZIE'S VOICE is ragged and stressed.

I catch certain key words. *JJ. Car accident. Hospital.*

I'm turning the car around to head to the hospital before I even hang up.

It's like déjà vu.

I'm drunk, lying in my dorm and thinking about her. I can still feel the softness of her sweater and the coolness of her skin against my warm hand. I'm thinking about those mile-long legs in dark jeans that hugged her curves.

I can hear one of the twins tell me how That Asshole Jake—that's what Phillip and I called him whenever Jay wasn't around—brought another girl to the party. He goes on about the girl's massive boobs while I watch Jay struggle to get across the field in the high heels she's wearing. As much as I want to immediately go beat the living shit out of Jake, I find myself jogging after her.

She has a little meltdown. The cutest babbling meltdown. Of course, my horny teen mind focuses on one detail. The thong she says she's wearing. Jay has always been cute. She's always been my friend. And, really, she is the only girl friend I have. Every other girl is just sex.

And, suddenly, I see my chance—that perfect crease in the defense where I know I can run straight through to the end zone.

I shut her up with my lips.

She's surprised when I kiss her, but her lips quickly get in sync. Kind of like when I taught her how to kiss and we kissed for hours—but hotter. She's better at it. Her tongue not unsure.

I want to throw her in the backseat of Lisa's car, strip her clothes off, and do her.

And, if she were any other girl, that's exactly what I'd do.

But this is Jay. She deserves better.

I stop kissing her. I have to, or I'll go against my better judgment.

She freaks out. Worries she's become a bad kisser.

And from somewhere in my memory comes the perfect line straight from her own smart-ass lips.

"Well, I can't be sure." I laugh. "The line judge didn't have a clear view, the side judge over there was watching the cheerleaders, and since there's no instant replay available"—I shrug my shoulders and tilt my head—"I'm just gonna have to call a do-over."

"You're a cheater," she says.

"Better than being a liar," I fire back.

But it's the sexy way she looks at me that causes my mouth to find hers again.

I don't want to stop kissing her.

But I have to.

Or I'm going to do something I'll regret. Because, right now, my dick is voting for the backseat.

"Uh, let's go get a beer, Jay."

She doesn't look convinced and gives me a pout. It's that face, that look, that has always stopped both Phillip and me dead in our tracks.

It's not her sassiness. Or her intelligence. Those things we'll fight her tooth and nail on, but when she whips out the pout, she always wins.

When I first moved to the neighborhood in sixth grade, I made her cry. Phillip told me, if I ever made her cry again, he'd punch me until I cried. He had a fierceness about him, and to this day, I've never doubted that he would.

It's that look and those words echoing in my head that make me grab her hand and drag her back to the party.

Phillip gives me a similar fierce look when I slide my hands around her waist.

And, when she leaves to go to the bathroom with Lisa, he raises his chin and almost imperceptibly shakes his head. It's the same thing he does on the football field. It means he's not open, so don't throw him the ball.

It's a warning.

And, right now, he's clearly warning me not to mess with her.

I chug some of the Warren twins' whiskey and decide she needs my attention to cheer her up.

I tell myself I'm doing it for her.

That I'm kissing those soft lips just to make her feel better.

I know, at some point, the shit's going to hit the fan. Either Phillip and I will come to blows or we'll team up on Jake.

Since I don't want to have it out with my best friend, I decide to push Jake's buttons and come up with the idea of making him jealous.

Her eyes sparkle like they always do when she knows we're going to do something exciting, something that will most likely get us into trouble.

It's that sparkle that makes me think about the backseat again.

I make a snap decision.

Jake first. Backseat later.

Or maybe I'll take her back to my dorm. My roommates are gone for the weekend.

We get in clear view of Jake, and I turn on the charm, for both Jake and my own reasons. Jake insults Jay and laughs about the fact that he went elsewhere for sex.

I pull Jay closer and suggestively run my hand up her thigh. "Hey, Jake, ya think maybe there's a reason she's never done it with you?" I cock my head and shrug. "Might explain all them trips to Lincoln ..." Then, I give Jay a hungry look, one driven by my own need as much as my wanting to put this asshole in his place.

Jake lunges at me.

The Warren twins and I make fast work of Jake, even when his friends get involved.

But, when I turn around to claim a victory kiss, she's gone.

"Lisa, where's Jay?" I ask.

"Phillip dragged her out of here. They left."

It always has to be Phillip. He always has to play the knight in shining armor.

Damn him.

I'm tipsy and horny, and I have no intention of sleeping alone tonight, so I grab my phone, intending to booty call the hot girl who's been sending me dirty pictures all week.

I'll be with her. Get my head straight.

Then, tomorrow, I'll drive home.

Screw studying for finals. I'll take Jay out for lunch.

Kiss her again.

Make a decision on how to proceed while I'm sober.

When I look at my phone, I notice three missed calls from my mom. It's a little unusual for her to call so late, but I'll deal with her tomorrow. She would've left a message if it was important.

But then I see I have a missed call and a voice mail from Phillip.

I listen to it.

"Jay parents. Accident. Life-flighted. It's not good. Call me."

When I call him back, I feel sick to my stomach. The alcohol I consumed tonight is suddenly not sitting well with the late-night Taco Bell drive-through.

Phillip says, "Hey, hang on."

I can hear him walking.

He tells me about the crash. "Head-on. Mom dead. She got to say good-bye to her dad. He's dead, too."

I can barely speak when he hands the phone to her.

What do you say when your best friend just lost her parents, and you've been thinking about how to get into her pants?

"Jay, I'm so sorry."

And I know it. I know I'm going to get to the hospital, and Phillip is going to say similar words about her and the baby.

They never had a chance.

I think about the funeral. How Jay asked me, without a tear, to be a pallbearer. How I nodded even though carrying a coffin was the last thing I wanted to do. I wanted to pull her into my arms and tell her it would be all right, that I'd take care of her.

But she clung to Phillip. He was always touching her. Holding her hand. She held his hand with such force; we were all convinced it was the only thing keeping her upright.

Then, the whole prom thing came up.

My parents thinking she needed to go. Phillip not wanting her to go with Jake.

His offer to ditch his date and take Jay instead.

I stepped up to the plate.

I would take her.

After we take some pre-prom photos, Phillip pulls me aside and says, "Don't you dare hurt my girl. She's been through enough."

I know what he's talking about.

Know she's a virgin.

Know I shouldn't take advantage of the situation, but the competitor in me wants to do just that. I want to hold her and touch her in ways Phillip's only dreamed about. And I know he dreams about her. He pretends like it's some hot model, but the things the model does are all things Jay does. I'm pretty sure he's in love with her.

Am I in love with her? No.

I love her. Like, as a friend. I think we'd have a lot of fun together. I think, with a little coaching, she'd be wild in bed.

I'm always nice when I end things with girls. I'd be nice to her when it was over.

And it would be over.

I adore her, but she also drives me flipping nuts. Always fighting me about something.

We'd definitely have fun while it lasted.

But my mind is wrestling between wanting to get with her and not wanting to hurt her. Even though she hides it well, the way she clings to Phillip tells me she's not okay. She hasn't even cried. Not once. Not at the funeral.

Nothing.

What if we do it, and she hates me for taking advantage of her?

The more I dance with her and kiss her, the less I worry about all of this, and by the time we get to the hotel room, I'm drunk and horny.

I try to be romantic and pop some champagne. I try not to think about how there's something else I'll be popping shortly. And, with the way she's been kissing me, I know she wants to.

I pull her close and kiss her, running my fingers through her hair. Her hair is up in a bun, and I want it down, flowing around her face.

I take out the pins and toss them to the ground.

"Danny, wait," she says.

And I think, Shit, she's changing her mind.

Good thing I can be very persuasive.

One of my many off-field talents.

I pour some more champagne, drain it, and kiss her again.

Then, she says, "I want to get into something more comfortable."

I want to tell her lingerie isn't necessary. That I'm just going to take it off. That naked is always best.

But then I remember it's her first time. She probably has some plan. Virgins always have a plan.

While she goes into the bathroom, I take my jacket and shirt off and put them on the dresser. I push my pants down over my boner and about fall over, trying to get my shoes off while my pants are down around my ankles.

I know she and Jake have done stuff, but I've seen him in the locker room with his little pencil dick. I opt to leave my boxers on. I don't want to scare the poor girl.

I remember one girl—Brittany or Bethany, some B name, what-

ever—telling me she didn't think it would fit. I proceeded to show her it fit just fine.

I get a condom out of my wallet and set it on the nightstand. Even drunk, I remember, No glove, no love.

As I lie down on the bed, it spins a little. Shit. I don't feel so good.

I grab the trash can and heave into it.

Then, I lie back down and close my eyes for just a minute.

I wake up, freezing.

I survey my surroundings and see I'm lying in a hotel bed, wearing only boxers.

And what is that smell? I gag and then grab the trash can and throw up in it—again, apparently.

"Jay?" I say.

What happened? What did we do? Did we have sex? Did I puke in the middle of it? Oh God. That would probably scar her for life.

Then, I see the condom still lying on the nightstand and try harder to remember.

"Jay?" I say again, checking the bathroom.

I'm half-afraid she's in there, bawling. Her prom dress is hung up. There's some lace half-shoved in a duffel bag.

I pull out the red nightie.

She would've looked hot in this. She would have put this on and come out, excited to show me.

And what did she find?

Me half-naked, passed out next to a trash can full of puke.

I grab a glass, fill it with tap water, and down it. I'm thirsty. Then, I grab my toothbrush and brush my teeth.

She must have gone to Billy's party.

Some date I am.

I throw on a pair of shorts and go to the party. Turning down a beer and learning no one has seen her. I know she can't be with

Phillip because he had plans with Carrie. Even went all out on a room with a hot tub.

I go knock on his door anyway because I'm getting a little worried. If she left with Jake, Phillip would be pissed at me.

When Phillip answers, I peek toward the bed, hoping to see Carrie naked. Instead, Jay sits up and rubs her sleepy eyes.

What is she doing in bed with Phillip? And where the heck is Carrie?

But then I realize they both have clothes on.

I'm either still drunk or too hungover to process.

So, I tease her, offering a threesome, and end up in bed with her and Phillip, doing nothing but sleeping.

Later, I wake up, extremely hungover, and get a nasty dose of reality.

Jay is sleeping peacefully, her long hair splayed out across Phillip's arm, her head resting on his shirtless shoulder, her face snuggled into his neck, and his arm wrapped possessively around her.

I'm never one to back down from a challenge or a dare. I never quit when I'm behind in a game.

I never give up.

But I know better than to play a game I'll never win.

I'm almost to the hospital when my phone buzzes again. I glance down and see Coach's name.

"Danny, where are you?"

"I'm headed to the hospital. My friend Jadyn was in an accident."

"That's why I was calling you. Marcus told me about the accident, and I drove by the scene on my way home. Um, have you gotten an update on her, uh, condition?"

"No, I'm almost at the hospital. I don't know much yet."

"Do you know for sure they were taking her to the hospital?"

His tone is off. Coach is always so direct.

"What aren't you saying?"

He sighs. "There was a coroner's van there."

My heart sinks into my stomach.

"But, but … they told me they were taking her to the hospital."

"I'm saying a prayer she made it, son. Text me and let me know if things are okay."

I don't reply as the phone slides out of my hand.

I GET TO the hospital, find somewhere to park, and stagger into the emergency room.

A nurse recognizes me right away.

"You're Danny Diamond, aren't you?" she says in that flustered tone older women get when they meet me.

Jay says it's because they've been picturing me naked. She always knows how to make me laugh. How to make me forget I'm nervous.

"My friend Jadyn Reynolds—er, Mackenzie was in a car accident. She's pregnant. I'm looking for her husband."

She looks motherly and less flustered when she hears Jadyn's name. She takes my hand in hers and pats it.

"I'm sorry," she says as she leads me down the hall.

I see Phillip.

He's wearing scrubs and sitting on a folding chair outside of an operating room.

All by himself.

His head is down, and he's sobbing uncontrollably.

I rush over, sliding onto my knees in front of him.

He looks at me through tear-drowned eyes, raises his chin, and almost imperceptibly shakes his head.

Just shakes his head.

Like he used to do on the football field.

Like he did that night at the party.

And I know my best friend is dead.

Jadyn is dead.

And I'll never be the same.

WE'RE BOTH CRYING like girls.

Sobbing.

Phillip is hysterical. "How am I going to make it without her?" he cries. He keeps asking me over and over, "How am I going to make it without her?"

I don't have an answer.

The hole in my own heart feels big enough to kill me.

Please, God, give him back his Princess.

Give me back my best friend.

My partner in crime.

Because I don't know what I'm going to do without her either.

"I'm here for you," I say, putting my arm around his shoulders.

It sounds lame, but it's all I've got.

JADYN

I FLOAT UP to the bright lights in the surgery room and see a man walking toward me.

A man I recognize even before I can clearly make out his features.

"Dad!" I say, running to him and tightly hugging him.

He doesn't say anything, just takes my hand and points at what's going on below us.

Phillip is standing beside me, holding my hand.

They've cut my abdomen open, and they are pulling the baby out.

The baby looks bluish and doesn't make a sound. They quickly whisk it out of the room.

I turn to my dad and cry out, "Are they going to be able to save the baby? Is that why we're watching? Where did they take the baby? How does this all work?"

My dad kisses me on the cheek but doesn't answer my questions.

"Why isn't Mom here?" I ask, but he just nods again toward what's going on below.

The surgeon says the abruption is worse than they thought.

Someone else says that I've lost too much blood.

Someone announces that I've coded.

A nurse grabs Phillip and tries to drag him away from me, but he resists.

"Code blue?" he asks, panic spreading across his face.

"Get him out of here!" someone yells.

"NO!" he screams. "I'm not going anywhere! Someone needs to tell me what's happening!"

"Sir, you need to leave."

He grabs Phillip by the shoulder and tries to force him away from me. There are tears in Phillip's eyes, but he looks pissed. Like he's going to punch the guy.

"We need you to leave now."

Phillip is holding my hand and won't let go. I turn my palm over and study it. Even though it's empty, I can somehow still feel Phillip's firm grip.

"I'm not leaving," Phillip says, standing up straighter, showing the man six foot three inches of muscle.

Phillip doesn't want to leave me.

I don't want him to leave either.

I don't want him to let go of my hand.

But I know he has to. He doesn't need to see this.

I don't want him to watch me die.

Two people grab ahold of him, but he still manages to bend down next to me. I can tell that he's yelling at me, but his voice is muted.

Like a whisper.

I can hear his voice, but it sounds almost like an echo. Like he's really far away even though he's standing right next to me.

"Stay with me, Princess. I need you. Don't you leave me. Don't you dare leave me. I need you."

"I said, get him out of here!" the doctor's voice booms, but I feel it more in my chest than I hear it with my ears.

Phillip is being forcefully removed from the room, but his hand is still outstretched toward mine, not wanting to let go.

IT REMINDS ME of when my dad pulled me out of the tree when we were little. How Phillip's hand was still stretched out, trying to hold on to me.

Tears start streaming down my face.

But, as I touch my cheek to brush them away, I can't feel them.

"You'll always be my Angel," Dad says to me, snapping his finger and causing Jesus to appear.

"Does Jesus greet everyone?" I whisper to my dad.

"I don't know," Dad says. "This is your deal."

"Why isn't he talking?"

Dad shrugs.

"Ohmigawd—I mean, gosh. He knows, doesn't he?"

"Knows what?"

"I wasn't always an angel, Dad."

I start telling Dad all the bad things I did. "I lusted after my neighbor's father. I stole your car when I was fourteen and drove it with my friend."

"Danny?" Dad asks.

I nod. So does Jesus. He doesn't seem surprised.

So, I keep going.

"We did stuff to our neighbor's house one Halloween, but it was all in good fun. Really, everything I've done that is bad was mostly in good fun. I might have been a glutton for alcohol and possibly Mrs. Mac's food. I was disrespectful to her today, and she's my elder. And, oh gosh, I had sex in the church parking lot—not to mention, sex before marriage. I might have made an effigy of a pastor and burned it in my mind, but I would never do that or make hot dogs that looked like him in real life. I've lied sometimes but mostly white lies. I cussed in church but not out loud. I did drugs"—I speak to Jesus directly—"but only the natural kind that *your* father made."

I study Jesus more closely.

"You know, you look exactly like the picture that hangs in the Sunday school room at my church." I take in his long hair, robe, and the crown of flowers on his head. "Jesus, are you a hippie?" I ask.

Jesus smiles and flashes me a peace sign.

"Why isn't Mom here? And where is my baby?"

Jesus pulls a wand out from under the sleeve of his robe and says a spell, causing my mother to appear.

"Wait, are you a wizard? Did you go to Hogwarts, like ever?"

Jesus and my dad disappear as my mom sits down next to me on a slipcovered white couch. I realize everything around us has changed. The room we are in now looks like my mom decorated it.

"Is this heaven or, like, the waiting room?"

"Jadyn," Mom says, touching my arm, "there's something you need to see." She picks up a remote from a coffee table made from a polished tree log and hits a button, causing a picture to appear on the wall.

"Is that how you keep up with your loved ones on Earth? Did you know I was pregnant? Did you get to watch my wedding? Will I get to see Phillip that way? You know, when you died, I was on my way to the hospital, and I swear that I felt you holding my shoulder. Was that you?"

"Watch," she says.

On the screen is what appears to be a video of Phillip and me in the police car on the way to the hospital. Only, somehow, I hear my own thoughts.

Please let them be okay.

Whooh, whooh, whooh.

Please let them be okay.

Whooh, whooh, whooh.

Please let them be okay.

Maybe this whole night is just some bad, horrible, messed up dream.

I look around to see if Jesus heard me swearing in my mind. Thankfully, he is gone.

I watch myself slowly open my eyes. I remember hoping it was a dream. But, instead, I see Phillip looking scared.

So, it's not a dream.

Okay. I need to mentally prepare myself. Be rational. Whatever this is, I can handle it. Obviously, they are hurt badly if they are being airlifted. But lots of people get better after bad car wrecks. You see it on television all the time. Broken bones heal; scars can be fixed.

They are going to be fine. Everything is going to be fine.

We're almost to the hospital. I can see it up ahead. I feel a hand on my shoulder, so I lean my head toward it and touch my cheek to it. I take a long, slow breath and feel myself relax. I feel comforted.

Only this version is different. I can actually see the faint image of my mother standing next to me, holding my shoulder. "It was you," I say.

"Of course. Always trust your heart, Jadyn. There are some other things you need to see."

She changes the channel, and up on the screen is my father, sitting in a rocking chair. He's surrounded by clouds but in what appears to be the nursery I designed.

She zooms in closer, and I see what he's holding.

A baby.

My baby.

I freak out.

"No!" I cry out. "I told them to save the baby! Where is the baby? Why can't I see it? Hold it? Oh God. What's Phillip going to do without us?"

My mom flips the channel again.

Now, I see Phillip. He's sitting in an empty hallway at the hospital, scrubs on. His head is down, and he's sobbing.

That makes me cry harder even though I can't feel the tears.

I move toward the screen, putting my hand on top of his shoulder. He reaches up and puts his hand on top of mine.

And I feel it.

"Can he feel that, too? Does he know it's me?" I ask Mom.

"When the love is strong, yes," she says.

I start sobbing hysterically. "Mom, heaven won't be heaven without Phillip."

She flips the channel again, the screen turning completely black.

I can't see anything, but I can feel everything.

And I mean, everything.

Not pain exactly.

More like emotions.

So many conflicting emotions, but rising to the top is an overwhelming sadness that our baby didn't make it. When I signed the directive, somehow, I knew. Knew this was happening. But I hoped our baby would survive and be with Phillip.

In a happy fairy-tale world, I'd be fine. The baby would be fine. They'd smile, tell us the baby's sex, and then gently lay it into my arms as Phillip cut the cord.

That was the plan.

I remember my grandma telling me something about God's plans versus our plans.

I look over my shoulder and see a group of people behind a sheer curtain. And I know my grandma is there. Waiting for me. I can feel her presence.

Then, I hear Grandpa's voice in my head. *"If you can't dazzle them with brilliance, baffle them with bullshit."*

Is he telling me I can bullshit my way through this?

Is that why I'm in heaven?

Is there some way I can affect the baby not dying?

I see a flash of white.

No, I *feel* a flash of white.

Like lightning.

Then, I'm overcome with extreme panic.

Our baby. Our baby.

Our baby.

Our baby.

Save our baby.

Please, save our baby.

Words are clawing inside my throat but unable to be released.

I feel hysteria.

Pain.

"Clear."

Chaos.

Peace.

Then, more white, brighter now than ever before.

I know intuitively that they are trying to revive me.

But I also know it's not meant to be because the picture comes back on the wall.

I SEE PHILLIP in our backyard, building a swing set.

This makes me mad.

"It's not fair, Mom! I don't understand. First, Phillip loses you and Dad and then me and the baby. How is he going to handle that?"

Mom nods toward the screen, causing me to look more closely at Phillip.

He looks different. There are little crinkles around his eyes, his hair looks darker, and he's heavier.

"Wait, what is this? *When* is this? Why would Phillip be building a swing set?"

"Watch," she says.

A few moments later, Danny, Lori, and a bunch of children join him in the backyard.

Two adorable dark-haired boys yell at him. "Daddy, Daddy! Is it done? Can we swing now?"

He picks up the younger of the two, twirls him around, and then sets him on the top of the slide. The child happily screams his way down. He tickles the other boy, throws him up over his shoulder, and then puts him on one of the swings and starts pushing him.

"Higher, Daddy! Higher!"

It's a sweet moment. The love Phillip has for his children is apparent, and my heart fills with joy, seeing him happy.

Until a dark-haired woman walks into the picture, kisses Phillip, and hands him a beer.

My heart drops.

Falls.

Shatters.

Breaks in two.

No.

Please.

No.

But then I realize that's selfish of me.

Of course I want Phillip to go on with life.

Without me.

I want him to be happy. And he looks happy with her. I also notice there is no blonde child.

Our baby didn't survive.

Phillip runs his hand across a spot on the wood. Through his eyes, I see what he touched. Carved in the wood, just like he carved it into the tree in his backyard when we were young, are three sets of initials.

J.R.

+

P.M.

+

D.D.

=

BFFs 4Ever

Danny stands next to him. "I miss her."

"I'll miss her forever," Phillip says.

From behind me, I hear the sound of someone yelling, "Clear," again.

"Is this the future?" I ask Mom.

Mom shrugs. "Time doesn't exist here. Not in the way you're used to. Time folds on top of itself."

"So, past, present, and future as one? Predetermined?"

Mom hesitates and then nods.

"So, what I saw, there with Phillip, it's already happened, or it is happening?"

She shrugs.

"I thought, when you got to heaven, all would be revealed?"

She shrugs again, which is very frustrating.

"What the hell, Mom?"

"Jadyn James! Watch your language!"

Then, she disappears.

Apparently, that's a word you don't say when you are in heaven.

Maybe unless you want to end up there.

And I don't.

I close my eyes and see Phillip with someone else.

My eyes burst open, and I grab the remote.

Maybe this thing goes backward, so I can see Phillip when we were together. So, while I'm here, I can relive all our happy moments.

Isn't that what heaven is supposed to be about?

I click the rewind button, stopping on a time when Phillip and I are about four years old.

Then, I close my eyes. I don't need a TV to remember all the precious moments with him.

His lips are ringed with purple as he smiles at me, breaks the Popsicle, and hands me half.

His sword slices through the air as he pretends to protect me from a dragon.

His eyes hold mine as my dad pulls me out of the tree and tells me I can't play with him anymore.

His lips touch mine when we're on the swings behind school.

He runs up the hill, turns around, and yells back, "Will you marry me someday?"

One beautiful brown eye winks at me as he throws a soccer ball to me during recess. "I'll play with you."

The shy grin he gives me when I tell him he acted like a prince today.

The dreamy sound of his voice as he says, "Hey, Princess."

His warm arms wrapping around me.

Finding me in the stands after he catches a game-winning pass.

His hand in mine, squeezing it and keeping me going when I need it most.

Standing in front of me, dressed for a date, tire iron in hand. "Phillip to the rescue."

A worried look when he discovers I have a fever and his shocked voice. "Princess, you're burning up!"

Kicked back on the couch, a beer in hand, looking scrumptious. "I'll play Spin the Bottle with you."

Heartbreak written across his face when I place my engagement ring on his desk and walk out.

Sweetness and love in his voice when he drops to his knee in the snow and asks me to marry him again.

Happiness and lust as he rushes up the stairs to see me in my wedding dress.

Panic in his eyes when he thinks I'm upset because he turned my parents' wedding rings into a beautiful necklace.

Love and devotion as we're standing under an altar made of branches and his promise to always rescue me.

A sexy smirk when we're on our honeymoon before he pounces on me.

His happy, surprised look when I tell him I'm pregnant.

The joy written all over his face and vibrating from his body when he hears the baby's heartbeat for the first time.

Sincerity in his voice when he tells me he understands about the nursery. "Love is all that matters."

I could do this forever, reliving every perfect moment with him.

I open my eyes and look around at the all-white room.

I can see the people behind the curtain now, like they're just outside a window.

I can't see their faces clearly, and I'm not sure who they all are, but I know that I know them.

And I know they are waiting for me.

Waiting for me to join them.

And maybe waiting for me to understand.

What they don't know is that I do understand. I know exactly what *my* heaven is.

It's Phillip.

I'm not going to join them. I can't. I'm staying here and watching Phillip TV until he joins me in eternity.

But then I think about our baby.

About my dad holding it.

And I know I have to go.

I need to be with our baby.

A scene flicks on the screen even though I didn't touch the

remote.

Danny is rushing down the hall.

He spots Phillip, who is still sitting on the folding chair, sobbing.

Danny slides on his knees in front of Phillip.

Phillip looks up for a moment and barely shakes his head, letting Danny know that I didn't make it.

Danny puts his head down. He's sobbing, too.

I watch as he reaches up and puts his hand on top of Phillip's.

I'm drawn back to the screen.

I love them in entirely different ways, but I love them both with all my heart.

I put my hand on top of Danny's, hoping I can console them.

I look at the TV and see myself. I look faded and faint, but I'm standing there, next to them, with my hand at the top of the pile.

It's fitting really.

That it looks like this. Our hands stacked on top of each other, looking like we're getting ready to break as we go out onto a sports field before a game.

On what I know will be the last time I ever touch either one of them.

DANNY

AFTER A WHILE, the nurse who helped me find Phillip gently relocates us to a waiting room.

Phillip's parents are here.

"How is she?" Mrs. Mac asks, but Phillip's body language says everything as he plops down into a chair, taking up the same position he had in the other one.

"She had a placental abruption. Lost too much blood," I say quietly, repeating one of the few shreds of information Phillip was muttering but knowing the look on our faces says more than my words could convey.

Mrs. Mac's hand immediately goes to her face, sadness washing over the concern that was there before. Mr. Mac, who was standing, sits down very slowly, grief written all over his face.

"Oh my God," Mrs. Mac slowly says, dropping to a chair next to him as the reality of Jadyn's death sinks in.

The sounds of the busy hospital blur around me as I sit next to Phillip, not knowing what to do.

My phone buzzes with a text from Lori, asking where I am and if I'll stop and pick up milk on the way home. I realize that she has no idea what's happened.

I start to send her a text to let her know Jadyn was in an accident.

But I can't bring myself to do it.

Part of me keeps thinking that this can't really be happening. Can't possibly be real.

"Phillip Mackenzie?" a nurse announces to the waiting room.

Phillip doesn't even look up.

I stand and point to him. "Uh, he's right here."

"Sir, could you come with me?" she says to him. "The doctor would like to speak with you."

Phillip tightly shuts his eyes and shakes his head. "I can't," he mutters. "I can't."

I squeeze his shoulder. "Come on, Mac. We'll do it together."

His eyes fill with tears again. "That's what I said to her at her parents' funeral. When she didn't want to drop the roses in their graves."

He stands up, and together, we numbly follow the nurse to a small room.

We sit in the little white cubicle for at least fifteen minutes.

Waiting.

For what, I have no idea.

What happens when someone dies like this?

Dies.

The word grips my heart and squeezes, the pain intense.

I want to say something to comfort Phillip, but I know nothing will.

So, we just sit together in silence.

I JUMP WHEN the door opens, and a doctor wearing clean blue scrubs enters the room.

"I'm Dr. Evans," he says, shaking both our hands and smiling at us.

I want to punch the freaking smile off his face. How can he be smiling at a time like this?

But then he says three miraculous words. "We revived her."

"What? Really?" Phillip says, hope flooding him as he stands up, hugs me, hugs him, and starts crying again.

"We've been working on her since she flatlined. She's not out of the woods yet, but we were able to bring her back and get her stabilized."

"Can I see her?" Phillip asks. "Is she going to be okay?"

"She's in critical but stable condition. She lost a lot of blood, but I did want to let you know that we were able to stop the bleeding without doing a hysterectomy. She's so young. I figured, if she survived, she'd probably want to have more children."

As soon as the doctor mentions more children, Phillip takes in a sharp breath. He hasn't said a word about the baby, and I've been too afraid to ask.

"What about the baby?" Phillip says in a tone barely above a whisper.

"I don't know about the baby. I was only responsible for your wife," he replies. "And, to answer your other question, she's being moved to the ICU now. Once she's set up there, you can go see her. She's heavily sedated, and we're giving her multiple blood products. She's also intubated, and we'll need to keep her that way until she's hemodynamically stable. The ICU staff will be monitoring her overnight, checking her blood levels, blood pressure, and heart rate."

"So, she's going to be okay?" I ask, mostly because I have no freaking idea what hemody—whatever means.

"Like I said, she's in critical condition, so the next twenty-four hours are crucial. We kept her oxygenated while we worked on her, but we never know how a patient's internal organs and brain will react to that stress. We'll know more tomorrow."

When the doctor leaves, Phillip puts his arm around me, his hand in a fist.

The man hug.

"Screw that," I say, wrapping both my arms around him, giving him the girliest hug ever.

But I don't care.

Because she's not dead.

"They revived her," he cries over and over again. "They revived her."

DANNY

I DON'T LEAVE Jadyn's side.

I can't.

They aren't letting anyone other than Phillip and me into the ICU. I finally told Lori what had happened but told her to stay home with Devaney. I have enough to worry about without dealing with her right now.

Phillip's parents and my parents have been here off and on. They've been rotating shifts to sleep, take care of Angel, and get Phillip and me to eat.

I walk down the hall to give them an update—which is nothing yet—and am assaulted by flashes of cameras and reporters.

"Are you playing today, Danny?"

I don't even know what day it is. Sunday? Game day?

I stop and look at them. All they care about is football. And, right now, football is the last thing on my mind.

But then I have a flashback. Lying on the hammock with Jay on the day after prom.

"Greatness is in you. Don't you know that? You're doing what you've always wanted, what you're meant to do."

Her friendship and unwavering support helped give me the confidence to do so many things.

I step into the nurses' office, realizing that I never did text Coach to let him know what happened. I call the stadium and let them know I won't make the game.

Then, I deal with the reporters.

My response is simple. "It's true that I love my job. But I'm a husband, a father, and a friend before I'm a quarterback."

Friendship—the people who touch your heart—that's what matters most in our lives. Something I knew before, but it is now permanently ingrained in me.

I'm thankful that, after I reply, the hospital security herds the reporters outside.

I go down the hall to grab a cup of coffee and find Lori in the waiting room.

"How's she doing?" She gives me a tight hug, and even though things between us have been strained, I'm grateful for it.

"No change yet. How's my little monkey doing this morning?"

"Good," she says. "She misses her daddy. What are you going to do about the game today?"

"I'm not playing. I don't give a shit about football, Lori. I'm not leaving until she wakes up. Until I know she'll be okay."

Lori frowns. "So, that's it? You're choosing her over your family?"

"My family? What are you talking about? No, I'm choosing her over a *game*."

"Football is your career, Danny. It's how you provide for your family. What if they fire you?"

"You're worried about the *money*? You've gotta be kidding me. If my job and the money are more important to you than our friendship, then, all of a sudden, you've developed some messed up values. Is that why you came here? To ask me about the game? Do you even care about her anymore?"

"Do you wish you were Phillip? Do you love her?"

I shake my head at her, not believing she'd bring this up again. Not now. But I say calmly, "Of course I love her. She and

Phillip are my best friends."

"Well, if she wakes up, maybe you should just sleep with her and get it over with," she snaps.

"Where is this even coming from? Why are you bringing this bullshit up again?"

"You're putting your family's future in jeopardy because of her. *Our* future. What am I supposed to think? Maybe, if you slept with her, it would ruin you once and for all."

I don't want to deal with this right now, her ridiculous jealousy. But she needs to know. I need her to know and understand why I told Jay that. Why I lied to her in the hammock. Maybe it will make a difference.

"Sit down," I say sternly.

She sits.

"I know you think, just because Jay is the only girl in my life besides my mother who I haven't slept with that, it makes her special. You think I have some unrequited crush. I lied to her that day in the hammock, Lori. If Jay and I had dated or slept together, it wouldn't have ruined us. I'm on good terms with every girl I ever dated."

"So, why didn't you?"

"Because it would have ruined my relationship with Phillip. It's always been her and Phillip. He's always been who she runs to. You should have seen how he took care of her when her parents died. Phillip is like my brother. And I'm not leaving this hospital until *he's* okay. And he won't be okay until she wakes up. Do you understand?" I start to tear up. I need her to understand that I chose her. I could have chosen Jennifer. I probably should have. But I didn't. "I need you to understand, Lori. You and our baby mean everything to me, but I need to be here for him. I *have* to."

Tears stream down her face. Tears of relief, I hope.

"I love you," I tell her. "I also owe Jay big time. She bribed you into going out with me."

"She came over before the accident. Said you made her. I said something that wasn't very nice," Lori admits.

"What did you say?"

"I just got jealous. She walks around, looking like a pregnant Barbie doll. And I said—"

"What did you say?"

"I'm embarrassed to even tell you. I feel horrible now."

"Horrible because she's lying in ICU or horrible because you *actually* regret what you said?"

"I'm sorry I said it."

"What did you say?" I ask again.

"I told her that, because her pregnancy had been so easy, it meant she'd have a hard delivery. She got really upset. Stormed out." She sobs. "It's like I cursed her. I didn't mean it. I didn't wish for this. I haven't been very nice to her. When she wakes up—and she will wake up—I promise you that I'm going to apologize for being such an ass about her morning sickness, for yelling about the skybox, about accusing her of cheating with you. I'll beg her to forgive me. And I'm sorry for the way I've been treating you. I really love you, Danny. Will you forgive me? Do you think she will forgive me?"

"That's all she wanted, Lori—was for you to apologize. There's something else I need to tell you. Something she didn't want you to know. Remember when we came home from the hospital and the kitchen was miraculously finished?"

"What's that got to do with any—"

"It was Jay. She's the one who got the construction crew together. She's the one who got them to work for thirty-six hours straight. She's the one who helped the designer. She's the one who got my mom and Mrs. Mac to make all that food and stock our pantry. And she's the one who paid the workers double overtime to get it done."

"But ... why did she do that?"

"Because that's the kind of friend she is. I hope you never forget that."

She shakes her head and cries. "I won't. I promise I won't. What about you, Danny? Will you forgive me?"

"That depends on your answer to my next question. Do you understand why I don't care about football right now?"

"Yes, I understand."

"Good," I say, giving my wife a kiss.

JADYN

I HEAR PHILLIP'S voice. My eyelids are heavy, but I push them open, squinting against the light.

"Phillip?" I mutter, my throat feeling as raw as it sounds.

"Princess, you're awake," he says, his voice like music to my ears. He has tears in his eyes but a smile on his face.

I raise my hand and see the IV in it, and then I see a room filled with flowers. "I'm in the hospital?"

"You got in a car accident."

It all flashes back. The car running a red light, coming toward me. The impact.

"You scared me—no, you devastated me when I thought you had ..."

I don't let him finish. I start crying, knowing how badly I've let him down. How I'll never forgive myself for losing our baby. He might have me, but what did I do to our life? There were no pictures of the two of us with a bunch of kids on heaven TV.

While I'm so happy to see Phillip, I know I'm not supposed to be here. I know that I messed up both our lives when I left our house. It's funny; had I run the light, I would be home now—still pregnant and feeling Baby Mac kicking me.

Instead, I feel an emptiness I can't contain, like I'm a shell of what I once was.

Emotionless.

Unfeeling.

Empty.

What kind of wife could I be to Phillip after this?

And, now, I know why they showed me that scene of Phillip in the backyard with his dark-haired children. So, I'd know I have to let the picture play out.

And, as much as it's going to hurt, I know I have to let him go. Let him find the happiness he deserves. The happiness he doesn't know he's fated to have without me.

"Do you remember the accident?" he asks gently.

"Yes. I turned on the arrow. A car ran the light. I saw it coming toward me and tried to speed up."

"And am I ever lucky I bought you the new Mercedes. The driver who hit you died at the scene."

Visions flash through my mind as Phillip speaks.

Watching them take the baby from my stomach. The baby not making a sound.

I touch my stomach and cry hysterically. "I'm so sorry, Phillip. I don't know why I'm here. It's all my fault; that's why, isn't it? I'm being punished for being mean to your mom. I wasn't really mad at her; I was upset with Lori. I shouldn't have been at that intersection. I should've never left the house. And my dad—"

"Your dad?"

I nod, but I'm still hysterical.

I need to get out of here.

Right now.

I grab my IV, ready to pull it out so that I can bolt from this bed.

This place.

The walls of the hospital are quickly closing in around me.

"Jadyn," Phillip says sternly, "calm down. If you don't calm down, they'll sedate you."

"How am I supposed to calm down, Phillip? I killed our baby!

I wish I were dead, too!"

Phillip's eyes widen in shock. "Princess, I sat by your side and told you over and over that the baby was okay. That we needed you to get better. They said you'd hear me."

I freeze. Stop crying. Shake my head.

Try to find my voice.

"What? No! The baby is okay? Really? It's not dead?"

"No, he isn't," Phillip says, running his hand across my face. "He had a low Apgar score at first, but he's fine now. Do you wanna meet him?"

I put my hand over my mouth, my whole body shaking, unable to control the emotions flooding me.

I can't get the words out. "*Him?* It's ... a ... boy?"

"Yes. *Him.*"

"Phillip, is he okay? Normal? Healthy? He was blue. He didn't cry."

"He looked blue to me, too. Really blue. I thought he was dead. They took him away so fast, and I just assumed ... then everything happened with you." He squeezes my hand and gives me a reassuring smile. "They said, as soon as he took his first breath, he turned the normal pink color. He's perfect. I promise."

"Where is he?"

"In the nursery."

"You're supposed to lay the baby on the mother's chest right away. What if he doesn't recognize me? What if we don't bond? How long have I been out?"

"You were in the ICU for thirty-six hours. It's Sunday morning. I couldn't bring the baby into the ICU, but he and I have been talking about you the whole time."

"Talking about me?"

"Yes, I explained that giving birth was difficult for you, and you needed a little time to get better but that you couldn't wait to meet him. He understands." Phillip looks so tired but so incredibly sweet. "I've been reading him stories, too. The ones you bought."

"*Barnyard Dance?*"

"That's his absolute favorite," Phillip says. "He coos when I read it to him. I'll have Danny come sit with you while I go get him."

"Danny's here?"

"Danny hasn't left your side. I don't think I would've gotten through this without him. It was a relief to have him stay with you when I needed to be with our baby."

Our baby.

He rushes to the door but stops and comes back.

He kisses my hand. Kisses my forehead. Kisses my dry lips.

"I love you, Princess."

"I love you, too, Phillip."

I watch the man of my dreams, my heaven on Earth, walk out of the room.

Part of me wonders if I'm dreaming.

Or if I'm finally in the real heaven.

BUT THEN DANNY wanders into the room, looking lost. It's obvious he hasn't slept much. The dark circles under his eyes have always shown a lack of sleep on his light skin.

"You look like crap," I say and smile, realizing this is real. That I'm alive.

He shakes his head at me and runs his hand through his hair. "I should look like crap. Do you know how badly you scared us? You *died*, Jay."

"Phillip said you've been here the whole time."

He sits next to me and grabs my hand, his eyes filling with tears. "I wasn't there for you when your parents died. No way was I going to leave when Phillip needed me."

I laugh. "Oh, so it was just for his sake, huh?"

"That, and I love you. You look like you've been crying."

"I love you, too. I thought the baby had died, Danny. It sounds weird—don't tell anyone—but I saw my dad, and he and I watched them take the baby out of me. There was blood everywhere. The baby didn't cry. I thought we were waiting for the baby to come to heaven with us."

"Then, what happened?"

"I heard Phillip yell, 'Princess, don't you dare leave me.'"

"But you did."

"I saw kids playing on a swing set Phillip built. You and Lori were there, but he was with someone else. It broke my heart."

"He'd never get over losing you. You know that. Neither would I." He hands me a water bottle and says, "Drink this. Your voice sounds hoarse."

I sip from a straw, savoring the coolness on my throat.

"Speaking of *losing*, Phillip said it's Sunday morning. Aren't you supposed to be playing football today?"

"Hey," he says. "I'm not a loser, and that's not a very nice thing to say to someone who has been worried about you."

"How am I supposed to watch you play if you're here?"

He smacks my hand. "What part of *you were dead* don't you understand?"

"Was I really dead?"

"Phillip was with you in surgery when your heart stopped. They rushed him out of the room. Called code red or blue or whatever they do. When I got here, Phillip told me you were gone. But I guess they worked on you. Zapped you or whatever they do to make your heart start beating again. They didn't tell us they'd revived you for almost an hour. It was the longest hour of my life. Phillip was inconsolable. And, even once they told us they had revived you, they couldn't assure us you'd be fine, and we didn't know what to expect when you woke up."

"You always said my mom must have dropped me on my head

when I was a kid." I laugh.

He rolls his eyes at me. "Well, obviously, your memory is still intact."

"You should also know that I drafted you as my fantasy football quarterback, and if you don't play tonight, I'll start the season in last place."

"Out of all the quarterbacks you could have drafted, you chose me? You must have gotten a shitty pick."

"I had first pick, Danny."

"But you should have taken Brady or Manning. Rogers."

"Danny, this is your first full season. It's your team. You're not the replacement or the backup. You're the starting quarterback for a professional football team. Exactly where we all knew you'd be. It's your time to shine. There's no other quarterback I'd want on my team. I don't care how many rings they have. And, if I win, I'll get, like, seventy-two dollars."

He pips my finger and looks at his watch. "Oh, sure. That's why you're trying to get rid of me."

I look at him seriously. "I really appreciate you being here with Phillip. A lot, Danny."

"Nowhere else I'd be. His parents are here, too. I understand you were upset with Phillip's mom before you left."

"I blew up."

"She chewed his ass, just so you know."

"Why?"

"Because he should've talked to her about it."

"I should have talked to her about it, too, but I didn't want to hurt her feelings. Honestly, it was Lori—"

"I'm sorry I made you go over there. She told me what she said. She feels really bad about everything that's happened lately. When she apologizes, do you think you can forgive her? For me?"

I nod. "Of course I will."

Danny smiles at me. "I'm glad you're not dead."

"I am, too."

Phillip walks into the room, carrying a little bundle wrapped in the blue-and-white cloud blanket I bought just the other day. I don't think I've ever seen him look more handsome. When he was in here a few minutes ago, he looked exhausted. Now, he's practically glowing.

The beaming look of pride he has trumps every single moment I saw on Heaven TV.

I can't believe he's carrying *our* baby.

He lays the bundle in my arms.

The most perfect baby stares up at me with wide blue eyes. His eyes are framed with dark eyelashes even though he has a tuft of blonde hair. He has adorably chubby cheeks and perfect lips. His mouth forms a little O-shape, and he coos at me.

"He's so beautiful," I whisper, still in awe of how perfectly perfect he is. I rub my lips across his feather-soft hair. "And he smells so good."

I try to open up the blanket, but my IV gets caught.

Phillip helps me, revealing ten toes.

"Oh my gosh, he has your feet, Phillip!" I laugh, looking at his long, bony toes. "Look, Danny! He has Skeletor toes already!"

Danny laughs.

"But he looks just like you," Phillip says dreamily.

"Do you really think so?"

"Looks like a little old man to me," Danny teases.

Phillip ignores him. "My mom has a picture of us as babies, and he looks just like you did."

"But he has your mouth," I say.

"Did Phillip tell you he named the baby?" Danny asks with a naughty smirk.

"Oh, Phillip, you didn't. If you named him Otto, I swear—"

He puts his pinkie next to the baby's hand, and I watch in marvelous wonder as the baby grasps ahold of it.

"What? I thought you loved that name."

I nod my head toward the door and motion to Danny with my eyes. "Don't you have somewhere you need to be?"

"I'm not sure if I should play."

"Danny, you need to."

He kisses my head. "Yeah, I suppose you're right."

When he gets to the doorway, he stops, turns around, and lets out a deep sigh.

"What?" I ask.

He grabs the duffel bag that we had packed for the hospital. "After what you went through with your heart and all, I probably shouldn't scare you." He pulls the Nebraska gnome out of the bag and sets it on the bedside table.

"I wondered when that thing was going to turn up." Phillip laughs.

"It's been in your bag since you packed it. I thought you'd get a kick out of having it during the labor process, but Jay ruined my brilliant plan with all of her drama."

I laugh with them but purposefully roll my eyes toward the door.

He holds up his hands. "Fine! I'm going!"

"I need lots of passing yards, please."

Danny plugs his ears as he walks out. "I didn't hear you."

PHILLIP SITS ON the bed and grins at me. Then, he runs his hand across the baby's forehead, just like he does mine when I'm stressed.

"Chase Michael Mackenzie, meet your mommy."

"You gave him my dad's middle name? We didn't talk about that."

"I know, but it just felt right. Did Danny tell you any of what happened?"

"Yeah, kind of."

"Did he tell you that we thought you were dead for what felt like an eternity?"

"He did. I'm sorry you had to go through that, Phillip."

Phillip nods, tears welling up in his eyes. He wraps his arm around me. "I love you."

"I heard you, Phillip."

"What do you mean?"

"I didn't hear you when you talked to me after the surgery, but when you said, 'Don't leave me, Princess,' I heard you. I never want to leave you."

Emotions rip through me. Joy. Happiness. Relief.

And love.

Most of all, an overwhelming, deep-in-my-soul, all-consuming love.

"We have a present for you," he says with a grin.

"*We?*"

"Yes, me and Chase." He pulls my charm bracelet out of his pocket and puts it on my wrist.

I immediately spot the new charm. A star that's sparkling with diamonds.

"It's beautiful," I say.

"Do you know why we got a star?"

"Heaven?" I guess.

"At the swings, before I proposed again, you told me that you'd always loved me but that our love felt too big and you felt small in comparison. I didn't completely understand what you meant. But I do now. The love I feel for you and this little guy," he says, squeezing my hand, "is almost overwhelming. Like the stars we used to stare at. My love for you both is the size of the universe."

I kiss the baby's head. "I love you, Chase Michael Mackenzie. Thank you for the charm."

And then I kiss Phillip.

DANNY IS PLAYING on the TV, the baby is sleeping in my arms, and Phillip is asleep in the recliner next to the bed. I stare at both of them in a happy daze. I notice the baby journal tucked into the chair next to Phillip, so I carefully reach over and grab it, deciding I need to write something.

I'm shocked to find out that Phillip already has.

Dear Baby Mac,

You were born three weeks early on September 7th, weighed in at six pounds five ounces, and were nineteen and a half inches long. You were early because you and Mommy got into a car accident, and it caused her to have something called a placental abruption. That's a bad thing because it meant she was bleeding, and you were not getting all the oxygen you needed.

When you were born, you were a little blue, and your Apgar score was low, but the nurses took care of you, and the next time they did the score, you were almost perfect. Your mom had a rougher time, and for a while, I thought we had lost her.

It was the worst pain I've ever experienced. Way worse than any of the bones I've broken. Even the time I fell out of a tree and they had to screw my arm back together.

But, when you love someone the way I love your mom, you'd happily take physical pain over the emotional kind.

She's in the ICU now. Stable but critical. They say the next twenty-four hours are crucial.

And I'll admit, I'm scared.

My parents are here—your grandparents.

And Danny. Danny is my best friend, and he's never left my side through all of this. I hope, someday, you will have a friend like him.

Everyone has been asking me what your name is. To be honest, I thought you were going to be a girl. We had agreed on a girl's name but not a boy's.

But your mom's favorite was Chase, so I decided on Chase Michael Mackenzie. You have a grandpa and grandma in heaven.

And it might sound crazy, but when I was crying in the waiting room, out of the corner of my eye, I thought I saw him rocking you. When I turned to see if I was just hallucinating, he was gone. But I'm pretty sure he was there. Helping us get through it.

So, I gave you his middle name—Michael.

I have to admit, I always thought most babies were kinda ugly.

But not you.

You're perfect.

I've been holding you and feeding you until your mom is able to. And staring in wonder at your ten perfect fingers, ten perfect toes, and the cute little way you ball your fists up before you start crying.

It's been killing your grandparents, but I won't let anyone else hold you until she has.

She went through a lot to bring you into this world, and she deserves that honor.

And I've been telling you all about her. About how she's been writing in this journal. About how she couldn't wait to meet you.

About how much she loves you.

When your mom and I were young, we'd lie in a hammock and stare up at the stars. We'd talk about how infinitely big the universe was and how small we were in comparison. Your mom once told me that she felt small compared to how big our love felt.

I didn't completely understand what she meant that day, but I certainly do now.

The love I feel for the two of you is almost overwhelming, like the size of the universe.

Your mom has a special charm bracelet, and I sent my dad out to buy her a diamond star, so she'll always know we feel the same way about her.

When she wakes up, we'll give it to her together.

I love you, Chase Michael Mackenzie, and I know your mommy can't wait to meet you.

And, as soon as she finds out you're a boy, she'll probably tell me she told me so. Sleep well, my precious baby boy.

All my love,
Daddy

Tears stream down my face. Phillip gave me this journal, so I could write to the baby, but that isn't really what I did. The journal was written more for me than for him.

I wrote some things that probably weren't appropriate.

I wrote some things that were probably stupid.

I wrote some things that were probably silly.

But this journal represents my real journey. It's not a sugar-coated fluff piece.

And, someday, I'll tell him that nothing in this journal prepared me for the way I feel right now.

Nothing.

No childbirth class.

No books read.

Nothing could have prepared me because there is nothing in the world that compares to the feeling of holding your baby for the first time.

I smile, realizing I know now exactly when I'll let him read it. When he's expecting his own baby someday.

Because I'll want him to know that, sometimes, life doesn't always go the way you planned it.

And, sometimes, tragedy can strike when you least expect it.

But, sometimes, it can be even more incredible than you ever imagined.

I grab a pen and start writing.

Dear Chase Michael Mackenzie,

My perfect, sweet baby boy.

We're still in the hospital. Your dad is taking a nap, and I've got your uncle Danny's football game on, but mostly, I'm watching you sleep in my arms. You're making the cutest little faces as you dream, and I can't wait until the day you smile at me for real.

I wish my parents were here to see you, but I know for sure that they are watching over us.

There's something I want you to always remember.

You and I could have had a very different outcome. We're both lucky to be alive. I'll be thankful for every single day I get to spend with you.

And something else I know …

You are destined for greatness.

I don't know what you'll do or be, but I know it as surely as I feel my own heartbeat.

And I'm going to do everything I can to prepare you for it.

All my love,
Mommy

Epilogue
JULY 4TH

I GLANCE OUT the window as I'm dragging three-year-old Madden out of the bathroom. He's been doing great at potty-training, but I have to watch him closely because he's obsessed with water and would flush the toilet all day if we let him.

Phillip is in the backyard, putting the finishing touches on the big play set he's spent the last two weekends building. He built a smaller one when the kids were little, but since they're getting older, he's decided they need something bigger. This one takes up a fourth of the backyard with its rock-climbing wall, monkey bars, two slides, a sandbox, rope and regular swings, and a crow's nest.

His shirt is off, and sweat is rolling down his muscles. I'd like to pull him in the house for a quickie before the older kids get home from getting fireworks, but a quick peek at my watch tells me there's no time.

"Come on, Madden," I say, kissing the top of his head. "Let's go outside and check on Daddy."

"Da-ddy!" he screams and takes off running.

There's a reason we stopped after four kids. Madden's been an adorable, energy-filled terror since birth.

As he tears through the kitchen, I stop to turn down the heat on the ribs that have been cooking all day in preparation for the

Fourth of July party we're having. Earlier today, the kids decorated and rode their bikes in the annual neighborhood parade, and later tonight, there will be a big fireworks display over the lake.

"Da-ddy!" Madden screams again, beating his head against the French doors.

I move fast, hoping to avoid a tantrum. I scoop him up, open the door, carry him down the stairs, and then let him loose in the backyard. He runs—well, sort of waddles—and then trips on the hose and crashes to the ground. I run up behind him to see if he's okay, but he pops up and keeps going. Danny says he's going to be a lineman.

Angel slowly follows us down the steps, her hips stiff with arthritis. I know she won't be with us much longer. Phillip and I have actually started talking about getting a puppy to make it a little easier on the kids when she passes.

"Hey, Crusher," Phillip says, calling Madden by his nickname. "You want to swing?"

"No! I slide!"

Phillip helps him climb up the ladder and lets him go down the twister slide. I run to the bottom to catch him.

"Let him do it himself," Phillip says. "So, he gets the hang of—"

"Wahhh!" Madden screeches as he gets to the bottom and face-plants into the grass. He stands up, his eyes full of crocodile tears as he runs to me.

"Did you go boom?" I ask him.

Madden giggles when Angel, who's protective of the kids, licks his entire face. Then, he yells, "Again!"

"See, he's tough," Phillip says, pulling me into his arms and kissing my neck. "By the way, my wife looks sexy."

"I didn't think I was ever going to get rid of the baby weight from him, but I'm finally back—almost—to normal," I say, looking down at the new bikini I'm wearing.

"You look amazing. Always. And very patriotic."

"You're just horny." I laugh, kissing him again. "I am, too, actually. I was watching you work out here with no shirt on. It's too bad we can't still put Madden in a playpen."

"Well, what did you expect when you're wearing a skimpy little red-white-and-blue bikini that reminds me of the one you had in high school?"

I don't get to answer because his mouth covers mine in a deep, sexy kiss.

"Tonight, after the kids go to sleep and everyone goes home, you and me have a date in the hot tub," he purrs. "We'll make some fireworks of our own."

"That sounds amazing." I press against him, wrapping my arms around his neck and kissing him again.

"Oh, gross," Chase says, flinging the back gate open, causing Angel to bound across the yard, her tail wagging furiously and making her look young again.

Angel loves all of us, but she loves Chase the most. She slept under his crib when he was a baby and has slept in his room pretty much ever since.

As Chase bends down and rubs her ears, he says, "Look, Dani, they're kissing."

Devaney Diamond—who Chase, much to Danny and Lori's chagrin, has called Dani since he was old enough to attempt her name and who made it stick—puts her hands on her hips.

"Kissing is for grown-ups," she says, repeating what Lori must have told her when she caught Dani giving Chase a kiss the other day.

Chase came home upset. He might look like me, but his personality is all Phillip. He's smart and thoughtful. When I asked what happened, he told me that Dani kissed him but that Miss Lori got mad and sent him home. We had one of our most in-depth conversations to date about the birds and the bees.

Chase—who at almost ten is very tall for his age—grabs Dani's hand, pulling her toward the play set, and yells, "Dad, can we climb on the rock wall now?"

Phillip reluctantly lets go of me. "Yeah, come over here, and I'll show you how to do it."

"We already know how, Dad," our daughter, Haley James, says, rolling her eyes.

She's only eight, but she has already mastered the teen eye roll. She's also a walking contradiction—tough as nails but always wearing something pink or glittery. Because she's our only girl—and I know my mom would have done it if she were here—I totally indulge and encourage her love of all things sparkly and girlie. She's a beast on the soccer field and a good gymnast, and both she and Dani are on competitive cheer teams.

Danny, Lori, and their son, Damon—who will be a fourth grader this fall with Chase—let themselves in the backyard, carrying sacks of fireworks.

"We got a ton of sparklers!" Damon says. "And Dad says Chase, Dani, and I can light smoke bombs and snakes all by ourselves this year, if it's okay with you."

"I'm okay with that," I say. "As long as you're care—"

"Damon," Lori chastises, "I told you that I don't know if *I'm* okay with it. I think you're all too young to be playing with fire."

Damon and Danny both roll their eyes, giving Lori the same look. It makes me laugh. Damon is going to give them hell as a teen. Lori will freak out, and Danny will secretly be proud.

"He's not going to be playing with fire, Lori," Danny says. "Didn't you ever get to light smoke bombs?"

"I'm sure I wasn't allowed until I was in high school," she states.

"We did when we were young," I tell her. "And they won't have fire. They'll have a punk. And I'm sure the guys will give them a safety lesson first."

"Says the girl who used to have bottle rocket wars with us," Phillip says to me under his breath.

"Mommy, Mommy!" our middle son, Ryder, says. "Do I get to, too?"

I bend down and push his sweaty bangs out of his big brown eyes, ready to explain to him that he can't until he's older, but Dani beats me to it.

"Ry, *you* can't yet because you're only a kindergartener. When you are big like us, then you can."

He points to his chest. "I'm not a kindergartener. I'll be in first grade!"

"How about we let you choose the colors?" Dani says sweetly, herding him toward the swing set. "Get on, I'll push you."

"Look at me, Dani!" Chase yells, showing off as he swings his way across the monkey bars without falling.

"I can do that, too, I think," Damon says, running over to try it.

Even though they are in the same grade, Damon is almost a year younger than Chase and is always trying to keep up.

Chase effortlessly leaps to the ground and says to Phillip, "Dad, can I do it now? Remember that thing you promised?"

Phillip nods his head, pulls out his pocketknife, and hands it to Chase.

I watch as Chase starts carving something on the new swing set.

"What's he doing?" I ask Phillip.

"Just wait and see," he says.

Chase works slowly and intently, and I can tell whatever he's doing is important to him.

When he's finished, he stands back and looks at his work, folds the knife up, and says, "Dani! Damon! Come look!"

Damon stops playing, looks at Chase's carving, and goes, "Cool," but Dani stares at it, a broad grin spreading across her face. It's the same grin I used to see on her dad when he wanted to do something that was going to get us in trouble.

She punches Chase in the shoulder and says, "Tag, you're it."

I tightly close my eyes, praying he didn't carve bad words into the swing set.

While the kids are running around, Phillip leads me over to the carving.

D.D.

+

C.M.

+

D.D.

=

BFFs 4Ever

Tears fill my eyes as I run my hand over the letters, instantly remembering the dream I had when I was in the hospital so many years ago. "How did he know about your carving?" I ask Phillip.

"I showed him the tree when we were up at my parents' last month. He asked me if he could do it on the new swing set. We'll never be able to tear it down now."

"We're really lucky, Phillip."

"Every morning when I wake up next to you, I remember the day I thought I'd lost you both. I'm grateful for every day we're together."

"Me, too," I say as Madden pulls on my shorts.

"Wadder," he says.

"Does he want a drink?" Phillip asks.

"No." I laugh. "He wants to play with the water."

Phillip turns on the garden hose and hands it to him.

Madden puts his finger across the end of the hose and sprays Phillip as a thank-you.

"Ah, shit, that's cold," he yells.

"Shit cold!" Madden repeats. "Shit cold!"

"I think we need a beer," Danny says, heading up to the deck where we'll be able to sit down and still keep an eye on the kids.

Lori, Phillip, and I follow him. By the time we're all sitting down, Danny has beers open and passed around.

"Here's to the good life," he says as we raise our bottles in a toast.

I giggle. "Remember the first time you said that?"

"I do," Phillip says. "Eighth grade. That was the night we got drunk in the tent."

"I didn't get drunk, Lori. I was a good girl," I say in my defense.

Lori takes a swig of beer and then teases, "Was that the one time you were good?"

"Probably," Phillip teases back. "Just think, it won't be too much longer, and our kids will be doing the same thing."

Danny shakes his head. "I still feel like a kid. It's hard to believe *we* have six kids running around down there."

"And just think, Dani will start middle school soon," Phillip says. "They say, once that happens, the next thing you know, they're off to college."

"That's sad," I say, looking down on our children.

Life is wonderfully crazy hectic for all of us with sports and jobs and life, but we can't imagine it any other way.

"I was throwing the ball with Chase and Damon the other day," Danny says. "Chase has a strong arm and a naturally good throwing motion. He could be a great quarterback someday. He's going to be tall, too, I think."

"The doctor thinks he'll end up about six-five," I say.

"Your son has magic hands," Phillip says. "He can catch better than anyone on their team."

Danny gets a proud father grin. "I think we should do another toast." We hold up our bottles again. "Here's to our children."

"Here's to our children," Phillip and I repeat, looking into each other's eyes.

I feel so incredibly blessed to be married to him. He's so sweet, and he still treats me like a princess. My eyes wander down his shirtless body.

"And our beautiful wives," Danny adds.

"And to our husbands' abs," I say, giving Phillip a wink and then clinking Lori's bottle.

"Hear, hear," she agrees.

I mentioned in the dedication that this book was difficult to write. When I plan out a story, I always know the ending first.

I knew the basics of this story since before I even wrote *That Wedding*. I knew JJ would be in an accident similar to that of her parents while pregnant. And I knew she would survive.

It was the part in between that I struggled with. I knew this story would take me back to a time in my own life that, for the most part, I've tried to forget.

Most of you know that I am very blessed to have two wonderful children. What few people know is that, when I was pregnant with our third child, we lost the baby when I was four months pregnant. We'd had a miscarriage before, and we knew that we would be able to deal with it and move on. But, when I went in for a routine D & C, things did not go well. My uterus and bladder were ruptured during surgery along with my uterine artery. In the short time it took for the doctor to figure out what had happened, I'd lost a whole lot of blood.

I'm told I'm lucky to be alive.

But, in the process, our dreams of being a family of six were shattered.

Dreams are interesting things. They keep you going when times are tough. They give you hope that things will get better. During the months that followed, I felt very lost. I felt like a failure. Not only was I physically unable to do a lot of things as I recovered from multiple surgeries, but I also felt like I was letting my husband down. The things that we had dreamed about as a couple were gone in an instant. And, while it might be true that I'm lucky to be alive, I feel even luckier that my marriage survived. Because I was a mess.

While writing this book, I did something I hadn't done since the surgery.

I read the journal I had written when I was pregnant for the last time.

That was difficult for me.

It was like I had read the ending of the book first and known the outcome before the story even started. And I dreaded the end.

Writing this book was both trying and therapeutic for me.

Most of the scenes from JJ's time in the hospital mimic my own experiences. I'm pretty open about my life, but this is an event that I don't talk about much. Much like JJ refusing to go to counseling after her parents died, I refused counseling, too.

I felt like I'd lost my dreams that day, and it's taken me a long time to recover.

To have new dreams and to be thankful for all the blessings I have in my life.

If you've ever suffered a miscarriage or with infertility, you know how I felt.

Just kinda, sorta empty. I couldn't even cry.

So, please know the scenes in the book weren't just to torture you. They are many of the things I felt, dreamed, saw, experienced, or hallucinated about while things were going on around me during my own time in the hospital.

None of these experiences have ever left me even though they happened almost twenty years ago. They are as painful as they are hopeful. Tragic as they are happy.

I hope that you enjoyed the That Boy trilogy. And thank you for being so patient with me. I hope it was worth the wait.

I also have a few special people I need to thank.

Mollie Harper—Thank you for your medical expertise and helping me make Jadyn's wreck and subsequent medical care to be grounded in realism. It's been almost two years since we stayed up late one night in a New Orleans hotel room, eating room service desserts and brainstorming ways to both kill and save JJ and the baby. And your thoughts on how you love seeing a strong man break down made this book that much better. I also can't thank you enough for being one of the very first bloggers to read *That Boy* back when bloggers weren't reading indie books. Your knock-my-socks-off review helped get Danny, Phillip, and JJ into the hands of so many readers. And yay for becoming The Vegas Ass Girl.

Nigel Blackwell—My brilliant brainstorming partner who probably got sick of me shooting down his storyline ideas. Him: Well, could someone have an affair? Me: OMG! No! Phillip would never do that! Pretty much every suggestion he had, I shot down with, *He would never do that.* It wasn't until I was about three-quarters of the way through the writing process that I realized I'd used many of our original brainstorming ideas, just spun them a bit differently.

Diane Capri—Thank you for helping me figure out what type of accident Jadyn could have that would allow both she and the baby to survive. With your guidance, I learned more about auto accident reports than I ever wanted to know. London was such an amazing trip, and I appreciate all the help and guidance you've given me on the business side of things.

Beth Suit—I think it's possible that you were one of the very first people to message me and tell me you'd read *That Boy*. What started as chatting on Goodreads became a wonderful friendship. I suck as a friend. I get involved in my characters and forget the world around me. But you are always there when I come up for air. Thank you for also making sure my books are, like, mostly, usually grammatically-ish correct.

Jenn Sterling—Thank you for your no-bullshit, kick-me-in-the-pants talk about this book. I greatly value your friendship and am constantly amazed at your ability to make new friends whenever we travel together. And for giving me a moment in Boston where I think I laughed the hardest I ever have in. My. Entire. Life.

Venus, Baby J, and Mandy—Thank you so much for your quick beta-reading. It meant I got to enjoy Chaos in Cocoa with you all instead of working. I love how much you all love these characters and how this book affected you. Sorry for the ugly cries!

Connor—Your humor always uplifts me after a day of sitting at my computer and crying. Maybe, someday, you'll read my books. :)

Kenzie—Once again, your input on my stories is invaluable. You are by far my toughest critic, and none of my books would be as good if it wasn't for you.

Mom—You've been with me on this from the start, reading and rereading this series until I'm sure you were probably sick of it. You listened patiently as I talked myself through each and every story. You made suggestions that made me wonder if you knew the characters better than I did. You've had a profound effect on each and every That Boy book. Although I dedicated this book in a different way, this one is really for you.

Scotty—It's been almost eighteen years since we lost Chelsea

Nicole along with the ability to have more kids. I know I was a wreck back then. I know the tables in our relationship were turned upside down. But, throughout it all, you loved me. Supported me. Let me find my way. You are my Phillip. My Prince Charming. My fairy tale. I love you.

And to my readers—Thank you for reading my stories.

ABOUT THE AUTHOR

Jillian is a *USA TODAY* bestselling author who writes fun romances with characters her readers fall in love with, from the boy next door in the *That Boy* trilogy to the daughter of a famous actress in *The Keatyn Chronicles* to a kick-ass young assassin in the *Spy Girl* series.

She lives in a small Florida beach town, is married to her college sweetheart, has two grown children, and two Labrador Retrievers named Cali and Camber. When she's not working, she likes to travel, paint, shop for shoes, watch football, and go to the beach.

www.jilliandodd.net